"Far less preachy than *1984* or *Brave New World*, it's much funnier too."

*The New York Times*

"A stunning satire conceived with mock-heroic intensity, peopled by absurd but recognizable human beings, and written with a gusto that makes most doomsday books look like effete comic strips."

*Saturday Review*

"Profoundly moving...One of the major novels of our time."

*Milwaukee Journal*

"Brilliant and hilarious...Some of the most fascinating characters you'll ever encounter."

*Dallas Morning News*

*Also by Walker Percy:*

*Fiction*
THE MOVIEGOER*
THE LAST GENTLEMAN*
LANCELOT*
THE SECOND COMING*
THE THANATOS SYNDROME*

*Nonfiction*
THE MESSAGE IN THE BOTTLE
LOST IN THE COSMOS

*Published by Ivy Books

# LOVE
# IN THE
# RUINS

## The Adventures of a Bad Catholic at a Time Near the End of the World

## Walker Percy

IVY BOOKS • NEW YORK

Ivy Books
Published by Ballantine Books
Copyright © 1971 by Walker Percy

Library of Congress Catalog Card Number: 71-143301

ISBN 0-8041-0378-X

This edition published by arrangement with
Farrar, Straus & Giroux

Manufactured in the United States of America

First Ballantine Books Edition: February 1989
Sixth Printing: November 1990

Cover paintings by Charles Burchfield, 1916, Courtesy of
Kennedy Galleries, Inc., New York.

*For Shelby Foote*

# JULY FOURTH

# IN A PINE GROVE ON THE SOUTHWEST CUSP OF THE INTERSTATE CLOVERLEAF

## 5 P.M. / JULY 4

Now in these dread latter days of the old violent beloved U.S.A. and of the Christ-forgetting Christ-haunted death-dealing Western world I came to myself in a grove of young pines and the question came to me: has it happened at last?

Two more hours should tell the story. One way or the other. Either I am right and a catastrophe will occur, or it won't and I'm crazy. In either case the outlook is not so good.

Here I sit, in any case, against a young pine, broken out in hives and waiting for the end of the world. Safe here for the moment though, flanks protected by a rise of ground on the left and an approach ramp on the right. The carbine lies across my lap.

Just below the cloverleaf, in the ruined motel, the three girls are waiting for me.

Undoubtedly something is about to happen.

Or is it that something has stopped happening?

Is it that God has at last removed his blessing from the U.S.A. and what we feel now is just the clank of the old historical machinery, the sudden jerking ahead of the roller-coaster cars as the chain catches hold and carries us back into history with its ordinary catastrophes, carries us out and up toward the brink from that felicitous and privileged siding where even unbelievers admitted that if it was not God who blessed the U.S.A., then at least some great good luck had befallen us, and that now the blessing or the luck is over, the machinery clanks, the chain catches hold, and the cars jerk forward?

3

\* \* \*

It is still hot as midafternoon. The sky is a clear rinsed cobalt after the rain. Wet pine growth reflects the sunlight like steel knitting needles. The grove steams and smells of turpentine. Far away the thunderhead, traveling fast, humps over on the horizon like a troll. Directly above, a hawk balances on a column of air rising from the concrete geometry of the cloverleaf. Not a breath stirs.

The young pine I am sitting against has a tumor and is bowed to fit my back. I am sweating and broken out in hives from drinking gin fizzes but otherwise quite comfortable. This spot, on the lower reaches of the southwest cusp, was chosen carefully. From it I command three directions of the interstates and by leaning over the lip of the culvert can look through to the fourth, eastern approach.

Traffic is light, an occasional milk tanker and produce trailer.

The hawk slants off in a long flat glide toward the swamp. From the angle of its wings one can tell it is a marsh hawk.

One of the roof tiles of the motel falls and breaks on the concrete.

The orange roof of the Howard Johnson motel reminds me of the three girls in rooms 203, 204, and 205. Thoughts of the girls and the coming catastrophe cause my scalp to tingle with a peculiar emotion. If the catastrophe occurs, I stand a good chance, knowing what I know about it, of surviving it. So do the girls. Surviving with one girl who likes you is not such a bad prospect. But surviving with three girls, all of whom like you and each of whom detests the other two, is both horrible and pleasant, certainly enough to make one's scalp tingle with a peculiar emotion.

Another reason for the prickling sensation is that the hives are worse. Fiery wheals bloom on my neck. My scalp feels airy and quilted and now and then pops a hair root like a dirigible popping its hawsers one by one.

These are bad times.

Principalities and powers are everywhere victorious. Wickedness flourishes in high places.

There is a clearer and more present danger, however. For I have reason to believe that within the next two hours an unprecedented fallout of noxious particles will settle hereabouts and perhaps in other places as well. It is a catastrophe whose cause and effects—and prevention—are known only to me. The effects of the evil particles are psychic rather than physical. They do not burn the skin and rot the marrow; rather do they inflame and worsen the secret ills of the spirit and rive the very self from itself. If a man is already prone to anger, he'll go mad with rage. If he lives affrighted, he will quake with terror. If he's already abstracted from himself, he'll be sundered from himself and roam the world like Ishmael.

Here in my pocket is the very means of inoculating persons against such an eventuality or of curing them should it overtake them.

Yet so far only four persons have been inoculated: myself and the three girls yonder in the motel.

Just below me, abutting the deserted shopping plaza, rises the yellow brick barn-and-silo of Saint Michael's. A surprisingly large parish it was, big enough to rate a monsignor. But the church is empty now, abandoned five years ago. The stained glass is broken out. Cliffs swallows nest in the fenestrae of its concrete screen.

Our Catholic church here split into three pieces: (1) the American Catholic Church whose new Rome is Cicero, Illinois; (2) the Dutch schismatics who believe in relevance but not God; (3) the Roman Catholic remnant, a tiny scattered flock with no place to go.

The American Catholic Church, which emphasizes property rights and the integrity of neighborhoods, retained the Latin mass and plays *The Star-spangled Banner* at the elevation.

The Dutch schismatics in this area comprise several priests and nuns who left Rome to get married. They threw in with the Dutch schismatic Catholics. Now several divorced priests and nuns are importuning the Dutch cardinal to allow them to remarry.

The Roman Catholics hereabouts are scattered and demoralized. The one priest, an obscure curate, who remained faithful to Rome, could not support himself and had to hire out as a fire-watcher. It is his job to climb the fire tower by night and watch for brushfires below and for signs and portents in the skies.

I, for example, am a Roman Catholic, albeit a bad one. I believe in the Holy Catholic Apostolic and Roman Church, in God the Father, in the election of the Jews, in Jesus Christ His Son our Lord, who founded the Church on Peter his first vicar, which will last until the end of the world. Some years ago, however, I stopped eating Christ in Communion, stopped going to mass, and have since fallen into a disorderly life. I believe in God and the whole business but I love women best, music and science next, whiskey next, God fourth, and my fellowman hardly at all. Generally I do as I please. A man, wrote John, who says he believes in God and does not keep his commandments is a liar. If John is right, then I am a liar. Nevertheless, I still believe.

A couple of buzzards circle the interchange a mile high. Do I imagine it, or does one cock his head and eye me for meat? Don't count on it, old fellow!

Thoughts about the coming catastrophe and the three girls cause my scalp to tingle with a peculiar emotion. Or perhaps it is the hives from drinking gin fizzes. A catastrophe, however, has both pleasant and unpleasant aspects familiar to everyone—though no one likes to admit the pleasantness. Just now the prospect is unpleasant, but not for the reasons you might imagine.

Let me confess that what worries me most is that the catastrophe will overtake us before my scientific article is published and so before my discovery can create a sensation in the scientific world.

The vanity of scientists! My article, it is true, is an extremely important one, perhaps even epochal in its significance. With it, my little invention, in hand, any doctor can probe the very secrets of the soul, diagnose the maladies that poison the wellsprings of man's hope. It could save the world or destroy it—and in the next two hours will very likely do one or the other—for as any doctor knows, the more effective a treatment, the more dangerous it is in the wrong hands.

But the question remains: which prospect is more unpleasant, the destruction of the world, or that the destruction may come before my achievement is made known? The latter I must confess, because I keep imagining the scene in the Director's office the day the Nobel Prize is awarded. I enter. The secretaries blush. My colleagues horse around. The Director breaks out the champagne and paper cups (like Houston Control after the moon landing.) "Hats off, gentlemen!" cries the Director in his best derisive style (from him the highest accolade). "A toast to our local Pasteur! No, rather the new Copernicus! The latter-day

Archimedes who found the place to insert his lever and turn the world not upside down but right side up!"

If the truth be known, scientists are neither more nor less vain than other people. It is rather that their vanity is the more striking as it appears side by side with their well-known objectivity. The layman is scandalized, but the scandal is not so much the fault of the scientist as it is the layman's canonization of scientists, which the latter never asked for.

The prayer of the scientist if he prayed, which is not likely: Lord, grant that my discovery may increase knowledge and help other men. Failing that, Lord, grant that it will not lead to man's destruction. Failing that, Lord, grant that my article in *Brain* be published before the destruction takes place.

Room 202 in the motel is my room. Room 206 is stacked to the roof with canned food, mostly Vienna sausage and Campbell's soup, fifteen cases of Early Times bourbon whiskey, and the World's Great Books. In the rooms intervening, 203, 204, and 205, are to be found Ellen, Moira, and Lola respectively.

My spirits rise. My quilted scalp pops another hair root. The silky albumen from the gin fizzes coats my brain membranes. Even if worst comes to worst, is there any reason why the four of us cannot live happily together, sip toddies, eat Campbell's chicken-and-rice, and spend the long summer evenings listening to Lola play the cello and reading aloud from the World's Great Books stacked right alongside the cases of Early Times, beginning with Homer's first words: "Sing, O Goddess, the anger of Achilles," and ending with Freud's last words: "—but we cannot help them and cannot change our own way of thinking on their account"? Then we can read the Great Ideas, beginning with the first volumne, Angel to Love. Then we can start over—until the Campbell's soup and Early Times run out.

The sun makes bursts and halos through the screen of pine needles. The marsh hawk ends his long glide into the line of cypresses, which are green as paint against the purple thunderhead.

At first glance all seems normal hereabouts. But a sharp eye might notice one or two things amiss. For one thing, the inner lanes of the interstate, the ones ordinarily used for passing, are in disrepair. The tar strips are broken. A lichen grows in the oil stain. Young mimosas sprout on the shoulders.

For another thing, there is something wrong with the motel.

The roof tiles are broken. The swimming pool is an opaque jade green, a bad color for pools. A large turtle suns himself on the diving board, which is broken and slanted into the water. Two cars are parked in the near lot, a rusty Cadillac and an Impala convertible with vines sprouting through its rotting top.

The cars and the shopping center were burnt out during the Christmas riot five years ago. The motel, though not burned, was abandoned and its rooms inhabited first by lovers, then by bums, and finally by the native denizens of the swamp, dirt daubers, moccasins, screech owls, and raccoons.

In recent months the vines have begun to sprout in earnest. Possum grape festoons Rexall Drugs yonder in the plaza. Scuppernong all but conceals the A & P supermarket. Poison ivy has captured the speaker posts in the drive-in movie, making a perfect geometrical forest of short cylindrical trees.

Beyond the glass wall of the motel dining room still hangs the Rotary banner:

> Is it the truth?
> Is it fair to all concerned?
> Will it build goodwill and better friendship?

But the banner is rent, top to bottom, like the temple veil.

The vines began to sprout in earnest a couple of months ago. People do not like to talk about it. For some reason they'd much rather talk about the atrocities that have been occurring ever more often: entire families murdered in their beds for no good reason. "The work of a madman!" people exclaim.

Last Sunday as I was walking past the house of a neighbor, Barry Bocock, a Boeing engineer transplanted from Seattle, I spied him riding his tiny tractor-mower like a big gringo astride a burro. The next moment my eye was caught by many tiny vines sprouting through cracks in the concrete slab and beginning to cover the antique bricks that Barry had salvaged from an old sugar mill.

Barry got off his tractor simply by standing up and walking.

"It looks as though your slab is cracked, Barry," I told him.

Barry frowned and, seeming not to hear, began to show me how the tractor could cut grass right up to the bark of a tree without injuring the tree.

Barry Bocock is the sort of fellow who gives the most careful attention to details, especially to those smaller problems caused by germs. A very clean man, he walks around his yard in his shorts and if he should find a pustule or hickey on his clean hairy muscular legs, he takes infinite pains examining it, squeezing it, noting the character of the pus. One has the feeling that to Barry there is nothing wrong with the world that couldn't be set right by controlling germs and human wastes. One Sunday he invited me into his back yard and showed me the effluence from his new septic tank, letting it run into a drinking glass, where in fact it did look as clear as water.

But when I called his attention to the vines cracking his slab, he seemed not to hear and instead showed me his new mower.

"But, Barry, the vines are cracking your slab."

"That'll be the day," said Barry, flushing angrily. Then, drawing me close to his clean perfect West-Coast body, he asked me if I'd heard of the latest atrocity.

"Yes. What do you think?"

"The work of a madman!" he exclaimed and mounted his burro-size tractor.

Barry is a widower, his wife having died of alcoholism before he left Seattle. "Firing the sunset gun" he called her drinking. "Every day she'd be at it as early as one o'clock." "At what?" "Firing the sunset gun."

The buzzards are lower and more hopeful, rocking their wings this way and that and craning down for a look.

When I think of Barry, I can't help but wonder whether he, not I, should be the doctor, what with his keen interest in germs, boils, hickeys, bo-bos, pustules, scabs, and such. Moreover, I could tell from Barry's veiled expression when I mentioned the vines sprouting that he knew of my own troubles and that he was accordingly discounting my alarm. Physician, heal thyself. . . .

The truth is that, though I am a physician, my health, especially my mental health, has been very poor lately. I am subject to attacks of elation and depression, as well as occasional seizures of morning terror. A few years ago my wife left me, running off with an Englishman, and I've led an irregular life ever since.

But to admit my infirmities is not necessarily to discredit my discoveries, which stand or fall on scientific evidence. After all, van Gogh was depressed and Beethoven had a poor time of it. The prophet Hosea, if you will recall, had a bad home life.

Some of the best psychiatrists, it is hardly necessary to add, have a few problems of their own, little rancors and terrors and such.

Who am I? you well might wonder. Let me give a little dossier.

I am a physician, a not very successful psychiatrist; an alcoholic, a shaky middle-aged man subject to depressions and elations and morning terrors, but a genius nevertheless who sees into the hidden causes of things and erects simple hypotheses to account for the glut of everyday events; a bad Catholic; a widower and cuckold whose wife ran off with a heathen Englishman and died on the island of Cozumel, where she hoped to begin a new life and see things afresh.

My afflictions attract some patients, repel others. People are generally tolerant. Some patients, knowing my frailties, calculate I'll understand theirs. I am something like old Doc in Western movies: if you catch old Doc sober, he's all right, etcetera. In fact, he's some kind of genius, I heard he went to Harvard, etcetera etcetera.

Not that I make much money. Sensible folk, after all, don't have much use for a doctor who sips toddies during office hours. So I'm obliged to take all kinds of patients, not merely terrified and depressed people, but people suffering with bowel complaints, drugheads with beriberi and hepatitis, Bantus shot up by the cops, cops shot up by Bantus.

Lately, however, I've discouraged patients in order to work on my invention. I don't need the money. Fortunately for me, my wife, who left me and later died, either didn't or wouldn't change her will and so bequeathed me forty thousand shares of R. J. Reynolds stock she inherited from her father.

Loose bark from the pine is beginning to work through my shirt. My scalp is still quilted, my throat is whistling with hives—albumen molecules from the gin fizzes hum like bees in the ventricles of my brain—yet I feel quite well.

Where is the sniper? Shading my eyes, I examine every inch of the terrain.

A flag stirs fitfully on its pole beside the green rectangle dug into the slope of the near ridge like a step. It is the football field of the Valley Forge Academy, our private school, which was founded on religious and patriotic principles and to keep Negroes out. Earlier today—could it have been today?—the Christian Kaydettes, our champion baton twirlers, practiced their twirling, little suspecting what dread misadventure would befall them.

Beyond the empty shopping plaza at my foot rise the low green hills of Paradise Estates. The fairways of the golf links make notches in the tree line. Pretty cubes and loaves of new houses are strewn among the pines like sugar lumps. It is even possible to pick out my own house, a spot of hot pink and a wink of glass under the old TV transmitter. By a trick of perspective the transmitter tower seems to rise from the dumpy silo of old Saint Michael's Church in the plaza.

Here in the old days I used to go to mass with my daughter, Samantha. My wife, an ex-Episcopal girl from Virginia, named our daughter Samantha in the expectation that this dark gracile pagan name would somehow inform the child, but alas for Doris, Samantha turned out to be chubby, fair, acned, and pious, the sort who likes to hang around after school and beat Sister's erasers.

The best of times were after mass on summer evenings when Samantha and I would walk home in the violet dusk, we having received Communion and I rejoicing afterwards, caring nought for my fellow Catholics but only for myself and Samantha and Christ swallowed, remembering what he promised me for eating him, that I would have life in me, and I did, feeling so good that I'd sing and cut the fool all the way home like King David before the Ark. Once home, light up the charcoal briquets out under the TV transmitter, which lofted its red light next to Venus like a ruby and a diamond in the plum velvet sky. Snug down Samantha with the *Wonderful World of Color* in the den (the picture better than life, having traveled only one hundred feet straight down), back to the briquets, take four, five, six long pulls from the quart of Early Times, shout with joy for the beauty of the world, sing "Finch 'han dal vino" from *Don Giovanni* and "Holy God We Praise Thy Name," conceive a great heart-leaping desire for Doris, go fetch Doris, whose lip would curl at my proposal but who was nonetheless willing, who in fact now that she thought of it was as lusty as could be, her old self once again, a lusty Shenandoah Valley girl, Apple Queen of the Apple Blossom Festival in Winchester. Lead her by the hand beyond the azaleas where we'd fling ourselves upon each other and fall down on the zoysia grass, thick-napped here as a Kerman rug.

* * *

A flutter of white in the motel window. The sniper? I tighten my elbow against the carbine belt. No, it is one of the girls' rooms. Moira's. Moira washing her things out and hanging them out to dry as if it were any other Tuesday. A good omen, Moira washing her underwear. Her I always think of so, standing barefoot in her slip at the washstand, legs planted far apart and straight, even a bit past straight, so that the pad at the back of her knees stands out as firm as rubber; yellow eyes musing and unfocused as she puts her things to soak in Lux.

Lola, on the other hand, I always see playing the Dvořák concerto, hissing the melody with her tongue against her teeth, straddling the cello with her splendid knees.

Ellen Oglethorpe appears in my mind as in fact she is, a stern but voluptuous Presbyterian nurse, color high in her cheeks, eyes bright with disapproval. I think of her as having her fists planted on her hips, as they used to say, akimbo.


All quiet in front. Could he, the sniper, have gotten behind me? I turn around slowly, keeping under the low spreading limbs of the longleaf.

Beyond the hump of the interchange rise the monoliths of "Fedville," the federal complex including the hospital (where I've spent almost as much time as a patient as doctoring), the medical school, the NASA facility, the Behavioral Institute, the Geriatrics Center, and the Love Clinic.

In "Love," as it is called, volunteers perform sexual acts singly, in couples, and in groups, beyond viewing mirrors in order that man might learn more about the human sexual response.

Next door is Geriatrics Rehabilitation or "Gerry Rehab," a far-flung complex of pleasant low-lying white-roofed Daytona-type buildings. Here old folk from Tampa to Tucson are treated for the blues and boredoms of old age. These good folk, whose physical ailments are mostly cured nowadays, who at eighty-five, ninety, even a hundred, are as spry as can be, limber-jointed, smooth-faced, supple of artery, nevertheless often grow inexplicably sad. Though they may live in the pleasantest Senior Settlements where their every need is filled, every recreation provided, every sort of hobby encouraged, nevertheless many grow despondent in their happiness, sit slack and empty-eyed at shuffleboard and ceramic oven. Fishing poles fall from tanned and healthy hands. Golf clubs rust. *Reader's Digests* go unread. Many old folk pine away and even die from unknown causes like victims of a voodoo curse. Here in Gerry Rehab, these sad oldsters are encouraged to develop their "creative and altruistic potential." Yet mysterious deaths, and suicides too, continue to mount. The last Surgeon General's report named the nation's number-one killer as "Senior Citizens' anomie," known locally as the St. Petersburg blues.

To my left, white among the cypresses, are the old frame buildings of the Little Sisters of the Poor. During the week the Little Sisters run a school for poor children, black and white, feed and clothe them, and on weekends conduct religious retreats for Christian folk. The scientists help the sisters with the children during the week. On weekends Christians come to make retreats and pray for the conversion of Communists.

The scientists, who are mostly liberals and unbelievers, and the businessmen, who are mostly conservative and Christian, live side by side in Paradise Estates. Though the two make much of their differences—one speaking of "outworn dogmas and creeds," the other of "atheism and immorality," etcetera etcetera—to tell the truth, I do not notice a great deal of difference between the two. Both sorts are generally good fellows, good fathers and husbands who work hard all day, come home at five-thirty to their pretty homes, kiss their wives, toss their rosy babes in the air, light up their charcoal briquets, or perhaps mount their tiny tractor mowers. There are minor differences. When conservative Christian housewives drive to town to pick up their maids in the Hollow, the latter ride on the back seat in the old style. Liberal housewives make their maids ride on the front seat. On Sundays Christian businessmen dress up and take their families to church, whereas unbelieving scientists are apt to put on their worst clothes and go bird-watching. As one of my behaviorist friends put it, "my cathedral is the blue sky and my pilgrimage is for the ivory-billed woodpecker," the fabulous and lordly bird that some say still inhabits the fastness of the swamp.

Beyond the cypresses, stretching away to the horizon, as misty as a southern sea, lies the vast Honey Island Swamp. Smudges of hummocks dot its savanna-like islands. The north-south interstate, crossing it on a causeway, flies due south straight as two lines drawn with a ruler to converge at a point on the horizon.

From the hummocks arise one or two wisps of smoke. Yonder in the fastness of the swamp dwell the dropouts from and castoffs of and rebels against our society: ferocious black Bantus who use the wilderness both as a refuge and as a guerrilla base from which to mount forays against outlying subdivisions and shopping plazas; all manner of young white derelicts who live drowsy sloth-like lives, sustaining themselves on wild melons and catfish and green turtles and smoking Choctaw cannabis the livelong day. The lonely hummocks, once the haunt of raccoon and alligator, are now rubbed bare as monkey islands at the zoo by all manner of disaffected folk: Bantu guerrillas, dropouts from Tulane and Vanderbilt, M.I.T. and Loyola; draft dodgers, deserters from the Swedish army, psychopaths and pederasts from Memphis and New Orleans whose practices were not even to be tolerated in New Orleans; antipapal Catholics, malcontented Methodists, ESPers, UFOers, Aquarians, ex–Ayn Randers, Choctaw Zionists who have returned to their ancestral hunting grounds, and even a few old graybeard Kerouac beats, wiry old sourdoughs of the spirit who carry pilgrim staffs, recite sutras, and leap from hummock to hummock as agile as mountain goats.

The town where I keep an office is north and to my right. By contrast with the swamp, the town has become a refuge for all manner of conservative folk, graduates of Bob Jones University, retired Air Force colonels, passed-over Navy commanders, ex–Washington, D.C., policemen, patriotic chiropractors, two officials of the National Rifle Association, and six conservative proctologists.

Paradise Estates, where I live now, is another matter. Directly opposite me, between swamp and town, its houses sparkle like jewelry in the sunlight. Emerald fairways run alongside sleepy bayous. Here everyone gets along well, heathen and Christian, Jew and Gentile, Northerner and Southerner, liberal and conservative. The Northerners, mostly businessmen and engineers from places like Kenosha and Sheboygan and Grosse Pointe, actually outnumber the Southerners. But they, the Northerners, have taken to Southern ways like ducks to water. They drink toddies and mint juleps and hold fish fries with hush puppies. Little black jockeys fish from mirrors in their front yards. Lifesize mammy-dolls preside over their patios. Nearly everyone treats his servants well, picking them up in Happy Hollow and taking them home, allowing "totin' privileges" and giving them "Christmas gifts."

The Negroes around here are generally held to be a bad lot.

The older Negroes are mostly trifling and no-account, while the young Negroes have turned mean as yard dogs. Nearly all the latter have left town, many to join the Bantus in the swamp. Here the conservatives and liberals of Paradise agree. The conservatives say that Negroes always have been trifling and no-account or else mean as yard dogs. The liberals, arguing with the conservatives at the country club, say yes, Negroes are trifling and no-account or else mean as yard dogs, but why shouldn't they be, etcetera etcetera. So it goes.

Our servants in Paradise are the exceptions, however: faithful black mammies who take care of our children as if they were their own, dignified gardeners who work and doff their caps in the old style.

Paradise Estates, where I live, is a paradise indeed, an oasis of concord in a troubled land. For our beloved old U.S.A. is in a bad way. Americans have turned against each other; race against race, right against left, believer against heathen, San Francisco against Los Angeles, Chicago against Cicero. Vines sprout in sections of New York where not even Negroes will live. Wolves have been seen in downtown Cleveland, like Rome during the Black Plague. Some Southern states have established diplomatic ties with Rhodesia. Minnesota and Oregon have their own consulates in Sweden (where so many deserters from these states dwell.)

The old Republican Party has become the Knothead Party, so named during the last Republican convention in Montgomery when a change of name was proposed, the first suggestion being the Christian Conservative Constitutional Party, and campaign buttons were even printed with the letters CCCP before an Eastern-liberal commentator noted the similarity to the initials printed on the backs of the Soviet cosmonauts and called it the most knotheaded political bungle of the century — which the conservatives, in the best tradition, turned to their own advantage, printing a million more buttons reading "Knotheads for America" and banners proclaiming "No Man Can Be Too Knotheaded in the Service of His Country."

The old Democrats gave way to the new Left Party. They too were stuck with a nickname not of their own devising and the nickname stuck: in this case a derisive acronym that the Right made up and the Left accepted, accepted in that same curious American tradition by which we allow our enemies to name us, give currency to their curses, perhaps from the need to concede the headstart they want and still beat them, perhaps

also from the secret inkling that our enemies know the worst
of us best and it's best for them to say it. LEFT usually it is,
often LEFTPAPA, sometimes LEFTPAPASAN (with a little
Jap bow), hardly ever the original LEFTPAPASANE, which
stood for what, according to the Right, the Left believed in:
Liberty, Equality, Fraternity, The Pill, Atheism, Pot, Anti-
Pollution, Sex, Abortion Now, Euthanasia.

The center did not hold.
    However, the Gross National Product continues to rise.
    There are Left states and Knothead states, Left towns and
Knothead towns but no center towns (for example, my old
hometown over yonder is Knothead, Fedville behind me is
Left, and Paradise Estates where I live now does not belong to
the center—there is no center—but is that rare thing, a pleasant place where Knothead and Left—but not black—dwell
side by side in peace), Left networks and Knothead networks,
Left movies and Knothead movies. The most popular Left
films are dirty movies from Sweden. All-time Knothead favorites, on the other hand, include *The Sound of Music*, *Flub-
ber*, and *Ice Capades of 1981*, clean movies all.
    I've stopped going to movies. It is hard to say which is
more unendurable, the sentimental blasphemy of Knothead
movies like *The Sound of Music* or sitting in a theater with
strangers watching other strangers engage in sexual intercourse and sodomy on the giant 3-D Pan-a-Vision screen.
    American literature is not having its finest hour. The
Southern gothic novel yielded to the Jewish masturbatory
novel, which in turn gave way to the WASP homosexual
novel, which has nearly run its course. The Catholic literary
renascence, long awaited, failed to materialize. But old favorites endure, like venerable Harold Robbins and Jacqueline Su-
sann, who continue to write the dirty clean books so beloved
by the American housewife. Gore Vidal is the grand old man
of American letters.
    Both political parties have had their triumphs.
    The Lefts succeeded in removing "In God We Trust" from
pennies.
    The Knotheads enacted a law requiring compulsory prayers
in the black public schools and made funds available for birth
control in Africa, Asia, and Alabama.
    But here in Paradise, Knothead lives next to Leftist in
peace. On Wednesday nights one goes to a meeting of

Birchers, the other to the ACLU. Sunday one goes to church, the other in search of the lordly ivory-billed woodpecker, but both play golf, ski in the same bayou, and give "Christmas gifs" to the same waiters at the club.

The war in Ecuador has been going on for fifteen years and has divided the country further. Not exactly our best war. The U.S.A. sided with South Ecuador, which is largely Christian, believing in God and the sacredness of the individual, etcetera etcetera. The only trouble is that South Ecuador is owned by ninety-eight Catholic families with Swiss bank accounts, is governed by a general, and so is not what you would call an ideal democracy. North Ecuador, on the other hand, which many U.S. liberals support, is Maoist-Communist and has so far murdered two hundred thousand civilians, including liberals, who did not welcome Communism with open arms. Not exactly our best war, and now in its sixteenth year.

Even so, most Americans do well enough. In fact, until lately, nearly everyone tried and succeeded in being happy but me. My unhappiness is not the fault of Paradise. I was unlucky. My daughter died, my wife ran off with a heathen Englishman, and I fell prey to bouts of depression and morning terror, to say nothing of abstract furies and desultory lusts for strangers.

Here's the puzzle: what is an unhappy psychiatrist to do in a place were everyone else is happier than he is? Physician, heal thy...

Fortunately for me, many other people have become unhappy of late. Certain psychiatric disorders have cropped up in both Lefts and Knotheads.

Conservatives have begun to fall victim to unseasonable rages, delusions of conspiracies, high blood pressure, and large-bowel complaints.

Liberals are more apt to contract sexual impotence, morning terror, and a feeling of abstraction of the self from itself.

So it is that a small Knothead city like my hometown yonder can support half a dozen proctologists, while places like Berkeley or Beverly Hills have a psychiatrist in every block.

It is my misfortune—and—blessing—that I suffer from both liberal and conservative complaints, e.g., both morning terror and large-bowel disorders, excessive abstraction and unseasonable rage, alternating impotence and satyriasis. So that at one and the same time I have great sympathy for my patients and lead a fairly miserable life.

But my invention has changed all this. Now I know how to be happy and make others happy. With my little machine I can diagnose and treat with equal success the morning terror of liberals and the apoplexy of conservatives. In fact it could save the U.S.A. if we can get through the next hour or so.

What's wrong with my eyes? My field of vision is narrowing from top to bottom. The world looks as if it were seen through the slit of a gun turret. But of course! My eyes are swelling with hives! It could only come from the delicious gin fizzes prepared for me by Lola, my lovely cellist.

Still I feel very well. My brain, lubricated by egg white from the gin fizzes, hums like a top; pangs of love for the three girls—two anyhow—pierce my heart (how beautiful did God make woman!). Yet I am able to observe every detail of the terrain through my turret slit. A single rank week, I notice, has sprouted overnight in the sand trap of number 12 fairly next to the interstate right-of-way—this despite the fact that the champs are to play here tonight "under the arcs."

Far away church steeples puncture the globy oaks. Ordinary fat grayish clouds sail over the town blown by map winds with pencil lines.

The sand trap and the clouds put me in mind of being ten years old and in love and full of longing. The first thing a man remembers is longing and the last thing he is conscious of before death is exactly the same longing. I have never seen a man die who did not die in longing. When I was ten years old I woke one summer morning to a sensation of longing. Besides the longing I was in love with a girl named Louise, and so the same morning I went out to this same sand trap where I hoped chance would bring us together. At the breakfast table, I took a look at my father with his round head, his iron-colored hair, his chipper red cheeks, and I wondered to myself: at what age does a man get over this longing?

The answer is, he doesn't. My father was so overwhelmed with longing that it unfitted him for anything but building martin houses.

My father, also a physician, had his office in town and I kept it, poor place though it was, even after I became a professor at the medical center.

We are not exactly a distinguished family. My father was a

failed physician who also drank. In early middle age he got himself elected coroner and more or less retired, sat alone in his office between the infrequent autopsies and made spectacular bird houses, martin hotels, and wren houses of cypress with brass fittings.

My mother, a "realtor" and a whiz at getting buyer and seller together, really supported us.

Our family's only claim to singularity, if not distinction, is that we are one of that rare breed, Anglo-Saxon Catholics who were Catholic from the beginning and stayed Catholic. My forebears remained steadfast in the old faith both in Hertfordshire, where Elizabeth got after them, and in Maryland, where the Episcopalians finally kicked them out. Sir Thomas More, in fact, is a collateral ancestor. Our name anyhow is More. But if such antecedents seem illustrious, recent reality is less so. It is as if the effort of clinging to the faith took such a toll that we were not fit for much else. Evicted from Maryland, my ancestor removed to Bardstown, Kentucky, where he and his sons founded a whiskey distillery—and failed at that.

My grandfather took dentistry at Loyola of the South and upon graduation married a Creole heiress with timberlands and never drilled a tooth.

All Mores, until I came along, were good Catholics and went to mass—I too until a few years ago. Wanderers we became, like the Jews in the wilderness. For we were Catholic English-Americans and most other English-Americans were Protestant and most Catholics were either Mediterranean or Irish. In the end we settled for Louisiana, where religious and ethnic confusion is sufficiently widespread and good-natured that no one keeps track of such matters—except the Baptists, who don't like Catholics no matter what. My forefathers donned Knights of Columbus robes, wore swords and plumed hats, attended French shrimp boils and Irish wakes, made retreats with Germans, were pallbearers at Italian funerals. Like the French and Germans here, we became easygoing Louisianians and didn't think twice about our origins. We fought with Beauregard next to old blue-light Presbyterian Stonewall Jackson and it seemed natural enough. My father was only a third-degree Knight of Columbus, but he too went regularly to Holy Name shrimp boils and Lady of the Lake barbecues and was right content. For twenty-five years he sat out the long afternoons in his dim little coroner's office, sipping Early

Times between autopsies and watching purple martins come skimming up to his splendid cypress-and-brass hotel.

The asphalt of the empty plaza still bubbles under the hot July sun. Through the shimmer of heat one can see the broken store fronts beyond the plaza. A green line wavers in midair above the pavement, like the hanging gardens of Babylon. It is not a mirage, however. I know what it is. A green growth has taken root on the flat roofs of the stores.

As for me, I was a smart boy and at the age of twenty-six bade fair to add luster to the family name for the first time since Sir Thomas More himself, the great soul, the dearest best noblest merriest of Englishmen. My contribution, I hasten to add, was in the realm of science not sanctity. Why can't I follow More's example, love myself less, God and my fellowman more, and leave whiskey and women alone? Sir Thomas More was merry in life and death and he loved and was loved by everyone, even his executioner, with whom he cracked jokes, By contrast, I am possessed by terror and desire and live a solitary life. My life is a longing, longings for women, for the Nobel Prize, for the hot bosky bite of bourbon whiskey, and other great heart-wrenching longings that have no name. Sir Thomas was right, of course, and I am wrong. But on the other hand these are peculiar times. . . .

When I was a young man, the question at the time was: where are the Catholic Einsteins, Salks, Oppenheimers? And the answer came, at least from my family: well, here comes one, namely me. The local Catholic paper and the K.C. magazine wrote me up, along with some well-known baseball players, bandleaders, and TV personalities. It was the end of the era of Lawrence Welk, Perry Como, Bing Crosby, Stan Musial, Ed McMahon, all good Catholics, good fellows, decent family men, etcetera etcetera, though not exactly the luminaries of the age—John Kennedy was the exception—and the question was, who was going to take their place, let alone measure up to Einstein.

One proof of the divine origin of the Catholic Church: that I found myself in the same Church as Lawrence Welk and Danny Thomas and all those Irishmen and did not feel in the least peculiar.

What happened was that as a young physician in New Orleans I stumbled onto an extraordinary medical discovery, wrote an article for the *Journal of the American Medical Association* that was picked up by *Time*, *Newsweek*, and the papers. Caption under *Time* photo: "Psychic Fallout?" In *Newsweek*: "Doctor Treats Doctors in Switch." Headline in New York *Daily News*: "Beautiful Girl Interne Disrobes—Fallout Cause Says Doc."

I was the doc and a very promising doc at that. How many doctors achieve fame in their twenties?

Alas, the promise didn't pan out. On the contrary. There followed twenty years of silence and decline. My daughter, Samantha died; my wife ran off with a heathen Englishman—come to think of it, I haven't seen a Christian Englishman for years—and I left off research, left off eating Christ in Communion, and took to sipping Early Times instead and seeking the company of the fair sex, as they used to say.

My wife and I lived a good life. We used to get up in the morning in a beautiful house, sit down to breakfast in our "enclosed patio," watch Barbara Walters talk about sexual intercourse on the *Today* show. Nevertheless, I fell prey to morning terror, shook like a leaf at the breakfast table, and began to drink vodka with my grits. At the same time that I developed liberal anxiety, I also contracted conservative rage and large-bowel complaints.

But—and here is the point—the period of my decline was also a period of lying fallow and of the germination of some strange quirky ideas. Toynbee, I believe, speaks of the Return, of the man who fails and goes away, is exiled, takes counsel with himself, hits on something, sees daylight—and returns to triumph.

First, reader and especially my fellow physicians, let me set forth my credentials, recall to your mind my modest discovery twenty years ago, as well as give you an inkling of my recent breakthrough.

Do you recall the Heavy Sodium experiments that were conducted years ago in New Orleans under the stands of the Sugar Bowl stadium? and the mysterious accident that put an end to the same? There occurred an almost soundless explosion, a *whssssk* like tearing silk, a few people were killed, and a curious yellow lens-shaped cloud hung over the French Quarter for a day or two.

Here's what happened. At the time I was encephalographer-in-residence at Tulane University. Part of my job was to do encephalograms on students with the hope of eliminating those who were subject to the sundry fits and seizures that were plaguing universities at the time, conservative fits and radical seizures. Another duty was to assist the team of physicists assigned to the secret Vieux Carré project under the Sugar Bowl. I doubled as medical officer and radiation monitor. The physicists were tinkering with a Heavy Sodium pile by means of which they hoped to hit on a better source of anticancer radiation than the old cobalt treatment. The Heavy Sodium was obtained from the massive salt domes of southern Louisiana where it occurs (along with the Heavy Chloride iron) as a trace element. The experiment was promising for two reasons. One was that Heavy Sodium radiation was thought not to injure normal tissues—hence no X-ray burns. The other was evidence that it destroyed cancer cells in mice.

The long and short of it is that the reactor got loose, killed a brace of physicists, sent up an odd yellow cloud, and accordingly rated a headline on the second page of the New York *Daily News*, as might a similar accident at Oak Ridge or Los Alamos.

In the weeks that followed, however, I noticed something curious and so made my, to date, sole contribution to medical annals. You may still find it in the textbooks, where it usually rates a footnote as "More's Paradoxical Sodium Radiation Syndrome." Something peculiar happened in the Tulane Psychiatric Hospital, where I was based. Nobody thought to make a connection between these peculiar events and the yellow cloud. Was it not John Locke who said that the mark of genius is the ability to discern not this thing or that thing but rather the connection between the two?

At any rate I noticed a remarkable change in the hospital people. Some of the patients got better and some of the psychiatrists got worse. Indeed, many of our most disturbed patients, the suicidal, the manic, the naked, the catatonic, in short the mad, were found one morning sitting fully clothed and in their right minds. A number of residents and staff physicians, on the other hand, developed acute symptoms out of the blue. One doctor, for example, a noted authority on schizophrenia, uttered a hoarse cry on rounds, hurled himself through a window, ran over the levee, and disappeared into the waters of the mighty Mississippi. Another, a lady psychologist and by the way a very attractive person and something of a radio-TV personality, stripped off her clothing in staff conference and made gross sexual overtures to several male colleagues—hence the somewhat inaccurate headline in the New York *Daily News*.

A third case, a fellow resident and good friend of mine, a merry outgoing person both at work and play, underwent a marked personality change. In the hospital he became extremely cold in mien, abstracted and so absorbed with laboratory data that he treated his patients like guinea pigs in a cage, while in his off-duty hours he began to exhibit the lewdest sort of behavior, laying hands on strange women like a drunken sailor.

Shortly thereafter I awoke one morning and it occurred to me that there might be a connection between these peculiar events and the lens-shaped cloud. For though I attached no weight to the superstitions flying around—one good soul, a chambermaid in the hospital, said that the yellow cloud had driven the demons out of the mad patients and into the doctors—nevertheless, it did occur to me that the cloud might have contained, and turned loose, something besides demons. I ordered esoteric blood chemistry on both sane patients and mad doctors. Sure enough, both groups had significant levels of Heavy Sodium and Chloride in their blood.

What I didn't know at the time and what took me twenty years to figure out was why some got better and others got worse. I know now that the heavy ions have different effects on different brain centers. For example, Heavy Sodium radiation stimulates Brodmann Area 32, the center of abstractive activity or tendencies toward angelism, while Heavy Chloride stimulates the thalamus, which promotes adjustment to the environment, or, as I call it without prejudice, bestialism. The two conditions are not mutually exclusive. It is not uncommon nowadays to see patients suffering from angelism-bestialism. A man, for example, can feel at one and the same time extremely abstracted and inordinately lustful toward lovely young women who may be perfect strangers.

So ran my report in the *J.A.M.A.*, a bald observation of a connection, without theory. The explanation, now that I look back on it, seems so simple now. Then I was like Benjamin Franklin getting a jolt from his kite and having no notion what hit him. Now I know.

A second thunderhead, larger and more globular, is approaching from the north. A breeze springs up. There is no thunder but lightning flickers around inside the cloud like a defective light bulb.

While there is still time, let me tell you what my invention does, just in case worst comes to worst and my article in *Brain* can't be published. Since catastrophe may overtake us within the hour, I am dictating these words into a pocket recorder so that survivors poking around the ruins of Howard Johnson's a hundred years from now will have a chance of avoiding a repetition.

My discovery, like all great scientific breakthroughs, is simplicity itself. The notion came to me during my work with the encephalograph, with which instrument, as you know, one tapes electrodes to the skull and records brain waves, which in turn may reveal such abnormalities as tumors, strokes, fits, and so on.

It happened while I was ill.

One stormy night I lay in a hospital bed recovering from seizures of alternating terror and delight with intervening periods of immense longing. These attacks are followed in my case by periods of extraordinary tranquility of mind, of heightened perception, clairvoyance, and increased inductive powers. The storm roared and crashed outside the acute ward; I lay on my back in bed, hands at my side, surrounded by thirty-nine other madmen moaning and whimpering like souls in the inner circle of hell. Yet I felt extraordinarily happy. Thoughts flew into my head like little birds. Then it was that my great idea came to me. So confident was I of its value that I leapt out of bed at the height of the storm and yelled at my fellow patients:

"Don't be afraid, brothers! Don't cry! Don't tremble! I have made a discovery that will cure you! Believe me, brothers!"

"We believe you, Doc!" the madmen cried in the crashing thunder, and they did. Madmen, like possessed souls in the Gospels, know when you are telling the truth.

It was my fellow physicians who gave me trouble.

My idea was simply this: if the encephalograph works, why not devise a gadget without wires that will measure the electrical activity of the separate centers of the brain? Hardly a radical idea. But here was the problem: given such a machine, given such readings, could the readings then be correlated with the manifold woes of the Western world, its terrors and rages and murderous impulses? And if so, could the latter be treated by treating the former?

A large order, yes, but so was Edward Jenner's dream of eradicating the great pox.

A bit of luck came my way. Once I got out of the acute wing, they put me to work as assistant to the resident encephalographer, one of those super-Negroes who speak five languages, quote the sutras, and are wizards in electronics as well. He, Colley Wilkes, got interested in my ideas and helped me rig up my first working model. Another break came my way from Kino Yamaiuchi, a classmate, presently with Osaka Instruments, who cut every piece of red tape and got the first five hundred production models turned out in record time—a little order that cost me $150,000 worth of my wife's R. J. Reynold's stock.

My invention unites two principles familiar to any sophomore in high school physics. One is the principle of electrical induction. Any electrical activity creates a magnetic field, which in turn will induce a current in a wire passed through the field. The other is the principle of location by triangulation. Using micro-circuitry techniques, Colley and I rigged up two tiny electronic "listeners," something like the parabolic reflectors with which one can hear a whisper at two hundred feet. Using our double receiver, we could "hear" the electrical activity of a pinhead sized area anywhere in the brain: in the cortex, the pineal body, the midbrain—anywhere.

So we "listened." Colley was interested in locating brain tumors and such, but I was after bigger game. We listened and sure enough Colley found his brain tumors. What I found was a horse of a different color.

Colley, I will admit, has not gone along with my idea of measuring and treating the deep perturbations of the soul. Unfortunately, there still persists in the medical profession the quaint superstition that only that which is visible is real. Thus the soul is not real. Uncaused terror cannot exist. Then, friend, how come you are shaking?

No matter, though. Later I was made a professor and didn't need Colley's help.

I have called my machine More's Qualitative Quantitative Ontological Lapsometer.

A curtain moves in a window of the front wing of the motel, opposite the girls' rooms. Could it be that some Bantu S.O.B. is still trying to shoot me?

* * *

Allow me to cite, in simplified terms, a couple of my early case histories.

## PATIENT #1

One hot summer afternoon as I sat at my father's old coroner's desk by the open back door sipping Early Times, watching the flight patterns of the martins, and pondering the singularity of being forty-four years old, my nurse, whom I mainly employ to keep patients away, brought in a patient.

Nothing changes in a man, I was thinking. I felt exactly as I felt when I was ten years old. Only accidentals change. Hair begins to sprout from your ears, your toes rotate, showing more skin.

My nurse first put away the bottle. She is a beautiful though dour Georgia Presbyterian of the strict observance named Ellen Oglethorpe. Her eyes, blue as Lake Geneva, glittered in triumph as she stowed the Early Times and closed the door behind the patient. For she had, to her way of thinking, killed two birds with one stone. She was striking a blow at my drinking and at the same time delivering one of the "better sort" of patients, the sort who have money. She approves of money on religious grounds.

The patient was P. T. Bledsoe, president of Brown-Betterbag Paper Company. The poor man had his usual blinding sick headache. I gave him a shot of corticaine and sat and looked at him.

P. T. Bledsoe is a sixty-year-old man, an upright citizen, a generous Knothead, good hunting companion, churchgoer, deacon, devoted husband and father, Lion, Kiwanian, 33rd-degree Mason who, however, is subject to seizures of rage and blinding headaches and is convinced of several conspiracies against him. The Negroes for one, he told me, were giving him a hard time at the plant, wanting to be promoted and all. He was certain that the Negroes and Communists were after him (as a matter of fact, the Negroes *were* after him, I happened to know) as well as a Jewish organization that he called the "Bildebergers" and that he had reason to believe had taken over the Federal Reserve system. Though he lived on the ninth hole squarely in the middle of Paradise Estates, which is protected by an electrified ten-foot fence, a guard house at every entrance, and a private patrol, he kept two fierce Rhodesian ridgebacks, one outside and one inside the house. His ambi-

tion was to move to Australia. He never tired of telling of the
year in his youth he spent in the Outback.

"Look, P.T.," I said at last. "Why don't you move to Australia?"

"Yeah," said P.T. sourly, disappointed at what he took to be
a conversational gambit.

"No, I mean it."

"I'm not ready to retire."

"Doesn't your company have a million acres in Queensland?"

"I'm not walking away from anything."

I sighed. Perhaps he was right. It's just that in recent
months I've found it an effective rule of therapy to accept as
more self-evident every day a certain state of affairs, namely,
that most people nowadays are possessed, harboring as they
do all manner of demonic hatred and terrors and lusts and
envies, that principalities and powers are nearly everywhere
victorious, and that therefore a doctor's first duty to his patient
is to help him find breathing room and so keep him from
going crazy. If P.T. can't stand blacks and Bildebergers, my
experience is that there is not time enough to get him over it
even if I could. Nor can I cast out his demon nor forgive his
sin if that's what it is. Why not then move to the Outback, if
that is what you like and especially if there is not a Jew or a
black for a hundred miles around?

But we'd been over this ground before and P.T. now sat
wearily in his chair.

Catching sight of the first crude model of my invention in
an open drawer, I had an idea. Until that moment I had not
tried it on anyone but myself—where I confess I had uncovered a regular museum of pathology, something like passing a
metal detector over the battlefield of Iwo Jima.

Why not begin my clinical series with P.T. Bledsoe?

His blood pressure and other physical signs were normal.
So, standing behind P.T., I passed the lapsometer over his
skull, taking readings and feeling a bit like a phrenologist.

His cortical readings were normal, as was his pineal selfhood. Then, having a hunch, I focused upon the red nucleus in
the floor of the fourth ventricle and asked him about the Bildebergers.

To my astonishment and even as I watched, the needle
swung from a moderate 2.6 mmv to a great whacking rage
level of 9.4 mmv.

"Your headache's coming back, isn't it?"

P.T. looked up in surprise, his eyes hazed with pain, and spied my machine, which at this stage looked for all the world like a Brownie box camera.

"Does that thing register headaches?"

"In a way."

"Can you cure them?"

Now it was his turn to be excited and mine to be depressed.

"No, not yet." At the time I had not yet made my second breakthrough.

I could not cure his headache then. Now I can. But here's the curious thing. The very act of locating the site, touching the sore spot, so to speak, seemed to make him feel better. He refused a second shot and left quite cheerfully.

## PATIENT #2

Later the same afternoon I saw Ted Tennis, a well-educated, somewhat abstracted graduate student who suffered from massive free-floating terror, identity crisis, and sexual impotence.

It didn't take my machine to size him up. Every psychiatrist knows the type: the well-spoken slender young man who recites his symptoms with precision and objectivity—so objective that they seem to be somebody else's symptoms—and above all with that eagerness, don't you know, as if nothing would please him more than that his symptom, his dream, should turn out to be interesting, a textbook case. *Allow me to have a proper disease, Doctor,* he all but tells me.

As we watched the sooty martins through the doorway come skimming up to the hotel—it helps with some patients if we can look a the martins and not at each other—he tells me his troubles with the usual precision, using medical words—he's read more medical books than I have—like a case history! The usual story: daytime terror and nighttime impotence, even though he feels "considerable warmth and tenderness" toward his wife, Tanya (why doesn't he just say he loves her?), and so forth. He is wondering again about the "etiology" of the impotence. Dear God, how could he be anything other than impotent? How can a man quaking with terror make love to his wife?

But today he's got a new idea. If I'd been as sharp-witted and alert to small clues as a good psychiatrist should be, I should have guessed from the way his eye kept straying to my big bottom drawer. Here I keep my samples. The untreatable maladies of any age, reader, may be ascertained from the free samples a doctor receives. My desk drawer contains hundreds of suppositories, thousands of pills for treating terror, and dozens of rayon "training" organs for relieving male impotence.

None of these things works very well.

In short, my patient asked—for the first time and in a halting, scarcely audible voice—to be fitted with a rayon organ.

If he could not "achieve an adequate response" himself, he said—why doesn't he say "make love"—he could at least see that his wife did.

Again we cast an eye toward my bottom drawer, which did in fact contain a regular arsenal of male organs, the best of which are for some reason manufactured in Bayonne, New Jersey.

"Very well, Ted," I said, opening the drawer and taking out not a Bayonne-rayon organ but my invention.

"What's that?"

"I'd like to do a personality profile using a new tele-encephalographic technique." This is the way you talk to Ted.

"Eh? How's that?" asked Ted, pricking up his ears. "You mean you can measure electrical activity with that?"

"Yes."

"Without electrodes?"

"Yes."

"And correlate the readings with personality traits?"

"Yes."

"Wow."

He was willing enough, of course. He sees something magic in it, scientific magic, like being touched by the king for the king's evil. But it is more than that. When I touched him—strange, but this happened earlier with P.T. Bledsoe—he already seemed better. Who of us now is not so strangely alone that it is the cool clinical touch of the stranger that serves best to treat his loneliness?

"Should be interesting," said Ted, bowing his head.

It was. He registered a dizzy 7.6 mmv over Brodmann 32, the area of abstractive activity. Since that time I have learned that a reading over 6 generally means that a person has so abstracted himself from himself and from the world around him, seeing things as theories and himself as a shadow, that he cannot, so to speak, reenter the lovely ordinary world. Instead he orbits the earth and himself. Such a person, and there are millions, is destined to haunt the human condition like the Flying Dutchman.

Ellen Oglethorpe peeped in and closed the door again as

discreetly as if we were lovers. Her eyes sparkled. She was having a good day. Two rich patients in one day! Ted Tennis's wife, Tanya, is a Milwaukee beer heiress and their house in Paradise is bigger than mine.

Over his coeliac plexus, soothed though he was, he still clocked a thunderous anxiety of 8.7 mmv. His hand trembled slightly against mine. And all at once I could see how he lived his life: shuddering in orbit around the great globe, seeking some way to get back. Don't I know? We are two of a kind, winging it like Jupiter and spying comely maids below and having to take the forms of swans and bulls to approach them. Except that he, good heathen that he is, wished only to reenter his own wife. I, the Christian, am the fornicator.

"Well?" he asked anxiously when I finished.

So I told him my findings and he listened with the intensest interest, but I made the mistake of using such words as "angelism," "spiritual apogee," etcetera, all of which are just technical words to me but had the wrong connotations to him. He's a biologist. So he looked disappointed.

"Look, Tom," said Ted patiently. "All I want is a Bayonne-rayon training member. Would you—"

"O.K. You can take your pick—if." I open the drawer of members.

"If?"

"If you follow my prescription first."

"Oh, very well."

"First, take these. . . . " I write him a prescription. "Now, tomorrow, here's what you do."

"Yes?"

"Instead of taking the car pool home tomorrow, walk."

"Walk twenty-five miles on the interstate?"

"No, walk six miles through the swamp."

"Through the swamp." He nodded dolefully, worst fears realized.

"Yes. Unfortunately, until we make a therapeutic breakthrough comparable to this diagnostic breakthrough"—I wave my invention at him— "the only way to treat a disorder like this is by rough-and-ready empirical methods. Like putting an ice pack on a toothache. We don't know much about angelism."

"Angelism," repeated Ted sourly. "So to treat angelism, you walk through a swamp."

"Is that worse than the indignity of strapping on a Bayonne rayon member?" I gave him a few technical details about

Layer V of Brodmann Area 32. He brightened. If it's scientific, he'll do it.

"Well, it's worth a try. I'll do it for Tanya's sake. I'd do anything to restore our relationship along the entire spectrum."

"Very well. Get a compass and after work tomorrow on Monkey Island, strike out due north across the swamp."

Ted does his research on Monkey Island in the middle of the swamp. There dwells a colony of killer apes, *Gorilla gorilla malignans,* thought to be an unevolved descendant of one of man's ancestors. No other ape kills for pleasure.

The question is: how to account for man's wickedness? Biologists, for some reason, find it natural to look for a wicked monkey in the family tree. I find it more reasonable to suppose that monkeys are blameless and that something went wrong with man. Many people hereabouts, by the way, blame the recent wave of atrocities on escaped killer apes. Some Knothead whites, however, blame black guerrillas. Some liberals blame white Knotheads.

If you measure the pineal activity of a monkey—or any other subhuman animal—with my lapsometer, you will invariably record identical readings at Layers I and II. Its self, that is to say, coincides with itself. Only in man do you find a discrepancy: Layer I, the outer social self, ticking over, say, at a sprightly 5.4 mmv, while Layer II just lies there, barely alive at 0.7 mmv, or even zero!—a nought, a gap, an aching wound. Only in man does the self miss itself, *fall* from itself (hence *laps*ometer!) Suppose—! Suppose I could hit on the right dosage and weld the broken self whole! What if man could reenter paradise, so to speak, and live there both as man and spirit, whole and intact man-spirit, as solid flesh as a speckled trout, a dappled thing, yet aware of itself as a self!

But we were speaking of Ted. Yes, I prescribed for Ted, Ted promised to follow the prescription, and he did. The next afternoon, instead of leaving Monkey Island at five, climbing into a sealed refrigerated bubbletop and gliding home on the interstate, home where in his glass-walled "enclosed patio" he would surely sit quaking with terror, abstracting himself from himself and corrupting the here-and-now—instead he wore jeans and tennis shoes and, taking a compass reading bearing nor'-nor'east, struck out through Honey Island Swamp. The six miles took him five hours. At ten o'clock that night he staggered up his back yard past the barbecue grill, half dead of fatigue, having been devoured by mosquitoes, leeches, vampire bats, tsetse flies, snapped at by alligators, moccasins, copperheads, chased by Bantu guerrillas and once even set upon and cuffed about by a couple of Michigan State dropouts on a bummer who mistook him for a parent. It was every bit the ordeal I had hoped.

At that time the only treatment of angelism, that is, excessive abstraction of the self from itself, was recovery of the self through ordeal.

So it came to pass that half-dead and stinking like a catfish, he fell into the arms of his good wife, Tanya, and made lusty love to her the rest of the night.

The freshening wind smells of rain and trees.

Behind the motel a tumbleweed blows through the vineclad posts of the drive-in movie. Its sign has advertised the same film for the past five years:

> **HOMO HIJINKS**
> **ZANY LAFF RIOT**

It took a lot to get people out to movies in the last days of the old Auto Age. A gimmick was needed. In *Homo Hijinks* it was an act of fellatio performed by two skydivers in a free fall on 3-D Ektachrome on a two-hundred-foot screen.

## PATIENT #3

Charley Parker, the Paradise golf pro, came to see me last year for a life insurance examination. In the physical, he checked out well in all categories, being indeed a superb physical specimen as well as a genial outgoing sort of fellow. A fifty-year-old blond stud pony of a man, he once made the winter tour with the champs and even placed at Augusta. But Charley is best known for having been the first pro to introduce night golf to a major course. Paradise Country Club, thanks to Charley Parker, inaugurated the famous Southern "Moonlight" summer tour of the champs, played "under the arcs" in the cool of the evening. It is a "new concept" in tournament golf. Making use of cheap electricity and cheap sodium vapor, Charley concealed hundreds of lamps in cypress trees, behind Spanish moss. To Charley goes the credit for delighting the fans with the romance of golf and repelling insects as well.

I made routine readings with my lapsometer. Hm, what's this? Healthy as he was, and with every reason to be happy,

Charley's deep pineal, the site of inner selfhood, was barely ticking over at a miserable o.1 mmv.

I asked Charley if he was sure he felt all right, no insomnia? no nervousness? no depression? no feelings of disorientation or strangeness?

"Are you kidding, Doc?" Charley began, ticking off his assets: his lovely wife, Ramona; one boy at M.I.T.; the other boy at fourteen winner of the J.C. tournament; his success in bringing the champs to Paradise (this very weekend, by the way) for a Pro-Am tournament; boosting the prize money to a cool million; being voted Man of the Year by the Optimists, etcetera etcetera.

But he paused in his counting. "Nervousness? strangeness? It's funny that you should ask."

"Why?"

As I waited, I was thinking: surely my machine is wrong this time. Charley never looked better, tan skin crinkled in healthy crow's-feet, blond, almost albino, eyelashes thick and sand-sprinkled as so many athletes' are. He's a healthy bourbon-cured stud of a man with a charming little-kid openness about him: it does not occur to him not to say how he feels. Charley's the sort of fellow, you know, who always turns up in a pinch and does what needs doing. Maybe he's the best American type, the sergeant-yeoman out of the hills, the good cop. When the hurricane comes, he's the fellow with the truck: come on, we got to get those folks out of there.

Charley blinked his sandy lashes and passed a hand across his eyes.

"I mean like this morning I looked at myself in the mirror and I said, Charley, who in the hell are you? What does it all mean? It was strange, Doc. What does it all mean, is the thing."

"What does what all mean?"

"What about you, Doc?" asked Charley, with a glint in his eye, meaning: look who's asking about nervousness. But he forgave me as quickly. "Doc, you ought to stay in condition. You got a good build. What you need is eighteen every night under the arcs, like the other docs."

I nodded, taking hope. He could be right.

A note for physicians: if you listen carefully to what patients say, they will often tell you not only what is wrong with them but also what is wrong with you.

Six months later I was called out to Charley's house by his wife, Ramona. Charley was in an acute depression. As a matter of fact, I was not feeling well myself. My feet moved in glue. It was March 2, the anniversary of Samantha's death and the date too of the return of the first martin scouts from the Amazon basin. I had been sitting at the back door of my office waiting for them and putting off going to see Charley.

It was four o'clock when I got there. Ramona and I sat there in the cathedral living room and watched Charley in his Naugehyde recliner set uncomfortably in the up position. Ramona had just got back from a garden club luncheon and still had her hat on, bright blue and fur-trimmed to match her suit. A thick white droning afternoon light filled the room. Through the open pantry door I could see Lou Ann, the cook, fixing to leave the kitchen with her plastic bag of scraps. The dishwasher had already shifted into the wash cycle *chug-chug-chug*.

Charley's appearance was shocking. He was dressed in sport clothes but wore them like an old man, aloha shirt, high-stomached shorts, but business shoes and socks. His elbows had grown tabs. His tan had an undertone of jaundice. The crow's-feet around his eyes were ironed out, showing white troughs.

"Did you want to see me, Charley?"

He cupped his hand to hear. Not that he was deaf, but it was hard to hear in that room. Voices sounded reedy. The vaulted ceiling crossed by simulated hand-hewn beams roared like a conch.

Charley looked at me.

"You look like hell, Doc."

"I know."

"You got a good build. You ought to stay in shape."

"You're right." I was feeling bad. Samantha was dead and the martins had not come back. It was a bad white winter day.

"What did you mean when you asked me if I felt strange?" Charley asked me, resuming our conversation of six months earlier.

"What? Oh. As I recall, it was a routine question."

"Why in hell should I feel strange?" Charley's reedy voice buzzed up into the vaulted ceiling like a cicada. He felt very low, but my own low spirits revived him sufficiently so that he pulled a lever and lay back in the recliner.

"He loves to talk to you," said Ramona in a loud drone as if Charley were not talking, were not even present. Discovering that she still had her hat on, she clucked and, feeling for hatpins, stood up and went into the pantry. Her inner calves still had the tender straight undeveloped lines of pretty girls in the Lower Piedmont, the sort who sit drinking Coke for twenty years. She is from Spartanburg, South Carolina.

It seemed permissible to slump as low as Charley. Charley and I could talk along the floor while we went sailing through the roaring upper air as if it were her medium.

Charley was depressed but he didn't know why. Nothing much had changed in his life, except that his son had dropped out of M.I.T. and taken to the swamp, hardly an uncommon occurrence these days. But he and his son had never been close.

"So what?" said Charley. "My old man ran me off when I was fourteen."

So there seemed to be no external cause for Charley's distress. On the contrary. Just the week before, the champs had signed up again to play under the arcs on the Moonlight Summer Tour. The new Paradise 36 was finished. A new concept in golf courses, its initial cost of forty million was also its final cost. What with its fleet of carts, elimination of caddies, its automatic sprinkler system with each outlet regulated by a moisture sensor, its new Tifton 451 Bermuda, which required neither mowing nor fertilizing, labor costs were eliminated.

Then what was the trouble?

Charley shrugged. "I don't know, Doc. I mean, what's the use? You know what I mean?"

"Yes." Something occurred to me. "When did you see your son last?"

"What's that got to do with it?"

"When?"

"Last month. On his way to Honey Island Swamp."

"Did you quarrel with him?"

"Do you know what that sapsucker wanted to do?"

"No."

"Move the three of them into his old room while he looks for a new cave."

"The three of them?"

"Him and his little yehudi and their cute little bastard. Up they go to bed without a by-your-leave."

"Yehudi?"

"Introduces her as Ethel Ginsberg or Finklestein."

"Yes?"

"What do you mean, yes? I mean, don't you think he could at least have had enough consideration for his mother to pretend they were married?"

"What happened then?"

"What do you mean, what happened? I threw his ass out. Wouldn't you have?"

"I don't know."

I was thinking of my daughter, dead these seven years. Would I have thrown her ass out if she had gone up to bed with a Ginsberg? Yes. No. I don't know.

Rising unsteadily, I blew my nose and reached for my lapsometer. What I was curious about was whether his deep pineal reading stayed low during his excitement. Charley was so wound up that he didn't even notice that I was going over his head like a barber. He kept swinging around to tell me something. It was like giving a haircut to a three-year-old.

(The reading was up: getting mad helped him. Or was it the talking?)

"Be still, Charley."

Charley shut up. But he had to do something, so he started pressing buttons on his recliner. The stereo-V came booming on and stayed on.

In a minute Ramona came in and turned it down. Her hat was off and her hair was piled up in tiers like a garden-club arrangement.

"It's a goddamn lie," said Charley.

"What's a lie?" Was he talking about the news or his son?

"That's what he does all day," Ramona told me, as if Charley were absent. "Fusses about the news and can't wait till the next. He listens to the news every hour."

"Fusses" seemed to be the wrong word for Charley's anger.

Then it was that the idea first occurred to me: what would happen if one were able to apply electrical stimulation to the pineal region?

But the best I could do in those days was a kind of "historical therapy," as I called it then: a recapture of the past and one's self.

Only one thing worked with Charley. After his anger had subsided (something in the news—the Negroes, the Lefts, the love people, I didn't notice—made him mad), I picked up the glass paperweight and I gave it a shake to set the snow whirling. The scene was the Battle above the Clouds atop Lookout Mountain. "Remember when we got this, honey," Charley would usually say. "Yes. At Ruby Falls on our honeymoon."

But that day Charley was either too angry still or too low to notice the paperweight.

"Ain't nobody starving in no swamp," he muttered.

I nodded, thinking he meant his son.

Ramona, who is quick and intuitive, saw my mistake and corrected me (women are smarter than psychiatrists).

"He" —still the absent *he*— "was talking about the news. You know, niggers supposed to be starving around here like in Beauford."

"I see."

Ramona gave me another hint. "He thinks they're accusing him."

"They?"

"That's humbug," said Charley.

"Guess what he told him," said Ramona. "He told him it was his fault."

He? Him? His? Which *he* is Charley and which his son and whose fault is it?

"Well of course," I said somewhat vaguely, "everyone knows that Charley is a generous—"

"No! No!" They both turned on me. I hadn't got the straight of it yet. I felt stupid, but on the other hand some married people, you know, carry on these mysterious six-layered conversations with all manner of secret signs.

Ramona set me straight. "Why should anyone blame Charley when all he did was build a golf course and invent the arcs? It wasn't his forty million dollars that filled in the swamp. He was just doing his job. Is it Charley's fault that Tifton 451 eliminates labor?"

"Yes. Hm," I said in the best psychiatric style, pretending I knew all along. "You mean he and Chuck quarreled?"

"Quarreled, hell," said Charley. "I kicked his ass out."

"You should have heard them," said Ramona. "Both of them acted ugly." Ramona tried to put it down to menfolk's ordinary foolishness. They had a fuss. But it was more than that. So serious was the quarrel that Charley was still worried about not winning it.

"I told him exactly like I'm telling you now: get your little yehudi and your little bastard and get your ass out."

"They used to go hunting together," said Ramona in her Spartanburg drone. But she was crying. "They never missed a dove season."

"You know what he accused me of?" Charley asked me.

"No."

"Starving niggers. You know what he called me?"

"No."

"A hypocritical son of a bitch."

"He didn't actually say—" began Ramona. "That was ugly, though."

"You too, Doc," said Charley.

"Me?"

"You were included. All of us here are hypocritical sons of bitches."

"I see."

"He told me he knew for a fact that niggers come up from the swamp at night and eat soybean meal off the greens. Now you know that's a lie."

"Well, I've never heard—"

"In the first place, we haven't used soybean meal since last summer. Tifton 451 doesn't need it. As a matter of fact, I've got a whole barnful left over I've got to get rid of."

"I see."

I shook the paperweight again and in the end succeeded in getting Charley to tell me about his first tour when he had to borrow a hundred dollars to qualify at Fort Worth because Ramona had spent their last money on Sears sport clothes for him so he wouldn't look like a caddy. But he was a caddy and wore sneakers instead of spiked shoes.

He told me about placing at Augusta. His deep pineal reading got up to 6 mmv.

"Doc, have you ever played thirty-six holes on three Baby Ruths?"

"No."

"Do you think I'm a hypocritical son of a bitch?"

"No."

"What do you think I am?"

What do I think? The mystery of evil is the mystery of limited goodness. Charley is a good man. Then how did things turn out so badly? What went wrong? I gave the paperweight a shake and sent snow swirling around Lookout Mountain.

Charley wanted to talk about whether the niggers were starving or not, etcetera, but what interested me and where my duty lay was with Charley. I saw how his life was and what he needed. Charley was a tinkerer, like GM's famous Charley Kettering, a fellow who has to have one idea to worry with twenty-four hours a day. Without it he's blown up. Charley's the sort of fellow who retires to Florida hale and hearty and perishes in six months.

Here's what happened.

Some months later I made my second breakthrough and added the ionizer to my lapsometer. I was able to treat an area as well as "listen" to it. It worked. Accordingly, a few days ago—when was it? a day? two days? dear Lord, how much has happened—I gave him a pineal massage and he came to himself, his old self, and began to have one idea after another. One idea: an electronic unlosable golf ball that sends signals from the deepest rough. Another: a "golfarama," a mystical idea of combining a week of golf on a Caribbean island with the Greatest Pro of Them All—a week of revivals conducted by a member of the old Billy Graham team, the same revivalist, incidentally, who is in Paradise this weekend.

The interstate swelters in the sun.

My eyes are almost swelled shut, breath whistles in my throat, but my heart is full of love. Love of what? Women. Which women? All women. The first night I ever spent on the acute ward, a madman looked at me and said, not knowing me from Adam: "You want to know your trouble? You don't love God, you love pussy."

It might be true. Madmen like possessed men usually tell the truth. At any rate, through a crack of daylight I catch sight of a face, a blurred oval in the window of room 203. Lola.

The question is: if worst comes to worst, what is the prospect of a new life in a new dead world with Lola Rhoades, to say nothing of Moira Schaffner and Ellen Oglethorpe? Late summer and fall lie ahead, but will they be full of ghosts? That was the trouble with long summer evenings and the sparkling days of fall, they were haunted. What broke the heart was the cicadas starting up in the sycamores in October. Everyone was happy but our hearts broke with happiness. The golf links canceled themselves. Happy children grew up with haunted expressions and ran away. No more of that. Vines sprout in the plaza now. Fletcher Christian began a new life with three wives on faraway Pitcairn, green as green and unhaunted by old Western ghosts. I shall be happy with my three girls. Only Ellen, a Presbyterian, may make trouble.

## PATIENT #4

Late last night a love couple crept up out of the swamp and appeared in my "enclosed patio." This often happens. Even though I am a psychiatrist, denizens of the swamp appear at all hours suffering from malaria, dengue, flukes, bummers, hepatitis, and simple starvation. Nobody else will treat them.

I saw them from my bedroom window. It was three o'clock. I had been reading my usual late-night fare, Stedmann's *History of World War I*. For weeks now I've been on the Battle of Verdun, which killed half a million men, lasted a year, and left the battle lines unchanged. Here began the hemorrhage and death by suicide of the old Western world: white Christian Caucasian Europeans, sentimental music-loving Germans and rational clear-minded Frenchmen, slaughtering each other without passion. "The men in the trenches did not hate each other," wrote Stedmann. "As for the generals, they respected or contemned each other precisely as colleagues in the same profession."

Comes a tap at the door. Is it guerrilla, drughead, Ku Kluxer, Choctaw, or love couple?

Love couple.

What seems to be the trouble? It seems their child, a love child, is very sick. I know you're not a pediatrician but the other doctors won't come, etcetera. Will I come? O.K.

Grab my bag, and down through the azaleas and into a pirogue, I squatting amidships, boy and girl paddling as expertly as Cajuns. A sinking yellow moon shatters in the ripples.

They speak freely of themselves. He's a tousled blond lad with a splendid fan-shaped beard like Jeb Stuart (I can tell he's from these parts by the way he says *fo'teen* for *fourteen*, *Bugaloosa* for *Bogalusa*), gold-haired, gray-jeaned, bare-chested and -footed. She's a dark little Pocahontas from Brooklyn (I judge, for she speaks of *hang-gups*). They've given up city, home, family, career, religion, to live a perfect life of love and peace with a dozen others on a hummock with nothing else for a shelter in the beginning than an abandoned Confederate salt mine. There they've revived a few of the pleasanter Choctaw customs such as building chickees and smoking rabbit cannab, a variety of *Cannabis indica* that grows wild in the swamp.

"You don't remember me, Dr. More." The boy speaks behind me.

"No."

"I'm Chuck."

"Chuck?"

"Chuck Parker."

"Yes of course. I know your father very well."

"My poor father."

How is it that children can be more beautiful than the sum of their parents' beauty? Ramona is a stork-legged, high-hipped, lacquer-headed garden-clubber from Spartanburg. Charley is a pocked-nosed, beat-up, mashed-down Gene Sarazen. And here is golden-haired golden-limbed Chuck looking like Phoebus Apollo or Sir Lancelot in hip-huggers.

When we reach the hummock, the sky in the east has turned sickly and tentative with dawn.

They're camping near the mouth of old Empire Number Two, the salt mine that supplied Dick Taylor during the Red River campaign. Except for an ember or two there is no sign of the others. In a swale springy with cypress needles Chuck has built a chickee of loblolly chinked with blue bayou clay.

As we enter the chickee, fragrant with bayberry smoke, a tall brown-haired girl rises and closes a book on her finger, for all the world like a baby-sitter in Paradise when the folks come home—except that her reading light is a candle made from wax myrtle and bayberries. Chuck stops her and introduces us. Her name is Hester. Instead of leaving, she squats cross-legged on the cypress needles.

Afterwards Chuck tells me in her hearing, "Hester has her own chickee."

"Is that so," I answer, scratching my head.

I take a look at Hester's book, still closed on her finger. A good way to size up people. It is not what you might think, Oriental or revolutionary. It is, of all things under the sun, Erle Stanley Gardner's first novel, *The Case of the Velvet Claws*.

The baby, as I had reason from experience to expect and had in fact prepared my bag for, suffers from dehydration. He's dried up like a prune. The treatment is simple and the results spectacular. Slip a needle in his scalp vein and hang a bottle of glucose from a loblolly twig.

Mama watched her baby get well before her eyes, reviving like a wilted hydrangea stuck in a bucket of water. I watched Mama. Ethel is a dark, quick little Pocahontas with hairbraids, blue Keds, jean shorts, and sharp soiled knees. She's not my type, being a certain kind of Smith girl, a thin moody Smithie who props cheek on knee, doesn't speak to freshmen, doesn't focus her eyes, and is prone to quick sullen decisions, leaping onto her little basketed bike and riding off without explanation.

(Hester is my type: post-Protestant, post-rebellion, post-ideology—reading Perry Mason here on a little ideological island!—reverted all the way she is, clear back to pagan innocence like a shepherd girl piping a tune on a Greek vase.)

When the sun clears the hummock, we sit on the bayou bank feeling the warmth on our backs, Ethel holding the baby, Chuck holding the infusion bottle. Hester sits cross-legged and stare-eyed, looking at nothing, smoothing her calves with her hands.

"How about that?" murmurs Chuck, as the baby's wrinkles disappear. What a lordly youth, with a smooth simple chest, simple large golden arms and legs, the large wrists and boxy knees of a tennis player.

Now the sun, breaking through the morning fog and live oaks, strikes shafts into the tea-colored water. Mullet jump. Two orange-colored warblers fly at each other in the sunlight, claws upraised like cockerels. A swarm of gnats hangs over the water motionless and furious, like a molecule. I eat a scuppernong. It is fat and tart.

"It wouldn't be bad to live here," I tell Chuck.

"Why don't you? Come and live with us." He turns to Ethel but she gives him her hooded Smithie look.

"Where would I live?"

"Here," says Hester. "There's my chickee."

Does she mean live with her or build my own chickee close by? She's from Massachusetts or Rhode Island. For car she says *cǎ*.

"What have you got to lose, Doc?" asks Chuck.

"Well—"

The glucose bottle is empty. Ethel frowns and takes baby and bottle inside.

"Are you happy over there?"

"Happy?"

"We're happy here."

"Good."

"Everyone here lives a life of perfect freedom and peace."

"Good."

"We help each other. We love."

"Very good."

"That is, all except Hester. She hasn't found anyone she likes yet. Eh, Hester?"

"I'm not quite sure," says Hester, not blushing.

Oh those lovely hollowed-out Holyoke vowels. Her voice is a Congregational bell.

"We're basically religious here, Doc."

"Good."

"We have God every minute."

"Good."

"Don't you see that I am God, you are God, that prothonotary warbler is God?"

"No."

"We always tell the exact truth. Will you answer me honestly, Doc?"

"All right."

"What is your life like? Are you happy?"

"No."

"What's wrong?"

"It's hard to say." For some reason I blush under Hester's clear gaze.

"But you don't have a good life."

"No."

"Then why do you live it?"

"I don't know."

"We have a good life here."

"Good."

"There's nothing wrong with sex, Doc. You shouldn't put it down."

"I don't."

"It's not even the most important thing."

"It's not?"

"With us it's far down the list."

"Hm." I look at my watch. "You can take me back."

"O.K. if I pay you later? Or do you want some Choctaw cannab?"

"No thanks. Don't worry about it." Some time ago Chuck lit up a calumet of Choctaw or "rabbit" cannabis and has now begun to jump a bit, feet together, kangaroo style. He passes the calumet around. Hester smokes and passes it to me.

"No thanks."

Ethel, returning from her chickee, also refuses. "Pay the man," she tells Chuck. "Can't you tell he wants to be paid?"

"You're all right, Doc," says Chuck, jumping. "I've always liked you. I've always liked Catholics. We've got some liberated Catholics here."

"I'm not a liberated Catholic."

"What's this about your invention?"

"Did your father tell you?" I am surprised. Perhaps Chuck and his father have patched things up.

"No. My mother. She said you passed a miracle. Have a drag, Doc?"

"No thanks."

I tell them briefly about my lapsometer and about the new breakthrough, my ionizer that corrects electrical malfunctions. High though he's getting, Chuck, what with his three years at M.I.T. and 800 SAT score, is digging me utterly.

"Wow, Doc! Great! Wild!" cries Chuck, jumping straight up and down like a Choctaw at the jibiya dance. "You got to stay! We'll massage everybody on the mainland with your lapsometer and get rid of the old sad things!"

"Do you mean you can actually treat personality hang-gups?" asks little Brooklyn-Pocahontas Ethel.

"Well, yes."

"Do you have it with you?"

"As a matter of fact I do."

"Give us a reading, Doc!" says Chuck.

Even Hester shows a spark of interest.

"Treat Hester, Doc!" cries Chuck. "She's still Springfield bourgeois. Look at her! She likes you, Doc."

"This is the last place I'd treat anybody."

"Why?" asks Ethel, frowning.

"Too much heavy salt hereabouts." I pick up a chunk of dirty Confederate salt. "This stuff assays at about point oh-seven percent heavy salt. I wouldn't dare use my ionizer."

Chuck snaps his fingers. "You mean sub-chain reaction? Silent implosion? Whssssk?"

"Yes."

"Wowee! Hot damn!" Now Chuck is jumping like a pogo.

"But you could do the diagnostic part?" asks Hester in her lovely hollow-throat voice.

"Yes."

"Do one on me," says Ethel.

"Doc, tell me the truth now," says Chuck, capering and jerking his elbows.

"All right."

"Are you telling me that with that thing you can actually register the knotheadedness of the Knotheads, the nutty objectivity of the scientists, and the mad spasms of the liberals?"

"That's an odd way of putting it, but yes."

"And you're also telling me that you can treat 'em, fry 'em with your ray and make 'em human?"

"With the same qualification, yes."

"And you're also telling me that something is afoot with all those nuts over yonder and that today on the glorious Fourth of July something is going to happen and they're all going to do each other in?"

"Well, not quite but—"

"And finally you're saying that some of your gadgets have fallen into the wrong hands and there's a chance the whole swamp might go up in a Heavy-Sodium reaction?"

"Yes."

"Wow! Whee! Hot damn!" Off he goes in his goat dance.

"Will you sit down, you idiot," says Ethel crossly. "What's got into you?"

"It's so *funny.* And Doc here. Doc, man you the wildest of all. Doc, you got to stay here with us. Who's going to believe all that great wild stuff over there?"

"You don't believe me?"

"Believe? Sure. Because you're putting down on all of them, including the scientists."

"I'm a scientist."

"You're better. You're a shaman. The scientists have blown it."

"Still and all, scientists are after the truth."

"I believe you," says Hester suddenly, clear post-Puritan Holyoke eyes full on me.

"I said, do one on me," says Ethel, handing my bag to me.

"Why?"

"Because I don't believe you."

"That's all right."

"I think you're afraid to."

"No, I'm not afraid."

"I wish you would," Hester says, pulling her brown heels across her calves.

"I can do a diagnosis here but not a treatment."

"Do it!"

I shrug. "Very well."

It takes three minutes to run a standard profile, Ethel bows her head so that her Pocahontas braids fall along her cheeks.

"Hm."

"Doc, you kill me," says Chuck.

"Hm. She's got a contradictory reading."

"A what?"

"Look here. She's got a strong amplitude and high milli-voltage over the temporal lobe, Brodmann 28, which corre-

lates in my experience with singular concrete historical aware-
ness, vivid childhood memories, you know, as well as a sense
of the uniqueness of one's tradition. But see here: an even
stronger reading over parietal lobe, Brodmann 18. That's the
site of ahistoric perceptions that are both concrete and abstract. You should be an excellent artist, Ethel."

"You see there, Ethel! She is, Doc."

"Tch," says Ethel sourly. "I've got the same thing from
fortune cookies."

"Are you Jewish, Ethel?"

"What? Yes. What do you mean by asking?"

"You exhibit here what I have termed contradictory Ju-
daism."

"What in hell do you mean?" Ethel swings around on her
knees and looks at me squarely for the first time.

"Because you believe at one and the same time that the Jews
are unique and that they are not. Thus you would be offended if a
Jew told you the Jews were chosen by God, but you would also
be offended if a non-Jew told you they were not."

"You hear that, Ethel," yells Chuck, beginning to jump
again. "Why only last week—"

Ethel has picked up my lapsometer. "You better take Dr.
More home," she tells Chuck without taking her eyes from me.

"O.K., honey, but I mean, gee—Look, I'm sorry, Doc—"

"I'm not listening to some bastard tell me I have a Jewish
brain."

"Well actually," I tell Ethel, "I show the same reading,
believing as I do both that God—" I stop, mouth wide open.
"*Look out!—don't throw it!*— Jesus!"

But she threw it and in doing so must have flipped the
adaptor switch because, before I can catch it, the laspometer
swings through a slow arc, adaptor down. The dirty salt on the
bank spits and smokes.

"Good God, what is that?" asks Chuck, instantly sober.

"That was close." Turning off the switch, I pack the lapsometer with trembling hands.

"Yeah, but what was that stuff? Was it what I think it was?"

"Brimstone, no doubt," says Ethel drily.

"As a matter of fact, it was."

"What else?" says Ethel.

"It's the sulfur in the salt. Don't worry. No harm done.
Now I've got to go."

"Right," says Chuck soberly. "I want to thank you for—"

"Never mind. Goodbye, Hester."

"Goodbye. Come back."

"All right."

How stands it with a forty-five-year-old man who can fall in love on the spot with a twenty-year-old stranger, a clear-eyed vacant simple Massachusetts girl, and desire nothing more in this life than to move into her chickee?

# On the Interstate

IT IS GETTING DARK. LIGHTNING FLICKERS LIKE A GENIE IN-side the bottle-shaped cloud.

Why am I so sleepy? It is almost impossible to keep my eyes open! Fireflies of albumen molecules spark in my brain. Yet I don't feel bad. Then concentrate! The next few minutes are critical.

At this moment the President is beginning to speak in New Orleans and the Vice-President is mounting the platform at NASA a few miles away. Both are making a plea for unity. The President, who is an integrationist Mormon married to a liberated Catholic, will appeal to Leftists to respect law and order. The Vice-President, a Southern Baptist Knothead married to a conservative Unitarian, is asking Knotheads for toler-ance and understanding, etcetera.

The poor U.S.A.!

Even now, late as it is, nobody can really believe that it didn't work after all. The U.S.A. didn't work! Is it even possible that from the beginning it never did work? that the thing always had a flaw in it, a place where it would shear, and that all this time we were not really different from Ecuador and Bosnia-Herzego-vina, just richer. Moon Mullins blames it on the niggers. Hm. Was it the nigger business from the beginning? What a bad joke: God saying, here it is, the new Eden, and it is yours because you're the apple of my eye; because you the lordly Westerners, the fierce Caucasian-Gentile-Visigoths, believed in me and in the outlandish Jewish Event even though you were nowhere near it and had to hear the news of it from strangers. But you believed and so I gave it all to you, gave you Israel and Greece and

48

science and art and the lordship of the earth, and finally even gave you the new world that I blessed for you. And all you had to do was pass one little test, which was surely child's play for you because you had already passed the big one. One little test: here's a helpless man in Africa, all you have to do is not violate him. That's all.

One little test: you flunk!

God, was it always the nigger business, now, just as in 1883, 1783, 1683, and hasn't it always been that ever since the first tough God-believing Christ-haunted cunning violent rapacious Visigoth-Western-Gentile first set foot here with the first black man, the one willing to risk everything, take all or lose all, the other willing just to wait and outlast because once he was violated all he had to do was wait because sooner or later the first would wake up and know that he had flunked, been proved a liar where he lived, and no man can live with that. And sooner or later the lordly Visigoth-Western-Gentile-Christian-Americans would have to falter, fall out, turn upon themselves like scorpions in a bottle.

No! No fair! Foul! The test was too much! What do you expect of a man? Yet even so we almost passed. There was a time . . . You tested us because bad as we were there was no one else, and everybody knew it, even our enemies, and that is why they curse us. Who curses the Chinese? Who ever imagined the Chinese were blessed by God and asked to save the world? Who ever expected anything else from them than what they did? What a laugh. And as for Russia and the Russian Christ who was going to save Europe from itself: ha ha.

Flunked! Christendom down the drain. The dream over. Back to history and Bosnia-Herzegovina.

No! No fair!

But wait. It is still not too late. I can save you, America! I know something! I know what is wrong! I hit on something, made a breakthrough, came on a discovery! I can save the terrible God-blessed Americans from themselves! With my invention! Listen to me. Don't give up. It is not too late. You are still the last hope. There is no one else. Bad as we are, there is no one else.

I crack one eye. Through my turret slit, I notice that the sand trap is smoking. The champs, swinging sand wedges, are converging in the fiery bunker.

It has begun.

A yellow lens-shaped cloud hangs like a zeppelin over the horizon beyond the swamp. From the direction of NASA to the north comes a rattle of gunfire.

Then why don't I get up and go down to the motel and see to the girls?

Because I am so sleepy. One little catnap . . .

# JULY FIRST

# At home

SOMEONE TOOK A SHOT AT ME AT THE BREAKFAST TABLE.

At this moment I am lying in a corner out of the line of fire and thinking to myself: why is it better down here?

The shots, three of them, came from the direction of the swamp. I was eating breakfast in my "enclosed patio." First there was the sound of the shot heard through the glass, not close, not alarming, not even noteworthy. Undoubtedly a gunshot, though it is too early for squirrel season. Then more or less at the same time as the second shot, the glass panel shattered. I say more or less at the same time because I did not infer a connection between the two, the shot and the glass shattering.

The third shot was lower, closer, louder. It made a hole in the glass, and in my mind the shot bore a relation to the hole. Somebody is shooting at me, I thought as I drank a warm orange drink named Tang. As I as considering this at the top of my head, something at the heart of me knew better and I found myself diving for the corner even as I ruminated. Saved by a reflex learned with the First Air Cav in the fifteen-year war in Ecuador.

The corner is a good choice, flanked as it is by two low walls of brick that support the glass panels, high enough for protection and low enough to see over if I crane up. But I don't have to crane up. There is a fenestration in the bricks at eye level.

Here I used to tell Samantha the story of Rikki-Tikki-Tavi, how the cobra got into the house by crawling through a hole in the bricks. Samantha shivered with delight and stopped up the hole with newspapers.

A description of my wife: the sort of woman who would

53

name our daughter Samantha though there was no one in our families with this name.

A plan takes shape. Wait a few minutes, get the Smith & Wesson, leave the house by the lower "woods" door, circle the yard under cover of the sumacs, and get behind the sniper.

Is someone after my invention? By craning my head I can catch a glimpse of the box in the hall, the lovely crafted crate from Osaka Instruments. It is the first shipment of the More Qualitative-Quantitative Ontological Lapsometer, the stethoscope of the spirit, one hundred compact pocket-sized machines of brushed chrome. I've come a long way since my Brownie model.

I am lying on the floor drinking warm Tang to which two duck eggs have been added plus two ounces of vodka plus a dash of Tabasco.

The reason the Tang is warm is that the refrigerator doesn't work. Nothing works. All my household motors are silent: air-conditioner, vacuum, dishwasher, dryer, automobile. Appliances and automobiles are more splendid than ever, but when they break down nobody will fix them. My car broke down at the A & P three weeks ago and nobody would come fix it so I abandoned it. Paradise is littered with the rusting hulks of splendid Pontiacs, Olds, and Chryslers that developed vapor locks and dead batteries and were abandoned. Nowadays people buy cars, drive them until they break down, abandon them and buy another. Most of my friends have switched to Toyotas, which have one moving part.

Don't tell me the U.S.A. went down the drain because of Leftism, Knotheadism, apostasy, pornography, polarization, etcetera etcetera. All these things may have happened, but what finally tore it was that things stopped working and nobody wanted to be a repairman.

The bricks smell of old wax. After all these years particles of Pledge wax still adhere to the cindery pits that pock the glaze. Doris used to wax the bricks once a week. "Annie Mae," she'd tell the maid, "Go Pledge the bricks."

I polish off the Tang-plus-vodka-plus-duck-eggs-plus-Tabasco. I feel better.

Another peep through the cobra hole: nothing moves in the swamp, but there is a flash of light. A telescopic sight?

By moving back a few inches I can see the curving loess slope on which my house stands. The house next door has

been abandoned, its slab cracked and reclaimed by the
swamp, by creeper and anise with its star-shaped funky-smell-
ing flower. Wild grape festoons the carport.

Honeysuckle has invaded Doris's azaleas. A particularly
malignant vine with rank racemose leaves has laid hold of her
Saint Francis, who appears to be lifting his birdbath above
these evil serpents Titmice and cardinals used to drink here.
Saint Francis was Doris's favorite saint, not because he loved
Christ but because he loved titmice.

The evil vine, I notice, has reached the house. A tendril
pokes through the cobra hole and curls up looking for purchase.

Wait! Something moves.

But it is only a swamp bird, a gloomy purplish-green heron
that flaps down out of a cypress and lights on Saint Francis's
birdlimed head. There he perches, neck drawn into his
shoulders, yellow bill pointed straight up. He looks as frowsty
and ill-conceived as a bird drawn by a child.

Now I've got my revolver, by crawling to the closet and back.
The carbine is downstairs.

No sign of the sniper. Has he gone?

Directly above my head on the glass-topped coffee table are
Doris's favorite books just as she left them in the "enclosed
patio." That was before I roofed it, and the books are swollen by
old rains to fat wads of pulp, but still stacked so:

> *Siddhartha*
> *Atlas Shrugged*
> *ESP and the New Spirituality*

Books matter. My poor wife, Doris, was ruined by books,
by books and a heathen Englishman, not by dirty books but by
clean books, not by depraved books but by spiritual books.
God, if you recall, did not warn his people against dirty
books. He warned them against high places. My wife, who
began life as a cheerful Episcopalian from Virginia, became a
priestess of the high places. I loved her dearly and loved to lie
with her and would and did whene'er she would allow it, but
most especially in the morning, at breakfast, in the nine
o'clock sunlight out here on the "enclosed patio." But books
ruined her. Beware of Episcopal women who take up with
Ayn Rand and the Buddha and Dr. Rhine formerly of Duke
University. A certain type of Episcopal girl has a weakness

that comes on them just past youth, just as sure as Italian girls get fat. They fall pry to Gnostic pride, commence buying antiques, and develop a yearning for esoteric doctrine.

Doris stood on these black pebbles, which we brought from Mexico, and told me she was leaving me.

Samantha had been dead some months. Doris began talking of going to the Isle of Jersey or New Zealand where she hoped to recover herself, learn quiet breathing in a simple place, etcetera etcetera, perhaps in the bright shadow of a 'dobe wall or perhaps in a stone cottage under a great green fell. She wanted to leave the bad thing here and go away and make a fresh start. That was all right with me. I was ready to go. I wanted out from the bad thing too. What I didn't know at the time was that I was, for her, part of the bad thing.

"I'm leaving, Tom."

"Where are you going?"

She did not reply.

The morning sun, just beginning to slant down into the "enclosed patio," struck the top of her yellow hair, sending off fiery aureoles like sunflares. I never got over the splendor of her person in the morning, her royal green-linen-clad self, fragrant and golden-fleshed. Her flesh was gold amorphous stuff. Though it was possible to believe that her arm had the usual layers of fat, muscle, artery, bone, these gross tissues were in her somehow transformed by her girl-chemistry, bejeweled by her double-X chromosome. Those were the days of short skirts, and she looked like long-thighed Mercury, god of morning. Her heels had wings. Her legs were long and deepfleshed, bound laterally in the thigh by a strap of fascia that flattened the triceps. Was it her slight maleness, long-leggedness—perhaps 10 percent tunic-clad Mercury was she—that set my heart pounding over breakfast?

No, that's foolishness. I loved her, that's all.

"Where are you going?" I asked again, buttering the grits and watching her hair flame like the sun's corolla.

"I'm going in search of myself."

My heart sank. This was not really her way of talking. It was the one tactic against which I was defenseless, the portentous gravity of her new beliefs. When she was an ordinary ex-Episcopalian, a good-humored Virginia girl with nothing left of her religion but a fondness for old brick chapels, St. John o' the Woods, and the superb English of the King James Version, we had common ground.

"Don't leave, Doris," I said, feeling my head grow heavy and sink toward the grits.

"I have to leave. It is the one thing I must do."

"Why do you have to leave?"

"We're so dead, Tom. Dead inside. I must go somewhere and recover myself. To the lake isle of Innisfree."

"Jesus, let's go to the lake isle together."

"We don't relate any more, Tom."

"I'd like to relate now."

"I know, I know. That's how you see it."

"How?"

"As physical."

"What's wrong with physical?"

Doris sighed, her eyes full of sunlight. "Who was it who said the physical is the lowest common denominator of love?"

"I don't know. Probably a Hindoo. Would you sit here?"

"What a travesty of love, the assertion of one's conjugal rights."

"I wasn't thinking of my conjugal rights. I was thinking of you."

"Love should be a joyous encounter."

"I'm joyous."

She was right. Lately her mournful spirituality had provoked in me the most primitive impulses. In ten seconds' time my spirits had revived. My heart's desire was that she sit on my lap in the yellow muscadine sunlight.

I took her about the hips. No Mercury she, here.

She neither came nor left.

"But we don't relate," said Doris absently, still not leaving though, eyes fixed on Saint Francis who was swarming with titmice. "There are no overtones in our relationship, no nuances, no upper mansions. Build thee more stately mansions, O my soul."

"All right."

"It's not your fault or my fault. People grow away from each other. Spiritual growth is the law of life. Our obligation is to be true to ourselves and to relate to this law of life."

"Isn't marriage a relation?"

"Our marriage is a collapsed morality, like a burnt-our star which collapses into itself, gives no light and is heavy heavy heavy."

Collapsed morality. Law of life. More stately mansions. Here are unmistakable echoes of her friend Alistair Fuchs-

Forbes. A few years ago Doris, who joined the Unity church got in the habit of putting up English lecturers of various Oriental persuasions, Brahmin, Buddhist, Sikh, Zoroastrian. Two things Doris loved, the English people and Eastern religion. Put the two together, Alistair Fuchs-Forbes reciting *I Ching* in a B.B.C. accent, and poor Episcopal Doris, Apple Queen, from Winchester, Virginia, was a goner.

Alistair Fuchs-Forbes, who came once to lecture at Doris's Unity church, took to coming back and staying longer. He and his boy friend Raymond. Here they would sit, in my "enclosed patio," on their broad potato-fed English asses, and speak of the higher things, of the law of life—and of the financial needs of their handicraft retreat in Mexico. There in Cozumel, it seemed, was the last hope of the Western world. Transcendental religion could rescue Western materialism. How? by making-and-meditation, meditating and making things with one's hands, simple good earthbound things like clay pots. Not a bad idea really—I'd have gone with her to Cozumel and made pots—but here they sat on my patio, these two fake English gurus, speaking of the law of spiritual growth, all the while swilling my scotch and eating three-dollar rib-eye steaks that I barbecued on my patio grill. They spoke of Hindoo reverence for life, including cattle, and fell upon my steaks like jackals.

It didn't take Alistair long to discover it was Doris, not I, who was rich.

"A collapsed morality?"

"I am truly sorry, Tom."

"I'm not sure I know what a collapsed morality means."

"That's it. It's meaning we've lost. What is meaningful between us? We simply follow rules and habit like poor beasts on a treadmill."

"There is something in that. Especially since Samantha died. But why don't we work at it together. I love you."

"I love you too, Tom. I'm extremely devoted to you and I always will be. But don't you see that people grow away from each other. A part of one dies, but the rest grows and encysts the old part. Like the chambered nautilus. We're dead."

"I love you dead. At this moment."

My arms are calipers measuring the noble breadth of her hips. She doesn't yield, but she doesn't leave.

"Dead, dead," she whispered above me in the sunlight.

"Love," I whispered.

We were speaking in calm matutinal voices like a pair of wood thrushes fluting in the swamp.

"My God, how can you speak of love?"

"Come here, I'll show you."

"Here?" she said crossly. "I'm here."

"Here."

We had not made love since Samantha's death. I had wanted to, but Doris had a way of ducking her head and sighing and looking elegaic that put me off and made me feel guilty besides. There is this damnable female talent for making a man ashamed, not merely turning him down but putting the guilt of it on him. She made me feel like a high school boy with impure thoughts. Worse than that: a husband with "conjugal rights," and that's enough to chill the warmest heart.

But not mine this morning. I pick up the napkin from my lap.

"Come here."

"What for?" A tiny spark of old Virginny, the Shenandoah Valley, rekindling in her: her saying "what for" and not "why."

"Come and see."

What she did was the nicest compromise between her faraway stare, her sun worship, and lovemaking. She came closer, yet kept her eye on the titmice.

"But you don't love *me*," she said to Saint Francis.

"Yes I do."

She gave me a friendly jostle, the first, and looked down.

"Tch. For pity's sake!" Again, a revival of her old Shenandoah good humor. "Annie Mae is coming, you idiot."

"Close the curtains then."

"I'm leaving," she said but stood closer, again a nicely calculated ambiguity: is she standing close to be close or to get between me and the window so Annie Mae can't see?

"Don't leave," I say with soaring hopes.

"I have to leave."

Then I made a mistake and asked her where she was going. Again her eyes went away.

"East of the sun and west of the moon."

"What crap."

She shrugged. "I'm packed."

*Knowing* I was wrong, I argued.

"Are you going to meet Alistair and that gang of fags?"

Doris was rich and there was much talk of her financing the Cozumel retreat and even of her coming down and making herself whole.

"Don't call him that. He's searching like me. And he's almost found peace. Underneath all that charm he's—"

"What charm?"

"A very tragic person. But he's a searcher like me, a pilgrim."

"Pilgrim my ass."

"Did you know that for two years he took up a begging bowl and wandered the byways with a disciple of Ramakrishna, the greatest fakir of our time?"

"He's a fakir all right. What he is is a fake Hindoo English fag son of a bitch." Why did I say the very thing that would send her away?

Here was where I had set a record: that of all cuckolds in history, I am the first American to be cuckolded by *two* English fruits.

"Is that what he is?" said Doris gravely.

"Yes."

"What are you, Tom?"

"I couldn't say."

She nodded absently, but now (!) her hand is on my head, ruffling my hair and strumming just as she used to strum her fingers on the Formica in the kitchen.

"Who was it who said: if I were offered the choice between having the truth and searching for it, I'd take the search?"

"I don't know. Probably Hermann Hesse."

"Hadn't we better close the curtains?"

"Yes. You do it. I can't get up."

She laughed for the first time in six months. "Boy, you are a mess."

We're back in Virginia, at school, under the apple blossoms. She looked down at me. "Annie Mae's going to see you."

"She'd be proud of me."

"Don't be vulgar."

Annie Mae is a big hefty black girl whom Doris dressed up like a French maid with a tiny white cap and a big butterfly bow on her tail.

"Sit in my lap."

"How?"

"This way."

"O.K."

"Easy!"

"Oh boy," she said, nodding and tucking her lip in her old style. Her hand rested as lightly on my shoulder as it did at the Washington and Lee Black-and-White formal. What a lovely funny Valley girl she was before the goddamn heathen Oriental English got her.

"You know the trouble with you, Tom?" She was always telling me the trouble with me.

"What?"

"You're not a seeker after the truth. You think you have the truth, and what good does it do you?"

"Here's the truth." Nobody can blaspheme like a bad Catholic.

"Say what you like about Alistair," she said—and settled herself! "He's a seeker and so am I."

"I know what he seeks."

"What?"

"Your money."

"That's how you would see it."

"That's how I see it."

"Even if it were true, would it be worse than wanting just my body?"

"Yes. But I don't want just your body."

"What do you want?"

"You."

"But not the real me."

"Jesus."

But she was jostling me, bumping me carelessly like a fraternity brother in a stagline.

"You know the trouble with you, Tom?"

"What?"

"You don't understand a purely spiritual relationship."

"That's true."

Somewhere Doris had got the idea that love is spiritual. So lately she'd had no use for my carrying on, as she called it, or messing about, putting her down in the zoysia grass, etcetera, with friendly whacks on the thick parts and shouts of joy for the beauty of the morning, hola! I do truly believe that she came to look upon her solemn spiritual adultery with that fag Alistair as somehow more elevating than ordinary morning love with her husband.

"You never grasped that," said Doris, but leaning closer and giving me a hug.

We sat in the chair, the chair not being an ordinary chair, which would have been fine, but a Danish sling, since in those days ordinary chairs had canceled out and could not be sat on. Married as we were and what with marriage tending to cancel itself and beds having come not to be places for making love in or chairs for sitting on, we had no place to lie or sit. We were like forlorn lovers in the street with no place to go.

But love conquers all, even a Danish sling.

"Darling," said Doris, forgetting for once all the foolishness.

"Let's lie down," I said.

"Fine, but how?"

"Just hold still. I'll pick you up."

Have you ever tried to get up out of a Danish sling with a hundred-and-forty-pound Apple Queen in your lap?

But I got up.

We lay on the bricks, here in this spot. Perhaps that is why I feel better lying here now. Here, at any rate, we lay and made love for the last time. We thought no more of Hermann Hesse that day.

In two weeks she was gone. Why? I think it was because she never forgave me or God for Samantha's death.

"That's a loving God you have there," she told me toward the end, when the neuroblastoma had pushed one eye out and around the nosebridge so that Samantha looked like a two-eyed Picasso profile. After that, Doris went spiritual and I became coarse and disorderly. She took the high road and I took the low. She said I was like a Polack miner coming up out of the earth every night with no thought but to fill his belly and hump his wife. The expression "hump" shocked me and was unlike her. She may have lost her faith but she'd always kept her Virginia-Episcopal decorum. But she'd been reading current novels, which at the time spoke of "humping" a great deal, though to tell the truth I had not heard the expression. Was this a word invented by New York novelists?

## 2

At last, getting up and keeping clear of the windows, I fetch my medical bag, which is packed this morning not merely with medicines but with other articles that I shall presently describe, and stick the revolver in my belt and slip out the lower "woods" door at the back of the house where it is impossible to be seen by an assailant lurking in the swamp.

The door, unused since Doris left, is jammed by vines. I squeeze through into the hot muscadine sunlight. Here the undergrowth has almost reached the house. Wistaria has taken the stereo-V antenna.

Two strides and I'm swallowed up in a plantation of sumac. It is easy to keep cover and circle around to the swamp edge and have a long look. Nothing stirring. Egrets sail peacefully over the prairie. A wisp of smoke rises from a hummock. There some drughead from Michigan State lies around smoking Choctaw cannab while his girl fries catfish.

I rub my eyes. Did I imagine the sniper's shots? Was it part and parcel of the long night's dream of Verdun, of the terrible assault of the French infantry on Fort Douaumont? No. There is the shattered window of the "enclosed patio."

What to do? The best course: walk to town by a route known only to me in order to avoid ambush. Call the police at the first telephone.

But in the thick chablis sunlight humming with bees, it is hard to credit assassination. A stray guerrilla perhaps, using my plate glass for target practice.

Anyhow, I have other fish to fry. First to the Center, where I hope to have a word with Max Gottlieb, ask a favor of him; then perhaps catch a glimpse of Moira in Love Clinic; thence to Howard Johnson's to arrange a trysting place, a lover's rendezvous with Moira my love from Love.

Afterwards there should be time for a long Saturday afternoon in my office—no patients, no nurse today—where I shall sip Early Times and listen to my father's old tape of *Don Giovanni* with commentary by Milton Cross.

Using my bag to fend off blackberries, I angle off to a curve of Paradise Drive where the woods notch in close.

Standing in the schoolbus shelter, now a cave of creeper and muscadine, I get my bearings. Across the road and fifty feet of open space, a forest of longleaf begins. A hundred yards into it and I should pick up the old caddy path that leads from town to country club.

Wait five minutes to be sure. No sound but the droning of bees in honeysuckle.

Step out and—bad luck! In the split second of starting across, a car rounds the curve. There's no not seeing him or he me. It's like turning the corner of a building and walking into someone's arms.

He stops. It is no stranger. But do I want to see friends now? I get along with everybody except people. Psychiatrist, heal—

It is Dr. George "Dusty" Rhoades in his new electric Toyota

bubbletop, a great black saucer of a car and silent as a hearse.

He's waving me in. Hm, not exactly my choice for a companion. Why? Because he's Lola's father and he may believe I have injured him, though I have not. Shall I accept the lift? The question does not arise. The fierce usages of friendship take command. Dusty leans out waving and grinning. Before I know what I'm doing I'm grinning too and hopping around to the door with every appearance of delight.

"There you go!" cries Dusty in an eccentric greeting that has evolved between us over the years. Renewed friendship sweeps all before it. We are like lovers after a quarrel.

Dusty is a big surgeon with heavy freckled hands that like to feel your bones and a red rooster shock of hair gone straw-colored in middle age. It is his manner to pay terrific attention to the controls of his car, the dials of the dashboard, while shouting eccentric offhand remarks. So does he also shout, I know, at his operating nurse, not to be answered or even to be heard but to make an occupational sound, so to speak.

"Fine, fine," I say, settling myself. He nods and keeps on nodding.

Dusty Rhoades is a conservative proctologist, though he does other surgery as well, from Tyler, Texas. He played tackle for Texas A & M, is a reserve Air Force colonel. An excellent surgeon, he works fourteen hours a day, caring nought for his own comfort, and owns a chain of Chicken Delight stands. The money rolls in faster than he can spend it even though he bought Tara, the showplace of Paradise, and an $80,000 Guarnerius cello for his daughter Lola.

Like saints of old, Dusty spends himself tirelessly for other men, not for love, he would surely say, or even for money, for he has no use for it, but because people need him and call him and what else would he do with himself? His waking hours are spent in a dream of work, nodding, smiling, groping for you, not really listening. Instead, his big freckled hands feel your bones like a blind man's. He's conservative and patriotic too, but in the same buzzing, tune-humming way. His office is stacked with pamphlets of the Liberty Lobby. In you come with a large-bowel complaint, over you go upside down on the rack, in goes the scope, ech! and Dusty humming away somewhere above. "Hm, a diverticulum opening here. The real enemy is within, don't you think?" Within me or the U.S.A., you are wondering, gazing at the floor three inches from your nose, and in goes the long scope. "You know as well as I do who's really causing the trouble, don't you?" "Do you mean—?" "I mean the Lefts and Commonists, right?" "Yes, but on the other hand—" In goes the scope the full twenty-six inches up to your spleen. "Oof, yessir!"

"Am I glad to see you, you rascal!" cries Dusty, coming out of his trance and looking over at me. His hand, going its own way, explores the crevices of my knee.

I blink back the beginning of a tear. He's forgiven me! Why do I forget there is such a thing as friends?

He's forgiven what he could only have understood as my misconduct with his daughter Lola, and misconduct it was, though in another sense it was not. Lola and I were discovered by him lying in one another's arms in the deep canyon-size bunker of the eighteenth hole. Though Lola is twenty-six, single, and presumably had the right to embrace whomever she chose, I fancied nevertheless that Dusty took offense. Though he was careful not to let me know it and I was careful not to find out. Certainly no offense was intended. Lola is a big, beautiful, talented girl who teaches cello at Texas A & M. We fell in love for a few hours last Christmas Eve, literally fell, came upon each other like strangers in a forest and fell to the ground in one another's arms, and the next day went our separate ways, she back to Texas and I to the nuthouse broken out with giant hives and quaking with morning terror and night exaltations.

The consequences of this misbehavior in Paradise, where everyone else behaves very well, were muted by my self-commitment to the mental hospital. Thus, it is possible that I have been expelled from the local medical society: no notices have come in the mail—but on the other hand, perhaps notices were suspended because of my illness. I dare not inquire. One consequence was certain: an anonymous communication did come in the mail, a copy of the Hippocratic oath with that passage underlined which admonishes physicians about their relations with female patients. But Lola was not, at the time, my patient.

"You making house calls, Doctor!" Dusty shouts.

I jump. "No no. I was . . . I felt like walking to town." For some reason I do not wish to speak of the sniper.

Dusty nods vigorously, as if my stepping out of the woods with my medical bag was no more or less than he expected. But even as he speaks, his eyes caress the mahogany dashboard and brass knobs and dials. These days it is the fashion to do car interiors in wood and brass like Jules Verne vehicles.

When we shake hands, he opens his meaty hand to me in his old tentative way like a porter taking a tip.

"I wish I could work like you!" he shouts at the rushing pines. "It must take discipline to cut down hack work and make time for research and writing."

How graceful and kind of him. Though Dusty knows all there is to know about me, my family troubles, my cuckoldry, my irregular life, my alcoholism—he connives at the best available myth about me, that I am "smart" but unlucky. People are kind. They find it easy to forgive you in the name of tragedy or insanity and most of all if you are smart. Certain mythic sayings come easily to the lips of my doctor friends when they wish to speak well of me, and lately they do since they know I've had a bad time of it. They'll speak of a mythic, storied diagnosis I made ten years ago. . . .

"No, I'm not working today," I tell Dusty. "I have a few errands to run, then I'm going down to my office and fix myself a little drink and listen to the opera."

"Yes! Right! Absolutely!" cries Dusty joyfully and strikes himself eccentrically in several places.

He fiddles with the controls. All of a sudden a hundred-piece orchestra is blasting away on the back seat, playing Viennese Waltz Favorites. The hot glistening pines fall away as the road climbs along the ridge. The dry refrigerated air evaporates my sweat. Strains of *Wienerblut* lilt us over the pines. We might be drifting along in a Jules Verne gondola over happy old Austria.

I feel better. There are no ruins here. We are beginning to pass sparkling new houses with well-kept lawns. What a lovely silent car. What lovely things money can buy. I have money. Why not spend it? Until this moment it has never occurred to me to spend a penny of Doris's two million on myself. I look down at my frayed cuffs, grubby fingernails. Why not dress well, groom myself, buy a good car, meet friends for lunch, good fellows like Dusty, chaff with them, take up golf? Money is splendid!

But today I have other fish to fry.

"Would you mind dropping me off at the plaza?"

"What the hell for?" asks Dusty, frowning. But his freckled hand continues to browse among the knobs and dials.

"I have a date."

When I left the hospital, I resolved not to lie. Lying cuts one off. Lying to someone is like blindfolding him: you cannot see the other's eyes to see how he sees you and so you do not know how it stands with yourself.

'Like the fellow says, that's a hell of a place to take a woman. All those tramps, outlaws . . ."

"Yes, well . . . I think it's safe."

"Is that why you're wearing your handgun?"

"What?" I had forgotten my pistol and didn't see Dusty look at it. The gun had worked its way around to my belt buckle where it sticks out like Billy the Kid's sixshooter. "The fact is somebody took a shot at me this morning."

"That a fact?" says Dusty with routine astonishment expressing both incredulity and affection. "I tell you the truth, nothing would surprise me nowadays."

"It was probably a wild shot from some nut in the swamp," I say, shoving the pistol out of sight. Indeed, is anything less likely than a *sniper* on this lovely old-fashioned Viennese morning?

"I happened to notice it is all. You're not going to the club?"

"The club?"

"For the Pro-Am."

"Oh, of course!" I laugh heartily. How could I have forgotten the most important event of the year, the Paradise Moonlight Pro-Am tournament played every Fourth of July weekend under the arcs? "But the champs don't tee off till tonight, do they?"

"Right. I thought you might be going to the Bible Brunch."

"No. No, I have to go to the Center."

"O.K. I'll take you over to the plaza."

"No no! Go on to the club. I'll walk from there. I need to walk."

"O.K.," says Dusty, frowning thoughtfully. The freckled hand browses like a small animal patrolling its burrow. "You know, it's something my running into you like this. It's really something."

"It is?"

"I've been looking for you."

"You have?" I look at him with interest. "Did you read my paper?"

"Paper? Well, I haven't finished it."

I sent Dusty a copy of my breakthrough article. He is president-elect of the American Christian Proctological Society and could be useful when I apply for N.I.M.H. funds. Dusty is highly regarded, both in Knothead and Left circles.

"As a matter of fact, I have one of the new models here," I say, taking out a lapsometer and putting it on the seat between us.

Dusty moves away an inch.

"Tom," says Dusty as we go lilting along to *Wine, Women, and Song*. "I want you to take my clinic for me."

Dusty holds a fat clinic on Tuesdays and Thursdays, dispensing thousands of pills to women and encouraging them in their dieting.

We've stopped at a gate and sentry box where a red-faced colonel of Security gives us the once-over before admitting us to the inner circle of Paradise. He's dressed like General Patton, in helmet, jacket, and pearl-handle revolvers.

"O.K., Doc," says Colonel Ringo, stooping down to the window. "Two docs! Ha ha." He waves us on.

Now we've stopped again, this time in front of Tara, Dusty's house. Thinking he's dropping me off, I open the door to go my way. But Dusty's browsing hand finds my knee and holds me fast.

"You know, life is funny, Tom."

"Yes, it is."

"You a brilliant profession and you losing your wife and all."

"Yes."

"And Lola coming home."

"Coming home?"

"Coming here, that is."

"I see."

"She's come to stay."

Tara is on the right, and to see it, Dusty leans over me. He makes himself surprisingly free of my person, coming much closer than men, American men, usually do. His strong breath, smelling of breakfast, breathes on me. An artery socks away at his huge lion-head causing it to make tiny rhythmic nods as if he were affirming this view of his beautiful house, Tara.

"Tom," says Dusty, taking his hand off my knee and fingering the tape deck. A Victor Herbert medley comes on.

"Yes?"

"I'm going home."

"O.K., I'll get out."

But the knuckle of his hand turns hard into my knee, detaining me.

"No, I mean I'm going back to Texas."

"I see."

"No, my old daddy died and I'm going back to the ranch outside of Tyler."

"You mean you're retiring?"

"Oh I reckon I'll work some—"

"I reckon you'll have to."

"Right!" Dusty laughs. "But I'm slacking off before I kill myself."

"I'm glad to hear it." But I'm also concerned about the knuckle turning hard into my knee.

"Lola is not leaving. She's staying here. This is what she wants. So I'm giving her Tara," muses Dusty, gazing past me. The huge head is in my lap, so to speak, nodding as the artery socks away.

"Is that right? You mean she's going to live here by herself?"

"Yep. She's home for good."

"Is that so?"

"You know, this is home to her. And she's got her Eastern gaited horses here, why I don't know."

"Yes."

"And to tell you the damn truth," Dusty goes on in exactly the same voice, lidded eyes peering past me at the white columns of Tara, breathing his breakfast breath on me, "that girl is ever more crazy about you, Tom."

"She is? Well, she is a wonderful girl and I am extremely—"

"In fact, your mother was only saying yesterday," Dusty breaks in, and his head swivels a few degrees, nodding now at the hipped roof of my mother's cozy saltbox next door. "She said: you know Tom and Lola are a match if ever I saw one. You know your mother."

"Yes." I know my mother and I can hear her say it in her trite exclamatory style: they're a match if ever I saw one!

For some reason I am nodding too, in time with Dusty. From the point where Dusty's knuckle is turning into my knee, waves of prickling spread out in all directions.

Now the hand lets go my knee and settles in a soft fist on my shoulder.

"I'm giving Tara to Lola, Tom."

"You are?"

"You want to know the reason she's staying?"

"No. That is, yes."

"You."

"Me?"

"She thinks the world of you."

"And I of her."

"She can't live here by herself."

"No?"

"No way. Tom, you see this place?"

"Yes?"

"I'm putting it and my little girl in your hands."

"You are?"

"Ha ha, that will give you something to think about, won't it?"

"Yes."

"You know, neither one a y'all got good sense."

"No?"

"You laying up in the bed with a bottle, shooting rats, out in the woods by yourself, talking about snipers and all. Lola taking long rides by herself in the backcountry where some crazy nigger's going to knock her in the head. I'm counting on you to take care her." Dusty gazes attentively at the kingbird sitting on the white Kentucky fence.

"All right."

"Both a y'all can damn well straighten up and fly right! That's what I told your mama I was going to tell you and now I done told you." For some reason Dusty begins to talk in a broad Texas accent. He gives a final joky-serious nod with his big head. "You reading me, Doctor?"

"Yes."

"That's settled then." Dusty settles back with a sigh. "I told your mama you would."

"Would what?"

"Do the right thing."

I sigh, relieved at least to have Dusty's great lion-head off my chest.

Again the car drifts along, a silent gondola. With a sudden inspiration, Dusty presses a button and a thousand violins play *Hills of Home*, the Tara theme.

"That's my favorite music," muses Dusty.

"Very nice."

"I'll tell Lola."

"Tell her what?"

"About our understanding."

"What understanding?"

"Ha ha, you're a card, Tom. I always thought you had the most wonderful sense of humor."

As we approach the clubhouse, more people are abroad. The Christian Kaydettes are practicing in the schoolyard. Suntanned golfers ply the fairways in quaint surrey-like carts, householders bestride tiny tractors, children splash in pools, their brown bodies flashing like minnows.

"Will you also take my Tuesday clinic?"

Also? Does that mean that I've agreed to take Tara and Lola?

"Thanks, Dusty. But I'm using all my spare time developing my lapsometer. I'm applying for an N.I.M.H. grant. You could help."

"Use it in the clinic!" cries Dusty, socking himself eccentrically in several places. He's in the best of humors. "Read their frontal lobes with your gadget and they'll believe you! They'll believe you anyhow! You know, Tom, you're the best diagnostician around here. If you wanted to, you could be—" Dusty shrugs and falls silent.

Then he did read my paper! Dusty's nobody's fool. Though he pretends to be a country boy, his mind can devour a scientific article with one snap of its jaws.

"Since you've read my paper, you know that my lapsometer has more important uses than treating fat women."

"Sho now. But is there anything wrong with treating fat women?"

"In fact," I tell Dusty earnestly, "with this device in hand any physician can make early diagnoses of potential suicides, paranoiacs, impotence, stroke, anxiety, and angelism/bestialism. Think of the significance of it!"

"Chk." Dusty winks and clucks tongue against teeth, signifying both a marveling and an unseriousness.

"This country is in deep trouble, Dusty."

"You don't have to tell me that."

"This device could be decisive."

"Well, I'm just a country doctor."

"Did you read about the atrocity last night?"

"Yeah."

"What do you think?"

"The work of a madman."

"Yeah, but there's a reason."

"Reason? You mean you're going to cure all the crazy niggers?"

"And crazy whites, crazy Lefts, and crazy Knotheads."

"I don't know about you, but me I see very few Lefts and no niggers at all."

We've reached the clubhouse. Pennants stream from the twin copper peaks of the roof, like a castle at tournament time. Gaily colored pavilions are scattered through the pines.

A few pros and ams, early arrivals, enter the clubhouse for the Bible Brunch. A banner strung the length of the eaves announces: Jesus Christ, the Greatest Pro of Them All.

"Come on in with me," says Dusty impulsively.

"Thank you, but I've got to be going."

"Many devout Catholics are coming."

"I'm not a devout Catholic."

"Cliff Barrow Junior is preaching."

"Good."

"Lola and I will be looking for you at the fish fry tonight."

As he talks, Dusty picks up the new lapsometer on the seat between us. He hefts it.

"Very compact."

"Yes."

It *is* a lovely device, all brushed chrome, pointer and dial, and a jade oscilloscope screen the size of a half-dollar, the whole as solid as a good camera. Just the thing, I see now, to take Dusty's fancy.

"You take readings?" says Dusty, turning it every which way. He's all business now, buzzing away while his big fleshy hand hefts, balances, knows.

"That's right."

"What do you take readings of?"

I shrug. "You know. Local electrical activity in cortical and subcortical centers. It's nothing but an EEG without wires, with a stereotactic device for triangulating."

"Yeah, I see. Here you measure your micromillivolts." The lizard scales have fallen from his blue eyes, which bear down like gimlets. His thumb rubs the jade screen as if it were a lucky piece. "And this here—"

"That's your oscilloscope to display your wave patterns, with this, see?—a hold-and-stack device. You can stack ten patterns and flip back at will."

"You take your readings, then what?"

"Like the article says, you correlate the readings with various personality traits, attitudes."

"You mean, like emotions?" asks Dusty, frowning.

"Well, yes, among other things."

"Isn't that all rather . . . subjective?"

"Is a pointer reading subjective?"

"But there's a lot of room for interpretation."

"Isn't there also in an electroencephalogram?" I turn it over.

"Here on the back you've got your normal readings at key centers."

"Yeah. Like a light meter." He takes it back. The freckled hand can't leave it alone. Again the thumb tests the grain of the brushed chrome, strokes the jade screen.

"How long does it take to do a, uh what? An examination?"

"A reading. I can do a standard profile in less than three minutes." I look at my watch and open the door. "Thanks for the ride."

"Do one on me."

"What?"

"Couldn't you do a reading right here and now?"

"Sure, but—"

"But what?"

"It's not a play toy."

"Well, damn it, does it work or doesn't it?"

"It works."

"Show me."

"I've learned that it's not to be used lightly."

Dusty nods ironically. We're both thinking of the same thing. It was using my first Brownie model on Lola that got me into trouble. That Christmas Eve six months ago I'd made my breakthrough and had the first inkling what I'd got hold of. I was abstracted, victorious, lonely, drunk, and full of love, and lo, there was Lola, also victorious (she'd had a triumphant concert in Tyler, Texas) and also lonely and full of love. My lapsometer revealed these things. But it was not the cause of our falling in love. Rather the occasion.

"You need controls for your series, don't you?" Dusty asks shrewdly.

"Yes."

"Then use me as a control."

"You wouldn't stick a proctoscope up me here in the car, would you?"

Dusty laughs, but his knuckle turns into my knee. "If you want my endorsement, I'd like to see how it works."

"I see." Why do I feel uneasy? "Oh very well. Take off your coat and lean over the steering wheel, like a sleepy truck driver."

"O.K., Doctor." Dusty says "Doctor" with exactly the same irony priests use in calling each other "Father."

It takes two and a half minutes to clock seven readings. There is one surprise. He registers good pineal selfhood, which I expected; an all but absent coeliac anxiety—he is, after all, an ex-fullback and hardworking surgeon, a man at home with himself and too busy to worry about it. That is to say: he may fear one thing or another but he's not afraid of no-thing, which is the worst of fears. His abstractive index is not excessive—he lets his hands do the knowing and working. His red nucleus shows no vagal rage.

But—

His love-sex ratio is reversed.

That is to say: the reading from Brodmann Area 24, the locus of "higher" or interpersonal relations, is a tiny o.5 mmv while the hypothalamus, seat of organic sexual activity, registers a whacking stud-level 7.9 mmv. The display wave of the latter is well developed. It is the wave of a powerful, frequently satisfied, but indiscriminate sexual appetite. Dusty is divorced.

"Well?" asks Dusty, buttoning his collar.

"No real pathology," I say, pocketing the lapsometer and adjusting my six-gun. I seize the door handle.

"Hold it, son!" cries Dusty, laughing. "Don't pull that!"

"What?"

"Tell me, you rascal!" Joyfully he socks me with a few eccentric blows.

"Very well," I say doubtfully, remembering my vow to tell the truth.

I show him, clicking back over the wave-displays stacked in the oscilloscope circuit, and tell him, glossing over as best I can the love-sex reversal. But I have not reckoned with Dusty's acuteness.

"I see," he says at last, looking straight ahead, lizard scales lowering over his eyes. "What you're saying is I'm messing around with my nurses."

"I said no such thing. You asked for the readings. I gave them to you. Make your own interpretation."

"Is that thing nonpartisan?" he asks in the same voice, yet somehow more ominously.

"How do you mean?"

"Does it also measure alcoholism, treachery, laziness, and whitetrash morals?"

"If you like," I reply in a low voice, but relieved to have him strike at me so hard.

The freckled hand browses. A switch clicks, locking the doors. It clicks again, unlocking, locking. Is Dusty thinking of beating me up?

"There's the door, Doctor." Click, unlock.

"Very well. Thanks for the ride."

"Don't mention it. Once piece of advice."

"Yes?"

Dusty begins his rhythmic nodding again as the artery pounds away.

"Lola has a lot more use for you than I do, though I used to. I know you been through a bad time. But let us understand each other." He still looks straight ahead.

"All right."

"You going to do right by Lola or, Doctor, I'm going to have your ass. Is that clear?"

"Yes."

"Goodbye, Doctor."

"Goodbye."


3

Leaving Dusty's car, I skirt the festive booths of the Bible Brunch.

The heat of the concrete pool apron strikes up like the Sahara sands. The sun strikes down into the top of my head. Chunks of Styrofoam water-toys are scattered in the weeds like dirty wedding cake. The pool is empty and drifted with leaves.

Why has the pool been abandoned?

A breath of cool air stirs in the doorway of the old pro shop bearing the smell of leather and of splintered pine flooring. The shop too is empty save for a life-size cutout of Gene Sarazen dipping toward the floor. Gene is dressed in knickerbockers and a British cap. A trumpet vine sprouts through the floor and twines around a rusty mashie.

Why is the pro shop empty? Is there a new pro shop in another part of the building?

It was not empty when I stood here and kissed Lola.

I went to the catfish fry and fell in love with Lola and performed with her the act of love in the grassy kidney-shaped bunker of number 18 green (par 4, 275 yards).

I was standing in the Paradise Country Club bar shaking the worn leather cup of poker dice and gazing at the rows of bottles lined up against the brand-new antiqued wormholed cypress, when I noticed something. The vines had begun to sprout. It was the first time I had noticed it. A whitish tendril of vine, perhaps ivy, had sprouted through a wormhole and twined about a bottle of Southern Comfort.

"Give me a drink of Southern Comfort," I told Ruby, the bartender, and watched to see if he would notice anything amiss.

Ruby, a thin sly Chinese-type Negro, took the bottle without noticing the tendril, which broke off in his hand.

"How long has that vine been here?"

"What vine?"

"In your hand."

He shrugged.

"How long has it been since anybody asked for Southern Comfort?"

"It been a while," said Ruby with a sly smile. "Christmas gif, Doc."

Absently I gave him a bill, a dollar.

Ruby's face went inscrutable like an Oriental's. He expected, rightly, a higher tip at Christmas. The dollar was received as an insult. We dislike each other. He sucked his teeth. Leaving him and my drink, I went out among the catfish crowd and found myself hemmed up with Lola Rhoades against a stretch of artificially wormholed cypress.

The pro shop seems to darken in the morning light. Gene Sarazen straightens. I sit on a pedestal holding a display of irons arranged in a fan. There is a chill in the room. The summer spins back to chilly azalea crucifixion spring, back further to Christmas with its month of cheerful commerical jingling shopping nights and drinking parties.

I see Lola clearly, holding her gin fizz.

"I am glad to see you," says Lola, who is five feet nine and in her high heels looks me straight in the eye and says what she thinks.

"So am I," I say, feeling a wonder that there should be such a thing as a beautiful six-foot woman who is glad to see me. Women are mythical creatures. They have no more connection with the ordinary run of things than do centaurs. I see her clearly, gin fizz in one hand, the other held against her sacrum, palm out, pushing herself rhythmically off the wall. Women! Music! Love! Life! Joy! Gin fizzes!

She is home for Christmas from Texas A & M. She looks like her father but the resemblance is a lovely joke, a droll commentary on him. His colorlessness, straw hair, straw skin, becomes in her a healthy pallor, milkiness over rose, lymph over blood. Her hair is a black-auburn with not enough red to ruin her skin, which has none of the green chloral undertones of some redheads. Her glance is mild and unguarded. It is the same to her whether she drinks or does not drink, talks or does not talk, looks one in he eye or does not look.

She drinks and hisses a cello tune in her teeth and pushes herself off the wall.

The gin fizzes come and go. We find we can look into each other's eyes without the usual fearfulness and shamefulness of eye meeting eye. I am in love.

A Negro band, dressed in unpressed Santa suits, is blasting out Christmas carols. Bridge-playing ladies surround us, not playing bridge but honking their Wednesday bridge-playing honks and uttering Jewish-guttural *yuchs* which are fashionable this season.

Lola asks me something. I cannot hear and, stooping, put my ear to her mouth, registering as I go past a jeweled reflection of red and green Christmas lights in a web of saliva spinning between parted rows of perfect teeth.

"Don't you want to ask about your patient?"

"You look well. How are you?" I had treated her last summer for a mild depression and a sensation of strangeness, quite common these days, upon waking in the morning.

"Well enough," she says, nodding in order to lever her sacrum off the wall. "But you seem—odd."

"Odd?" I speak into her ear, which crimsons in the canal like a white orchid.

"You look both happy and—sad."

It is true. Women are so smart. In truth I am suffering from simultaneous depression and exaltation. So I tell her about it: that this very day I perfected my invention and finished my article, which will undoubtedly be recognized as one of the three great scientific breakthroughs of the Christian era, the others being Newton hitting on his principles and Einstein on his field theory, perhaps even the greatest of all because my discovery alone gives promise of bridging the dread chasm between body and mind that has sundered the soul of Western man for five hundred years.

She believes me. "Then why do you feel bad?"

I explain my symptoms in terms of my discovery: that when one records the thalamic radiation, a good index of one's emotional state, it can register either as a soaring up, a sine curve, or a dipping down, a cosine curve. "Mine registers both at the same time, sine and cosine, mountain on a valley."

She laughs, thinking I am joking.

"Why should that be?"

Since I am in love, I can feel with her, feel my sacrum tingle when hers hits the wall.

"Well, I've won, you see. Won the big one. But it's Christmas Eve and I'm alone. My family is dead. There's nobody to tell."

"Tell me."

"Do you know what I planned to do tonight?"

"No."

"Go home and watch Perry Como's Christmas show on stereo-V." Perry Como is seventy and still going strong.

Lola nods sympathetically, ducks her head, drinks, and hisses a tune in her teeth. I bend to listen. It is the Dvořák cello concerto.

Trays pass. I begin to drink Ramos gin fizzes with one swallow. At one time I was allergic to egg white but that was long ago. These drinks feel silky and benign. The waiters too are dressed as Santa. They grin sideways from their skewed Santa hoods and shout "Christmas gif!" I give them money, a dollar, ten dollars, whatever.

"Listen to this," I tell Lola and hum the *Don Quixote* theme in her ear.

"Very good. You have absolute pitch. And you look better! Your face is fuller."

I feel my face. It is fuller.

"I feel fine. I am never happier than when I am in love."

"Are you in love?"

"Yes."

"Who with?"

"You."

"Ah huh," says Lola, nodding, but I can't tell whether the nodding is just to get her sacrum off the wall.

"Christmas gif!"

Another black Santa passes and I take three gin fizzes. The tingling sacrum should have been a warning, but love made me happy, love and the sight of tiny jewels strung along the glittering web of saliva. Her membranes are clear as light, the body fluids like jeweler's oil under a watch crystal. A lovely inorganic girl.

Her company stabilizes me. Abstracted still, my orbit becomes lower. Bending close to her, close to the upper reaches of her breast, is like skimming in silence, power off, over the snowy slopes of Kilimanjaro. I close my eyes.

"When I close my eyes, I can see you teaching cello in the Texas A & M cello class, a drafty gym-like room, the cello between your knees. It is during a break and you're wearing a sweatshirt and resting your arm on the cello."

"Ah huh." She nods. "It gets cold in there." She believes everything I say, knowing it is true.

Handing Lola her gin fizz, I touch her. A hive, a tiny red wheal, leaps out at the point of touch, as if to keep touch. The touch of her is, as they say, a thrill.

"Why did you bring your physician's bag here?" Lola asks me.

"I haven't been home yet. The first working model of my lapsometer is inside, can't afford to lose it."

"Can you really measure a person's innermost self?"

"In a manner of speaking."

"Can you measure mine?"

"Sure."

"Do it."

"Where? Right here?"

"Yes."

"Well—over here." Taking her by the hand, I lead her through the bridge women to the pro shop. We stand behind Gene Sarazen while I take a few snapshots of her with my Brownie.

She registers zero anxiety—music saves her! she goes dreaming through the world as safe and sure as Schubert's trout—but her interpersonal wave is notable in two respects: it is both powerful and truncated, lopped off at the peak like Popocatepetl.

"Well?"

"You see?" I show her the snail tracks on jade, a faint cratered Fuji in a green dawn.

"What does that mean?"

"It means you have a heart full of love and no one to give it to, but that is not so bad because you have your music, which means a great deal to you."

"Yes. I don't. It does. Yes!"

Now it is she who does the hemming up and I who am backed up against the cypress, sacrum fiery and quilted. My head is turning against the wormholes. Hairs catch and pop.

"Why is that?" she asks, brown eyes level with mine.

"Why is what?"

"Why is there—no one?"

"Well, you're a bit much, you know. You scare most men. Also, your music is hard to compete with. You always hear singing." I show her the lilting curve of her aesthetic radiation.

"Yes! I understand! It is true! Can love be like that?"

She takes my hand urgently, her cello calluses whispering in my palm.

"Yes, it can, if the love is like that, singing."

"Do you love me like that?"

"Yes."

"How do I know?"

I kiss her hand. My lip leaps out to keep touch, ridges with a wheal.

She feels it. "Good heavens!"

We are laughing and touching.

"Christmas gif!"

A waiter comes up. We take four gin fizzes. Under the monklike Santa hood, I recognize a Negro named Willard Amadie. Long ago he used to be a caddy, before the electric surreys came along. A very strong short black man, he would stand down the fairway for the drive and with the heavy bag still on his shoulder take a full swing at the clover with an iron. It is a surprise to see him. Years ago he went off to the Ecuadorian wars and became, I heard, a career soldier. Somber even as a youth, he'd stand waiting at the lie, club selected and proffered handle first, face bitter-black, bee-stung, welted laterally like an Indian's.

Now he's dressed like Santa and grinning a ghastly grin.

"Christmas gif, Doc!"

I look at him.

"What's wrong, Willard?"

"Nothing, Doc! Christmas gif to you and missee."

"Missee?" The outer corners of my eyes are filling up with hives, forming a prism. Willard and Lola are edged in rainbows. "What in hell are you talking about?"

Willard doesn't leave but stands watching. His sclerae are yellow as egg yolk. At last I give Willard ten dollars, blushing, as I do so, with rage or shame, I'm not sure which.

"Thankee, Doc!" says Willard in the same goofy Gullah accent. "May you and missee have many a more!"

I refuse to look at Willard, watching instead sections of a road map, pieces of highway, dots of towns, drifting across my retina.

But Lola is pleased. She sees Willard's courtliness (what is wrong with him?) as a sanction. Christmas is sanctioned. Our love is sanctioned. Willard's nutty good manners (something is up, I know that, like the vines sprouting, but what?) are part of the singing, life made to lilt.

"Let's go outside," I say, to go outside but mainly to get away from Willard, and take her again by the hand, her left hand, her fingering hand, calluses whispering in my palm.

Out into the gloaming we go.

It is a warm Christmas Eve. A south wind blows fat little calypso clouds over a new moon.

We kiss in the grassy bunker. She kisses oddly, stooping to it, developing a torque and twisting down and away, seeming to grow shorter. Her breath catches. What she puts me in mind of is not a Texas girl at all but a smart Northern girl, a prodigy who has always played the cello ten hours a day, then one day finds herself at a summer festival and twenty-one and decides it is time to be kissed. So she stoops to it with an odd, shy yet practiced movement, what I fancy to be the Juilliard summer-festival style of kissing.

Now her hands are clasped in the small of my back. My hands are clasped in the small of her back. She hisses Dvořák. My hot chicken blood sings with albumen molecules. Her hand is warm and whispery as a horn.

We lie in the grassy bunker, she gazing at the winter constellations wheeling in their courses, I singing like a cello between her knees. Fiery Betelgeuse hangs like a topaz in the south. We kiss hungrily, I going around after her.

"Doris," I whisper, forgetting she is Lola. Fortunately my breath whistles in my throat and she doesn't hear me.

She is like Doris, except for her Juilliard torque and her odd going-away persimmon-tasting kisses. A big lovely girl, big and white and cool-warm, a marble Venus with a warm horned hand. Her callused fingertips strew stars along my flanks. Hot wheals of love leap forth at her touch.

"What's the matter with you?" Lola asks, leaning out of the moon's shadow to inspect my bumps.

"I've got hives."

"You've got bobos on your shoulder" she says, minding my bobos attentively and curiously like a child.

When I look sideways, the wedge of sky is narrower.

"Hold still, hon," she whispers, from Tyler Texas now, Juilliard forgotten. "You'll be all right. Lola'll hold you tight."

"I have to go."

"Where you going?"

"For a walk. Stay here, I'll be right back."

I can't hold still. Why? The longing is back. Longing for what? I don't know. For Doris? For the Valley of Virginia and sycamore trees and cicadas unwinding in October? I don't know. God knows.

Now running down 18 fairway, knowing it in the black dark (for the "old" 18 is the terrain of my youth), to the tee and back, eyes squeezed shut like a Chinaman's. Back to the bunker to lie at Lola's breast, a blind babe. My scalp quilts and pops. Lymph engorges me. Love returns. Again I sing between Lola's knees, blind as a bat.

Go now, I try to tell her, you better leave, but my larynx squeaked shut.

So it was that Lola, noble cellist, saved my life at the cost of her reputation. She could have gone, left me to die in the bunker, swell up and die and be found stiff as a poker in the foggy dew. But she fetched her brother, who fetched Willard Amadie, and they both fetched me home, finding me in some disarray, I think, for Lola, putting first things first, had thought only to save my life.

Did I dream it or do I have a recollection of Willard Amadie bending over me, his Santa hood pushed back on his shoulders like a Carmelite's, his face no longer farcical but serious and tender but also risible in his old style. "—If you ain't something now," did he not say, bending over to pick me up and seeming in the same motion to adjust my clothes before Dusty came up.

So it was not even a great scandal but just enough to allow the possibility that Dusty could have been offended, though perhaps not, and the possibility that my name was dropped by the medical society, though perhaps it wasn't. I did receive the anonymous Hippocratic oath, however. But I was in love and Lola was not my patient at the time.

Dusty saved my life, finding me without breath, shot me full of epinephrine, helped Willard carry me home, where he, Dusty, put a tube in my nose and stayed with me until I came to myself.

All this, if you can believe it, in less than an hour's time from the moment I hoisted the first gin fizz until I opened my Chinaman's eyes in my own bed.

Christmas Eve fell out thereafter as planned. With the last of my strength I pressed the button on the headboard and saw Perry Como's Christmas show after all.

There came Perry, seventy years young and snowy-thatched but hale as old Saint Nick himself, still wearing his open cardigan, color off a bit, face orange, lips violet, but all in good 3-D.

He sang *Silent Night* sitting on his stool.

It was during the following week, between Christmas and New Year, that I became ill, suffering simultaneous depressions and exaltations, assaulted at night by longings, succubi, and the hideous shellfire of Verdun, and in the morning by terror of unknown origin. One morning—was it Christmas morning after listening to Perry Como?—my wrists were cut and bleeding. Seeing the blood, I came to myself, saw myself as itself and the world for what it is, and began to love life. Hm, better stop the bleeding in that case. After all, why not live? Bad as things are still when all is said and done, one can sit on a doorstep in the winter sunlight and watch sparrows kick leaves. So, hugging myself, I stuck a wrist in each armpit like a hobo, squeezed the arteries shut, and walked to Max's house. Max mostly sewed me up without making much over it, fetched a surgeon to suture a tendon, and at my request allowed me to commit myself to the federal hospital.

4

Going to see Max. Is the sniper following?

As I walk across the pool apron, powdered by chlorine dust and littered by dirty cakes of Styrofoam, I try to collect my wits, badly scattered by memories of Lola and by Dusty Rhoades's plans for me. Lola did not come to see me in the hospital. But perhaps she returned to Texas A & M without knowing I was ill.

Two things to do today—no, three things: (1) see Max Gottlieb, who knows the value of my discovery, and ask him to speak to the Director about sponsoring my article in *Brain* and my application for funding from N.I.M.H.; (2) complete arrangements for a trysting place at the ruined Howard Johnson motel for my date with Moira on the Fourth; (3) go to my office where, undisturbed by patients or my shrewish nurse (it is Saturday), I can put the finishing touches on my article, sip a toddy or two, listen to music, and watch the martins fly home in the evening.

Shortest and safest route is by foot. Across the fairways of the old 18 waist-high in Johnson grass, past the old Bledsoe house, a streaked Spanish stucco from the thirties, in the dog-leg of number 5. Here for fifty years lived the Bledsoes, locked in, while golf balls caromed around the patio, rico-cheted off Spanish balconies and window grills.

*Clink clink. Clink clink.*

A great thunderhead hides the sun, but it is dry on the fairways. The anthills are abandoned, worn away to a comb of cells.

*Clink clink. Clink clink.*

Stop and listen.

Someone is following me. But there is no sound but the whir and snap of grasshoppers.

*Clink clink.*

There it is again: a sound very much like—yes, the very sound my caddy Willard Amadie used to make when he'd hump it for the angle of the dogleg to watch the drive, running level and flat out and holding the clubheads in the crook of his arm so they wouldn't rattle and disturb the drivers already poised over their balls, but even so the faces of the irons would slap *clink clink*.

There is no one. I stop on a high bald green dotted with palmetto. The flagpole flies a pennant of wistaria.

Now into a dry wash out of bounds and among the flared bladed trunks of tupelo gums. *Clink clink*, it's ahead of me.

Stop and calculate: really it seems unlikely that anyone is trying to shoot you here or even following you or, if he is, that he would be carrying a golf bag.

Nevertheless, suppose that he is. Suppose he has seen me and, knowing me, knows where I am going and is going ahead to wait. Where would he go?

One place: the "island" of number 11, a sporty hole where the drive has to carry a neck of the swamp, which the golfers cross by two Chinese footbridges connecting a little loess lump in the swamp. Here I'd cross if I were going to the Center and here on the island stands a pagoda shelter that commands both bridges.

Instead of using the bridge, drop down the soft cliff, using a boy's trick of walking along the face dropping two steps for every step forward.

Now behind the "Quarters," a long rowhouse, a ruin of soft warm brick which housed sugar-plantation slaves and which, set just above water level of the bayou, was thought of by the Paradise developers as a kind of Natchez-under-the-hill and so restored and reroofed for domestic servants, even a chapel added so that strains of good old spirituals would come floating up to our patios in the evening, but the domestic preferred their Hollow, dank and fetid though it was. So back to the jungle went the Quarters, new tin roof and all.

A crashing in the vines ahead of me. My heart stops: if it is a sniper, there's an army of them. Wait. Yes, whew. I spot Colley's pith helmet and Gottlieb's fishing cap. It is the Audubon Society, on the trail of the lordly ivorybill.

Moving swiftly in deep shade and without sound on the moss bank of the bayou, I reach the hogback of the island, high and dry now, and climb its gentlest slope, angling for the path and keeping an eye peeled for the roof of the pagoda.

There it is, directly above, but the loess loam, soft as meal, has eroded badly under the near quadrant of the pagoda so that one may no longer walk into it but has to climb up through the vines. Thunder rumbles. A big sour drop spatters on my hand. The wind smells of trees. It is a simple matter to climb into the quadrant, put bag on seat, hold pistol, stand on seat to see over the partition.

Is anyone there?

The two adjacent quadrants are empty. The opposite quadrant? It is difficult to see because the angle between partitions is choked with potato vine and dirt-dauber nests. The space between the eaves and the intersecting rafters allows a view of a stretch of the coast with a church steeple and parade ground. There the Kaydettes are drilling, the sun is shining. By a trick of light and distance, the field seems to be tilted like an Andes farm. Tiny figures march up and down. The twirling batons make silver coins in the sunlight.

Safe in the thunder and wrapped in potato vine, I wait. The wind is sour with raindrops but the storm is veering off.

In a brief quiet between thunder rolls, close as close, a man clears his throat. So close that I feel my head incline politely as if he were addressing me. In a panic I grip the center post and hollow my throat to keep breathing quiet.

"That's a pretty sight now." The voice is so close that the dry wood of the partition vibrates like a sounding board.

"They fixing to parade." A second voice, the sentence uttered civilly, an observation.

"They'll parade all right." A third voice, even closer, grim, rich in ironies.

Thunder rolls, covering the voices. Dropping slowly, I sit

in the angle, feeling behind me the press and creak of wood as bodies shift weight.

"What do we need with him?" asks the third voice.

"Victor's all right now. He know how to get along with people. Victor what you call our contract man." First voice: a familiar two-layered voice, one layer speaking to meaning, the other risible, soliciting routine funniness: we might as well be funny as not.

"Contract? Do you mean contact?"

"Contract, contact."

I recognize two voices but not the third.

The rolling thunder becomes more discrete, coming after lightning cracks. I count the intervals. Two seconds, three. The storm is going away. At the next crack I count four and stand up in the thunder.

Use the potato vine as screen, crane up and over into it, far enough to see through the leaves but not be seen.

The man sitting at the end of the seat, facing the path toward the club, is, I know already, Willard Amadie. Bent forward, forearms on knees, he can look up and see the others, see the path, only by wrinkling his low wide welted forehead. He wears a Marine camouflaged coverall. Beside him, propped against the bench, butts grounded, are a rifle and shotgun fitted with straps. Then it was they, not golf irons, that clinked.

Stretched out on the bench, only its forequarters visible, head lolling to the ground, tongue smeared with dust, is a young buck deer.

"No reason why people can't get along," says the first voice in the style of uttering platitudes agreeably.

"People?" Voice number three. "What people? I'll tell the truth, I never know what he's talking about."

I know what he's talking about. *People* uttered so, in a slight flatting of tone, means white people. Uttered another way, it means black. A third way means people in general.

"I'll tell you this!" exclaims the first voice, shouting a platitude. "I'm not going have anything to do with people"—second meaning—"who looking to hurt other people." First meaning. "That's not what the good Lord intend."

"The good Lord," says the third voice. "What is it with this dude? Jesus."

"Victor is all right. He's with us. In fact, we couldn't do without him," says Willard, looking up from his black welted brow. "He's for the plan, he's for the school, don't worry.

Aren't you, Brother?" The *brother* too I recognize, though I doubt if number three does. This is Baptist brother: Victor is a deacon in Starlight Baptist Church.

"Sure I'm for it! Education is good for everybody and everybody is entitled to it!"

"I'll tell you this, Uru," says Willard. "We need Victor more than he needs us. Where do you think we get our medicine? People respect him." All kind of people.

"I don't understand anybody down here. This dude sounds like some old uncle from Memphis."

"Those old uncles in Memphis are tougher than you think," says Willard, grinning.

Victor Charles sits opposite Willard, feet planted flat on the ground, hands prone on his knees. A strong, grave, heavy-thighed man, he is purple-black and of an uncertain age. He could be forty and looking older for his dignity. Or he could be sixty and flat-bellied from his life as a laborer. Dressed like a hospital attendant in white duck trousers, white shirt, white interne shoes, he does in fact work in the animal shelter as caretaker. A black belt circles his wide, flat hips, buckle worn to the side and I recall why: so the buckle won't scrape against the high metal table when he holds the big dogs.

"Look like he not coming," says Willard after a pause, squeezing his fist in his hand.

Who's not coming? Me? A corkscrew tightens in my sacrum.

"Where are they going now?" asks the third man.

The other two look toward the coast.

"They marching over to the club for a show this evening," says Willard. Willard has a slight stammer. Once in a while the words hang in this throat, he touches his eye and out they come, hooting.

"All right. Now you know the route Tuesday."

"Sure I know the route," hoots Willard.

"How about the brother here?"

Willard and Victor look at each other and laugh.

"I know," says Victor gravely.

"Here," says Willard, bending over. Something scrapes in the dirt. He's drawing a map. "Intercept the bus here. Brother, we counting on you to watch them."

"I'm going to be watching more than them," says Victor, spreading his fingers over his knees.

"What does he mean?" asks the third man.

"He means you, Brother Uru," says Willard, laughing.

"Ain't nobody going to hurt anybody long as I got anything to do with it!" cries Victor. "I mean nobody!"

"I don't know. I just don't know," mutters number three to himself. "What kind of damn country is this?"

"Victor's going to lead them to Honey Island."

"That's right and I'm staying there."

"What you worrying about, old man?"

"You."

"Me?"

"Ain't nobody bothering those little ladies."

"What in the hell—"

Willard opens his mouth, touches his eye: "Listen!"

There is a crackling in the swamp, a sound that becomes louder and more measured. It is the little safari of bird-watchers.

"See. I told you," says Willard softly. "They pass here every Saturday this time of day, and on Tuesday the Fourth they'll do the same."

"Well well well," says the third man, pleased for the first time. "Here come our teachers."

"Teachers?" says Victor Charles. "What you talking about. They the doctors from the Center out for a walk. With their spyglasses."

"They going too," says Willard quietly. "We need teachers at the school."

"You mean they going out to Honey Island too!" cries Victor.

"That's right, Brother. Some of them, anyhow."

"Lord to God. Now I done heard it all."

"Why not, Uncle," says the third man. "I think it proper and fitting that our children be taught by Ph.D.'s."

"I think ever'body entitled to an education!" exclaims Victor in his singsong.

The crashing grows louder as the safari works around the hogback. Presently, by standing at the end of the bench, I can see them: Colley and Gottlieb still in the lead, Colley in pith helmet, bermuda shorts, and bush jacket; Gottlieb in his long-billed meshtop hat, the sort retirees wear in Fort Lauderdale. There follow a dozen or so behaviorists, physicians, Love counselors, plus a NASA engineer or two.

Returning to the corner, I discover I can hear by putting an ear to the partition, which acts as a sounding board.

"And I'll tell you something else," says the voice at the center pole, a voice without antecedents, black yes, Midwestern perhaps, but mainly stereo-V, an announcer's voice, a

Detroit disc jockey's voice. "This is war and don't you forget it. All this talk about some people being nice, listen. They're nice all right. They're so nice and polite that you mothers been castrated without knowing it."

"What you talking about, my mother being—" begins Victor, outraged.

"No, what he means, Victor," says Willard, touching his eye and hooting, "is—"

"Never mind," says the third man in disgust. "Jesus."

"I hear you say Jesus!" cries Victor.

"I said, never mind."

"I say bless Jesus!"

"O.K., O.K."

Guns clink together. Wood, lightened of its load, creaks. The deer carcass slides over the rough wood of the bench. A man grunts as the load is hefted.

"Well, they going to eat today," says a voice, Willard's, going away.

Wait five minutes to make sure.


5


Shortcut into rear of hospital and through the day room of my old ward. The attendant peering through the screened glass lets me in, though he is not clear about my position. Am I professor, patient, doctor, what? But he knows me from somewhere, sees my bag, lets me through. Did I remember to put pistol in bag? Yes.

Though the building is new, the day room already has the worn look of all day rooms. Its scuffed tile and hard-used blocky wooden furniture is for all the world like a child's playhouse. The picture on stereo-V rolls slowly. The room smells of idle man-flesh, pajamas stiffened by body dandruff and dried urine. Great sky-high windows let in the out-of-doors through heavy security screens that render the world gauzy green and pointillist.

Here dwell my old friends and fellow madmen. I recognize them. They gaze at me, knowing me and knowing me not. I am like a dream they have dreamed before. A man standing at the window twitters his fingers, sending out radar beams to the vague, gauzy world, and cocks his ear, listening for returning blips. *Who are you out there?* Another man carries his head under his arm. A blond youth, a pale handsome exchange student from Holland, remembers that he owes me a debt of some sort and pays me off with feces money, a small dry turd, which I accept in good part, folding it into my handkerchief and pocketing same.

Here I spent the best months of my life. In a few days my high-lows leveled out, my depression-exaltation melded into a serene skimming watchfulness. My terror-rage—cowardly lionheartedness and lionhearted cowardice—fused into a mild steady resolve. Here in the day room and in the ward we patients came to understand each other as only fellow prisoners and exiles can. Sane outside, I can't make head or tail of people. Mad inside, we signaled each other like auctioneers, a wink here, a wag of finger there. I listened and watched. Outside there is not time to listen. Sitting here in the day room the day after Christmas next to a mangy pine tree decorated with varicolored Kleenex (no glass!), the stereo-V showing the Blue-Gray game and rolling flip flip flip, my hands on my knees and wrists bandaged, I felt so bad that I groaned aloud an Old Testament lamentation AAAAIEOOOOOW! to which responded a great silent black man sitting next to me on the blocky couch: "Ain't it the truth though."

After that I felt better.

We love those who know the worst of us and don't turn their faces away. I loved my fellow patients and hearkened to them and they to me. I loved Max Gottlieb. He sewed up my wrists in his living room without making a fuss about it. How did I get to his house? By walking, I think. The last thing I remember clearly is Perry Como, hale as Saint Nick but orange of face and livid of lip.

As Max worked, he was holding my wrist pressed with pleasant pressure against his stomach, and I remember thinking he was like a trainer lacing up his fighter's gloves.

He clucked in mild irritation.

"What's the matter, Max?"

"Tch. I can't fix the tendon here. You'll have to wait. Sorry."

"That's all right, Max."

Here's an oddity. Max the unbeliever, a lapsed Jew, believes in the orderliness of creation, acts on it with energy and charity. I the believer, having swallowed the whole Thing, God Jews Christ Church, find the world a madhouse and a madhouse home. Max the atheist sees things like Saint

Thomas Aquinas, ranged, orderly, connected up.

Here it was in this very day room that I, watchful and prescient, tuned into the palpable radiations of my fellow patients and my colleagues as well, the tired hollow-eyed abstracted doctors, and hatched my great principle, as simple and elegant and obvious as all great principles are. It is easy to understand how men do their best work in prison or exile, men like Dostoevsky, Cervantes, Bonhoeffer, Sir Thomas More, Genet, and I, Dr. Thomas More. Pascal wrote as if he were in prison for life and so he was free. In prison or exile or a mental hospital one has time to watch and listen. My question was: how is it with you, fellow patient? how is it with you, fellow physician? and I saw how it was. Many men have done that, seen visions, dreamed dreams. But it is of no use in science unless you can measure it. My good luck came when I stumbled onto a way of measuring the length and breadth and motions of the very self. My little machine is the first caliper of the soul.

Then one day in May I had had enough of the ward and wanted out. I had made my breakthrough. I had done my job. Though I was still on the ward, I was working on the staff as well, even presenting cases to students in The Pit. But I still had to get out. What was it like out there in the gauzy pointillist world? Would my great discovery work out there?

So I went AWOL, walked out and haven't been back since. I walked to town along the interstate. Wham! there it was, the world, solid as a rock, dense as a doorknob. A beer can glinted malignantly on the shoulder. The grains of concrete were like rocks on the moon. Here came old friend, morning terror, corkscrewing up my spine. Dear God, let me out of here, back to the nuthouse where I can stay sane. Things are too naked out here. People look and talk and smile and are nice and the abyss yawns. The niceness is terrifying.

But I went on to town, to the Little Napoleon tavern where I greeted Leroy Ledbetter, the owner, and other old friends, sipped a few toddies and soon felt better. From the Little Napoleon I telephoned an acquaintance, Dr. Yamaiuchi of Osaka Instruments, with whom I had been in correspondence and who had my specifications, and placed an order for one hundred lapsometers, certified check to follow upon his estimate. The pay phone in the Little Napoleon cost me $47.65 in quarters and nickels.

Leroy and my pals did not find the call remarkable and fed

me coins: old Doc is making a call to Japan, scientific medical
business, etcetera, keep the money coming, fix him a drink.

Max and Colley, just back from birding, are sitting in the chief
resident's office. Max has donned his white clinical coat but
hasn't changed his boots. Colley, still wearing bush jacket and
bermuda shorts, lounges in a tattered aluminum chaise, puffing a briar that sends out wreaths of maple-sugar smoke.

Max is glad to see me, Colley is not. Colley is a super-
Negro, a regular black Leonardo. He is chief encephalographer, electronic wizard, ornithologist, holds the Black Belt
in karate, does the crossword in the Sunday *Times*. A native
of Dothan, Alabama, he is a graduate of Amherst and N.Y.U.
medical school. So he lounges around like an Amherst man,
cocking a quizzical eyebrow and sending out wreaths of
maple-sugar smoke, or else he humps off down the hall like a
Brooklyn intern, eyes rolled up in his eyebrows, shoes
pigeoning in and going *squee-gee* on the asphalt tile. Yet if he
gets excited enough or angry enough, the old Alabama hambone shows through. His voice will hit up into falsetto and he
might even say *aksed* instead of *asked*.

When I was in the open ward and working on staff, he was
very good to me. He immediately saw what I was getting at
and helped me wire up my first lapsometer, read my article
and refused to take credit as coauthor. "Too metaphysical for
me," he said politely, knocking out his briar. "I'll stick to
old-fashioned tumors and hemorrhages"—and off he went
humping it down the hall *squee-gee*.

But we were always wary of each other. Our eyes never quite
met. It was as if there was something between us, a shared
secret, an unmentionable common past, an unacknowledged
kinship. We were somehow on to each other. He recognized my
Southern trick of using manners and even madness guilefully
and for one's own ends. I was onto his trick of covering up
Alabama hambone with brave old Amherst and humping it like a
Brooklyn intern. What is more, he knew that I knew and I knew
that he knew. We were like two Jews who have changed their
names.

Max sits behind his desk in his perfectly fitted white coat,
erect as a young prince, light glancing from the planes of his
forehead. But when he rises, like Toulouse-Lautrec he doesn't
rise much.

Colley drums his fingers on his pith helmet in his lap, Jungle Jim after the safari.

"Well well," says Max with pure affection, an affection without irony. He loves me because he saved my life. "The prodigal has returned."

"Prodigal or prodigy?" asks Colley quizzically-Amherstly.

We're all three prodigies. Max is a prodigy. His performance on grand rounds is famous. There he stands at the foot of my bed in the ward, the small erect young prince, flanked by a semicircle of professors, psychiatrists, behaviorists, Love counselors, reminding me of the young Jesus confounding his elders.

He saved me twice. Once the night before by suturing my arteries. The next morning by naming my terror, giving it habitation, standing at the foot of my bed, knowing the worst of me, then naming it with ordinary words, English common nouns, smiling and moving on.

A bad night it had been, my wrists bandaged and lashed to the rails, crucified, I by turns exalted, depressed, terrified, lustful. Miss Oglethorpe, a handsome strapping nurse (she's now my nurse) came on at eleven and asked me what I wanted. "I want you, Miss Oglethorpe. You are so beautiful and I need you and love you. Will you lie here with me?" Since she was and I did, was beautiful and I did love and need her, and she being a woman knew the truth when she heard it, she almost did. She almost did! But of course she didn't and instead made a horrid nurse-joke about how I couldn't be so bad off what with chasing the nurses etcetera, but what a good nurse!

Later, lust gave way to sorrow and I prayed, arms stretched out like a Mexican, tears streaming down my face. Dear God, I can see it now, why can't I see it other times, that it is you I love in the beauty of the world and in all the lovely girls and dear good friends, and it is pilgrims we are, wayfarers on a journey, and not pigs, nor angels. Why can I not be merry and loving like my ancestor, a gentle pure-hearted knight for our Lady and our blessed Lord and Savior? Pray for me, Sir Thomas More.

Etcetera etcetera. A regular Walpurgis night of witches, devils, pitchforks, thorns in the flesh, upkneed girl-thighs. Followed by contrition and clear sight. Followed, of course, by old friend morning terror.

There stood Max at the foot of my bed flanked by my former colleagues, the ten o'clock sunlight glancing from the planes of his forehead and striking sparks from the silver of his reflex hammer and tuning fork in his breast pocket, Max smiling and spreading the skirts of his immaculate white coat and saying only, "Dr. More is having some troublesome mood swings— don't we all—but he's got excellent insight, so we hope we can enlist his services as soon as he'll let us, right, Tom?" And all at once it, the terror, had a habitation and name—I was having "mood swings," right, that's what they were—and the doctors nodded and smiled and moved to the next bed. And suddenly the morning sunlight became just what it was, the fresh lovely light of morning. The terror was gone.

That, sirs, is love.

In a week, I got up cheerfully and went about my business. Another week and, lying in my bed, I became prescient and clairvoyant, orbiting the earth like an angel and inducing instant angelic hypotheses. Another week and I had made my break- through.

"The prodigal returns," says Max, smiling his candid unironic smile (Max, who is from Pittsburgh, doesn't know all the dark things Colley and I know, so is not ironic). "This time to stay, I hope."

"No," I say quickly, taking a tiny shaft of fright. For I've just remembered that legally I'm still committed and that they could, if they wished, detain me.

"Yeah, very nice," says Colley, shaking hands without enthu- siasm. He appears to knock out two pipes at the same time. The smoke has leveled out in a layer like leaf smoke in Vermont.

"What can we do for you, Tom?" asks Max, his princely head shedding light.

"I've a favor to ask."

"Ask it."

For some reason I frown and fall silent.

"I thought you'd come by to prepare for The Pit," says Max.

"The Pit?"

"Sure, Tom," says Colley, cheering up at my confusion. "You're down for Monday. This is the last go-round of the year for the students, you know, the annual Donnybrook."

Max hastens to reassure me. "You've got quite a following among the students, Tom. You're the new matador, Manolete taking on Belmonte."

Buddy Brown, my enemy, must be Belmonte. O God, I had forgotten. The Pit is a seriocomic clinic, an end-of-year hijinks put on by the doctors for the students. Doctors, you

may know, have a somewhat retarded sense of humor. In medical school we dropped fingers and ears from cadavers on
pedestrians. Older doctors write doggerel and satirical verse.
When I was a young man, every conservative proctologist in
town had a cartoon in his office showing a jackass kicking up
his heels and farting a smoke ring: "LBJ has spoken!"

"God, I had forgotten. No, Max, I came to ask you a favor."

"Ask it."

"You know what it is. I want you to speak to the Director
about my article and my lapsometer before my appointment
with him Monday."

Colley straddles the chaise and rises.

"Wait, Colley. I want to tell you something too."

He shrugs, settles slowly, unfolds a silver pipe tool.

"Well, Max?"

"Sure sure." Max swivels around to the gold-green gauze.
"If—"

"If what?"

"If you'll come back."

"You mean as patient?"

"Patient-staff. As you were."

"Why?"

"You're not well."

"I'm well enough. I can't come back."

"Why not?"

"Something is afoot."

"What?"

I sit down slowly and close my eyes. "You were both out
birding this morning, weren't you? Down by the Quarters."

"Yeah!" says Max, lighting up. Rummaging in his desk for
something, he hands it to me, a piece of bark. "Take a look at
those cuttings."

"O.K."

"What do you think?"

"I don't know."

"That's from an overcup oak and it's not a pileated."

"You mean you think—"

"Ask Colley. He's the ornithologist."

"No question about it," says Colley, rubbing his briar on his
nose. "It's the ivorybill. He's out there. Just think of it, Max."

"Yes."

"No one's seen him since nineteen-three and he's out there.
Think of it. I think he's on Honey Island."

"Yes." Max's eyes are shining. For him the ivorybill, which the Negroes used to call the Lord-to-God, is the magic bird, the firebird, the sweet bird of youth. For the ivorybill to return after all these years—

Colley is different. The search for the bird is for him not a bona fide search. It is something he has got the knack of. How happy he is to have got the knack of searching for the ivorybill!

(No idle speculation this: once, before Colley and I fell out, I measured his pineal region. He had good readings at layer I, little or nothing at layer II. Diagnosis: a self successfully playing at being a self that is not itself. I told him this—he asked me!—and he took offense, rolled his eyes up in his eyebrows, and went humping off down the hall *squee-gee*).

Max is looking at me sharply. "Why do you ask? Did you see us? Why didn't you join us? It would be good—"

"I couldn't. I was trapped."

"Trapped?"

Colley, I see, is wondering whether he should risk an exchange of glances with Max. His eyes stray. He doesn't.

"Yes," I say and relate to them the events of the morning, beginning with the sniper and ending with my eavesdropping on the three conspirators in the pagoda. I don't tell it badly, using, in fact, Max's own low-keyed clinical style of reciting case histories on grand rounds.

Silence falls. Colley, who has lit up again, screws up an eye against the maple-sugar smoke. Max's expression does not change. He listens attentively, unironically. Daylight glances interestingly from his forehead.

"Let me be sure I understand you," says Max at last, swinging to and fro. "You are saying first that somebody tried to shoot you this morning; second, that there is a conspiracy planned for the Fourth of July, a conspiracy to kidnap the Paradise baton-twirlers as well as staff members here who participate in the Audubon outings?"

"Not exactly. The shooting is a fact. The other is what I heard."

"And they're planning to run a school on Honey Island for the Bantus and Choctaws," says Colley, drumming his fingers on his helmet.

"They said it."

Silence.

I rise. "Look. I felt obliged to pass it on to you. Make of it what you will. Perhaps it is foolishness. It is not even necessary that you believe me. I simply—"

"I didn't say I didn't believe you, Tom," says Max affectionately. "Belief. Truth values. These are relative things. What interests me is—"

"Yeah, don't give me that either. Skip it. Look, will you speak to the Director?"

"Of course. Will you come back?"

Colley beats me to the door. "I'm off. Max. Tom. You know your job is still open?"

"Thanks," I say sourly.

Colley gone, Max nods toward the lounge. "You look tired, Tom. Did you have a bad night?"

"Yes."

"How are you feeling?"

"Fine fine."

"No depression?"

"Not much."

"No highs?"

"They come together, sine-cosine."

"What?"

"Nothing. Max, you read my paper and you've seen my lapsometer."

"Yes."

"Do you think they're of value?"

"Yes. I think you've hit on something extremely intriguing. You've got a gift for correlation, but there's too much subjectivity here and your series is too short. You need to come back in the hospital and spend about a year at it."

"At what?" I ask him suspiciously.

"At this." He picks up my paper. "And at treatment."

"Whose treatment?"

"Your treatment of other patients and our treatment of you."

"I know my mental health is bad, but there's not much time."

"Let's talk about this sense of impending disaster."

"Bullshit, Max. Are you going to help me with the Director or aren't you?"

"I am. And you take the job back."

"What job?"

"Your same job. As a matter of fact, Kenneth Stryker over in Love just read your earlier paper and I told him something about this. He's quite excited and thinks you can help him out over there."

"Max, I don't seem to be getting across. You're talking about doing business at the same stand here. I'm talking about a crash program involving N.I.M.H. and twenty-five million dollars."

"A crash program? You mean on a national scale? You think there is a national emergency?"

"More even than that, Max! It's not even the U.S.A., it's the soul of Western man that is in the very act of flying apart HERE and NOW. Christ, Max, you read the paper. I can measure it, Max! Number one, I've got to get this thing mass-produced and in the hands of G.P.'s, number two, I've got to hit on a therapeutic equivalent of my diagnostic breakthrough. Don't you agree?"

"Well now. The soul of Western man, that's a large order, Tom. Besides being rather uh metaphysical—"

"Metaphysical is a word, Max. There is nothing metaphysical about the tenfold increase in atrocities in this area. There's nothing metaphysical about the vines sprouting. There's nothing metaphysical about the Bantu guerrillas and this country falling apart between the Knotheads and the Leftpapas. Did you know the President and Vice-President will both be in this area on the Fourth—"

"What was that about the vines?" asks Max, cocking an ear.

"Never mind," I say, blushing. I shouldn't have mentioned the vines.

Max is shifting about in his chair.

"I get uh uncomfortable when politics gets mixed with medicine, to say nothing of angels."

"Very well."

"Wait. What are your immediate plans?"

"For today? I'm headed for my office in town, stopping off on the way at old Howard Johnson's. I want to make sure it's safe. Moira and I have a date there on the Fourth."

"Moira? Isn't she the little popsy over in Love?"

"Yes. She's a secretary at the Love Clinic."

"Yes indeed. I saw her at the square dance with Buddy."

"Buddy?" I frown.

"She's a charmer."

Max calls all attractive young women "popsies." Though he is a neobehaviorist, he is old-fashioned, even courtly in sexual matters. Like Freud himself, he is both Victorian and anatomical, speaking one moment delicately of "paying court to the ladies" or "having an affair of the heart," and the next of genitalia and ejaculations and such. Whenever he mentions women, I picture heavy black feather-boa'd dresses clothing naked bodies and secret parts.

"Then will you come back, Tom?"

"Come back?"

"To the hospital. I'll work like a dog with you."

"I know you will."

"We were just getting the cards on the table when you left."

"What cards?"

"We found out what the hangup was and we were getting ready to condition you out of it."

"What hangup?"

"Your guilt feelings."

"I never did see that."

"You did see that your depression and suicide attempt were related to sexual guilt?"

"What sexual guilt?"

"Didn't you tell me that your depression followed *une affaire* of the heart with a popsy at the country club?"

"Lola is no popsy. She's a concert cellist."

"Oh." Max has a great respect for stringed instruments. "Nevertheless your guilt did follow *une affaire* of the heart."

"Are you speaking of my fornication with Lola in number 18 bunker?"

"Fornication," repeats Max, nodding. "You see?"

"See what?"

"That you are saying that lovemaking is not a natural activity, like eating and drinking."

"No, I didn't say it wasn't natural."

"But sinful and guilt-laden."

"Not guilt-laden."

"Then sinful?"

"Only between persons not married to each other."

"I am trying to see it as you see it."

"I know you are."

"If it is sinful, why do you do it?"

"It is a great pleasure."

"I understand. Then, since it is 'sinful,' guilt feelings follow, even though it is a pleasure."

"No, they don't follow."

"Then what worries you, if you don't feel guilty?"

"That's what worries me: not feeling guilty."

"Why does that worry you?"

"Because if I felt guilty, I could get rid of it."

"How?"

"By the sacrament of penance."

"I'm trying to see it as you see it."

"I know you are."

"What I don't see is that if there is no guilt after *une affaire*, what is the problem?"

"The problem is that if there is no guilt, contrition, and a purpose of amendment, the sin cannot be forgiven."

"What does that mean, operationally speaking?"

"It means that you don't have life in you."

"Life?"

"Yes."

"But you didn't seem much interested in life that night. On the contrary."

"I know."

"In any case, your depression and suicide attempt did follow your uh 'sin.'"

"That wasn't why I was depressed."

"Why were you depressed?"

"It was Christmas Eve and there I was watching Perry Como."

"You're blocking me."

"Yes."

"What does 'purpose of amendment' mean?"

"Promising to try not to do it again and meaning it."

"And you don't intend to do that?"

"No."

"Why not, if you believe it is sinful?"

"Because it is a great pleasure."

"I don't follow."

"I know."

"At least, in the matter of belief and action, you are half right."

"That's right."

"But there remains the tug of war between the two."

"There does."

"If you would come back and get in the Skinner box, we could straighten it out."

"The Skinner box wouldn't help."

"We could condition away the contradiction. You'd never feel guilt."

"Then I'd really be up the creek."

"I'm trying to see it."

"I know you are."

"I notice that in speaking of your date with the little popsy from Love, you choose a setting that emphasizes the anonymous, transient, and sordid character of the relationship as you see it."

"How's that?"

"Not merely a motel, but an abandoned motel, a ruin, a secret hole-in-corner place, an assignation."

"Yes, that's the beauty of it, isn't it?" I say, cheering up.

"No. No no. You misunderstand me. It's a question of maturity—"

"You're right, Max," I say, wringing his hand affectionately and rushing off. "You're a good friend!" I call back from the hall.

Poor Max did his best for me. Once he devised a psychological test, tailored to my peculiar complaint.

"You see those two doors," he said to me one day, sitting behind the same desk.

"Yes." I could tell from the sparkle in his eye and from the way light glanced interestingly from his forehead that he had cooked up something for me.

"Behind those two doors are not the lady and the tiger but two ladies."

"O.K.," I say, perking up. Max, I saw, had gone to some trouble devising a test that would reveal to me the nature of my problem.

"Behind the door," said Max, wheeling in his chair, "is a lovely person, a mature, well-educated person who is quite fond of you."

"Yes?"

"You have much in common. She can converse on a variety of topics, is psychiatrically-oriented, empathetic toward you, and is quite creative in the arts. She is equally at home discussing the World Bank or a novel by Mazo de la Roche."

"Mazo de la Roche? Jesus, Max. Look, do you have someone in mind?"

"And she is dressed in the most seductive garb"—Max would say garb—"and you find her reclining on a couch in a room furnished with the costliest, most tasteful fabrics. Exotic perfumes are wafted toward you"—Max says wäfted—"You talk. She responds warmly at all levels of the interpersonal spectrum. The most seductive music is playing—"

"What music in particular, Max?"

"What difference does it make? *Scheherazade*."

"God, Max, it all sounds so Oriental." What makes Max's attempt to find me a girl both odd and endearing is that he is so old-fashioned. He and his wife, Sylvia, are like Darwin and Mrs. Darwin at their fireside in Kent. "Who's behind the other door, Max?"

"Oh, a popsy in a motel room."

"What is she like?"

"Oh, ordinary. Say a stewardess. You've spoken to her once on a flight from Houston."

"She fancies me?"

"Yes."

"You want to know which I prefer?"

"Yes."

"The stewardess."

"Exactly!" cried Max triumphantly. "You prefer 'fornication,' as you call it, to a meaningful relation with another person qua person."

"Right, and you're saying the other case is not fornication."

"Yes."

Thus Max devised a specific test to reveal me to myself, I flunked the test, was in fact revealed to myself. But nothing came of it.

After saving my life, he tried to make it a good life. He invited me along on Audubon bird walks and to Center square dances and even introduced me to an attractive lady behaviorist named Grace Gould. Was this the lady behind the first door, I wondered. He even invited me to his home. Grace and I would sit in Max's living room while Max barbecued kebabs outside and his wife, Sylvia, a tall stooped one-shoulder-hitched-up ruddy-faced girl from Pittsburgh, passed around a dip. We spoke of politics, deplored Knotheads, listened to Rimski-Korsakov, played Scrabble, watched educational stereo-V. Max himself had many interests besides medicine and looking for the ivory-bill: tropical fish, square dancing, gem-polishing, tree-dwarf-ing—which he tried to interest me in, without success. Grace Gould was his last and best effort. Grace, who came from Pasadena, was indeed attractive, was nimble as a cat at square dancing, could spot a Louisiana waterthrush at one hundred feet, and could converse on a variety of topics. Max and Sylvia would retire early, leaving us to our devices downstairs. Upstairs the Gottliebs lay, quiet as mice, hoping something was cooking downstairs (for Max loved me and wanted for me what he had). Nothing was cooking, however, though Grace and I liked each other. But there seemed to be nothing to do but drink and look at the walls which, though the house was a new one in Paradise, nevertheless gave the effect of being dark and varnished inside like an old duplex in Queens. The bookshelves contained medical, psychiatric, and psychological texts, a whole shelf of *Reader's Digest* four-in-one novels, and the complete works of Mazo de la Roche. The night Max sewed up my wrists at his house, found a cut tendon, went out to beat the bushes for a surgeon, I read *Whiteoaks of Jalna* at one sitting. There we sat, Grace and I, agreeing on everything, until I developed a tic, commenced to wink, and so took her home, keeping one side of my face averted.

6

Passing through the geriatric cottages on the way to Love. Here in cold glassed porches sit despondent oldsters, exiled from Tampa and Tucson for crankiness, misanthropy, malcontent, solitariness, destructiveness, misery—in short, the St. Petersburg Blues.

Each has two electrodes in his head, like a Martian with antennae. They're being reconditioned, put in Skinner boxes, which are pleasant enough chambers furnished with that "recreational or avocational environment" which the patient shows highest aptitude for—pottery wheel, putting green, ceramic oven, square-dance therapist—and conditioned. Positively conditioned when he responds positively: spins wheel, hops to music—by a mild electric current flowing through electrode A inducing a pleasant sensation, an unlocated euphoria, hypothalamic joy. Negatively conditioned when he responds negatively: breaks wheel, kicks therapist, sits in corner—by a nasty shock through electrode B inducing a distinct but not overpowering malaise.

Those who respond? Back home to Senior Citizen compounds in Tampa and Tucson with other happy seniors.

Those who don't respond? Off they're packed to the Happy Isles of Georgia, the federal Good Time Garden where reconditioning is no longer attempted but rather the opposite: whenever they behave antisocially they're shocked into bliss, soon learning to press the button themselves, off and dreaming so blissful that they pass up meals—

Here's the hottest political issue of the day: euthanasia. Say the euthanasists not unreasonably: let's be honest, why should people suffer and cause suffering to other people? It is the quality of life that counts, not longevity, etcetera. Every man is entitled to live his life with freedom and to end it with dignity, etcetera etcetera. It came down to one curious squabble (like the biggest theology fight coming down to whether to add the *que* to the *filio*): the button *vs*. the switch. Should a man have the right merely to self-stimulation, pressing the button that delivers bliss precisely until the blissful thumb relaxes and lets go the button? Or does he not also have the right to throw a switch that stays on, inducing a permanent joy—no meals, no sleep, and a happy death in a week or so? The button *vs*. the switch.

And if he has such a right and is judged legally incompetent to throw the switch, cannot a relative throw it for him?

The debate rages. The qualitarians, as the euthanasists call themselves, have won in Maryland and New York and Hawaii where legislatures have passed laws that allow sane oldsters to choose a "joyful exitus" as it is called in Maryland, or a *kawanee-olaua* as it is called in Hawaii, and throw the on-switch on. In the case of the insane, the consent of both physician and spouse is necessary.

*Whup*. Up ahead I spy my enemy, Dr. Buddy Brown, sailing his coattails, and duck into Love Clinic just in time.

I don't want to talk to him about our coming shoot-out in The Pit. Am I afraid of him?

7

The small observation room in Love is not crowded. Moira is perched on a stool at the viewing mirror, steno pad open on her knees. My heart melts with love. Does not a faint color spread along her throat? She blushes! I nod merely—or do I blush?—and go on talking to Stryker. But her presence is like sunlight. No matter which way I turn I feel a ray of warmth, now on my cheek, now between my shoulder blades. There is a sextant in me that keeps her position.

Father Kev Kevin sits reading *Commonweal* at his console of vaginal indicators. Only the regular staff is present today— though there may be students in the amphitheater above—Dr.

Kenneth Stryker, chief of staff of Love; Dr. Helga Heine, his assistant, a West German interpersonal gynecologist; Father Kev Kevin, an ex-priest now a Love counselor; and Moira Schaffner, my own true love.

Stryker and Moira are glad to see me. Father Kev Kevin and Helga are not, though they are civil enough. Helga thinks I don't like Germans. I suspect, too, she believes I am Jewish because I was always with Gottlieb and I look somewhat Jewish, like my illustrious ancestor, Sir Thomas More.

Father Kev Kevin was a curate at Saint Michael's, my old parish church. So he is skittish toward me, behaving now too brightly, now too sullenly. I think he fears I might call him Father. A handsome Irishman, he is not merely chaplain of the clinic but jack of all trades: counsels persons in Love who cannot love—love or die! he tells them—takes clinical notes, operates the vaginal console. Imagine a young genial anticlerical Pat O'Brien who reads *Commonweal*.

The behavior room beyond the viewing mirror is presently unoccupied. It has an examining table with stirrups, a hospital bed, a tray of instruments, a tube of K-Y jelly, and a rack for the sensor wires with leads to the recording devices in the observation room.

A subject comes in, a solitary lover. I gaze at her, feeling somewhat big-nosed.

I recognize her. She is Lillian, Stryker's first subject. No doubt she will go down in history like Freud's first patient, Anna O. For it was she, Lonesome Lil as the students called her, who exhibited in classic form the "cruciform rash" of love that won for Stryker the Nobel Prize.

Lillian wears a sensible gray suit and sturdy brown low-heeled shoes. Her outfit, with shoulder bag and matching hat, a kind of beret with up-arching hoop inside, puts me in mind of Lois Lane of the old *Superman* comics of my childhood. Lillian is a good deal sturdier, however. As she opens her shoulder bag and begins to remove small fitted devices of clear Lucite, lining them up neatly on the surgical tray, she is for all the world like a visiting nurse come to minister to a complex ailment.

But, unlike a visiting nurse, she undresses. As briskly as a housewife getting ready for her evening bath and paying no more attention to the viewing mirror than if it were her vanity, she sheds jacket, skirt, underwear—the lower article a kind of stretch step-in garment, the upper a brassiere with a bodice-like extension—and finally her up-arched beret, holding a bobby pin in her teeth and giving her short dark hair a shake as any woman would do. Not fat, she is heavy-legged and heavy-breasted, her olive skin running to pigment. Though there is glass between us, there is the sense, almost palpable, of the broad, low, barefooted heft of her, of a clothed-in cottoned-off body heat and of the keratin-rasp of her bare feet on the cork floor.

Now, clipping Lucite fittings to sensor wires—and again with the impression of holding a bobby pin in her teeth—she inserts one after another into the body orifices, as handily and thriftily as a teen-ager popping in a contact lens.

Cameras whir, tapes jerk around, needles quiver, computers wink, and Lillian begins her autostimulation.

My eyes meet Moira's. She blushes and glances down. Here we meet, at Lillian's recording session, as shyly as two office workers at the water cooler, touch fingers and—! Yes, my hand strays along the vaginal computer, our fingers touch. A thrill pierces my heart like an arrow, as they say in old novels. I am in love.

Stryker tells me his problem, I listen attentively, and sure enough he offers me a job. It disconcerts me that he speaks in a loud voice, in the hearing of others, and pays no attention to Lillian, who is doing her usual yeoman-like job. Isn't it impolite not to watch her? Stryker is a tall, willowy doctor who feels obliged by the nature of his work to emphasize the propriety, even the solemnity of his own person. So he dresses somewhat like a funeral director in a dark suit, perfectly laundered shirt, and sober tie. Yet there persists about him the faint air of the dude: his collar has a tricky pin that lofts the knot of his tie. Overly long cuffs show their jeweled links and cover part of his hand, whose fingers are still withered from his years as a chemist before he went into behavior. He is a wonderful dancer, hopping nimbly through the complicated figures of the Center's square dances. Even now, in the observation room, there is about him a lightness of foot, a discreet bounciness, as if he were keeping time to an inner hoedown. His foot swings out. Yet there pervades the observation room a strong tone, at once solemn and brisk. Embarrassment is not to be thought of. Nor, on the other hand, would it be thinkable to crack vulgar jokes as surgeons do in the scrub room.

Dr. Helga Heine has caught the same note of brisk solemnity. She is a jolly matronly Bavarian gynecologist, neither young nor old, a regular hausfrau, hair done up in a bun, breast conformed to a single motherly outcurve. Moira tells me that Helga takes pains to remember the birthdays of staff members and veteran performers, brings a cake and plays *Zwei Herzen* on her little Bavarian guitar. I gaze big-nosed at her plump pink fingertips.

"Thanks to you," says Stryker solemnly, balancing lightly on the balls of his feet, "we've made a breakthrough in the whole area of sexual behavior."

"Oh, I wouldn't say—" I begin, sweeping out a foot like Stryker. So he's read my paper! In the corner of my eye Moira listens and registers pride. To Moira, who believes in Science without knowing much about it, my triumph has all the grace and warrant of a matador's.

"Your article in the *J.A.M.A.* delineated a new concept."

"Oh. I wouldn't say that."

And I wouldn't. The "article" he speaks of is not the epochal paper I just finished, but a minor clinical note, small potatoes indeed. It noted nothing more than a certain anomaly in the alpha wave of solitary lovers (as Colley's assistant, I read the EEG's of all the lovemakers in Love). Stryker's praise is something like congratulating Einstein for patenting a Swiss watch. I accept it for Moira's sake.

Moira's eyes were shining.

Lillian is going about her task at a fair clip. Drums revolve, heartbeats spike on a monitor, her skin conductivity ascends a gentle slope. Stryker keeps a casual eye on the dials, now and then dictates a clinical note to Moira. Helga and Father Kev Kevin, hearing my praises, look glum.

Moira perches on her stool, heels cocked on a rung, and manages both to take notes and keep her short skirt tucked under her knees. What lovely legs. Her kneecaps are smooth and tan as a beaten biscuit. To plant kisses on those perfect little biscuits, I'm thinking, as Stryker dances a step. Moira and I do not quite look at each other but my cheek is aware of hers.

> She never told her love
> But let concealment, like a worm i' the bud
> Feed on her damask cheek.

Lillian is going at a good clip now.

"There's the old methodology," says Stryker, waving a hand at Lillian without bothering to look. "Thanks to you, we're onto something new."

"I'm not sure I understand," I murmur out of Moira's hearing.

"Not that the old wasn't useful in its way—"

"Useful!" chime in Helga and Father Kev Kevin. "Useful enough to take the Nobel!"

But Stryker waves them off. "Useful, yes, to a point. But without your note on the alpha wave, we'd never have struck out on a new path."

"A new path?" I ask, puzzled. But my Moira-wards cheek glows.

> Her cheek like the rose is, but fresher, I ween,
> She's the loveliest lassie that trips on the green.

I ween she is.

Stryker sways closer, balancing lightly on his toes. "I think you might be interested to learn, Tom, that since June we've been using not one subject at a time"—he touches my arm with a withered finger—"but two."

"Two?"

"Yes. A man and a woman. Here's the breakthrough."

"Breakthrough?"

"Yes. And guess what?"

"What?"

"We've got rid of your alpha wave anomaly. You were right."

"Very good. But actually I was only reading EEG's and not making recommendations about future techniques, you understand—"

"Moral scruples, Doctor?" asks Father Kev Kevin, eyes alight. He clears the orgasm circuit.

"Perhaps."

"Oh, that's neither here nor there!" cries Stryker cheerfully. "All I'm saying is that using couples instead of singles we've got rid of your alpha wave anomaly and kept the cruciform rash. I thought you'd want to know."

"Yes," I say gloomily, watching Lillian. My nose is getting bigger. I try to think. "Then if that's the case, what's your problem?"

"Yeah, here's the thing." Stryker glances at Lillian like a good cook watching a pot of beans. I notice that as Lillian progresses, Stryker becomes ever more light-footed. His black pumps swing out. His watching Lillian is like a poet reading his best poem. "Our problem is that our couples do not perform regularly."

"Ted 'n Tanya do!" Helga objects.

"Not lately. Only one out of four couples interact successfully," says Stryker drily. "Hardly an adequate base for observation.

"Ted 'n Tanya?" I ask, scratching my head. There could only be one Ted 'n Tanya. It must mean that my prescription for Ted didn't, in the end, work, and that they've come here. "But what do you think I can do about it?"

Lillian seems to be looking at me. But I know she can only see mirror. It is herself she is watching. Her eyes are unfocused and faraway. Her eyebrows are unplucked, the heavy black sort one used to see in daguerreotypes of frontier women.

"Do some studies on our noninteracting couples!" cries Stryker. "I hear you've developed a special sort of EEG."

"Not exactly."

"Join our team! We're even funded for a full-time consultant."

"Well, thank you, Ken, but . . ." On the other hand, I could see Moira all day if I did.

"Twenty thousand a year, full professorship, and do as you please."

"Well . . ."

"We've hit a snag in the interpersonal area and both Max and I feel you could iron it out."

"The fact is . . ." What does Moira's cheek say, my cheek wonders.

*"Here-we-are,"* says Stryker in a routine rush, glancing at Lillian. All the quiet pride of a scientist demonstrating his best trick.

The Love team springs into action, each to his station.

Lillian turns to show her famous cruciform rash. She embraces herself. Her pale loins bloom. Stryker presses buttons with a routine skill, a practiced climactic.

"Beautiful!" murmurs Helga.

"Pathognomonic!" cries Father Kev Kevin.

Moira bends to her note-taking, scribbles furiously as Stryker dictates.

Helga speaks by microphone to Lillian.

"Turn around slowly, dear."

She addresses the unseen students, perched in their roost above us.

"You will notice please the cruciform morbilliform eruption extending bilaterally from the sacral area—"

Moira breaks her pencil and goes to sharpen it. The others are busy with Lillian and I see my chance. I follow her into a small closet-sized room, which houses a computer and a cot littered with dusty scientific journals. A metal label on the door reads Observer Stimulation Overflow Area. Standard equipment in all Love clinics. Known more familiarly to the students as the "chicken room," it is provided to accommodate those observers who are stimulated despite themselves by the behavior they observe. For although, as Stryker explained, the observer hopes to retain his scientific objectivity, it must be remembered that after all the observers belong to the same species as the observed and are subject to the same "environmental stimuli." Hither to the closet, alone or in pairs or severally, observers may discreetly repair, each to relieve himself or herself according to his needs. "It iss the same as a doctor having hiss own toilet, *nicht*?" Helga told me somewhat vulgarly. *"Nicht,"* I said but did not argue. I have other fish to fry.

While moral considerations are not supposed to enter into scientific investigation, "observer stimulation overflow" is nevertheless discouraged. It is Stryker's quiet boast, moreover, that whatever may happen in Palo Alto or Berkeley or Copenhagen, scientific objectivity has been scrupulously preserved in the Paradise Love Clinic. No observer has ever used the chicken room. The closet houses not lovers but dusty journals and a computer.

Moira, in fact, tells me she feels safer in Love than when she worked as secretary to the chief psychologist.

"Can I see you after work today?" I whisper and take her hand. It is cold. *Che gelida manina.* Thy tiny hand is frozen.

"Can't today!" she whispers back. "But I can't wait till the Fourth! Where are we going?" Her lovely gold eyes look at me over her steno pad like a Moslem woman's.

I frown. An ugly pang pierces my heart. Why can't she see me today? Does she have a date with Buddy? Here's the misery of love: I don't really want to see her today, was not prepared to, have other plans, yet despite myself hear myself insist on it.

"But—"

She shushes me, seals my lips with her finger, and, glancing through the open door at Lillian who is unwiring herself, brushes her lips with her fingers, brushes mine.

"You better go."

"Yes." Ah.

Returning to the observation room, I sink into a chair and dreamily watch Lillian dress. Here's my trouble with Moira. She's a romanticist and I'm not. She lives for what she considers rare perfect moments. What I long to share with her are ordinary summer evenings, cicadas in the sycamores.

She whispers behind me. "Where are we going this time? To Dry Tortugas again? Chichen Itza? Tombstone?"

I shrug and smile. She likes to visit ghost towns and jungle ruins, so I'll show her the one in our back yard, the ruined Howard Johnson motel. She'll savor the closeness of it. One weekend we flew to Silver City, Arizona, and stood in the deserted saloon and watched tumbleweeds blow past the door. "Can't you just hear the old rinky-dink piano?" she cried and hugged me tight. "Yeah," I said, taking delight in the very commonplaceness of her romanticism. "How about a glass of red-eye, Moira?" "Oh yes! Yes indeed!"

Lillian dresses quickly, pins on her Lois Lane hat, using the viewing mirror as her vanity, shoulders her bag, trudges out.

In comes the next subject. No, subjects. A couple. I recognize one, a medical student who is doubtlessly making money as a volunteer. He is J. T. Thigpen, a slightly built, acned youth who wears a blue shirt with cuffs turned up one turn. He carries a stack of inky books in the crook of his wrist. His partner, whom the chart identifies only as Gloria, is a largish blonde, a lab worker, to judge from her stained smock, with wiry bronze hair that springs out from her head. Volunteers in Love get paid fifty dollars a crack, which beats giving blood.

"These kids are our pioneers," Stryker tells me, speaking softly now for some reason. "And a case in point. Something has gone wrong. Yet they were our first and best interaction subjects. Our problem, of course, with using two subjects was one of visualization. Colley, who is a wizard, solved that for us with his Lucite devices. We can see around curves, you see, between bodies. So we figured if Colley could help us out in mechanics, you could help us out with interpersonal breakdowns. How about it?"

"Well . . ."

Gloria and J. T. are undressing. J. T. takes off his shirt, revealing an old-fashioned undershirt with shoulder straps. He's a country boy from hereabouts. The spots of acne strewn across his shoulders turn livid in the fluorescent light. Removing his wristwatch with expansion band, he hesitates for a moment, then hangs it on the crank handle of the hospital bed.

Gloria wears a half-slip, which comes just short of her plump white knees, and a half-brassiere whose upper cusps are missing.

"Okay, keeds!" cries Helga, clapping her hands into the microphone. *"Mach schnell!* Let's get the show on the road!"

"We have found," Stryker explains to me, "that you can inspire false modesty and that by the same token a brisk no-nonsense approach works wonders. Helga is great at it!"

I clear my throat and stretch up my heavy-lidded eyes. My nose is a snout.

"I've got to be going."

J. T. and Gloria, half-undressed, are standing around like strangers at a bus stop. J. T. sends his fingers browsing over his acned shoulder. Gloria stands foursquare, arms angled out past her hips as if she were carrying milkpails.

Father Kev Kevin clears the orgasm circuit. He won't look at me.

"I've got to be going, Stryker."

"Wait. How can you spot the hangup if you don't watch them?"

"Yeah. Well, later. Thank you very much, all of you. Hm. I'm already late—" I look at my watch and start for the door.

"Wait! Ted 'n Tanya are next. They're our best. Or were. Don't you want to—"

"No."

"What about the job?"

"I'll let you know."

"We're funded, man! The money is here!"

"Very good."

Leaving, I catch a final glimpse of J. T. Thigpen, bare-chested and goose-pimpled, gazing around the porcelain walls with the ruminant rapt expression of a naked draftee.

*"Mach schnell!* Keeds—" cries Helga, clapping her hands.

Whew! Escape! Escape, but just in time to run squarely into Buddy Brown, my enemy, in the corridor.

He smiles and nods and grips my arms as if we shared a lover's secret. What secret? Who is he waiting for?

I brush past and do not wait to find out. Am I afraid to find out?

8

To the motel to fix a room for a tryst with Moira on the Fourth.

No sign of sniper or anyone else for that matter. But I take no chances, slip into Howard Johnson's through the banquet room where the rent Rotary banner still flies from Tuesday's meeting five years ago:

> *Is it the truth?*
> *Is it fair to all concerned?*
> *Will it build goodwill and better friendships?*

and straight up the inside stairs without exposing myself to the patio.

Room 203, the most nearly intact, was nevertheless a mess when we first saw it: graffiti, illuminations of hairy pudendae, suspicious scraps of newspaper littering the floor. The beds moldy, the toilet fouled. I've been working on the room for a month, installed a generator for air-conditioner and TV and coffee-maker and lights and bed vibrators; brought in hose water from Esso station next door; laid in supplies for a day or so.

And I haven't finished. This weekend, knowing what I know, I'll lay in supplies for six months, plus clothes for Moira, books, games. All hell will break loose on the Fourth and Moira and I may need a place to stay. What safer place than a motel in no man's land, between the lines so to speak?

This is the place. Moira, in fact, picked it. She and I came here for a few minutes last month. She likes the byways. That weekend we hadn't time to fly to Merida or Tombstone. So we took a walk. A proper ruin this, and what is more, it has a bad reputation and people don't come here. But I think it is safe. The whites think the black guerrillas have it. The blacks think the white drugheads have it. Neither wants any part of the other, so both stay away. I think.

Moira was delighted with the motel. There was a soupçon of danger, just enough. She clutched my arm and shrank against me. We stood by the scummy pool. Spanish moss trailed from the balcony. Alligator grass choked the wading pool. A scarlet watersnake coiled under the lifeguard's perch. Moira found a pair of old 1960 harlequin glasses and an ancient vial of Coppertone.

"It's like Pompey!" she cried.

"Like what? Yes, right."

We kissed. Ruins make her passionate. Ghosts make her want to be touched. She is lovely, her quick upturned heart-shaped face and gold-brown eyes bright with a not quite genuine delight, a willingness rather to be delighted. Are you going to delight me? isn't this the time? aren't things falling out just right? Pleasing her is fathoming and fulfilling this expectation. Her face. Her cropped wheat-colored hair with a strong nap that aches my hand to brush against, her rather short tanned perfect legs drawn with strong simple strokes like the Draw Me girl in magazine contests. She's poor, having left her West Virginia parents early and supported herself in civil service, worked in Bethesda for N.I.M.H. before transferring here. I can see her in Washington in the evening washing out her things in the wash-stand, keeping her budget, minding herself. . . . But she has her own views and likes. She opposes the war in Ecuador, sub-scribes to *Playgirl*, a mildly liberated, mildly Left magazine, and carries in her purse a pocket edition of Rod McKuen, a minor poet of the old Auto Age, which she likes to read aloud to me: "Don't you just love that?" "Yes." But what I love is her loving it, her faintly spurious love of loving things that seem lovable.

A turtle plopped into the pool.

"Can't you just see them!" she whispered, swaying against me.

"Who?"

"All the salesmen and flappers."

"Yes."

"Aah!" said Moira, stretching out on a convex lounge which pushed her up in the middle. I perched somewhat pre-cariously beside her.

Moira, who is twenty-two and not strong on history, thinks that the great motels of the Auto Age were the haunt of salesmen and flappers of the Roaring Twenties. Whereas, of course, it was far more likely that it was the salesman and his wife and kids and station wagon who put up here in the sixties and seventies.

A green lizard did push-ups on Moira's lounge, blew out a red bladder. Moira screamed and hopped into my lap. We kissed. I kissed her smooth biscuit-shaped kneecaps. Her eyes went fond and faraway. "Just think," she said.

"What?"

"It's all gone. Gone with the wind."

"Yes."

"The lion and the lizard keep/The courts where Samson gloried and drank deep."

"Right." I held her close, melting with love, and whispered

in her ear: "The wild ass/Stamps o'er his head, but cannot break his sleep."

"Don't be nasty!" cried Moira, laughing and tossing her head like Miss Clairol of olden time.

"Sorry."

Taking my hand like a child, she led me exploring. In a rusted-out Coke machine in the arcade we found warm, five-year-old Cokes. I opened two, poured out half and filled the bottles with Early Times.

"This is how the salesmen and flappers used to drink."

"Wonderful!" She took a big swig.

The hot sun blazed in the patio. We could not swim in the foul pool. So we sweated and drank Coke and bourbon like a salesman and a flapper. The Spanish moss stirred on the balcony. We went up to get the breeze. Then we explored the rooms, sat on the moldering bed in 203 and drank some more.

"A penny for your thoughts," said Moira thoughtfully.

"I fancy you. Do you fancy me?"

"Yes."

"Let's lie down."

"On this? Ugh."

"Then let's sit in the chair."

"Not today, Josephine."

"Why not?"

"I didn't bring my Cupid's Quiver."

"Your what?"

"My sachet, silly."

"I'm not sure I understand. In any case, I don't mind."

"I do."

"Then let's have a drink."

Again she took a mighty pull. Again we kissed. Her gold eyes gleamed.

"Ugh," she said again, noticing the graffiti and pudendae on the walls. Damn, why didn't I clean the walls? But she refused to be shocked by dirty pictures. To prove it, we had to make a museum tour. Love, where is love now? We gazed at the poor penciled organs, same and different, same and different, like a figure in the wallpaper, and outside the swifts twittered down the sky and up sang the old skyey sounds of June and where was love?

So we walked hand in hand and read the graffiti. Moira had

taken a course in semantics and knew there was nothing in dirty words.

Above the Gideon Bible: *For a free suck call room 208.*

Moira shook her head sadly. "What an unhappy person must have written that."

"Yea. That is, yes." Desire for her had blown my speech center. "Love, I, you," I said.

"Love I you too," she said, kissing me, mouth open, gold eyes open.

Holding hands, we read the graffito under *The Laughing Cavalier: Room 204 has a cutout on her pussy.*

"The poor man."

"Yes."

"What is a cutout?"

"It is a device salesmen used to attach to their auto mufflers."

"But how—? Never mind. Ummm, what a good place for a picnic!"

"Yes."

"Far from the maddening crowd."

"That's true."

It was then that the notion occurred to me to fix the room up properly and spend a weekend here.

"Tom, do you remember the quaint little hotel in Merida?"

"Yes, I do."

"There's a small hotel/With a wishing well."

"Right."

"Remember the coins we threw in the fountain after our love and the wish we made?"

"Yes."

She is right. I must remember that women like to think of the act of love as a thing, "our love." There are three of us, like a family, Moira and I and our love.

"I wish you'd worn your Mexican pleated shirt."

"Why?"

"You look just like Rod McKuen, if you had more hair."

"He's an old man."

"No, he's not. Look." She showed me his picture on the back of her book, Rod hoofing it along a California beach, arms open to the sea gulls.

"That was twenty years ago."

"Let's have a picnic here."

"We will."

"A jug of wine, a loaf of bread, and thou."
"Yes, thou."


## 9

That was last month. I've been working on this room
ever since. Today I finish the job. No bowerbird ever prepared a bower for his love more carefully.

The hard work was done last week, Delco generator installed downstairs, hose run two hundred feet from the Esso
station faucet up through the bathroom window.

Room 203 still has suspicious smells. Pull back curtains,
open front panels and bathroom window to get a breeze. Un-
pack from doctor's bag and line up on dresser: one Sani-flush,
one wick deodorizer, and one tube of cold solder, one roll of
toilet paper, one boxed gift copy of *Stanyan Street*, one brass
shower head, one jar of instant coffee.

Half an hour and my work is done, floors mopped, fungoid
mattresses and horrid foam-rubber pillows slung over balcony
rail to sun, coffee-maker restocked, graffiti wiped from wall
revealing original hunt-and-hound design, *Laughing Cavalier*
straightened, ancient color TV and bed vibrator plugged into
Delco lead, shower head screwed onto hose from Esso station
and tested (hot bitter hose water), *Stanyan Street* lined up with
the Gideon.

Test vibrator: sit on bed and drop in quarter. Z-Z-Z-Z-Z goes
the vibrator and suddenly I am thinking not of Moira but of
Samantha, my dead daughter, and the times she and I and Doris
used to travel in the Auto Age all over the U.S.A. and Samantha
would explore the motel and drop coins in every slot. First off
she'd have found the Slepe-Eze and fed it a quarter.

Tears spurt from my eyes. Removing a pint of Early Times
from my bag, I sit on the humming bed and sip a few drinks.

Why does desire turn to grief and memory strike at the heart?


## 10

Off to town. Past empty Saint Michael's Church and
school, a yellow brick dairy-barn-with-silo.

Here I went to mass with Samantha, happy as a man could

be, ate Christ and held him to his word, if you eat me you'll
have life in you, so I had life in me. After mass we'd walk
home to Paradise through the violet evening, the evening star
hard by the red light of the TV tower like a ruby and diamond
in the plush velvet sky, and I'd skip with happiness, cut the
fool like David while Samantha told elephant jokes, go home,
light the briquets, drink six toddies, sing *Tantum Ergo*, and
"Deh vieni alla finestra" from *Don Giovanni* and, while
Samantha watched *Gentle Ben*, invite Doris out under the
Mobile pinks, Doris as lusty and merry a wife then as a man
could have, a fine ex-Episcopal ex-Apple Queen from the
Shenandoah Valley. Oh Shenandoah, I long to see you.

Cliff swallows are nesting in the fenestrated concrete
screen in front of Saint Michael's.

In this Catholic church, the center did not hold. It split in
three, Monsignor Schleifkopf cutting out to the right, Father
Kev Kevin to the left, leaving Father Smith. There is little to be
said about Father Smith since he is in no way remarkable, having
been a good and faithful if undistinguished priest for twenty-five
years, having baptized the newborn into a new life, married
lovers, shriven sinners, comforted the sick, visited the poor and
imprisoned, anointed the dying, buried the dead. He had his
faults. He was a gray stiff man. Like me, he was thought to drink
and on occasion was packed off, looking only a bit grayer and
stiffer than usual, to a Gulf Coast home for addled priests. Now
he and his little flock are looking for a new home, I hear, having
used for a while a Pentecostal church and later Paradise Lanes,
my bowling alley here in the plaza, until it became too dangerous.

The plaza is empty now save for the rusting hulks of cars
abandoned or burned in the time of troubles.

Five and a half years ago, on Christmas Eve, Paradise Plaza
was sacked by Bantu guerrillas foraying up out of the swamp.
Store windows were smashed, the new Sears looted, some stores
burned, cops shot up by Bantus, Bantus shot up by cops.
Noncombatants fled, Christmas shoppers, storekeepers, motel
occupants, drive-in movie patrons watching *Homo Hijinks*.
Monsignor Schleifkopf left by the front door of the church,
abandoning his burning Buick and golf clubs in the garage,
where they are to this day. Nobody came back these five and a
half years save lovers and bums and drugheads and in the end
only the original denizens of the swamp, owls, alligators, and
moccasins.

I should have known trouble was brewing. The night before, Leroy Ledbetter had kicked out a black couple from Tougaloo who wanted to bowl at Paradise Lanes. That very morning, walking to town, I met Nellie Bledsoe, who told me her cook had quit and she was ready "to shoot some niggers."

"Eh? What? What's that? My God," I said, "you don't mean you want to shoot some niggers because your cook quit."

"Oh yes I do!" she cried, laughing and winking and kneading her arm. "Don't you know what they do?"

"What?"

"They go on welfare and have little illegitimate nigger babies and get paid for it, paid more than they make working."

"Yes, but you're not saying that you're going out and—"

"Oh yes I am!" says Nellie, winking and laughing. "Ho ho HO!"

Earlier the same morning, at six, a young jaundiced Bantu came up out of the swamp and appeared at my "enclosed patio" to be treated for liver flukes.

After I gave him his shots, he too winked at me with his yellow eye.

"I can't pay you now, Doc, but since you're so nice, we won't shoot you when the shooting starts."

"Who are you planning to shoot?"

"Anybody who gets in our way."

"In the way of what?"

"In the way of our taking over this goddamn parish, Doc," he said, pulling out a copy of Fanon with one hand and patting a bulge under his coat with the other.

"My God, you're not really going to shoot anybody, are you?"

"We're taking over, Doc."

"Why don't you take over by the vote? You got the vote and there are more of you than of us."

"Shit on voting, Doc."

There was something in the air all right.


11


On McArthur Boulevard now: a defunct parkway that deadends in a weedy lot and an ancient putt-putt course. Follow it as far as the L & N overpass and take the shortcut to town through Happy Hollow.

A bit shaky now, faintified but not hungry. The Early Times is not sitting well.

The thunderhead fills the whole eastern sky. A hot wind blows me toward it over the asphalt playground of the school. A chain rings against a flagpole.

The short cut turns out to be a mistake. Happy Hollow is a hot airless hole. The sun slants down like a laser. My stomach churns acid. When did I eat last?

The bare ground between the shacks and under the chinaberry trees never dries out. Where the sun does strike, the earth steams and gives off a smell of dishwater and chicken fat. Duck eggs rise in my throat.

But people seem happy here. Happy pot-bellied picaninnies play in the alley. Old folk rock on the porches. The unhappy young men are gone. The kindly old folk doff their caps politely. Yellow yarddogs lie chained to the chinaberry trees. They lift an eyebrow and snarl as I pass.

It is collection day. Up one side of the alley goes Moon Mullins collecting rent for his shacks. Down the other side goes old Mr. Jack Bourgeois collecting burial-insurance premiums. Both are cheerful and good-humored with their clients, exchanging jokes and pleasantries at each shack before moving on. Both collect in exactly the same way. If the householder is sitting on his porch, he will pass the time of day and hand down the money to the collector, who stands on the ground. If the porch is vacant, the collector will put his foot on the second step, rest an elbow on his knee and rap the porch floor with his knuckles, all the while looking down at the ground with a musing expression. Old Mr. Jack bangs the porch with his fat premium book.

The collectors greet me cordially.

"Hot enough for you, Doc!" cries Moon.

"How you doing, Doc!" cries old Mr. Jack.

"Yes, it is. All right," I reply, weaving a bit.

The Negroes greet me uneasily. Why do the yarddogs snarl at me and not at Moon and old Mr. Jack? I am unwell.

How will I get up the hill to town? The sun laser bores into the top of my head, but my feet are blocks of ice. If only I could make it to the Little Napoleon, where I could sit in a dark nook and drink a little toddy to settle my stomach.

Halfway up the hill it becomes clear I won't make it. Flowers of darkness are blooming in the weeds. Rank vines sprout in the path. In times of ordeal one's prayers become simple. I pray only that I will faint in a private place where no one will disturb me and where especially Moon and old Mr. Jack won't see me.

I have drawn abreast of the new animal shelter, a glass-and-concrete air-conditioned block of a building cantilevered from the hillside like a Swiss sanitorium.

My knees knock.

But here's a good spot.

I sit down in a dry ditch under a chinaberry whose dense branches come down and make a private place. It is next to the dog-runs that slope down the hill under the pines. Where are the dogs?

Something in the ditch catches my eye. It is a Garrett snuff can. I lean forward to pick it up and faint. Not keel over but settle down comfortably propping my head on my bag. The weeds smell like iron.

Where are the dogs?


12

Here are the dogs. Inside where it is cool.

When I come to, I am lying on the large-dog table in the treatment room of the animal shelter. I feel well but so weak I cannot lift my head. Delicious cool air bathes my forehead. A great blue surgical lamp shines straight down. When my eyes get used to the glare, I notice the dogs, several dozen glossy-coated curs, seated behind grills and watching with interested expressions. This is why the outside runs are empty: the dogs have come inside to enjoy the cool breezes.

Gazing down at me, hands shoved deep in his pockets and fingering coins, stands Victor Charles. I know him without seeing his face. His flat abdomen engages the edge of the table. His belt buckle is to the side. The white duck is soiled by a horizontal streak I've seen before. Now I know where the streak comes from. It coincides with the metal edge of the table.

I try to get up.

"Hold it, Doc." Victor places skilled large-dog hands on my shoulders.

I close my eyes. There is a pleasant sense of being attended, of skills being practiced, strong hands laid on, of another's clothes rustling nearby.

I open my eyes. The lamp is reflected in one coppery highlight from Victor's forehead. The rest of his face is blue-black. I notice that his sclerae are lumpy and brown.

"How long have I been here?"

"No more than fifteen minutes, Doc."

"How did you find me?"

"I saw you sit down out yonder."

"Were you watching me?"

"Watching you?"

"And you carried me in?"

Victor nods.

I am thinking: it is true. All day I have had the sense of being watched.

"Where's my bag?"

"Right here, Doc."

"O.K., Victor. Thank you. I think I'll sit up."

He helps me. I am well but weak.

"Eat this, Doc."

Victor gives me a piece of corn bread and a cold glass of buttermilk. Though the bread is hard and unbuttered, it is very good. I don't remember anything ever tasting better. The buttermilk slides under the acid.

"Thank you again."

"You're welcome." Victor presses against the table and fingers his coins.

"I've got to go."

"You ought to take better care yourself, Doc. And be more careful where you takes a nap."

"Why?"

"Crazy folks everywhere now, Doc."

"Folks? What folks?"

"Folks. You know."

"You ought to be more careful too, Victor."

"How's that, Doc?" Victor, who has been pushing himself off the table with his stomach, stays off.

"I mean who you meet and where you meet, though it's none of my business."

"What you talking 'bout, Doc?"

For some reason all three tiers of dogs start barking.

Presently Victor shouts, "You'll be all right, Doc. Just rest here a while. You know what you need? Somebody to take care you. Why don't you move in with your mama, Miss Marva? She be glad to do for you."

I wait for the dogs to subside.

"You were there at number 11 on the old 18. This morning."

"What you talking 'bout, Doc?"

"I was there, Victor. On the island. In the pagoda."

"Oh, you talking about—!" Victor begins to shake a loose hand toward the east as if he just remembered.

"What the hell is going on, Victor?"

"Like I told you, Doc—"

"Like you told me! You haven't told me anything. I saw you, I saw Willard Amadie. Who was the third man?"

"Willard bringing meat for the swamp. Folks going hungry out there, Doc."

"I saw the deer. Was that all?"

"All? How you say, all?"

"Victor, I heard you. I was sitting in the pagoda."

"Oh, you talking about—" Again Victor salutes the east.

"Yes. Who was the third man?"

"Him? Doc, they say he *mean*," says Victor, laughing.

"They?"

"Everybody. You talk about mean and lowdown!"

"Then what are you laughing about?"

"You, Doc. You something else."

"Victor, is Willard trying to shoot me?"

"Shoot you! Willard!" Victor falls back.

"You mean somebody else is trying to shoot me?"

"Doc, why in the world anybody want to shoot you? You help folks. Like I tell people, you set up with my auntee when other doctors wouldn't even come out."

"You mean somebody is trying to shoot me and you tried to talk them out of it?"

"Doc, look. How long me and you known each other?"

"All our lives."

"How long did I work for y'all, first for Big Doc, then for Miss Marva clearing land?"

"I don't know. Twenty years."

"And didn't you set up with my auntee many a night before she died?"

"Yes."

"You think I wouldn't do the same for you?"

"I think you would. But—"

"Wasn't I working as a orderly in the hospital last year when they brought you in and didn't I take care you?"

"Yes, you did."

"When you said to me, Victor, there's something crawling on the wall, get it out of here, didn't I make out like I was throwing it out?"

"Yes."

Victor is laughing in such a way that I have to smile.

"I couldn't see but I threw it out anyhow."

"Yes, you did."

"You think I wouldn't tell you right?"

"I think you would."

"Then, Doc, listen." Victor comes close again, presses stomach against metal table. "Move in with Miss Marva. She'll do for you. Miss Marva, she'd love nothing better. I help you move over there, Doc."

"How come you want me out of my house?"

"I'm worried about you, Doc. Look at you. Fainting and falling out in a ditch."

"Victor, who were you waiting for in the pagoda?"

"Waiting?"

"I heard Willard say: Looks like he's not coming."

"Oh yeah. Willard."

"Was he waiting for me?"

Victor is silent.

"Did he or the third man intend to shoot me?"

"Shoot you! Lord, Doc. We just want to talk to you."

"Well, here I am."

"That's what I'm telling you. Move in with your mama."

"What's she got to do with it?"

Silence.

"What about that other stuff?"

"What other stuff?"

"All that stuff about the Kaydettes, the doctors, and the school."

"Doc, all in the world I want to do is help you. You say to me, do this, that, or the other, and I'll do it."

Victor's his old self, good-natured, reserved, with just the faintest risibility agleam in his muddy eyes.

"How you feeling, Doc?"

"I think I can make it."

But when I stand up, one knee jumps out.

"Whoa, look out now. Why don't you stay here till you are stronger? Ain't nobody going to bother you here."

"I got to get on up the hill."

"I was going up there too. I'll carry your bag—no wonder, Lord, what you got in here? Just hang on to Victor."

We are near the top. Victor wants me to hang on to him, but I don't feel like it.

"You never did like anybody to help you, did you, Doc?"

I stop, irritated with Victor and because the faintness is coming back. Flowers of darkness begin to bloom on the sidewalk.

We sit on the wooden steps of an abandoned Chinese grocery angled into the hill. Again I invite Victor to go back—I know he's along just to help me. He refuses.

"You've been away, haven't you, Victor?" I say to hide my irritation.

"I been back for two years, Doc."

"Where did you go?"

"I lived in Boston and worked in the shipyard. I made seven fifty an hour."

"Why did you come back?"

"You know something, Doc? You don't trust anybody, do you?"

I look at Victor with astonishment.

"What do you mean?"

"Nothing, Doc. I know that when you ask me a question like that, you really want to know."

I blink. "You're humbugging me, aren't you, Victor?"

"No, Doc. You know what I remember? You asked me why I came back. I don't know. But I remember something. I remembered in Boston and when I did, you were in it. You remember the shrimp jubilees?"

"Yes."

"The word would come that the shrimp were running and everybody would go to the coast at night and as far as you could see up and down the coast there were gas lamps of people catching shrimp, setting up all night with their chirren running around and their picnics, you remember? And long before that me and you learned to throw a cast-net holding it in your teeth."

"Yes. Those were the days."

"Not for you, Doc."

I, who am seldom astonished, am astonished twice in a minute. "What do you mean?"

"You never did like—you didn't even like the jubilees. You were always . . . to yourself."

I shrug. "Are you telling me you came back because of the jubilees?"

"I don't know. I just wanted to come back. You know, I been a deacon at Starlight Baptist for twenty years."

"I know."

"Mr. Leroy, though, he used to love the jubilees."

"So you and Leroy Ledbetter like the jubilees and that's why you came back?"

"Not exactly. But I remember when everybody used to come to the jubilees. I mean everybody. You and Mr. Leroy came one night, you and your family on one side of me and he on the other."

"In the first place the shrimp don't run any more. In the second place, even if they did, Leroy Ledbetter wouldn't be next to you now."

"That's right, but you know something, Doc?"

"What?"

"You ought to trust people more. You ought to trust in the good Lord, pick yourself out a nice lady like Miss Doris, have chirren and a fireside bright and take up with your old friends and enjoy yourself in the summertime."

"For Christ's sake."

"What say, Doc?" Victor, who is slightly deaf, cups an ear.

"You kill me."

"How's that?"

"Here're you complaining about me and acting like you and Leroy Ledbetter are sharing the good life. Hell, Leroy Ledbetter, your fellow Baptist, wants no part of you. And one reason you're living in this pigpen is that Leroy is on the council and has turned down housing five times."

"That's the truth!" says Victor, laughing. "And it's pitiful."

"You think it's funny?"

My only firm conclusion after twenty years of psychiatry: nothing is crazier than life. Here is a Baptist deacon telling me, a Catholic, to relax and enjoy festivals. Here's a black Southerner making common cause—against me!—with a white Southerner who wouldn't give him the time of day.

That's nothing. Once I was commiserating with a patient, an old man, a Jewish refugee from the Nazis—he'd got out with his skin but lost his family to Auschwitz—so I said something conventional against the Germans. The old fellow bristled like a Prussian and put me down hard and spoke of the superiority of German universities, German science, German music, German philosophy. My God, do you suppose the German Jews would have gone along with Hitler if he had let them? Nothing is quite like it's cracked up to be. And nobody is crazier than people.

"It would be funny if it wasn't so pitiful," says Victor. He looks at me from the corner of his eye. Something has occurred to him. "Do you think you could speak to Mr. Leroy?"

"About what?"

"About— Never mind. It's too late."

"Victor, what in the hell is going on?"

He is shaking his head. "It's so pitiful. You would think people with that much in common would want to save what they have."

"Are you talking about you and Leroy?"

"Now everything's got to go and everybody loses."

I rise unsteadily. "Everybody?"

Victor jumps up, takes my arm. "Not you, Doc. All you got to do is move in with your mama. She'll do for you."

# 13

Victor takes me as far as the Little Napoleon. There I make a mistake, a small one with small consequences but a mistake nevertheless, which I'd ordinarily not have made. But it has been a strange day. Hanging on to Victor, I did not let him go until we were inside. I should have either dismissed him outside or held on to him longer. As it was, letting go Victor when the bar was within reach, I let go a second too early, so that Leroy Ledbetter, turning toward me in the same second, did not see me let go but saw Victor just beside me and so registered a violation. Not even that: a borderline violation because Victor was not even at the bar but still a step away. What with his white attendant's clothes and if he had been a step closer to me, it would have been clear that he was attending me in some capacity or other. A step or two in the other direction and he'd have been past the end of the bar and in the loading traffic where Negroes often pass carrying sacks of oysters, Cokes, and such. As it was, he seemed to be standing, if not at the bar, then one step too close and Leroy, turning, saw him in the split second before Victor started to leave, Victor in the act of backing up when Leroy said as his eyes went past him, said not even quite to Victor, "The window's there," nodding toward the service window opening into the alley; even then giving Victor the benefit of the doubt and not even allowing the possibility that Victor was coming to the bar for a drink, but the possibility only that he had come to buy his flat pint of muscatel and for some reason had not known or had forgotten about the service window. In the same second that he speaks, Leroy knows better, for in that second Victor steps back and turns toward me and I can see that Leroy sees that

Victor is with me, sees it even before I can say, too late, "Thank you, Victor, for helping me up the hill," and signifies his error by a pass of his rag across the bar, a ritual glance past Victor at the storm cloud above the saloon door, a swinging back of his eyes past Victor and a saying in Victor's direction, "Looks like we going to get it yet," said almost to Victor but not quite because it had not been quite a violation so did not quite warrant a correction thereof. Victor nods, not quite acknowledging because total acknowledgment is not called for, withholding perhaps 20 percent acknowledgment (2 percent too much?). He leaves by the side door.

A near breach, an insignificant incident. A stranger observing the incident would not have been aware that anything had happened at all, much less that in the space of two seconds there had occurred a three-cornered transaction entailing an assignment of zones, a near infraction of zoning, a calling attention to the infraction, a triple simultaneous perception of the mistake, a correction thereof, and an acknowledgment of that—a minor breach with no consequences other than these: an artery beats for a second in Leroy's temple, there is a stiffness about Victor's back as he leaves, and there comes in my throat a metallic taste.

It is not even worth mentioning even though Victor withholds perhaps 2 percent of the acknowledgment that was due and his back is 2 percent stiffer than it might be.

"What's wrong with you, Tom?"

"I'm all right now. It was hot in the Hollow. I got dizzy."

He gives me my toddy. I peel an egg.

"Is that your lunch? No wonder you fainted. And you a doctor."

I look at the mirror. Behind the bar towers a mahogany piece, a miniature cathedral, an altarpiece, an intricate business of shelves for bottles, cupboards, stained-glass windows, and a huge mirror whose silvering is blighted with an advancing pox, clusters of vacuoles, expanding naughts. Most of the customers of the Little Napoleon have long since removed to the lounges of the suburbs, the nifty refrigerated windowless sealed-up Muzaked hideaways, leaving stranded here a small band of regulars and old-timers, some of whom have sat here in the same peaceable gloom open to the same twilight over the same swinging doors that swung their way straight through Prohibition and saw Kingfish Huey P. Long promise to make every man a king on the courthouse lawn across the street. Next door *Gone with the Wind* had its final run at the old Majestic Theater.

The vines are sprouting here in earnest. A huge wistaria with a tree-size trunk holds the Little Napoleon like a rock in a root. The building strains and creaks in its grip.

The storm is closer, the sun gone, and it is darker than dusk. The martins are skimming in from the swamp, sliding down the dark glassy sky like flecks of soot. Soon the bullbats will be thrumming.

Leroy Ledbetter stands by companionably. Like me he is seventh-generation Anglo-Saxon American, but unlike me he is Protestant, countrified, sweet-natured. He's the sort of fellow, don't you know, who if you run in a ditch or have a flat tire shows up to help you.

We were partners and owners of the old Paradise Bowling Lanes until the riot five years ago. In fact, the riot started when Leroy wouldn't let a bushy-haired Bantu couple from Tougaloo College have an alley. I wasn't there at the time. When Leroy told me about it later, an artery beat at his temple and the same metallic taste came in my throat. If I had been there. . . . But on the other hand, was I glad that I had not been there?

"Lucky I had my learner ready," Leroy told me.

"Your learner?" Then I saw his forearm flex and his big fist clench. "You mean you—"

"The only way to learn them is upside the head."

"You mean you—?" The taste in my mouth was like brass. Where did the terror come from? Not from the violence; violence gives release from terror. Not from Leroy's wrongness, for if he were altogether wrong, an evil man, the matter would be simple and no cause for terror. No, it came from Leroy's goodness, that he is a decent, sweet-natured man who would help you if you needed help, go out of his way and bind up a stranger's wounds. No, the terror comes from the goodness and what lies beneath, some fault in the soul's terrain so deep that all is well on top, evil grins like good, but something shears and tears deep down and the very ground stirs beneath one's feet.

"Ellen was looking for you," Leroy is saying, leaning close but not too close, a good drinking friend. He's fixed himself a toddy. "She's got some patients."

"That's impossible. I don't see patients Saturday afternoon."

"You're a doctor, aren't you?"

Leroy, like Ellen, believes that right is right and in doing right. You're a doctor, so you do what a doctor is supposed to do. Doctors cure sick people.

The terror comes from the piteousness, from good gone

wrong and not knowing it, from Southern sweetness and cruelty, God why do I stay here? In Louisiana people still stop and help strangers. Better to live in New York where life is simple, every man's your enemy, and you walk with your eyes straight ahead.

Leroy believes that doctors do wonders, transplant hearts, that's the way of it, right? Isn't that what doctors are supposed to do? He knows about my lapsometer, believes it will do what I say it will do—fathom the deep abscess in the soul of Western man—yes, that's what doctors do, so what? Then do it. Doctors see patients. Then see patients.

"Looks like it's going to freshen up," says Leroy. We drink toddies, eat eggs, and watch the martins come skimming home, sliding down the glassy sky.

In the dark mirror there is a dim hollow-eyed Spanish Christ. The pox is spreading on his face. Vacuoles are opening in his chest. It is the new Christ, the spotted Christ, the maculate Christ, the sinful Christ. The old Christ died for our sins and it didn't work, we were not reconciled. The new Christ shall reconcile man with his sins. The new Christ lies drunk in a ditch. Victor Charles and Leroy Ledbetter pass by and see him. "Victor, do you love me?" "Sho, Doc." "Leroy, do you love me?" "Cut it out, Tom, you know better than to ask that." "Then y'all help me." "O.K., Doc." They laugh and pick up the new Christ, making a fireman's carry, joining four hands. They love the new Christ and so they love each other.

"You all right now?" Leroy asks, watching me eat eggs and drink my toddy.

"I'm fine."

"You better get on over there."

"Yes."

I leave cheerfully, knowing full well that Ellen must be gone, that I shall be free to sit in my doorway, listen to *Don Giovanni*, sip Early Times, and watch the martins come home.

# 14

The back doors of the Little Napoleon and my father's old office let on to the ox-lot in the center of the block. It is getting dark. The thunderhead is upon us. A sour raindrop splashes on my nose. It smells of trees. The piles of brickbats scattered in the weeds are still warm. A dusty trumpet vine has taken the loading ramp of Sears and the fire escape of the old Majestic Theater. In the center of the ox-lot atop a fifteen-foot pole sits my father's only enduring creation: a brass-and-cedar martin hotel with rooms for a hundred couples. Overhead the martins wheel and utter their musical burr and rattle. They are summer residents. Already they are flocking with their young, preparing for their flight to the Amazon basin.

I sit at my desk and listen to *Don Giovanni* and watch the martins through the open door. From the lower desk drawer, where I also keep the free samples of Bayonne-rayon Skintone organs, I fetch a fresh bottle of Early Times.

My office is exactly as my father left it twenty years ago: three rooms, one behind the other like a shotgun cottage, but with a hall alongside, my office at the rear, treatment room in the middle, and at the front the waiting room furnished with the same sprung green wicker and even the same magazines: the *Ford Times*, *National Geographic*, the Knights of Columbus magazine, and the *S A E Record* (my father was an S A E).

The offices are dark. No sign of Ellen, my nurse, and no patient in the waiting room. A sigh of relief and a long happy evening.

No such luck.

A half hour of happiness, the fresh sour evening, the gathering storm, a warm toddy, and the singing god-like devilish music of *Don Giovanni* and—*bang*.

*Bang* up front, the door slams, and here comes Ellen clop-clopping down the hall.

It seems I've got not one but three patients. They went away all right, but they've come back. Ellen told them: don't worry, she'd find me.

I sigh and console myself: I should be able to polish them off in thirty minutes—and do right by them, Ellen! Leroy! Hippocrates!—and get back to my researches. I've the strongest feeling that the second breakthrough is imminent, that if I wait and be still and listen, it will come to me, the final refinement of my invention that will make it the perfect medicine. I've the strongest feeling that the solution is under my nose, one of those huge simple ideas that are so big you can't see them for being too close.

"Good heavens, Chief, where've you been? I've been looking for you all day."

"Why?"

"Why what?"

"Why have you been looking for me? Today is Saturday."

I lean back in my chair and watch Ellen sadly as she picks up the fifth of Early Times and puts it back in the drawer of organs. Then she rinses out my toddy glass, closes the back door, turns off Mozart, pops a chlorophyll tablet in my mouth, wets her thumb with her tongue and smooths my eyebrows with firm smoothings like a mother. My eyebrows feel wet and cool.

Ellen Oglethorpe is a beautiful but tyrannical Georgia Presbyterian. A ripe Georgia persimmon not a peach, she fairly pops the buttons of her nurse's uniform with her tart ripeness. She burgeons with marriageable Presbyterianism. It somehow happens that the strict observance of her religion gives her leave to be free with her own person. Her principles allow her a kind of chaste wantonness. She touches me, leans against me, puts spit on me. I shudder with horrible pleasure and pleasurable horror. Caught up by her strong female urgings, one to mother, one to marry, one to be a girl-child and lean against you, she muses and watches and is prodigal with herself—like an eleven-year-old who stands between your legs, eyes watching your eyes, elbows and knees engaging you in the lap, anywhere, each touch setting off in you horrid girl-child tingles. She doesn't know how close is close.

Now she stands in front of me even closer than usual, hands behind her. I have to look up. Her face is tilted back, the bones under her cheeks winged and wide as if the sculptor had spread out the alar ridges with two sure thumb thrusts. The short downy upper lip is lifted clear of the lower by its tendon. Her face, foreshortened, is simple and clear and scrubbed and peach-mottled, its beauty fortuitous like that of a Puritan woman leaning over her washtub and the blood going despite her to her face.

"Look, Ellen, it's Saturday. What are you doing here?"

"Not an ordinary Saturday."

"No?"

"It's your birthday."

And what she's hiding behind her is a present. She hands it to me. I feel a prickle of irritation. My birthday is but one more occasion for her tending to me, soliciting me, enlisting me. Yes, it is my birthday. I am forty-five. As I unwrap it, she comes round and leans on my chair arm and breathes on me.

It is the sort of present only a woman would buy. A gift set of Hell-for-Leather pre-shave and after-shave lotion. Through the chair arm comes the push of her heedless body weight. Her sweet breath comes through her parted lips. There is nothing to do but open a bottle. It smells like cloves.

"We've got customers, Chief."

Though she is an excellent nurse, I wish she would not call me Chief and herself my girl Friday.

Forty-five. It is strange how little one changes. The psychologists are all wrong about puberty. Puberty changes nothing. This morning I woke with exactly the same cosmic sexual-religious longing I woke with when I was ten years old. Nothing changes but accidentals: your toes rotate, showing more skin. Every molecule in your body has been replaced but you are exactly the same.

The scientists are wrong: man is not his own juices but a vortex, a traveling suck in his juices.

Ellen pats some Hell-for-Leather on me.

"How do you like it, Chief?"

"Very much," I say, eyes watering with cloves.

Ellen, though she is a strict churchgoer and a moral girl, does not believe in God. Rather does she believe in the Golden Rule and in doing right. On the whole she is embarrassed by the God business. But she does right. She doesn't need God. What does God have to do with being honest, hard-working, chaste, upright, unselfish, etcetera. I on the other hand believe in God, the Jews, Christ, the whole business. Yet I don't do right. I am a Renaissance pope, an immoral believer. Between the two of us we might have saved Christianity. Instead we lost it.

"Are you ready now, Chief?"

"Ready for what?"

"You've got two patients. Or rather three. But two are together."

"Who?"

"There's Mr. Ives and Mr. and Mrs. Tennis."

"Good God. Who is Mr. Ives?"

"You know. He's an old patient of yours."

"Wait a minute. Isn't he from Gerry Rehab over in Fedville?"

"Yes."

"Then what's he doing here?"

"He wanted to see you."

"He's the patient who's up for The Pit Monday, isn't he?"

"Yes."

"I still don't understand how he got here."

"He wanted to see you. I brought him."

"You?"

"Don't forget, Chief, I used to work over there."

She did. She even took care of me in the acute ward when I

was strung out, bound by the wrists, yet in the end free and happy as a bird, by turns lustful and exalted, winging it like a martin, inducing scientific theories, remembering everything, quoting whole pages of Gerard Manley Hopkins:

> Glory be to God for dappled things—
> For skies of couple-color as a branded cow;
> For rose moles all in stipple upon trout that swim;
> Fresh-firecoal chestnut-falls;

and inviting her into my bed, *her* of all people.

Nevertheless, when I left the hospital, she came with me and set up as my nurse. Toward me she feels strong Presbyterian mother-smoothings.

"Did Mr. Ives want to come or was it your idea?"

"My idea?"

"Did you think I needed a little briefing before appearing in The Pit?"

"Tch. What do you mean?"

"Are you afraid Dr. Brown is going to beat me?"

"He can't hold a candle to you as a doctor."

"But you were afraid?"

"Afraid? Oh yes, I'm afraid for Mr. Ives. Oh, Chief, do you think he'll be sent to the Happy Isles?"

"I don't know."

"Do they really throw the Switch there?"

"Yes."

"No!"

"You don't think they ought to?"

"Oh no, Chief!"

"Why not?" I ask her curiously.

"It's not right."

"I see."

"I think Mr. Ives is putting on."

"But if he were not?"

"Oh, Chief, why do you have anything to do with those people?"

"What people?"

"Those foul-mouthed students and that nasty Dr. Brown."

"It's all in good fun. End-of-year thing."

"You're much too fine to associate with them."

"Hm. Well, don't worry. I have other fish to fry."

"You mean you're not going to The Pit?"

I shrug. "What difference does it make? By the way, what's Brown's diagnosis of Mr. Ives?"

She reads: "Senile psychopathy and mutism."

"And his recommendation?"

"The Permanent Separation Center at Jekyll, Georgia. Doesn't that mean the Happy Isles?"

I nod.

"And the Euphoric On-Switch?"

"Yes. But you think the diagnosis is wrong?"

"Because you did."

"I did? Well, let's see him."

She wheels him in. Mr. Ives sits slumped in a folding chair, a little bald-headed monkey of a man, bright monkey eyes snapping at me. His scalp is a smooth cap of skin, heavily freckled, fitted over his low wrinkled brow. The backs of his hands are covered with liver spots and sun scabs. His eyes fairly hop with—what? rage or risibility? Is he angry or amused or just plain crazy? I leaf through his chart. He was born in Sherwood, Tennessee, worked for forty years as controller in a Hartford insurance company, lost his wife, retired to Louisiana, lived in the woods in a camper, dug up potsherds in a Choctaw burial mound, got sick, was transferred to a Tampa Senior Citizens' compound, where he misbehaved and was referred to Gerry Rehab here. I remember him from the old days. He used to call me for one complaint and another and we'd sit in his camper and play checkers and through the open door watch the wild turkeys come up and feed. He was lonely and liked to talk. Now he's mute.

I get up and open the back door. Ellen frowns.

"What's the trouble, Mr. Ives?"

He doesn't reply but he's already looking past me at the martins scudding past and turning upwind for a landing. Gusts of warm air sour with rain blow in the open doorway.

"Ecccc," says Mr. Ives.

The old man can't or won't speak but he lets me examine him. Physically he's in good order, chest clear, abdomen soft, blood pressure normal, eyegrounds nominal. His prostate is as round and elastic as a handball. Neurological signs normal.

I look at his chart. ". . . Did on August 5 last, expose himself and defecate on Flirtation Walk." Hm. He could still suffer from senile dementia.

I look at him. The little monkey eyes snap.

"Do you remember playing checkers out at the mound?"

The eyes snap.

"You never beat me, Mr. Ives." I never beat him.

No rise out of him. His eyes slide past me to the martins rolling and rattling around the hotel.

"He doesn't look senile to me," I tell Ellen. I take out my lapsometer and do a complete profile from cortex to coeliac plexus. Ellen jots down the readings as I call them out.

"No wonder he won't talk," I say, flipping back through his stack of wave patterns.

"Won't or can't?" Ellen asks me.

"Oh, he can. No organic lesion at all. Look at his cortical activity: humming away like a house afire. He's as sharp as you or I."

"Then why—?"

"And he's reading me right now, aren't you, Mr. Ives?"

"Ecccc," says Mr. Ives.

"You asked me why he won't talk," I tell her loudly. "He's too damn mad to talk. His red nucleus is red indeed. Look at that."

"You mean—"

"I mean he doesn't trust you or me or anybody."

"Who's he mad at?"

"Who are you mad at?" I ask Mr. Ives.

His eyes snap. I focus the lapsometer at his red nucleus.

"At me?" No change.

"At Communists?" No change.

"At Negroes?" No change.

"At Jews?" No change.

"At students?" No change.

"Hm. It's not ordinary Knothead anger," I tell Ellen.

"How do you know he understands you at all?" asks Ellen.

"Watch this." I aim in at the medio-temporal region, near Brodmann 28, the locus of concrete memory. "Do you remember our playing checkers in your camper ten years ago on summer evenings like this?"

The needle swings. The eyes snap, but merrily now.

"Chief!" cries Ellen. "You've done it!"

"Done what?"

"You've proved your point!"

"I haven't proved anything. He still won't talk or can't, won't walk or can't. All I've done is make a needle move."

"But, Chief—! You're a hundred years ahead of EEG."

"I can't prove it. I can't treat him. This thing is purely diagnostic and I can't even prove that." Mr. Ives and I watch the last of the martins come home. "I feel like a one-eyed man in the valley of the blind."

"You'll prove it, Chief," says Ellen confidently. She tells me a story about a famous Presbyterian (she said) named Robert the Bruce who sat discouraged in a cave and watched a spider try seven times to span the cave with its web before it succeeded. "Remember Robert the Bruce!"

"O.K. Who's the next patient?"

"Mr. and Mrs. Ted Tennis."

"Are you going to take Mr. Ives back to the hospital?"

"No. They'll send for him."

"Very well. Goodbye, Mr. Ives. Don't worry. You're going to be all right."

He takes my hand with his old wiry grip. I can't understand why he won't talk. His prefrontal gyrus is as normal as mine.

Ted 'n Tanya are next. They must have come directly from Love. It is a bit of a surprise that they've come here, since his former complaint of impotence had been pretty well cleared up by my prescription of an occasional tramp through the swamp, so successfully in fact that only today I've learned that Ted 'n Tanya have become star performers in Love.

They come in together and sit opposite me across the desk. Ellen closes the door and turns on the lights and leaves discreetly. Hm. Have they come to gloat, to tell me of the superiority of Love Clinic to the swamp? But no. They look glum.

But Ted is more than ever the alert young crop-headed narrow-necked Oppenheimer. Tanya is an angular brunette who has smoldering violet eyes, one of which is cocked, and wears a ringlet of hair at each temple like a gypsy. They love each other, do Ted 'n Tanya, and, though heathen, are irrevocably monogamous and faithful.

That much I know. Ted brings me up to date. The swamp treatment of impotence did indeed work for a while but wore off after a few months, as I had told Ted it might. Whereupon they applied for treatment at Love, where they were put in a Skinner box and conditioned so successfully that they became one of the first volunteer couples in the new program of "multiple-subject interaction." A breakthrough. Here too, encouraged by Stryker, Dr. Helga Heine, and Father Kev Kevin, they succeeded admirably.

"I understand that. The only thing that puzzles me is why you're here at all." Making sure Ellen is up front, I open the drawer of organs and recover my Early Times. Ted 'n Tanya don't mind my drinking.

"I know," says Ted glumly.

"Weren't you over at Love today?" I ask them, pouring a little toddy.

"Yes," whispers Tanya, one lovely violet eye fixed on me, the other drifting out a bit as if it were keeping track of my second self, my pneuma.

"Well?" They're sitting side by side on a bench, like children in the principal's office. "How did it go today in Love?"

Ted 'n Tanya look at each other. "It didn't," says Ted.

"It hasn't for weeks," whispers Tanya.

"Hm. I expect the effect of the conditioning is wearing off too, though to tell you the truth I've always suspected that the good results came more from the sympathetic third party, the observer, rather than—"

"Exactly!" cries Ted.

Puzzled, I wait.

Again Ted 'n Tanya exchange glances. "Shall we tell him, Tanya?" She nods.

"Tell me what?"

Ted leans forward, big Oppenheimer head bobbing on its slender neck. "That we never did succeed at home."

"You mean—"

"I mean even at the peak of our performances at Love, we were never able to achieve orgasm at home, except after floundering around the swamp, but even that wore off."

"Pity. Would you care for a drink?"

"No thanks, Tom."

We fall silent. The storm is closer. Thunder rumbles.

I sigh and open the drawer. "Well, I suppose you're here for a Bayonne-rayon member."

But Ted is shaking his head. "That's not the idea, Tom."

"You don't want a member?"

"No."

"Then what can I do for you?" I am genuinely puzzled.

Ted leans forward. "Tom, you were right in thinking that it was the presence of the sympathetic observer that was crucial."

"Yes?"

"The trouble with the observers in Love Clinic is precisely that, that they are too clinical."

"Yes?"

"We thought perhaps if we could enlist the services of an

observer-therapist team who were more sympathetic and in surroundings less clinical."

"Hm."

"When we put the two ingredients together, friend plus professional, naturally our thoughts turned in this direction."

"What direction?"

"To you and Miss Oglethorpe."

"You want me and Miss Oglethorpe . . ."

"We thought we could use your waiting room with that wonderful campy old couch, and you and Miss Oglethorpe could stay in the examining room with the door cracked and spy a bit, to add piquancy to the observer factor."

"Miss Oglethorpe is a Presbyterian."

"So what? Don't Presbyterian nurses treat patients?"

"I expect she's gone home."

"No, she said she'd wait."

I spill my drink. "You mean you asked her?"

"She said anything you wanted to do was all right with her." Ted turns to Tanya. "Do you know what that couch reminds me of?"

"I know, I know."

"The porch at the old dorm in Lansing."

"I know, I know," says Tanya, looking at Ted, but her out eye strays toward me.

"I'm feeling like a kid, wow," says Ted, rising. "I'll go get Miss Oglethorpe."

"Wait," I say.

"Yes?"

"Why Miss Oglethorpe? Why the two of us? Why not me?"

Ted frowns impatiently. "Studies in Palo Alto have shown that when observers are of both sexes, successful reconditioning increases by sixty-two percent."

"Yes. Hm. But I fear today is out of the question. I'm tied up." The prospect of watching Ted 'n Tanya make love is lugubrious enough, but it is the enlisting of Ellen Oglethorpe that makes me nervous. In fact, I've broken out in a cold sweat.

"You couldn't give us half an hour, Tom?" asks Tanya, patting a gypsy ringlet.

"I'm afraid not."

"What about Wednesday?" asks Ted.

"Yes!" I say, seizing at the straw. By Wednesday anything could happen. The world could end. "Check with Ellen for a new appointment."

"Dear?" Ted stretches out both hands to Tanya, lifts her up. Ted is smiling. Two spots of color glow in Tanya's cheeks. They exit, arms about each other like Rudolfo and Mimi.


# 15

I sit in the dark wondering where Ellen is. The storm breaks at last. My lapsometer gleams in the lightning flashes. If only . . . If only my lapsometer could treat as well as diagnose, I wouldn't be caught up in these farces.

The back door is open. The tape rolls. Don Giovanni begins his descent into hell. A bolt of lightning strikes a transformer with a great crack. Sparks fly. The ox-lot is filled with a rinsing blue-white light. Trees jump backward. The lights go out.

Ellen comes in to tell me she is leaving and that someone else wants to see me.

"I'm not seeing any more patients."

"I think he's a detail man. He said he wouldn't keep you long."

"But—"

"Don't forget, Chief, your mother expects you tomorrow."

"What? Wait—"

But she's gone. In the lightning flashes a man seems to come forward by jumps. He carries an outsize attaché case like a drug salesman.

"Look, I see detail men on weekdays."

But he's not a detail man.

"Art Immelmann is the name," he says, sticking his hand across the desk. "Funding is my game."

"Very good, Art, but—" I notice gloomily that he's sat down. Did he say Immerman, or Immelmann like the German ace and inventor of the Immelmann turn?

"It's a new concept in funding, Doctor." Art is shouting over the storm as he takes papers out of his attaché case. He frowns at the open door but I don't feel like closing it.

I try to turn on the lights to see him better, but the current is off. The lightning flashes, however, are almost continuous. He's an odd-looking fellow, curiously old-fashioned. Indeed, with his old-style flat-top haircut, white shirt with short sleeves, which even have vestigial cuff buttons, and neat dark trousers, he looks like a small-town businessman in the old Auto Age, one of those wiry old-young fifty-year-olds, perhaps a Southern Bell manager, who used to go to Howard Johnson's every Tuesday for Rotary luncheon. His face is both youthful and lined. The flat-top makes a tangent with the crown of his skull, giving the effect of a tonsure. Is it an early bald spot or a too-close flat-top?

When he leans across the desk to shake hands, air pushes ahead of him bearing to my nostrils a heavy complex odor, the intricate canceled smell of sweat neutralized by a strong deodorant.

"A lovely little lady, Doc," says the stranger, nodding at the closed door.

"Who? What's that?" I say sharply, frowning with irritation. Did he wink at me or is it the effect of the lightning?

"Very high-principled and efficient, yet most attractive. Most. I'd like to beat you out of her."

"How—! What in hell do you mean?" At a loss for words —I almost said, How dare you?—I jump up from the chair.

"No offense! Take it easy, Doc! Ha ha, made you come up for air, didn't I?"

"What do you want?"

"I only meant that I admire your nurse and wish I had someone as good to assist me in my own researches. What is the saying: All is fair in love and war and hiring cooks?"

"Are you selling something?" My hair prickles with an odd, almost pleasurable dislike.

"Not selling today, Doc. We're giving it away." With that, Art hands over what appear to be application forms. "Don't worry!" He laughs heartily. "They're already filled in."

I haven't been listening carefully. The papers seem to jump back and forth in the lightning. "What are these for?" (Why don't I throw him out?)

"For the money you need."

"Money? Who are you representing, Art?"

"I'm one of those liaison fellows from Washington."

"Liaison? Between whom?"

"Between the public and private sectors."

"What does that mean?"

"Ha ha, you might well ask." His young-old face, I notice, goes instantly serious between laughs. "In this case it is between the National Institute of Mental Health in the public sector and the Ford, Carnegie, and Rockefeller foundations in the private sector."

"Good."

"It does sound impressive, doesn't it?"

"I didn't say that."

"Actually, I'm a glorified errand boy."

"Is that so," I say gloomily, trying to read my watch.

"We of N.I.M.H. and"—for a moment his words are lost in a clap of thunder—"you may have come up with the most important integrative technique of our time."

"What's that?" I say. The wind shifts and a fine mist blows in the doorway. There is a smell of wet warm brick.

"You've done it, Dr. More!"

"Done what?"

"You've come up with a technique that maximizes and unites hardware and software capabilities."

"How's that?" I ask inattentively. What to make of this fellow who talks like a bureaucrat but looks—and smells—like a hardworking detail man? "What technique are you talking about?"

"The More Qualitative-Quantitative Ontological Lapsometer," says Art Immelmann, laughing. "What a mouthful. Everybody at the office calls it the MOQUOL. Sounds like a hole in the ground, doesn't it?"

I set down my toddy. My hand, feeling light and tremulous, levitates. I put it in my pocket.

"Surprised, eh, Doc?"

After a moment I decide to fix a drink. Though my hand feels normal, I decide to hold the glass in both hands.

"What I don't understand is how you knew about it."

"Think about it a moment, Doc, and you'll see."

I see in the next lightning flash. Either the Director has approved my article, or *Brain* has accepted it, or both, and either or both have leaked the news to N.I.M.H.

"You've won, Doctor," says Art gravely. Again the hand comes across the desk. We shake hands. Again comes the intricate canceled sweat-and-deodorant smell.

I've won.

Now I know how Einstein felt when the English astronomers flashed the news from Venezuela that sure enough, Arcturus's light had taken a little bend as it swept past the sun.

Victory.

I sat back and listen to the steady rain and the peepers tuning up in the ox-lot. What to do now? I recall my uncle's advice: guard against the sadness of hubris. How to do that? By going to the Little Napoleon and having a drink with Leroy Ledbetter.

"We're interested in funding truly innovative techniques. Yours is truly innovative."

"Yes."

"You've got your own built-in logistical factor. The results, moreover, are incremental."

"Yes." What in hell is he talking about? It doesn't matter. I've won.

"You are aware of the national implications?"

"Yes, I am."

"For the first time the behavioral sciences have a tool for dealing with the heretofore immeasurable and intangible stresses that are rending the national fabric."

"Yes."

"Dr. More." Again Art stands up, not to shake hands again I hope, no, but again there is the heavy mollified protein smell.

"Yes?"

"We're prepared to fund an interdisciplinary task force and implement a crash program that will put a MOQUOL in the hands of every physician and social scientist in the U.S. within one year's time."

"You are?" Why don't I feel excited? My eyes don't blink.

"As you know better than I, your MOQUOL has a multilevel capacity. It is operative at behavioral, political, and philosophical levels. I would even go so far as to say this, Doc—" Art pauses to hawk phlegm and adjust his crotch with an expert complicated pat.

"What's that, Art?"

"If the old U.S. of A. doesn't go down the drain in the next year, it will be thanks to your MOQUOL."

"Well, I wouldn't say that, but—"

In the last flash of lightning, a legal-size blue-jacketed document appears under my nose and a pen is pointed at my breastbone.

"What's this, Art?"

"A detail. A bureaucratic first step, ha ha." Art laughs his instant laugh and goes as sober as a mortician.

"Hey, this is a transfer of patent rights!"

"Boilerplate, Doc. Standard procedure for any contract with the private sector. And look at your return!" Expertly he flips pages. "Seventy-five percent!"

"Yeah, but I mean, goddamn, Art—!" I begin, but Art Immelmann turns white and falls back a step.

"Pardon. I only meant to say that the money doesn't interest me." Art must be a Holy Name man or a hard-shell Baptist.

"I told them you'd say that. But let's don't worry about it. The important thing is to get the MOQUOL distributed in time."

"Well, I've already got a hundred production models."

*"Where?"* Art nearly comes across the desk.

I sit back in surprise. "In a safe place. Don't worry."

"You don't want to leave something like MOQUOL lying around, Doc."

"I know." I tell him of my plans, my appointment with the Director Monday, the submission of my article to *Brain*. "I just don't see the necessity of signing over my patent rights."

"You know, you could be disappointed, Doc," says Art thoughtfully but beginning, I see with relief, to put the application forms back in his case.

"Well, I'm hopeful."

"You know how people resist a really radical innovation."

"Yes, but this thing works, Art."

"I know. Tell you what, Doc," says Art cheerfully, snapping up his attaché case. "I'll drop in next week."

"Can't the funding be arranged without signing over control of the MOQUOL?"

"No doubt. But I'll be seeing you in a day or two. Just in case."

"In case of what?"

"In case you hit a snag. You never know about people, Doc," says Art mysteriously.

"Very true," I say, anxious only to get rid of him and get over to the Little Napoleon, a snug and friendly haven in any storm.

Some seconds pass before I realize that Art left by the back door, striking out across the dark ox-lot. I shrug. Perhaps he's taking the short cut to the old Southern Hotel, where a few drummers and detail men still put up.

But how would he know about the short cut?

# JULY SECOND

# MY MOTHER'S HOUSE

## 10:00 A.M. / SUNDAY, JULY 2

SUNDAYS I EAT BREAKFAST WITH MY MOTHER. BUT TODAY IS special. Yesterday was my birthday. Today is Property Rights Sunday. My mother, who is president of the altar society and also of the Business & Professional Women, is leading an ecumenical delegation to Saint Pius XII Church (A.C.C.). (A.C.C. = American Catholic Church.)

The Summer Moonlight Tour of the Champs is in full swing. The fish fry will be held this afternoon. Later this morning the Kaydettes corps of Christian baton-twirlers will give a performance. Tuesday they leave for the nationals at Oxford, Mississippi.

It seems I promised to go to church with Mother—because it is my birthday, because it is Property Rights Sunday, and because she wants me to "come back to the Church."

We are sitting on a terrace overlooking the golf links where we are served a hearty breakfast by Eukie, Mother's little black houseboy. His white jacket is too dazzling to be looked at. The pile of steaming grits is also white and glittering in the morning sunlight. I've already had my warm Tang plus duck eggs plus vodka, and my pulse races along at a merry clip. I am both alert and shaky.

Everything is lovely and peaceful here. Towhees whistle in the azaleas. Golfers hum up and down the fairways in their quaint surrey-like carts. Householders mow their lawns, bestriding tiny burro-size tractors. Why am I so jumpy?

On the other hand, the vines are encroaching. Mother's yard is noticeably smaller.

My chair is placed so that I am facing Tara next door,

147

Dusty Rhoades's plantation house, which he purchased from Vince Marsaglia, a gangster from New Orleans who runs Louisiana.

Mother, I see, has all sorts of schemes afoot for me. She is saying:

"I can just see you and Lola walking up and down by moonlight while from the inside come the strains of lovely old-world music."

"Lola Rhoades?"

"Ho ho, you can't fool your mother! I know what's going on between you two."

"You do? What is going on?"

"I couldn't be more pleased. She's wild about you, Tom! What a wonderful girl!"

I am scratching my head: this is odd. Until now Mother hasn't had much use for Lola, considering her Texas-raw and Texas-horsy. Lola's cello-straddling always struck Mother as somehow unladylike. She's been talking to Dusty, I reckon.

"You're a Cancer and she's a Taurus. It couldn't be better!"

"That may be, Mother, but the fact is I don't really—"

"Beware of Aries and Libra."

"O.K., Mother, but—"

"Isn't that little nurse of yours an Aries?"

"Who? Ellen? Good Lord, I have no idea, Mother. In any case, Ellen and I have no—"

"And isn't that little Left snippet of yours a Libra?"

"Who? Moira? My Lord, Mother, how in the world do you know? And in any case why do you say 'of mine'?"

"She's not for you, son."

"Are you speaking of marriage? Moira has no intention of marrying me."

"Then all the more reason for breaking it off. But I'm not really worried about that. Here's what's been on my mind."

"Yes?"

"Being a Cancer means that you are deeply sensitive and that family strife tends to cause you much suffering. God knows this is true in your case."

"That it is."

"Ginger Rogers and Red Skelton were Cancers."

"I didn't know that."

"You are also under Moon rule, which means that you are emotionally unstable and tend to form will-o'-the-wisp relationships with more than one sweetheart."

"That's true."

"What I wanted to tell you is that in this, the first week of July, I believe that certain things are going to become clear to you and that you will make some important decisions, but—"

"I believe that too."

"But—! Do not make any real estate transfers until later in the month. I've told Dusty and Lola the same thing."

"Real estate transfers," I say, scratching my head.

"I've told Dusty and Lola and I'm telling you: whatever plans you all might have, don't sell anything now or buy anything now." She nods meaningfully at Tara.

"Sell anything? Mother, Lola and I have no plans. What did Dusty tell you?"

"Ho ho *ho*. I know a thing or two. And I know that Lola is a wonderful girl."

"It is true. Lola, a big beautiful cellist, is a wonderful girl. Last Christmas Eve we lay in one another's arms in the grassy bunker of number 18 and watched the summer constellations wheel in their courses—I, smashed out of my mind with love, with scientific triumph, and brain hives, she full of love and music, hissing cello tunes in my ear. A brave girl, she saved my life at the expense of her reputation, went to fetch her father as I lay dying of love and hives in the bunker.

What Mother doesn't understand is that we loved each other for one night and that was the end of it. One night I sang between her knees like an antique cello while she watched the wheeling constellations. A perfect encounter, but it is not to be thought that we could repeat it.

And yet—here's the wonder of love—even as I bend shivering over the glittering mound of grits, love revives! Love is always possible, even here in the ashes of my forty-five-year-old life. Something stirs, a phoenix. Bad as things are, perhaps just because they are so bad, why not go to the fish fry this afternoon, see Lola again, drink a gin fizz or two?

"Doris was not for you, Tom," Mother is saying. "God knows she was a wonderful person, but she was never for you. A Capricorn, your exact opposite. I told you!"

No, she didn't. The truth is she was all for Doris at the beginning, embracing her as a Virginia aristocrat, which she was not, being no more than a good-looking Shenandoah Valley girl.

"Doris was not for you, Tom!" says Mother, swishing her leg angrily.

"Evidently she wasn't."

Look at Mother! Look at the difference between us! I, a shaky decrepit forty-five, she in her sixties as pert as a sparrow and on good terms with the world. She sits bolt upright, handsome legs crossed, nylon swishing against nylon, one hand pressed deep into her waist to emphasize her good figure. This morning she's been up for hours, rooting around in her garden, ordering the help around, calling prospects—she's a "realtor," makes forty thousand a year, is more successful now than my father in his prime.

She sparkles with good health and is at one with herself. I? I am six feet ahead of myself, ricocheting between terror and elation. My toes are rotating. The out-of-doors doesn't suit me. I feel like Henry Miller, seedy and stove up, sitting in a park in Jacksonville, Florida. Her plate is clean. She eats like a longshoreman, yet is trim as can be, has a good skin and a clear eye. What a bowel she has! Unfortunately I have my father's bowel, which is subject to conservative rages and liberal terror.

"Tom," says Mother, lowering her voice and rolling her eyes. "I feel that something is about to happen. *They* are going to do something."

"I have the same feeling," I say, watching her curiously. "But what's your reason for thinking so?" Whenever Mother lowers her voice and rolls her eyes, it means she's going to talk about *them*, Negroes.

"I've seen them," Mother whispers, "riding around, looking."

"Who, the Bantus or the locals?"

"Both. But that's not the main thing."

"What's the main thing?"

"Last Sunday I saw a black cloud with something coiling in it hovering over the Infant Jesus of Prague."

"You took that to be a sign something is going to happen here soon?"

"Haven't I always been proved right in the past?"

"What was the 'something coiling'?"

"Entrails. Which is a sign of the Bantus. They divine and foretell by examining entrails. You think I'm ridiculous."

"I think you're right about something happening."

Mother has a reputation hereabouts as a seer and prophetess. What she is is a Catholic gnostic. Though she believes in God, she also relies on her crystal ball—she actually has a crystal ball, which she looks into—and her gift for seeing signs and divining hidden meanings. But she is quite brisk about it, puts on no psychic airs, has no truck with séances and such. Her clairvoyant powers have rather to do with business and politics. She will not close a deal with a Leo in May. Most of her visions and dreams are about plots of the Lefts against the Knotheads. She predicted four out of the last five assassinations.

"Don't ask me how it happens!" she chides her admirers. "All I know is it does. Why, I would no more sell a Capricorn to a Cancer than fly to the moon. Because I know what happens when I do. I not only lose the sale but also the deposit." She is referring to the astrology of the vendor and vendee. "And I also know, without knowing how it happens, that when I'm saying the third decade of the rosary on the third day of a novena and when I come to the third bead, I'm going to see something. Don't ask me why!" she cries, laughing at herself.

When she says see, she means it. Last year she saw a vision of a dragon fighting a bear over the statue of the Infant Jesus of Prague, to be specific: over the little globe the Infant Jesus held. War between Russia and China broke out the next week.

Her fame is spreading. "Marva, it's a gift from God," her friends tell her. "Why don't you share it with the world?" But she laughs it off.

She doesn't even interpret her visions, leaving that to others. But the meanings are clear to her friends and they usually have political overtones, auguring ill for conservatives and good for liberals. On the eve of the last national election, for example, she came to the third bead of the third decade of her rosary and saw Old Glory, the Stars and Stripes, slowly sinking into the waters of the Great Salt Lake. Her friends undestood. The new President is an integrationist Mormon from Salt Lake City.

It is only breakfast that Mother gets around to telling me that I received a telephone call earlier. She makes a face. She disapproves of the caller.

"He said for you to come see him. He said it was urgent. I deliver the message without comment."

"Who, Mother?"

"Your friend, the Roman priest."

"Roman?"

"*Father* Smith," she says, accenting *Father* sarcastically.

"What did he want?"

"He wouldn't tell me. Only that you were to come to see him."

"Where?"

"You'd never imagine."

"Well?"

"He said he'd be down in the Slave Quarters. Now wouldn't you know it?"

"Know what?"

"That that's where he'd end up."

"What do you mean?"

"You know," says my mother, pushing her hand deep into her waist and arching her back. "I think he's in with them."

"Who?" I ask. "You mean the guerrillas?"

"So I told him in my sweetest voice that you were coming over here and going to church with me. I just dared him to say there was anything wrong with our mass."

"You used to like him." She did. He was a favorite with the ladies. He had a courtly manner, used to look like Ricardo Montalban playing a lithe priest and saying things like "Do not worry about the bell, my children. God will provide the bell, you will see," etcetera. "What have you got against him now?" I ask Mother.

"He who is not with you is against you," says Mother darkly. Her eyes glitter. She's a bad enemy.

"Yes. Well—hm." I shiver in the sunlight. I notice that the vines are encroaching. A tendril has twined about Mother's antique wrought-iron Singer table.

Before we go to church, Dr. Dusty Rhoades hops the hedge. Eukie pours him a cup of coffee.

Dusty and Mother hit it off very well, I notice. Dusty winks at me and feels my bones. Then he's got nothing against me. They both kid me.

"Marva," says Dusty to Mother, but at the same time exploring my shoulder with his big freckled hand. "Do you think Tom's going to invite us white trash up to the big house?" Now he's gazing at Tara with his fond filmed-over eyes.

"Eh? What's that?" I ask.

"He better, the scamp!" cries Mother.

"What big house?" I ask them. They both laugh merrily. I find that I am grinning too.

But Dusty goes suddenly serious. He shakes his big lion head slowly.

"You know I'm leaving for Texas in a week. And I feel bad about leaving Lola over there alone. Do you know we haven't had a servant for a week? You don't know how lucky you are to have your little nigger."

Mother rolls her eyes and raises her finger to her lips. "Eukie is a treasure."

Eukie is worthless, but that is not what bothers me.

"Guess who is going to look after my little Lola when I leave," says Dusty past me. He and Mother are exchanging all manner of glances over my head.

"I wish the child would move in with me." Again a regular semaphore of eye messages.

"She's not about to leave Tara," muses Dusty. "She says her roots are there."

"You should have seen her over there this morning, feeding her horses, planting greens—"

"Where is Lola now?" I ask them.

"You'll see her this afternoon at the fish fry, it's all settled," says Mother. "But you should have seen her, standing there in that old garden, her hands potty black, her face glowing. She never looked prettier or more determined."

"I still don't like to leave her there alone," says Dusty, wagging his head.

"Do you remember what Scarlett said about the land?" asks Mother. "Or was it in *The Good Earth?*"

"Yes," says Dusty, popping his great jaw muscles.

Mother squeezes my hand. "We're making a foursome this evening, Tommy," she says in a strange soft voice, a rushing lowpitched thrilling voice, the sort women use on solemn occasions, funerals and weddings. "You and I and Dusty and Lola."

Hm. Is something cooking between Mother and Dusty? And are they cooking up something between me and Lola? Warning signals flash in my brain. Look out! They're making a match. And yet. And yet, despite all, love kindles. Lola is a lovely girl after all. And a brave girl. And what lovely sounds the Guarnerius makes clasped between her lovely knees. There are worse lives, after all, than sitting on the gallery of Tara and... I look at Tara, a preposterous fake house on a fake hill: even the hill is fake, dredged up from the swamp by the state of Louisiana for Vince Marsaglia. The very preposterousness of life in Tara with Lola inflames me with love.— Yes, sitting on the gallery sipping Early Times while Lola plants greens or plays *Don Quixote* or we hold hands, her cello-callused fingers whispering in my palm. Lovely Lola.

The question is: how can I bear not to marry Lola? Why did God make woman so beautiful and man with such a loving heart?

"Time for mass," says Mother, rising briskly. "Won't you come with us, Dusty?"

But Dusty, who is a Baptist, makes his excuses, socks himself in his joyful-eccentric style, and hops the hedge.

2

We walk over to Saint Pius XII's. Pius XII, the last Pope recognized by the American Catholic Church, was canonized by the Sacred College of Cicero, Illinois. The present "Pope" of the A.C.C., a native of Anaheim and Bishop of San Diego, took the name Pius XIII.

Property Rights Sunday is a major feast day in the A.C.C. A blue banner beside the crucifix shows Christ holding the American home, which has a picket fence, in his two hands.

Mother sits up front with the other Business & Professional Women. I skulk at the rear with the ushers, one foot in church, one foot in the vestibule. It is possible to leave at any time, since I told Mother I had to keep my appointment and might not see her after church.

I can leave any time I please, but it is deliciously cool in here. The superb air-conditioning always puts me in mind of the words of the old Latin mass (to which the A.C.C. has returned as a patriotic gesture): "Grant us we beseech Thee a *locum refrigerii. . . .*"

Monsignor Schleifkopf reads the Gospel from Matthew that relates how Joseph of Arimathea, a rich man, believed in Christ and gave him his tomb. He preaches on the resurrection of Lazarus, who was also well off.

"Dearly Beloved: we are reminded by the best commentators that Lazarus was not a poor man, that he lived comfortably with sisters in a home that he owned. Our Lord himself, remember, was not a social reformer, said nothing about freeing the slaves, nor are we obliged to."

After the sermon Monsignor Schleifkopf announced triumphantly that this week the congregation had paid off the debt on the new church, the air-conditioning, the electronic carillon that can be heard for five miles, and the new parochial school.

Moon Mullins, who is an usher, greets me in the vestibule. He stands around in true usher style, hawking phlegm and swinging his fist into his hand.

Monsignor Schleifkopf prays for victory over North Ecuador and for the welfare of our brothers in Christ and fellow property owners throughout Latin America and for the success of the Moonlight Tour of the Champs in the name of "the greatest pro of them all."

I begin to think impure thoughts. My heart, which was thumping for no good reason, begins to thump for love of Lola Rhoades and at the prospect of seeing her this very afternoon and later inviting her out into the gloaming.

When the congregation rises for the creed, I see my chance and slip out.

Christ have mercy on me. Sir Thomas More, pray for me. God bless Moon Mullins, a good fellow, a better man than I. Lord have mercy on your poor church.

Goodbye, Pius XII. Hello, Lola baby, big lovely cellist. Let us go out into the gloaming and lie in one another's arms and watch the constellations wheel in their courses.


3


Father Rinaldo Smith is sitting on the tin-roofed porch of the tiny slave-quarter chapel. In his rolled-up shirt sleeves he looks more than ever like Ricardo Montalban. He is waiting, I suppose, for his tiny flock. The Roman Catholics are a remnant of a remnant.

We sit on the steps.

"You know what we need, Tom?" he asks me with a sigh.

"What's that, Father?"

"A bell."

"Right, Father. And I have an idea where I might lay my hands on one."

"Splendid," says Father Smith, kicking a cottonmouth off the steps.

Though Father Smith is a good priest, a chaste and humble man who for twenty-five years had baptized the newborn into a new life, shriven sinners, married lovers, annointed the sick, buried the dead—he has had his troubles.

Once he turned up in the bed next to mine in the acute

wing. It seemed he had behaved oddly at the ten o'clock mass and created consternation among the faithful. This happened before the schism, when hundreds of the faithful packed old Saint Michael's. When he mounted the pulpit to make the announcements and deliver his sermon, he had instead—fallen silent. The silence lasted perhaps thirty seconds. Thirty seconds is a very long silence. Nothing is more uncomfortable than silence when speech is expected. People began to cough and shift around in the pews. There was a kind of foreboding. Silence prolonged can induce terror. "Excuse me," he said at last, "but the channels are jammed and the word is not getting through." When he absently blew on and thumped the microphone, as priests do, the faithful thought he was talking about the loudspeaker and breathed a sigh of relief. But Father Smith did not continue the mass. Instead he walked to the rectory in his chasuble, sat down in the Monsignor's chair in a gray funk and, according to the housekeeper, began to mutter something about "the news being jammed"—whereupon the housekeeper, thinking he meant the TV, turned it on (strange: no matter what one says, no matter how monstrous, garbled, unfittable, whoever hears it will somehow make it fit). Monsignor Schleifkopf later said to Father Kev Kevin, the other curate, "Beware of priests who don't play golf or enjoy a friendly card game or listen to *The Lawrence Welk Show*—sooner or later they'll turn their collar around and wear a necktie." This was before Father Kev Kevin married Sister Magdalene and took charge of the vaginal computer in Love.

So there was Father Rinaldo Smith in the next bed, stiff as a board, hands cloven to his side, eyes looking neither right nor left.

"What seems to be the trouble, Father?" asked Max, pens and flashlight and reflex hammer glittering like diamonds in his vest pocket.

"They're jamming the air waves," says Father Smith, looking straight ahead.

"Causing a breakdown in communication, eh, Father?" says Max immediately. He is quick to identify with the patient.

"They've put a gremlin in the circuit," says Father Smith.

"Ah, you mean a kind of spirit or gremlin is causing the breakdown in communication?"

"No no, Max!" I call out from the next bed. "That's not what he means." What Max doesn't understand is that Father

Smith is one of those priests, and there are a good many, who like to fool with ham radios, talk with their fellow hams, and so fall into the rather peculiar and dispirited jargon hams use. "When he said there was a gremlin in the circuit, he meant only that there is something wrong, not that there is a, um, spirit or gremlin causing it." Priests have a weakness for ham radio and seismology. Leading solitary lives and stranded in places like Pierre, South Dakota, or the Bronx or Waycross, Georgia, they hearken to other solitaries around the world or else bend an ear to the earth itself.

"Yes, they're jamming," says Father Smith.

When I spoke, Max and the other doctors looked at me disapprovingly. They had finished with me, passed my bed. I am like a dancing partner who's been cut in on and doesn't go away.

"They?" asks Max. "Who are they?"

"They've won and we've lost," says Father Smith.

"Who are they, Father?"

"The principalities and powers."

"Principalities and powers, hm," says Max, cocking his head attentively. Light glances from the planes of his temple. "You are speaking of two of the hierarchies of devils, are you not?"

The eyes of the psychiatrists and behaviorists sparkle with sympathetic interest.

"Yes," says Father Smith. "Their tactic has prevailed."

"You are speaking of devils now, Father?" asks Max.

"That is correct."

"Now what tactic, as you call it, has prevailed?"

"Death."

"Death?"

"Yes. Death is winning, life is losing."

"Ah, you mean the wars and the crime and violence and so on?"

"Not only that. I mean the living too."

"The living? Do you mean the living are dead?"

"Yes."

"How can that be, Father? How can the living be dead?"

"I mean their souls, of course."

"You mean their souls are dead," says Max with the liveliest sympathy.

"Yes," says Father Smith tonelessly. "I am surrounded by the corpses of souls. We live in a city of the dead."

"Are the devils here too, Father?" asks Max.

"Yes. But you fellows are safer than most."

"How is that, Father?"

"Because you don't know any better," says the priest, cheering up all of a sudden. He laughs. "Do you want to know the truth?"

"We always want to know the truth, Father," says Max gravely.

"I think it is you doctors who are doing the will of God, even though you do not believe in him. You stand for life. You are trying to help us in here, you are good fellows, God bless you all. Life is what—" begins the priest and, as suddenly as he laughed, now covers his face with his hands and bursts into tears.

The doctors nod silently, pat the foot of the bed, and move on.

But today at Natchez-under-the-Hill the priest is his old self, sits fully clothed and in his right mind, a gray-faced gray-haired gray man with flat hairy forearms like Ricardo Montalban. He looks at his wristwatch and, explaining that it is time for him to go into the confessional, makes as if to rise.

"Don't go on my account, Father," I say, noticing no other pentients.

"No?" Sighing, he sits down again.

"I'm sorry, Father, but you could not give me the sacrament of penance. One of the elements is missing."

"Which element?"

"Contrition. To say nothing of a firm purpose of amendment."

"I understand. I'll pray for you."

"Good."

"Um, pray for me."

"I haven't prayed much lately. But excuse me, Father."

"Yes?"

"I thought you wanted to see me about something."

"See you? Oh yes. Right. It occurred to me the other day," says the priest, working his expansion band around his wide hairy wrist (a Spanish athelete's futbol wrist), "that it would be a good idea for you to move out of your house."

I look at him curiously. "Why should I do that?"

"I am not at liberty to tell you why."

"You mean someone told you something under the seal of the confessional?"

"I am just telling you that it would be better for you to leave. Now. Today."

"Is something going to happen, Father?"

The priest shrugs.

"Father, if my life is in danger, I think you're obliged to tell me."

"You should move. Say, why don't you move down here with me? You know, it's quite cool down here." He nods toward the restored slave quarters, a long brick row house already engulfed by creeper and swamp cyrilla.

"But, Father—"

He rises. His parishioners are arriving. They're an odd lot, a remnant of a remnant, bits and pieces, leftovers, like the strays and stragglers after a battle. I know most of them. They recognize me and so signify by noncommittal nods. Am I one of them?

They are:

Three old-style Roman Catholics, the sort who are going to stick with the Roman Pope no matter what—let's hear it for the Pope!—Knights-of-Columbus types, Seven-Up Holy-Name Prudential Western-Auto types, and their wives, good solid chicken-gumbo and altar-society ladies.

A scoffing Irish behaviorist, the sort in whom irony is so piled up on irony, jokes so encrusted on jokes, winks and nudges and in-jokes so convoluted, that anticlericism has become anti-anticlerical, gone so far out that it has come back in as clericism and comes down on the side of Rome where he started.

An old scold, a seventy-year-old lady sacristan, the sort who's been lurking in the shadows of the tabernacle since the prophetess Anna.

A love couple from the swamp, dressed in rags and seashells, who, having lived a free life, chanted mantras, smoked Choctaw cannab, lain together dreaming in the gold-green world, conceived and bore children, dwelled in a salt mine— chanced one day upon a Confederate Bible, read it as if it had never been read before, the wildest unlikeliest doctrine imaginable, believed it, decided to be married and baptize their children.

An ordinary Knothead couple recently transferred from Jackson, he the new manager of Friendly Finance, they having inquired after the whereabouts of the local Catholic church and being directed here, perhaps as a joke, and now standing around, eyes rolled up in their eyebrows, wondering: could this be the right church, a tin-roofed hut in a briar patch? They're in the wrong place.

Two freejacks, light-skinned sloe-eyed men of color, also called "Creoles" by other Negroes but generally called freejacks ever since their ancestors were freed by Andy Jackson for services rendered in the Battle of New Orleans.

Two nuns who refused either to get married, quit, or teach in all-white Knothead schools and so have no place to go.

Three seminarians, two lusty white fellows, lusty Notre Dame types, the sort who run up and down basketball courts swinging sweaty Our Lady medals, and one graceful black youth, face set in a conventional piety, who reminds me of Saint Aloysius Gonzaga, the Jesuit boy-saint who was reputed never to have entertained an impure thought.

Two secretaries from the Center, you know the sort, good Catholic girls thirty-one or -two and not exactly gorgeous, one dumpy and pudding-faced, the other an Olive Oyl.

Everyone stands around at sixes and sevens, eyeing each other and wondering if he's in the right place. The love couple look at the K.C. types swinging their fists into their hands. The Friendly Finance Couple look at the freejacks and wonder if they are black or white.

Father Rinaldo Smith sighs and mounts the steps. The others follow silently.

"You coming, Tom?" he asks.

"Not today."

"Wouldn't it be wonderful to have a good old bell to summon the faithful and ring the angelus?"

"Yes. I believe I know where a good old plantation bell might be found."

"Grand."

4

In my "enclosed patio."

I decide to skip the fish fry and spend the afternoon sipping toddies and reading Stedmann's account of Verdun.

At six o'clock on the morning of May 23, 1916, the French

Thirty-fourth Infantry attacked the fort at Douaumont. The Germans had 2,200 artillery pieces, of which 1,730 were heavy. The French division advanced to the fort, losing four out of five men. The survivors reached the roof of the fort but could not get in. They were soon killed by artillery.

The slaughter of Verdun was an improvement over the nineteenth century, in which, for example, Grant lost 8,000 men, mostly white Anglo-Saxon Protestants named Smith, Jones, and Robinson, in forty minutes at Cold Harbor to Lee's army, also mainly Anglo-Saxon, white, and Protestant, named Smith, Jones, Robinson, and Armstrong.

Here's the riddle. Father Smith speaks of life. Life is better than death. Frenchmen and Germans now choose life. Frenchmen and Germans at Verdun in 1916 chose death, 500,000 of them. The question is, who has life, the Frenchman now who chooses life and will die for nothing or the Frenchman then who chose to die, for what? I forget.

Or a Pennsylvanian. This afternoon during the assault on Fort Douaumont, I heard a sportscaster listing the football powers of the coming season. Number one on his list were the Nittany Lions of Penn State. I do not care to hear about the Nittany Lions. But what would it be like to live in Pennsylvania and every day of your life hear sportscasters speak of the prospects of the Nittany Lions?

With my lapsometer I can measure the index of life, life in death and death in life. It is possible, I suspect, to be dying and alive at Verdun and alive and dying as a booster of the Nittany Lions.

An example of life in death: for fifty years following the Battle of Verdun, French and German veterans used to return every summer to seek out the trench where they spent the summer of 1916. Why did they choose the very domicile of death? Was there life here? Afterwards they would sit for hours in a café on the Sacred Way.

But I most prove my case. I must be present with my lapsometer in circumstances where the dying are alive and the living are dead. Observe, measure, verify: here's the business of the scientist.

Outside my "enclosed patio" the weeds are sprouting through the black pebbles Doris brought back from Mexico. Virginia creeper has taken the $500 lead statue of Saint Francis she ordered from Hammacher-Schlemmer. The birdbath and feeder Saint Francis holds are empty. Tough titty for the titmice.

Sunday night: awake till 5 A.M. Reading Stedmann on Verdun, listening to a screech owl crying like a baby in the swamp, assaulted by succubi, night exaltations, morning terror, and nameless longings; sipped twelve toddies.

But why should I be afraid? Tomorrow—today—I meet with the Director and hear the triumphant news about my lapsometer, the first caliper of the soul and the first hope of bridging the dread chasm that has rent the soul of Western man ever since the famous philosopher Descartes ripped body loose from mind and turned the very soul into a ghost that haunts its own house.

# JULY THIRD

# AT THE DIRECTOR'S OFFICE TO HEAR THE GOOD NEWS ABOUT MY ARTICLE AND INVENTION

## 11:00 A.M. / MONDAY, JULY 3

THIRTY MINUTES EARLY FOR MY APPOINTMENT. QUITE NERvous. But why? My article speaks for itself. The evidence is there. My invention works.

There is time to go the roundabout way through Love Clinic in hopes of catching a glimpse of Moira, my love.

No one is in but Father Kev Kevin, who is sitting at the vaginal computer reading a book, *Christianity Without God.*

"Is it good?"

"What? Oh. Yes, this is where it's at."

He jumps up and greets me with suspicious cordiality, flashing his handsome Pat O'Brien grin and shaking my hand with both of his just as he used to when he was chaplain for the Knights of Columbus. He must have bad news. He does.

"Are you looking for Miss Schaffner?"

"Yes."

"I'm afraid she's no longer with us," says Father Kev Kevin, rocking back on his heels in his old clerical style.

"Where is she?"

"She's working over in Geriatrics with Dr. Brown."

"Very good," I say, but my heart gives an ugly leap sideways. But really, why should I be jealous? Buddy Brown is a licentious man, but Moira knows this. Undoubtedly it is the hapless old folk who interest her and whom she wants to help.

"Thank you. Goodbye, Father," I say absently.

Father Kev Kevin frowns and returns to the vaginal computer. At the same moment Lonesome Lil enters the clinic, lines up her Lucite fittings on the table, and begins taking off her good gray suit.

It does not help matters when I run into Buddy Brown in the hall. He greets me even more effusively.

"See you in The Pit this afternoon," he says, coming close and pinching my flank in a loving kind of hate.

"The Pit?"

"At two o'clock. Me and you. Let's give them a real show, what do you say?"

"Yes. But just now I have an appointment with the Director."

"It's a good case. You saw him first, then I saw him. We both know him backwards and forwards."

"Which case? Oh, Mr. Ives."

"Which case! Ho ho." Buddy twists my flank a bit too hard for comfort. "Son, this time I got you by the short hairs."

"Perhaps. What do you think is wrong with him?"

"I know what's wrong with him."

"And you've got him down for the Happy Isles."

"What would you do with him?"

"I don't know." I am gazing down at Buddy's tanned bald head and lustrous spaniel eyes. His jaw muscles spread up like a fan under the healthy skin. Could Moira like him? There is to commend him his health, strength, brains, and cleanliness. He is very clean. His fingernails are like watch crystals. His soft white shirt and starched clinical coat sparkle like snow against his clear mahogany skin. Burnished hairs sprout through the heavy gold links of his expansion band.

Buddy is winking at me. "I understand that you diagnosed uh no pathology in Mr. Ives."

"Yes."

"You mean you think there's nothing wrong with him?"

"Yes."

"Then how come he can't walk or talk?"

"I don't know."

"Me and you going to have it."

"All right."

"This time you're wide open."

"How do you figure?"

"Because you have allowed nonscientific considerations to affect your judgment."

"Nonscientific considerations?"

"Religious considerations."

"I? Religious? How's that?"

"Tell the truth. You oppose in principle Happy Isles and the Euphoric Switch."

"Yes."

"And you don't want Mr. Ives to be sent there."

"That's true."

"Why?"

"Why what?"

"Why do you disapprove?"

I fall silent.

"Tom, you and I don't disagree," says Buddy in an earnest friendly voice.

"We don't?"

"It's the quality of life that counts."

"Yes."

"And the right of the individual to control his own body."

"Well—"

"And above all a man's sacred right to choose his own destiny and realize his own potential."

"Well—"

"Would you let your own mother suffer?"

"Yes."

"I don't believe you. I know you too well and know that you place a supreme value on human values."

"Yes."

"We believe in the same things, differing only in the best way to achieve them."

"We do?"

"See you in The Pit!"

One last squeeze—we are good friends now—and off he goes, white skirts sailing.

The Pit is a curious institution, a relic of medieval disputations and of doctors' hankering for horseplay, satiric verse, heavy-handed clinical jokes, and such. Once a month a clinical-pathological conference is held in the student amphitheater, before four hundred odd students, professors, nurses, and staff members. Local physicians are invited and sometimes come, if only to see what the Leftpapasan psychiatrists and behaviorists are up to. Today's Pit is the grand finale of the arduous ten-month school year. The seats of The Pit slope steeply to a small sunken arena, a miniature of the bullring at Pamplona. The Pit is popular with students because it is the one occasion when the Herr Professors try publicly to make fools of each other and the students can take sides (perhaps it is an Anglo-Saxon institution: no German Herr Professor would put up with it). They can clap, cheer, boo, point thumbs down, scrape their feet on the concrete. Contending physicians present and defend their diagnoses. Opponents are free to ridicule, even abuse each other. One doctor, none other than Buddy Brown in fact, routed an opponent who had diagnosed the "typical red butterfly rash of Lupus" by demonstrating that he, the opposing doctor, was color-blind.

Buddy exaggerates when he says I have my "following." My one small success in The Pit might be compared to a single well-executed *estocada* by an obscure matador. I was able to demonstrate that a lady suffering from frigidity and morning terror and said to have been malconditioned by her overly rigid Methodist parents was in truth terrified by her well-nigh perfect life, really death in life, in Paradise, where all her needs were satisfied and all she had to do was play golf and bridge and sit around the clubhouse watching swim-meets and the Christian baton-twirlers. She woke every morning to a perfect husband, perfect children, a perfect life—and shook like a leaf with morning terror. All efforts to recondition her in a Skinner box failed. I thought they had got it backward, that the frigidity followed from the terror, not vice versa. How can a lady quaking with terror make love to her husband? For the first time I produced my lapsometer in The Pit—yes, the students know about my invention but are not sure whether it is a serious diagnostic tool or a theatrical prop. It registered normal readings in both the erogenous and interpersonal zones. The lady had a loving heart. Ah, but what to do about it? How to demonstrate it in The Pit? An idea came to me. Sizing her up, noting her suggestibility—she was one of those quick slim ash-blondes whose gray eyes are onto you and onto what you want before you know it yourself and are willing to follow your lead: a superb dancing partner—I gambled on a quick hypnosis, put her under and implanted the posthypnotic suggestion that she had nothing to worry about, that as soon as possible she should make an excuse and leave in search of her husband. Whereupon she did, waking up, rising with parted lips and a high color, patting the back of her hair and looking at her watch: "Good heavens, I'm late. I've got to meet Harry. This is his day off and if I hurry, I'll be home before he finishes his nap." Exit, blushing. The students cheered and sang "I'm Just Wild About Harry."

My little triumph, of course, was more theatrical than medical. As you well know, medical colleagues, and as Freud proved long ago, hypnosis is without lasting benefit.

## 2

Five minutes to eleven. Time for a last visit to the men's room. Why am I so nervous? The Director has to be on my side. Else how would Art Immelmann have found out about my invention?

Speak of the devil. A man takes the urinal next to me though there are six urinals and mine is at the end. I frown. Here is a minor breach of the unspoken rules between men for the use of urinals. If there are six urinals and one uses the first, the second man properly takes the sixth or perhaps the fifth, maybe the fourth, tolerably the third, but not the second.

This fellow, however, hawks and spits in the standard fashion, zips and pats himself and moves to the washstand, again the next washstand. In the mirror I notice it is Art Immelmann, the man from the Rockefeller-Ford-Carnegie foundations who looks like a drug salesman.

"Well, well, Doc."

When I turn to speak, I notice another minor oddity. In the mirror, which reverses things, there was nothing amiss. But as Art adjusts his trousers, I notice that he "dresses" on the wrong side. He dresses, as tailors say, on the right, which not one American male in a thousand, ask any tailor, does. In fact, American pants are made for left-dressing. A small oddity, true, but slightly discommoding to the observer, like talking to a cross-eyed man.

"Well, Doc," says Art, turning on the hot water, "have you thought about our little proposition?"

"It's out of the question."

"May I ask why?"

"I wouldn't want my invention to fall into the wrong hands. It could be quite dangerous."

"Don't you trust the National Institute of Mental Health and the Ford, Carnegie, and Rockefeller foundations?"

"No. Besides, my invention is not perfected yet. I haven't finished with it."

"What's not perfected?" Art bends his knees, mambo style,

and combs his hair like a sailor with quick alternating strokes of comb and hand.

"My sensors won't penetrate melanin pigment in the skin."

"Hm." Art wets his comb. "You mean your MOQUOL doesn't work on darkies?"

"No, it doesn't." I look at him with surprise. Darkies?!

"Anything else wrong?"

"Yes. I don't yet have a therapeutic component. As it stands, my device is a diagnostic tool, no more."

"I know." Art goes on riffling his flat-top with a wet comb. Is he trying to make it lie down? Some hairs stick up like a wet airdale's. "What would you say, Doc, if I told you your invention has the capacities and is incremental for both components?"

"Eh?"

"That the solution to both the melanin problem and the therapeutic problem is under your nose."

"Where?"

Art laughs. "You know all I'm good for, Doc? I'm a coordinator. You've got the big ideas. I'm a tinkerer. In fact, I've got a little gadget right here that would fit your device—"

"Excuse me. I'm late. I've got to—"

"We'd make a team, Doc! All you've got to do is sign the funding application!"

"No."

But we say goodbye and shake hands agreeably enough. His is curiously inert, as if all he knew about shaking hands he had learned from watching others shake hands. A heavy smell of sweat neutralized by deodorant pushes to my nostrils.

Art holds my hand a second too long. "Doc. Just in case anything should go wrong, I'll be around."

"What could go wrong?"

"Just in case!"

As I leave him, he opens his attaché case on the window-sill. He looks like a traveling salesman doing business in the post office.

My hour of triumph is at hand.

3

In the outer office of the Director the typists do not look up, but the secretary is pleasant. She nods toward a bench.

There are no staff members present. A row of patients, dressed in the familiar string robes of the wards, sit on the bench, hands on their knees. They look at me without expression. There is no place to sit but the bench.

Quite correct of the Director not to make a fuss! Yet it is an annoyance when one of the patients is called before me. I do not mind. The encounter with Art Immelmann has left me thoughtful. Was he trying to tell me something?

When my turn does come, the Director greets me warmly, if somewhat vaguely, at the door. The first thing I catch sight of over his shoulder is—yes!—my *Brain* article and my lapsometer lined up side by side on his desk.

"You are very imaginative!" cries the Director, waving me to a chair opposite him.

"Thank you." What does he mean?

The Director is a tough old party, a lean leathery emeritus behaviorist with a white thatch and a single caliper crease in his withered brown cheek. Though he is reputed to have a cancer in his lung that is getting the better of him, one can easily believe that the growth is feeding on his nonvital parts, fats and body liquors, leaving the man himself worn fine and dusty and durable as Don Quixote. The only sign of his illness is a fruity cough and his handkerchiefs, which he uses expertly, folding them flat as a napkin over his sputum and popping them up his sleeve or into the slits of his white coat.

Though he is a behaviorist and accordingly not well disposed to such new ideas as an "ontological lapsometer," I take heart from two circumstances: one, that he is an honorable man of science and as such knows evidence when he sees it; two, that he is dying. A dying king, said Sir Thomas More, is apt to be wiser than a healthy king. A dying behaviorist may be a good behaviorist.

The Director coughs his fruity cough. His eyes bulge. Handkerchiefs pop in and out of his pockets.

"With your permission, Tom, we're going to do a feature about your project in the *Rehab Weekly*."

"The *Rehab Weekly?*"

"Yes. We think you've shown a great deal of imgination."

"Sir, the *Rehab Weekly* is the patients' mimeographed magazine."

"I know," says the Director, his eyes bulging amiably.

The unease that has been flickering up and down my spine

turns into a pool of heat in the hollow of my neck. Strange, but I feel only a mild embarrassment for him.

"Sir," I say presently. "Perhaps you have misunderstood me. You say there are plans to do a feature on my work in the *Rehab Weekly*. Very good. But the reason I submitted my article to you was to obtain your approval and support before submitting it to *Brain*."

"Yes, I know," says the Director, coughing.

"It is also necessary to obtain your sanction of my application to N.I.M.H. for funding."

"Yes. In the amount of—" The Director is leafing through —not my proposal but my medical chart!

"Twenty-five million," I say, blushing furiously. Why am I so embarrassed? What is shameful about twenty-five million?

"I see." The Director lays his head over, eyes bulging thoughtfully. "You are on patient-staff status."

"Technically, but—"

"Doctor, don't you think that before launching such a ah major undertaking, it might be well to wait until you are discharged?"

"Discharged?"

He slides the chart across the desk. "According to our records you are still a patient on A-4, which means that though you perform staff duties, you have not yet reached an open ward."

I find myself nodding respectfully, hands on my knees— like a patient! I blink at my trousers. Where is my string robe?

"Sir, I left the hospital five months ago."

"Left?" The glossy eyes bulge, the pages flip past. He's lost me somewhere in the chart. "Here. You're still on A-4."

"No sir."

"You're still on patient-staff status."

"Yes sir, technically."

"I remember that. It is the first time in my experience that a doctor-patient on A-4 has ever been put on patient-staff. Remarkable. We have great respect for your abilities, Doctor. Let's see, you're in encephalography with Dr. Wilkes. How is it going?"

"I was with Colley Wilkes. Five months ago."

"I noticed today you're down for The Pit, heh heh heh. I saw you once before, Doctor. Great, heh heh heh. What'll it be today, high medicine or hijinks or both? You know, Doctor, if you could ever get on top of your mood swings, you have a real contribution to make. Hm"—again poking through the chart—"too bad the Skinner box didn't do more for the anxiety and elation-depression. I wonder if we hadn't better get on with implanting electrodes—"

"Sir, excuse me. I believe I understand. Rather, there is a misunderstanding. You are under the impression that I am here as a patient, together with the other patients outside, for my monthly visit with you. Right, I'd forgotten, Monday is patient day."

"That reminds me." He consults his watch. "I fear we're running a bit over. But don't worry about it. Always glad to see you. I predict you'll soon make A-3 and permanent staff. For the time being, hang in right where you are."

"With Colley Wilkes."

"Tremendous fellow! A renaissance man."

We rise. There lying on the desk between us like a dog turd is my lapsometer. I can't bear to look at it. Neither can the Director.

"But, sir—"

"Dr. More, tell me the truth."

"Yes sir."

"Do you think you are well?"

"No sir, I'm not well."

"Well—?" He spreads his hands.

My God, he's right. $25,000,000. An ontological lapsometer. I'm mad as a hatter.

But the Director suddenly feels so much better that in an access of goodwill he does look at my machine and even gives it a poke with his pencil.

"Amazing! What workmanship. Say, why don't you use it in The Pit today, heh heh heh. Where did you get it machined?"

"In Japan," I say absently. "You remember Dr. Yamaiuchi."

"The Japanese are amazing, aren't they?"

We reflect on the recent excellence of Japanese workmanship.

"What do you call this thing, Doctor?" the Director asks, exploring the device with his pencil.

"Lapsometer." I am unable to tear my eyes from his strong brown farmer's hands.

"The name interests me."

"Yes sir?"

"It implies, I take it, a lapse or fall."

"Yes," I say tonelessly.

"A fall perhaps from a state of innocence?"

"Perhaps." My foot begins to wag briskly. I stop it.

"Does this measure the uh depth of the fall?"

I stand up.

"Sir?"

"Yes, Doctor?"

"Am I to understand then that you do not intend either to approve my article for *Brain* or my application for funding from N.I.M.H.?"

"We'll cross that bridge at our next month's meeting. Right now I'm more interested in the hijinks in The Pit, heh heh. And don't worry about being on A-4 much longer. I believe you're ready for A-3. Glad to have you aboard. You've no idea how hard it is to keep staff these days. Now back at the old hospital in Boston—"

"Sir?"

"Yes?"

"There is one thing I don't understand."

"What's that?" I've gone past my ten minutes. His glossy eyes bulge at his watch.

"Why did you tell Art Immelmann you had approved my application?"

"Who?"

"Art Immelmann."

"I never heard of him."

"He's a liaison man between N.I.M.H. and the funds."

"Oh my, one of those fellows. They're bad news. They all say the same things: the war in Ecuador has dried up the money."

"He says Ford, Carnegie, and Rockefeller are willing to fund me."

"Good!" He doesn't believe me.

"But you don't know him?"

"I steer clear of those fellows!" For some reason the Director laughs immoderately, which in turn sets him off into a fit of coughing.

"Then you've told no one about my invention or article?"

Handkerchiefs pop in and out. The Director, still red-faced, shakes his head and gazes past me. He has other patients!

The next patient passes me in the doorway, a sorrowful

angry man in a string robe who stares at me furiously, tapping his watch with trembling forefinger. His cheek quivers with rage. I've encroached upon his time. Rage shakes him like a terrier. I recall being possessed by this demon. Once, after brooding two days over a remark made by a fellow patient, I walked up to him with clenched fists. "I resent that remark you made two days ago. In fact, I can't stand it any longer. Take it back!" "O.K.," said the startled man and took it back.

## 4

My feet shuffle past the elevators, my hands groping for the pockets of my string robe.

Where am I going? Back to the wards?

The center is not holding.

Where am I going? Back to my narrow bed on A-4 with its hard mattress and seersucker spread stretched tight as a drum, a magic carpet where I can lie and wing it like a martin.

Why is it I feel better, see more clearly, can help more people when I am crazy? Not being crazy, being sane in a sane world, is the craziest business of all.

What I really want to do is practice medicine from my bed in A-4, lie happy and stiff on my bed, like a Hindoo on his bed of nails, and treat sane folk and sane doctors from the sane world, which is the maddest world of all.

Where am I? Going past Love. On the bench in the hall sit volunteers J. T. Thigpen and Gloria and Ted 'n Tanya. J. T. strokes his acne with his fingernails. Gloria reads a textbook open on her plump thighs. Through the diamond-shaped window I catch a glimpse of Father Kev Kevin reading *Commonweal* at the vaginal console.

"See you Wednesday!" whispers Ted.

"What's that? Oh."

On the lower level Buddy Brown and Moira are standing next to Mr. Ives in a wheelchair. Moira hangs her head. Buddy greets me with the cordiality of a good enemy.

"You're just in time, Tom!"

"In time for what?"

"To give Mr. Ives the once-over. Be my guest."

"No thanks."

"Look at this." Taking a reflex hammer from his pocket, he taps Mr. Ives's knee tendon with quick deft taps.

Mr. Ives dances a regular jig in his chair, all the while watching me with his mild blue gaze.

"Isn't that upper-motor-neurone damage, Doctor?" Buddy asks me.

"I don't think so."

"Try it yourself." He hands me his hammer, a splendid affair with a glittering shaft and a tomahawk head of red rubber.

"No fanks."

"What? Oh. Then I'll see you shortly."

"Fime."

I do not speak well. I've lost. I'm a patient. But Buddy doesn't notice. Like all enemies, he puts the best construction on his opponent. But Moira knows something is wrong. She hangs her head.

"Is something wrong?" she asks in a low voice.

"I'm fime." I notice that they are waiting outside the tunnel that leads into The Pit from the lower level.

"Don't forget Howard," says Moira.

"Who? Oh." Howard Johnson. "Nopes."

"Who is Howard?" Buddy asks.

"We can go now," whispers Moira. She sees the abyss and is willing to save me.

"When will you come in?" asks Buddy.

"Eins upon a oncy," I reply.

"O.K. *Eins zwei drei*," says Buddy, willing to give me the benefit of the doubt. "He's going to the men's room," he tells Moira, trying to make sense of me.

"Rike," I say.

"Rotsa ruck."


5

So I go back to the men's room.

At the washstand there is a step behind me. A familiar smell of sebum-sweat overlaid by unguents.

"Hello, Art." Where did he come from? He must live in a cubicle. Now he's wearing a tie and jacket, as if he were dressed for an occasion. But where did he get the tie and jacket? I take a closer look in the mirror. It is a tight gabardine "bi-swing" jacket, a style popular many years ago, with little plackets under each shoulder.

"How does it go, Doc?"

"Not so good."

"Win a few, lose a few, eh?"

"What? Yes."

I am gazing at my face in the mirror intently, like the man in Saint James's epistle. The image reverses on the retina and a hole opens. Removing the bottle of Early Times from my bag, I take two long pulls."

"Where to now, Doc?"

"I don't know. Back to A-4."

"As a patient."

"I suppose."

"Do you give up easily?"

I shrug.

"What about our little proposition?"

"What proposition?"

"Let me see your MOQUOL."

"Gladly." Taking the device from my bag, I loft it toward the used-towel bin.

Art intercepts it, rubs it on his shirt front like a street urchin finding a dime.

"You got to have faith, Doc."

"Faith?"

"Listen to me for a minute."

"Why?"

"Sit here." Taking my arm, he leads me to the shoeshine chair. I sit on the platform. Art hops up to the throne and fits his shoes to the treadles. The whiskey catches hold in my stomach like a gear. I feel better, engaged.

"And to make matters worse," says Art cheerfully, "somebody's beating your time with your girl." Beating my time. I haven't heard that expression since childhood.

"What do you want?" I ask him, slumping around the pleasant engaged gear in my stomach.

"To show you something." He hops over me, fumbles in his attaché case, which still lies open on the windowsill. It is a short barrel, like a telephoto lens, fitted with an adapter ring. He screws it onto my lapsometer.

"Life is funny, Doc."

"It is."

"There is such a thing as being too close to the woods to see the trees."

"What is that thing?"

"It's really your discovery. The principle is yours. This is just a bit of tinkering. If you want to give me credit in a footnote, ha ha—"

"What's it for?"

"Doc, the trouble with your invention has always been that you could diagnose but not treat, right?"

"That's right."

"Now you can treat." He tosses me the lapsometer.

"How's that?"

"Don't you know? You discovered it twenty years ago."

"What—"

A behaviorist comes in to take a leak. Art begins combing his hair again, wetting his comb and bending his knees mambo-style. The behaviorist washes his hands, nods at me, and leaves. Art hops nimbly up into the shoeshine chair.

"Doc, you recall that you discovered the effects of Heavy Sodium fallout?"

"Yes." I am wondering: if two drinks of Early Times makes me feel good, wouldn't three drinks make me feel better?

"You had the answer. Don't you see?"

"See what?"

The possibility of treating personality disorders with Heavy Sodium and Chloride."

"That would be like exploding a cobalt bomb over New Orleans to treat cancer."

"That's the point. How do you treat cancer with cobalt radiation?"

"I've thought of that. But you know, of course, that sodium radiation is a two-edged sword. In the same moment that you assuage frontal terror you might increase red-nucleus rage."

"Exactly!" Art's feet fairly dance on the treadles above my head. "And you of all people should know how to avoid that."

"How?"

"With this."

"What is that?"

"A differential stereotatic emission ionizer. Beams in either your Heavy Sodium or Chloride ion. Using your principle."

"How?"

"Don't you see? You don't even move your MOQUOL. Say you take a reading at the red nucleus and find a plus-five milli-volt pathology. All you do is swing your dial to a minus-five Chloride charge and ionize."

"And what will that do?"

"Tranquilize red-nucleus rage."

"Sure."

"You don't believe me? Where are you going?"

"To get a drink."

"That's the point, Doc. Drink this drink and you'll never want a drink. Let me show you something."

"What?"

"Sit down here."

As I sit on the lower platform, Art holds the machine to my head. It feels like barber's clippers.

"Now. Using your diagnostic circuit, I observe that you are registering a plus-three on the anxiety scale. A little high but not unusual considering the pace of modern living. Now suppose I keep the MOQUOL in place and switch over to a plus-two ion emission. You should feel a bit worse."

The machine hums like a tuning fork against my head.

I begin to shiver. My shoulders are rounded and I am gazing at my hands clenched in my lap. At last I raise my eyes. A horrid white light streams through the frosted window and falls into the glittering porcelain basins of the urinals. It is the Terror, but tolerable. The urinals, which are the wall variety, are shaped like skulls. The dripping water sounds hollow like water at the bottom of a well.

"Now. We'll reverse and give you a minus-seven Chloride dose, which should throw you over into minus-two anti-anxiety."

My head is leaning against the metal support of the treadle. Again the machine hums.

When I open my eyes, I am conscious first of breathing. Something in my diaphragm lets go. I realize I've been breathing at the top of my lungs for forty-five years. Now my diaphragm moves like a piston into my viscera, pulling great drafts of air into the base of my lungs.

Next I become aware of the cool metal of the support against my neck.

Then I notice my hand clenched into a fist on my knee. I open it slowly, turning it this way and that, inspecting every pore and crease. What a beautiful strong hand! The tendons! The bones! But the hand of a stranger! I have never seen it before.

How can a man spend forty-five years as a stranger to himself? No other creature would do such a thing. No animal would, for he is pure organism. No angel would, for he is pure spirit.

"Feeling better, Doc?"

"Yes."

"It's quite a device, isn't it?"

"Yes."

"And the Director doesn't appreciate it, does he?"

"No."

"Now." Art is at my head again, fiddling about, pressing bony protuberances, measuring salients of my skull with a cold metal centimeter scale. It feels good to be measured. "I'm going to show you something I think will interest you. I'm going to stimulate Brodmann 11 mildly. You know what that is?"

"Yes, but I'd like to hear what you think it is."

"It lies in the frontal-temporal sulcus of course, betwixt and between the abstractive areas of the frontal and the concrete auditory radiation of the frontal. It is the area of the musical-erotic."

"Hm, that's not my terminology."

"But you know what I mean. Here the abstract is experienced concretely and the concrete abstractly. Take women, for example. Here one neither loves a woman individually, for herself and no other, faithfully; nor does one love a woman organically as a dog loves a bitch. No, one loves a woman both in herself and insofar as she is a woman, a member of the class women. Conversely, one loves women not in the abstract but in a particular example, this woman. Loves her truly, moreover. One loves faithlessly but truly."

"Truly?"

"Loves her as one loves music. A woman is the concrete experienced abstractly, as women. Music is the abstract experienced as the concrete, namely sound."

"So?"

"Ha! Old stuff to you, eh, Doc? Well, that's not the end of it. Don't you see? Stimulate this area and you stimulate both the scientist and the lover but neither at the expense of the other. You stimulate the scientist-lover."

"I see."

But it is Art himself who interests me. How does Art, who looks like the sort of fellow who used to service condom vendors in the old Auto Age, know this?

"So that in the same moment one becomes victorious in

science one also becomes victorious in love. And all for the good of mankind! Science to help all men and a happy joyous love to help women. We are speaking here of happiness, joy, music, spontaneity, you understand. Fortunately we have put behind us such unhappy things as pure versus impure love, sin versus virtue, and so forth. This love has its counterpart in scientific knowledge: it is neutral morally, abstractive and godlike—"

"Godlike?"

"In the sense of being like a god in one's freedom and omniscience."

"You surprise me, Art."

"Hold still, Doc."

Again the cold steel hums like a tuning fork against my skull.

The tone of the tuning fork turns into music: first, a plaintive little piping, the dance of happy spirits in a high meadow; the flute trips along, hesitates, picks up again, and here's the beauty of it, in the catch, the stutter, and starting up again. Now comes the love music of man in particular for women in general: happy, faithless, seductive music: the race and rip of violins dancing, whipping, tricking, fizzing in a froth of May wine, sunshine sunshine, and cotton dresses in summertime.

Who am I?

I am he who loves. I am in love. I love.

Who do you love?

You.

Who is "you?"

A girl.

What girl?

Any girl you please. You.

How can that be?

Because all girls are lovable and I love them. I love you. I can make you happy and you me.

Only one thing can make you happy and it is not that.

Love makes me happy. Knowing makes me happy.

Love is God, bcause God is love. Knowing God is knowing all things.

Love is not God. Love is music.

"Who are you talking to, Doc?"

"What?"

"Why don't you sit down?"

"What was I doing?"

"It doesn't matter, as long as you feel good."

Art pushes up the frosted window. We gaze out into the gold-green. Fat white clouds are blown by map winds. Swallows dip. Cicadas go *zreeeee*.

"You look good, Doc. Look at yourself. You're not a bad-looking guy. You're still young, you got a good build if you took care of yourself. Here, wash your face in cold water and comb your hair." He hands me his pocket comb. "Now, no need to look like a hairy elf." In a flash he produces a pocket klipette, clips the hair in my nose, ears, and eyebrows. "Tch, your fingernails!"—and gives me a manicure on the spot. In two minutes my nails become glossy watchglasses like Buddy Brown's. Art comes close and sniffs: "Pardon, Doc, but you're a little high, you know. Here's a man's deodorant. Now!"

Art gazes at me. I gaze at the gold-green summer.

"How do you feel, Doc?"

"Fine."

"Isn't it better to feel good rather than bad?"

"Yes."

"Isn't it better to be happy than unhappy?"

"Yes."

"How can you take care of unhappy patients if you are unhappier than they are? Physician, heal thyself."

"Yes."

"Your terror is gone, you're breathing well, your large bowel should be slack as a string, clear as a bell. How is it?"

"Slack as a string, clear as a bell."

"O.K., Doc, now what?"

"I don't know. What?"

"Well, what is the purpose of life in a democratic society?"

"A democratic society?" I ask him, smiling.

"Sure. Isn't it for each man to develop his potential to the fullest?"

"I suppose so."

"What is your potential?"

"I don't know, what?"

"Doc, you have two great potentials: a first-class mind and a heart full of love."

"Yes."

"So what do you do with them?"

"I don't know, what?"

"Know and love, what else?"

"Yes."

"And win at both."

"Win?"

"Is there anything wrong with being victorious and happy? With curing patients, advancing science, loving women and making them happy?"

"No."

"Use your talents, Doc. What do you know how to do?"

"I know how to use this." I pick up the lapsometer.

"What can you do with that?"

"Make people happy."

"Who do you love, Doc?"

"Women, knowing, music, and Early Times."

"You're all set, Doc. One last thing—"

"Yes?"

"Where is your crate of MOQUOLs?"

"In a safe place."

"Let me have them. The situation is critical and I think we ought to get them in the right hands as soon as possible."

"No. I'd better not. That is not part of our contract."

"Why not?"

"There are dangers. I can't be too careful."

"What dangers?"

"Physical and political dangers."

"What do you mean?"

"I think you know what I mean. If one of these falls into the wrong hands, it could produce a chain reaction in the Heavy Sodium deposits hereabouts or a political explosion between the Knotheads and the Lefts. Do you realize that the President and Vice-President will be here tomorrow?"

"Realize it! Why do you think I want your MOQUOLs?" Coming close, he opens and closes his wallet, giving me a glimpse of a metal shield.

"F.B.I.?"

"A bit more exalted. Let's just say I make security reports from time to time. That's why we're interested in making sure your invention stays in the right hands."

"This seems a bit far afield from your work with mental health and foundations."

"Everything is interdisciplinary now, Doc. As well as being third-generational. You understand."

"No. But don't worry about my invention."

"O.K., Doc. Now. Sign here." He nods to the contract on

the windowsill. A ballpoint pen leaps to his hand, clicks, and backs toward my chest.

"Very well." Standing at the windowsill, which seems to be his place of business, I sign the blue-jacketed contract.

"You won't be sorry, Doc." All in one motion he takes pen and contract, clicks pen, stuffs both into his inside breast pocket. As usual, he stands too close and when he buttons his coat it exhales a heavy breath. "Now you can use your talents for the good of mankind and the increase of knowledge. All you have to do is never look back and never be sorry, as per agreement."

"As per what agreement?" I ask vaguely, frowning. But my colon is at peace and my heart beats in time to Mozart.

"We're in business, Doc."

"Yeah. Let's have a drink."

"What? Oh. Well—"

The bottle of Early Times passes between us. The whiskey catches hold in my stomach, gear engaging gear. Art chokes, his eyes water.

"That's good stuff," says Art, blinking. I could swear it was his first drink.

"Yes," I say, laughing.

It's like being back in Charlottesville, in the spring, in the men's room, at a dance, at old Saint Anthony's Hall.


6

The Pit is in an uproar. Students roost like chickens along the steep slopes of the amphitheater, cackling and fluttering their white jackets as they argue about the day's case. Bets are placed, doctors attacked and defended. The rightwing Knot-head Christian students occupy the right benches, the Lefts the left.

The lower reaches are reserved for professors, residents, consultants, and visiting physicians. The Director, for example, sits in the front row, elbows propped on the high retaining wall, next to his fellow Nobel laureate Dr. Kenneth Stryker, who first described the branny cruciform rash of love. Gottlieb is directly behind them, erect as a young prince, light glancing from his forehead. His eyes search mine with a questing puzzled glance, seeking to convey a meaning, but I do not take the meaning. In the same row sit Dr. Helga Heine, the West

German interpersonal gynecologist; Colley Wilkes, the super-Negro encephalographer and his wife, Fran, a light-colored behaviorist and bird-watcher; Ted 'n Tanya and two visiting proctologists from Paradise: my old friend Dr. Dusty Rhoades and Dr. Walter Bung, an extremely conservative albeit skillful proctologist recently removed from Birmingham.

The pit itself, a sunken area half the size of a handball court and enclosed by a high curving wall, is empty save for Dr. Buddy Brown, the patient, Mr. Ives, in a wheelchair, and behind him a strapping blond nurse named Winnie Gunn, whose stockings are rolled beneath her knees. Where is Moira? Ah, I see: sitting almost out of sight in the approach tunnel with no more of her visible than her beautiful gunmetal legs. Is she avoiding me?

I enter not through the tunnel but from the top, walking down the steep aisle like a relief pitcher beginning the long trek from the left-field bullpen. As I come abreast of successive rows of students, there occurs on the left a cutting away of eyes and the ironic expression of the fan confronted by the unfavorite. These are by and large Buddy's fans and mostly qualitarians ( = euthanasists).

From here and there on the right comes a muted cheer, a vigorous nodding and lively corroborative look from some student who remembers my small triumph and imagines that he and I share the same convictions.

I don't pay much attention to left or right.

Students are, if the truth be known, a bad lot. En masse they're as fickle as a mob, manipulable by any professor who'll stoop to it. They have, moreover, an infinite capacity for repeating dull truths and old lies with all the insistence of self-discovery. Nothing is drearier than the ideology of students, left or right. Half the students here revere Dr. Spiro T. Agnew, elder statesman and the honorary president of the American Christian Proctological Society; the other half admire Hermann Hesse, Dr. B. F. Skinner, inventor of the Skinner conditioning box, and the late Justice William O. Douglas, a famous qualitarian who improved the quality of life in India by serving as adviser in a successful program of 100,000,000 abortions and an equal number of painless "terminations" of miserable and unproductive old folk.

People talk a lot about how great "the kids" are, compared to kids in the past. The only difference in my opinion is that kids now don't have sense enough to know what they don't know.

On the other hand, my generation is an even bigger pain.

It seems today in The Pit I am favored by the Christian Knothead antieuthanasic faction, but I'm not sure I like them any better than the Hesse-Skinner-Douglas qualitarians.

But I do not, on the whole, feel bad. My large bowel is clear as a bell, my coeliac plexus is full of blood. Anxiety flickers over my sacrum but it is not the Terror, rather a useful and commensurate edginess. What I fear is not nothing, which is the Terror, but something, namely, getting beat by Buddy Brown in front of Moira. Otherwise I feel fine: my heart is full of love, my mind is like a meat grinder ready to receive the raw stuff of experience and turn out neat pattycake principles.

The thing to do, it occurs to me halfway down into the pit, is to concern myself with the patient and what ails him, and forget the rest.

In the pit itself a casual air is cultivated. Mr. Ives's bright monkey eyes snap at me. Buddy Brown leans against the high wall talking to the Director, who hangs over, cupping an ear. Nurse Winnie Gunn, who stands behind the wheelchair, gives me a big smile and shifts her weight, canting her pelvis six degrees starboard. Moira? Her face swims in the darkness of the tunnel. Are her eyes open or closed?

The uproar resumes. The doctors are free to unhorse each other by any means fair or foul. The students are free to boo or cheer. Last month one poor fellow, a psychiatrist who had diagnosed a case as paranoia, was routed and damned out of his own mouth, like Captain Queeg, by Buddy Brown, who led the man to the point of admitting that yes, he was convinced that all the students and the faculty as well had it in for him and were out to get him. Jeers from the students, right and left, who have no use for weakness in their elders.

The door opens at the top and in strolls Art Immelmann and perches in the back row. In the same row but not close sit two women. The two women are—good Lord!—my two women, Lola Rhoades and Ellen Oglethorpe. What are they doing together?

There is no time to speculate. The uproar subsides and Buddy Brown begins, flipping through the chart held above Mr. Ives, who sits slumped in his string robe, head jogging peacefully, monkey eyes gone blank for once and fixed on the wall in front of him.

Buddy presents the medical history, physical examination, and laboratory findings. He stands at his ease, looking fondly at Mr. Ives.

"My differential diagnosis: advanced atherosclerosis, senile psychosis, psychopathic and antisocial behavior, hemiplegia and aphasia following a cerebrovascular accident."

Murmurs and nods from the students.

"Doctor." With a flourish Buddy hands me the chart.

The Early Times is turning like a gear in my stomach. I am looking at my hand again. What a hand.

"Doctor?"

"Yes. Oh. By the way, Dr. Brown. You made no therapeutic recommendations."

Buddy spreads his fingers wide, shrugs an exaggerated Gallic shrug (he is part Cajun and comes from Thibodeaux).

"You have no recommendations?"

"Do you, Dr. More?"

"Then you plan to transfer him?"

"Yes."

"Where?"

"To the Happy Isles Separation Center."

This is what the students have been waiting for.

"Euphoric Switch! Euphoric Switch!" cry the euthanasists.

"Button! Button!" cry the right-benchers. "Not to Georgia!"

"Where would you send him, Doctor?" asks Buddy sarcastically.

The heavy warm gear is turning in my stomach. My hand is the hand of a stranger. Music is still playing. I must have swayed to the music because Winnie Gunn has seized my forearm with both hands.

"Are you all right, Doctor?" she whispers.

"Fine."

"We are still waiting for your diagnosis, Dr. More," says Buddy with the gentleness of victory.

"I found no significant pathology."

"Louder!" from the back benches. The Director cups his ear.

"I said I found no significant pathology."

"No significant pathology," says Buddy as gently as Perry Mason beating Hamilton Burger for the thousandth time. "And what is your recommendation, Doctor?"

"Discharge him."

"Discharge him," repeats Buddy. "He can't walk or talk, and if he could, he would presumably return to his former atrocious behavior. And yet you want to discharge him. As cured, Doctor?"

"If indeed there was anything wrong with him."

"You think there was nothing wrong with him?"

"No. That is, yes."

"Then what's he doing here in a wheelchair?"

Titters.

I shrug.

"Dr. More, what do you think his chances are of recovering from his stroke?"

"You mean, assuming he's had one."

"Very well. Assuming he's had one."

"Very small."

"And if he did recover, what are the chances he'd return to his former mode of behavior?"

"Very large."

"Do you recall his former behavior?"

I am silent.

"Allow me to refresh your memory, Doctor." Again Buddy flips through the chart. "These," he explains to the amphitheater, "are progress reports during the last year of the patient's residence at the Golden Years Senior Citizen Settlement in Tampa. I quote:

"'The subject has not only refused to participate in the various recreational, educational, creative, and group activities but has on occasion engaged in antisocial and disruptive behavior. He refused: shuffleboard tournament, senior softball, Golden Years gymkhana, papa putt-putt, donkey baseball, Guys and Gals à go-go, the redfish rodeo, and granddaddy golf. He refused: free trip to Los Angeles to participate in Art Linkletter III's "the young-olds," even though chosen for this trip by his own community.

"'Did on two occasions defecate on Flirtation Walk during the Merry Widow's promenade.

"'Did on occasion of the Ohio Day breakfast during the period of well-wishing and when the microphone was passed to him utter gross insults and obscenities to Ohioans, among the mildest of which was the expression, repeated many times: piss on all Ohioans!

"'Did in fact urinate on Ohio in the Garden of the Fifty States.

"'Was observed by his neighbors on Bide-a-wee Bayou to be digging furiously with a spade on the patio putt-putt, defacing same. When asked what he was digging for, he replied: the fountain of youth.'"

More titters from the student roosts.

Buddy goes on:

"'Despite extensive reconditioning in the Skinner box, the patient continued to exhibit antisocial behavior. This behavior,'" Buddy hastens to add, "'occurred before his stroke last month.'"

"If he had a stroke," I say.

"If he had a stroke," Buddy allows gravely. "Well, Doctor?"

"Well what?"

"What would you do with him?"

"Discharge him."

"To suffer another thirty years?" asks Buddy, smiling. "To cause other people suffering?"

"At least he'd have a sporting chance."

"A sporting chance to do what?"

"To avoid your packing him off to Georgia, where they'd sink electrodes in his head, plant him like a carrot in that hothouse which is nothing more than an anteroom to the funeral parlor. Then throw the Euphoric Switch—"

"Doctor!" interrupts the Director sternly.

"Aaah!" The students blush at the word *funeral*. Girls try to pull their dresses down over their knees.

Buddy flushes angrily.

The Director is angrier still.

"Doctor!" He levels a quivering finger at me, then crooks it, summoning me. Craning down, he croaks into my ear. "You know very well that the patient is present and that there is no guarantee that he cannot understand you."

"Excuse me, sir, but I hope—indeed I have reason to believe—that he does understand me."

The Director goes off into a fit of coughing. His eyes bulge glassily. Handerkerchiefs fly in and out of plackets in his coat. The students are in an uproar. Cheers from the Knotheads, boos from the Lefts.

"This is too much!" The Director throws up both hands. Now he's grabbed me, hooked me with his claws like the ancient mariner. "It's my mistake, Doctor," he croaks. "My putting you on patient-staff status. I beg your pardon. It is only too clear that your illness does not yet permit you to function."

"I can function, sir," I tell him, speaking into his great hairy convoluted ear. "You'll see."

"Be careful, Doctor!" The powerful old hands squeeze my arm by way of warning. "Proceed!"

Mr. Ives's bright monkey eyes have begun to snap again.

"I repeat," I say to the back rows. "If Mr. Ives is going to be referred to the Happy Isles of Georgia, which is nothing but a euthanasia facility, he has the right to know it and to prepare himself accordingly. And he has the right to know who his executioner is."

"I warned you, Doctor!" The Director is on his feet and shouting. "Perhaps you'd better go back to the ward, to A-4."

"Yes sir," I say. Perhaps he is right.

The students, struck dumb, gaze at me, gaze at each other. "Sir!"

It is Buddy, advancing toward me, hands clasped behind his back. He holds one hand up to quiet the uproar. The other hand is still behind him. "Sir!"—to the Director, in a loud voice. "I submit to you, sir, that you are mistaken!"

"Eh?" The Director cups his ear.

"Sir, you do an injustice both to Dr. More as well as to your own clinical judgment!"

"Eh? How's that?"

"Your first decision about Dr. More was quite correct. Your confidence in him is not misplaced. His illness does not in the least interfere with his functioning. In short, sir, I submit to you that his odd behavior today cannot be laid to his illness at all. The truth is—" Buddy, quick as a cat, steps behind me, embraces me with one arm, with the other hidden hand claps a mask over my face. His grip is like iron. There is nothing to do but squirm and, at length, gasp for breath. Three, four, five seconds and Buddy flings one arm up like a cowboy bulldogging a steer. He holds the dial aloft for all to see, presents it to the Director like the bull's ears. "Point three percent ethyl alcohol. The truth is Dr. More is drunk as a lord!"

Relieved laughter from the students—along with the gasps. At least they recognize a familiar note of buffoonery.

Even the Director looks relieved despite himself.

"Fun is fun," he announces to no one in particular. "But The Pit may be getting out of hand."

Moira has shrunk even farther into the tunnel.

Unbuckling my physician's bag, I take out my modified lapsometer. Buddy makes way for me, giving my arm a friendly squeeze, handing me on to the patient with a reassuring smile. *You see*, his smile tells the students, *it's all in the spirit of The Pit. Dr. More and I are not mad at each other.*

"Your patient, Doctor." Your witness, Mr. Burger. Twenty years and Ham Burger never won a case.

"Thank you, Doctor, but I don't want the patient. I want you."

A beehive murmur. Buddy holds up both hands.

"It's all right!" he cries, smiling. "Turnabout is fair play. Dr. More is going to diagnose me. Why not? He is going to measure, not my blood alcohol, but my metaphysical status. The device he holds there—correct me if I'm wrong, Doctor—is the More Quantitative-Qualitative Ontological Lapsometer."

Laughter from the left.

"Qualitative-Quantitative." I correct him.

More laughter from the left. Consternation from the right benches. Stony stares from my colleagues. But the Director's glossy eyes bulge amiably—at least he is relieved to see the tone change to the acceptable medical-farcical.

Moira is all but invisible. Have I lost her?

"Be my guest, Doctor," says Buddy, presenting his bald brown crown to me.

With Buddy standing at ironic attention, arms folded, I do a quick diagnostic pass from cortex to brain stem. Over the top of his head I catch a glimpse of Dr. Helga Heine's bare thighs crossed on the aisle, and far above in the shadows, Art Immelmann, who is standing like a bailiff in front of the swinging doors. Working up Buddy's brain stem now, I focus moderate inhibitory dosages over the frontal cerebrum and, letting it go at that, step back. It is enough, I calculate, to inhibit the inhibitory centers and let Buddy be what he is.

Buddy does not move. "Is that all, Doctor?" he asks in his broad stage voice. "How is my metaphysical ontology? Or is it my ontological metaphysics?"

Giggles. I wait. Silence. Throats are cleared. Could I be mistaken?

Again the Director stirs restlessly. Our crude theatrics don't bother him as much as my silence.

"Doctor," he begins patiently and coughs his fruity cough. "Please get on with it."

Helga uncrosses her thighs.

"Doctor, I really think that unless—" says the Director, eyes bulging with alarm.

"I see Christmas," says Buddy, peering up Helga's dress.

"What's that?" asks the Director, leaning forward.

"I see Christmas."

"What did he say?" the Director asks Max, cupping an ear. Max shrugs.

"Nurse!" cries the Director sternly. "This is too much. Remove the patient. What's wrong with that woman?" he asks Max, for now Winnie Gunn is standing transfixed at the tunnel entrance. Try as she might, she can't tear her eyes from Buddy Brown, who has swung around to face her.

"Nothing wrong with Winnie," Buddy tells me, winking and giving me an elbow in the ribs. "You know what they say about the great white whale: thar she blows, but not the first night out."

"Eh?" says the Director.

"Not so loud," I tell Buddy uneasily. It is not clear how much the students, who are gaping and shushing each other, can hear.

But Buddy pays no attention. He flexes his elbow in a vulgar Cajun gesture, forearm straight up. "*Voilà*! Eh, Winnie?"

Uproar among the students. The doctors blink at each other. Only Art Immelmann sees nothing amiss. Somehow, even though I don't watch him, his every movement makes itself known to me. He hawks and swallows and adjusts his uncomfortable right-dressed pants leg. Now he steps through the swinging doors and drags in a carton. My lapsometers! How did he get hold of them?

"Look at the leg of that woman," says Buddy and makes another crude Cajun gesture, common on the bayous. "*Ça va*! What say, old coonass?"

"It's all right, Buddy," I tell him.

"I think," says the Director, rising and looking at his watch, "that we will call it a day—"

"Sir—" I say, either so loudly or so urgently that everyone falls silent. "May I proceed with the case?"

"If only you would, Doctor!" cries the Director fervently, snatching handkerchiefs from several pockets.

The students laugh and settle back. They are telling themselves they must have heard wrong.

"Let 'em have it, little brother!" Buddy nods encourage-
ment to me and takes a stool. "Go!"

Winnie Gunn stands stolidly behind the wheelchair, eyes
rolled up.

Mr. Ives sits still as still, yet somehow twittering in his
stillness. His monkey eyes snap. There is something boyish
and quick about his narrow face. He is like one of those
young-old engineers at Boeing who at seventy wear bow ties
and tinker in their workshops.

"It is quite true that Mr. Ives has not walked or talked for a
month," I say loudly enough to be heard by Art Immelmann in
the back row. "It is also true that he is afflicted by some of the
pathologies listed by Dr. Brown. Dr. Brown is quite right
about the atherosclerosis."

"You old fucker," says Buddy affectionately, giving me the
Cajun arm. "Give 'em hell."

"I deny, however, that he is paralyzed or aphasic. His
pineal selfhood, as well as other cerebral centers, is intact."

"Spare us the metaphysics, Doctor," says the Director
bluntly. "The best proof that a man can talk is hearing him
talk. And walk."

"Yes sir," I say, nodding in admiration of the Director's
toughness. A tough old party he is, wasted by disease to his
essential fiber, a coat upon a stick. "Sir, I can assure you that
speech and locomotion are no problem here. What is interesting is the structure of his selfhood as it relates both to his
fellow seniors in the Tampa settlement and to the scientists
here."

"No metaphysics!" says the Director, coughing. "I'm a
simple man. Show me."

"Speech! Speech!" cry the students.

I shrug. Mr. Ives could, if he wanted, have spoken without
further ado. But, to make sure, I administer a light Chloride
dampening to his red nucleus (whence his rage) and a moderate Sodium massage to his speech area in the prefrontal gyrus.

Mr. Ives blinks, takes out a toothpick, and begins to suck
it.

"Mr. Ives, what was your occupation before you retired?"

"You know that as well as I do, Dr. More," says Mr. Ives,
cocking his lively monkey's head. He's got a deep drawling
voice!

"I know, but tell them."

"I was controller at Hartford Travelers Insurance. We lived

in Connecticut forty years until my wife, Myrtle, God rest her soul, died. I got restless."

"Mr. Ives, what were you digging for down there at the Golden Years Center in Tampa?"

"You know what I was digging for."

"The fountain of youth?"

"That's right."

"Did you find it?"

"I did."

"You see!" cries Buddy, whose ionization is wearing off. He blinks and shakes himself like a spaniel.

"The fountain of youth," says the Director in his old sour-civil style. "Why didn't you drink some? Or, better still, bring some back with you?"

The students, spiritual pimps that they are, reassured that things are back on the track and that laughing is in order, laugh.

"Mr. Ives," I say when the laughing subsides, "what was your avocation while you lived in Hartford?"

"Linguistics."

"And what were you especially interested in?"

Mr. Ives blows out his cheeks. "I've had the hunch for the last twenty years that I could decipher the Ocala frieze."

"What is the Ocala frieze?"

"A ceramic, an artifact discovered in the Yale dig and belonging to the proto-Creek culture. It has a row of glyphs so far undecipherable."

"Go on."

"I found a proto-Creek dictionary compiled by a Fray Bartolomeo who was with the original Narvaez expedition."

"How did you happen to find it?"

"Browsing through the Franciscan files in Salamanca."

"What were you doing there?"

"Looking for the dictionary."

"Did that decipher the glyphs?"

"No, but it gave me the Spanish for certain key proto-Creek words."

"But that wasn't enough."

"No."

"What else did you need?"

"One or two direct pairings of glyphs and Spanish words might break the cipher."

"Did you find such a pairing?"

"Yes."

"In the fountain of youth?"

Mr. Ives cackles and stomps his feet on the treadles of the wheelchair. "Sure!"

"There is such a fountain?"

"Oh sure. Not the fountain of youth and not de Leon, but there was a fountain, or at least a big spring, where Narvaez parleyed with Osceononta. It was known to be in the general area of the Oneco limestone springs near Tampa. Why else would I hang around that nuthouse?"

"So you had a hunch?"

"I knew there had been a spring there, and a mound that had been bulldozed. I was poking around. It wasn't the first time. I've been digging around there off and on for years."

"Did you find anything?"

"Enough."

"Enough for what?"

"To crack the cipher."

"You deciphered the frieze?"

"Oh sure. Look in next month's Annals."

"What did you find?"

"This." Mr. Ives hunches over and sticks his hand in his pocket.

"Could you bring it here?"

Lurching out of his chair, he comes weaving across The Pit like a jake-legged sailor and drops it in my hand, a crude coin that looks like a ten-dollar gold piece melted past its circumference.

"What is it?" I offer to help him back to his chair but he waves me off and goes weaving back. The students cheer.

"It's a do-it-yourself medal the Spaniards struck on the spot for the occasion of the Narvaez-Osceononta parley. What they did was take one of their own medals showing a salamander on one side and scratch a proto-Creek glyph on the reverse. My hypothesis was that the glyph meant fish. It worked."

I hand it to the Director, who holds it up. The students cheer again.

Mr. Ives watches nervously. "Be careful. There ain't but one of them."

The Director examines the medal intently.

"I'd just as soon have it back," says Mr. Ives, who is afraid the Director is going to pass it around.

The latter hands it back to me. I give it to Mr. Ives.

"Mr. Ives," says the Director. "Would you answer one question?"

"Sure."

"Why did you behave so badly toward the other retirees, hurling imprecations at folk who surely meant you no harm and"—coughing, snatching handkerchiefs—"defecating on, what was it? Flirtation Walk?"

"Doctor," says Mr. Ives, hunkering down in his chair, monkey eyes glittering, "how would you like it if during the most critical time of your experiments with the Skinner box that won you the Nobel Prize, you had been pestered without letup by a bunch of chickenshit Ohioans? Let's play shuffleboard, let's play granddaddy golf, Guys and Gals à go-go. Let's jump in our Airstream trailers and drive two hundred miles to Key West to meet more Ohioans and once we get there talk about—our Airstream trailers? Those fellows wouldn't let me alone."

"Is it fair to compare the work of science to the well-deserved recreational activities of retired people?"

"Sir, are you implying that what retired people do must necessarily be something less than the work of scientists? I mean is there any reason why a retired person should not go his own way and refuse to be importuned by a bunch of chickenshit Ohioans?"

"Excuse me." It is Stryker, rising slowly behind the Director. "I am not a chauvinistic man. But as a graduate of Western Reserve University and a native of Toledo, I must protest the repeated references to natives of the Buck-eye state as a 'bunch of chickenshit Ohioans.'"

"No offense, sir," says Mr. Ives, waving him off. "I've known some splendid Ohioans. But you get a bunch of retired Ohioans together in Florida—you know, they get together on the west coast to get away from the Jews in Miami. But I'll tell you the damn truth, to me it's six of one and half a dozen of the other."

"Just a minute," says Max, rising to a stoop. "I see no reason for the ethnic—"

"Where are you from?" Stryker asks Mr. Ives.

"Originally? Tennessee."

Stryker turns to Max. "I mean Jesus Christ, Tennessee."

"Yeah, but that's not the point, Ken," says Max, still aggrieved. "I still see no reason for the ethnic reference."

"But you have no objection to his referring to us as a bunch of chickenshit Ohioans?"

"You're missing my point."

"Let me quote you a figure!" cries Mr. Ives to Stryker, warming to it. "Did you know that there are three thousand and fifty-one TV and radio announcers in the South, of which twenty-two hundred are from Ohio, and that every last one of these twenty-two hundred says 'the difference between he and I'? In twenty years we'll all be talking like that."

But Max and Stryker, still arguing, pay no attention.

The students are both engrossed and discomfited. They chew their lips, pick their noses, fiddle with pencils, glance now at me, now at Mr. Ives. Who can tell them who's right? Students are a shaky dogmatic lot. And the "freer" they are, the more dogmatic. At heart they're totalitarians: they want either total dogmatic freedom or total dogmatic unfreedom, and the one thing that makes them unhappy is something in between.

Art Immelmann looks restive too. He fidgets around on the top step, hands in pockets hiking the skirts of his "bi-swing" jacket, and won't meet my eye. Now what the devil is he doing? He has removed one of the new lapsometers from the carton and is showing it to a student.

The doctors are unhappy too. The behaviorists, I know, don't like Mr. Ives dabbling in science. The visiting proctologists don't like anything they see. Colley Wilkes reverts to an old Alabama posture, hunched forward, hands clasped across wide-apart knees, pants hitched up black fuzzy shins. He clucks and shakes his head. "Man, what is all this?" I imagine him saying.

Moira has emerged from the shadows and taken charge of Mr. Ives's chair from Winnie Gunn, who is out of sight in the tunnel. Moira smiles at me!

Buddy Brown is trying to pick up the pieces of his anger but he's still out of it. He can't make out what happened to him.

Ellen Oglethorpe is torn between her disapproval of The Pit and what seems to be my triumph. But is it a triumph? She sits disgruntled, fingers shoved up into her cheek, shooting warm mothering glances at me, stern Calvinistic glances at the rowdy students.

Lola Rhoades is not paying strict attention. She moves to her own music, lips parted, hissing Brahms. Brahms, old

Brahms! We'll sing with you yet of a summer night.

Lola fills every inch of her seat with her splendid self, her arms use both arm rests, her noble knees press against the seat in front.

"Mr. Ives, a final question."

The Director is speaking.

"Why have you neither walked a step nor uttered a word during the past month?"

Mr. Ives scratches his head and squints up the slope. "Well sir, I'll tell you." He lays on the cracker style a bit much to suit me. "There is only one kind of response to those who would control your responses by throwing you in a Skinner box."

"And what would that be?" asks the Director sourly, knowing the answer.

"To refuse to respond at all."

"I see." The Director turns wearily to me. "Doctor, be good enough to give us your therapeutic recommendations and we'll wind this up."

"Yes sir. May I have a word with the patient?"

"By all means."

"Mr. Ives, what are your plans? I mean, if you were free to make plans."

"I intend to go home if I ever get out of this nuthouse."

"Where is home?"

"Sherwood, Tennessee. It's a village in a cove of the Cumberland Plateau. My farm is called Lost Cove."

"What are you going to do there?"

"Write a book, look at the hills, live till I die."

The students avert their eyes.

The Director looks at his watch. "Dr. More?"

"I recommend that Mr. Ives, instead of being sent to the Separation Center in Georgia, be released immediately and furnished with transportation to Sherwood, Tennessee."

"To Tennessee!" cries a student.

"To Tennessee! To Tennessee!" chime in both right-benchers and left-benchers.

Applause breaks out. I take some comfort in it, even though students are a bad lot, fickle as whores, and no professor should take pleasure in their approval.

"Hold it!" cries Buddy Brown, who has pulled himself together. He strides back and forth, sailing his white coat. "This may be good show-boating, but it's sorry damn science. Dr.

More has proved he's a good hypnotist, but as for his meta-physical machine—"

"To Tennessee!" cry the students.

Art is busy as a bee.

Some of the students, I notice, have acquired lapsometers from Art, which they wear about their necks like cameras and aim and focus at each other. Now Art Immelmann bounds up the aisle for a fresh supply. Feverishly he hands them out, squatting beside a student to explain the settings and point out skull topography. A dark circle of sweat spreads under his armpit.

A student near the top turns to the girl next to him, lifts her ponytail and places the MOQUOL muzzle on her occiput.

"Wait! No!" I yell at the top of my lungs and go bounding up the steps past the startled Director. "No, Art!"

But Art can't or won't hear. Lapsometers are stacked up his arm like a black marketeer wearing a dozen wristwatches.

Dr. Helga Heine aims a lapsometer at Stryker's midfrontal region.

"Wait, Helga!" I cry. "That thing is not a toy! It is not a prop for The Pit! It's for real! No, Helga!"

"But, *liebchen*, all we're doing is what you yourself suggested," says Helga as Stryker points his lapsometer at the region of her interpersonal sulcus.

"Yes, but my God, what's the setting? Let me see. Oh Lord, he's set the ionization at plus ten!"

Everywhere lapsometers are buzzing like a swarm of bees. Students and doctors and nurses either duck their heads or buzz away at their neighbors' heads with their new hair-dryers.

"STOP I BEG OF YOU!" I yell at the top of my voice.

But nobody pays attention except the Director, who plucks at my sleeve.

"Isn't this all part of the hijinks, Doctor, heh heh. Just what is it you fear?" he asks and cups his ear to hear me in the uproar.

"Goddamn sir," I yell into the hairy old ear. "As I told you earlier, this device is not a toy. It could produce the most serious psychic disturbances."

"Such as?"

"If it were focused over certain frontal areas or the region of the pineal body, which is the seat of selfhood, it could lead to severe angelism, abstraction of the self from itself, and what I call the Lucifer syndrome: that is, envy of the incarnate condition and a resulting caricature of the bodily appetites."

"Eh? What's that? Angelism? Pineal body? Seat of the self? Lucifer? Oh, I get it. Heh heh heh. Very good. Good show, Doctor. But really, I'm afraid The Pit is getting away from us."

"Sir, you don't understand. What I meant—" But Helga jostles me.

She has unwound her hair and let it down like Brunhilde. Placing her hand on her breast, she tells Stryker: "Everything is spirit. *Alles ist Geist.*"

"Right." Stryker nods and puts his hand on her other breast.

"Hold it," I tell Stryker and turn to the Director. "Sir, this is not what it appears."

A powerful grip, catching my arm, yanks me erect. I find myself standing between the two proctologists, Dusty Rhoades and Dr. Walter Bung. Have they—? Yes, Dr. Bung carries a lapsometer slung from his shoulder.

Yet they seem in the best of humors. They nod and wink at each other, claim me as an ally, and give every appearance of approval.

"Did you ever in your life," says Dr. Walter Bung, holding us close, "see this many commonists, atheists, hebes, and fags under one roof?"

"Excuse me, Dr. Bung," I say, unlimbering my lapsometer, "but the fact is that neither they nor you are quite yourselves."

"How's that, son?"

"I'll warrant you your red nucleus is at this moment abnormally active. May I take a reading?"

"What the hell you talking about, boy, my *red*—"

"The reason you're both so upset is this," I tell them both, but at that moment someone, perhaps one of them, pushes me violently and I stumble backward into the pit, nearly cracking my skull.

Moira is standing transfixed behind Mr. Ives's chair.

"Let's go to Howard Johnson's," she whispers, leaning over me as I struggle to get up.

"Get the patient out of here," I tell her.

Moira hesitates, opens and closes her mouth. Mr. Ives rises and takes her arm.

"I'll take care of her, Doctor."

"Thank you."

"Where shall I take her?"

"Are we going to Howard Johnson's?" Moira asks, coming close.

"Yes."

"Then I'll go to my room first."

"I'll take her to her room," Mr. Ives assures me.

"Thank you."

They disappear into the tunnel, Mr. Ives escorting Moira like the Tennessee gentleman that he is.

Colley Wilkes is trying to reach his wife, Fran, by detouring through the pit. But Buddy Brown stands in his way.

"Who you shoving?" asks Buddy.

"Out of my way."

"If there is anything I can't stand, it's a smart-mouth coon."

Buddy picked the wrong man. For Colley is no ordinary Negro, smart-mouthed or not, but a super-Negro who besides speaking five languages and being an electronic wizard, also holds the Black Belt in karate.

Colley pokes his hand, fingers held stiff as a plank, straight into Buddy's throat. Buddy sits down in Mr. Ives's wheelchair and tries to breathe.

I must see to Ellen and Lola.

Halfway up the aisle two students are fighting over a girl. I recognize J. T. Thigpen. The girl is Gloria, by no means a beauty, still dressed in her soiled lab coat, her brass-colored hair sprung out in a circle like a monstrance. The second student is a Knothead named Trasker Gluck. Seeing Trasker and Gloria together, I suddenly realize they are brother and sister.

Trasker and J.T. have each other elbow around neck, grunting and cursing, the way boys fight.

"Hold it, fellows." I try to stop them.

"You stay away from my sister, you son of a bitch," says Trasker, who is a clean-living athletic Baptist type like pole-vaulter Bob Richards.

"It's a meaningless relationship and nothing for you to take exception to," grunts J.T. "We get fifty bucks for a successful performance. Let me go, I need the money. Let me go! I feel if we can get over to Love right away we can make it for sure. Let me go! There is nothing between us. Ask your sister."

"Why you son of a bitch, that makes it worse," says Trasker, slamming J.T. squarely on the nose with his big fist.

"Do something, Dr. More!" pleads Gloria. "I love him!"

"Who?"

"J.T.!"

"Excuse me," I say, spying Ellen and Art Immelmann in the next aisle.

Ted 'n Tanya are lying under the seats. I almost step on Ted's back.

"Tom, you were wonderful," says Tanya over Ted's shoulder.

"Thank you."

"Your invention works! We can love. We are loving!"

"Good. Pardon." I step over them.

"All we feared was fear itself."

"I know."

"Stay with us! Share our joy!"

"I can't just now. Pardon."

Warm arms encircle my waist. I find myself sitting in Lola's lap.

"Hi, Sugah!"

"Hi, Lola."

"My, you're a big fine boy!" She gives me a hug.

Reaching back, I give her a hug. She warms my entire back from shoulders to calves.

"Do you love Lola?"

"Yes, I do." I do.

"Lola's got you."

"She sure has."

"When are you coming to see Lola?"

"Tomorrow. No, this evening."

"Lola will make you some gin fizzes and we'll go walking out in the moonlight."

"Absolutely. But you better go home now. I don't want you to get hurt."

"O.K., Sugah," says Lola, giving me a final tremendous squeeze.

Dusty seizes my shoulder in his huge hand, working the bones around like dice.

His face looms close, his breath reeks like a lion's.

"You listen here, Doctor."

"Yes, Dusty?"

"You mess with my daughter one more time without wedding bells and you done messed for the last time. You read me?"

"Yes."

"You all right, boy," says Dusty and, taking Dr. Walter Bung in one arm and me in the other, draws the three of us close.

Ellen is shouting angrily at Art Immelmann, who surveys the pit, swinging his arms idly and whistling loudly and accurately *Nola*, the piano theme of Vincent Lopez, a band leader in the Middle Auto Age.

I snatch Ellen away.

"Stay away from him."

"Chief, he's got your lapsometers!" Ellen is sobbing with rage.

"I know."

"What are we going to do?" asks Ellen, wringing her hands. "Just look."

Below us the pit writhes like a den of vipers. Now and then an arm is raised, fist clenched, to fall in a blow. Bare legs are upended.

"Listen." I whisper in Ellen's ear. "While I am talking to Art, take the rest of the lapsometers in the carton and put them in your car. I'll call you tomorrow."

"O.K., Chief. But are you leaving?"

"I have to collect all the loose ones."

"I'm not leaving without you!"

"You son of a bitch," I tell Art. "What did you pull this stunt for?"

"I am not a son of a bitch," says Art, looking puzzled. "Take it easy, Doc." As usual he has no sense of distance, comes too close, and blows Sen-Sen in my face.

"I told you specifically to leave my lapsometers alone."

"How are we going to run a pilot on your hardware without using your hardware?"

"Pilot! Is this what you call a pilot?"

"Doc, we can't go national until we test the interactions in a pilot. That's boilerplate, Doc."

"Boilerplate my ass. Goddamn it, don't you know the

dangers of what you're doing? We're sitting on a dome of Heavy Salt, the President is coming tomorrow, and what do you do? Turn loose my lapsometers cranked up to ten plus."

"Doc, does this look political to you?" He nods at the lovers and fist-fighters. "This is not political. It is a test of your hypotheses about vagal rage and abstract lust, as you of all people should know. And as for the dangers of a chain reaction, there's no Heavy Salt within three miles of here."

"We're through, Art. I'm canceling the contract."

"You'll be right as rain tomorrow, Doc. Just remember: music, love, and the dream of summer."

Max Gottlieb and Ellen hold me tight, one at each elbow.

"Let's go home, fella," says Max. "You've been great."

"Wait a minute. I'm needed here, Max."

"He's right, Chief. You're worn out."

"I'm not leaving until I collect all the lapsometers."

"I'll get them for you," says Max. "You go home and get a good night's sleep. Or better still, go back to A-4."

"Damn it, Max, don't you realize what's happening?"

"I'm afraid I do. Your device has triggered a mass hysteria. Like the St. Vitus's dance in the Middle Ages. These are strange times."

"Listen to me, Max. Number one, my lapsometer works. You saw it. Number two, it has fallen into the wrong hands. Number three, the effect here is mainly erotic but it could just as easily have been political. Number four, the President and Vice-President will be in this area tomorrow. Number five, there are plans to kidnap you and hold you prisoner in the Honey Island wilderness. Number six, we're sitting on the biggest Heavy Salt dome in North America."

"Oh boy," says Max to Ellen.

Ellen frowns. She is loyal to me.

"I believe you, Chief. But if what you say is true, you're going to need all your strength tomorrow."

"That's true. But I feel fine right now." How lovely you are, Ellen. Perspiration glitters like diamonds in the down of her short upper lip.

"What's that, Chief?" asks Ellen quickly. Did I say it aloud? She blushes and tugs at my arm. "Come on now!" At the same time I feel a pinprick in my other arm. Max has given me a shot through my coat sleeve.

"You're going to get a good night's sleep. Ellen will take

you home. I'll drop in on you tomorrow morning." He holds my hand affectionately. I see him look at the scars on my wrist. "Take care of yourself now."

"I feel fine, Max." I do. I can still hear music.

"Let's go out through the tunnel, Chief. My car is in the back."

I say goodbye to the Director, but he is engrossed with a young medical student. It is Carruthers Calhoun, scion of an old-line Southern family, a handsome peach-faced lad.

"Wasn't it Socrates," the Director is saying, a friendly arm flung across the boy's shoulders, "who said: A fair woman is a lovely thing, truth lovelier still, but a fair youth is the fairest of all?"

"No sir," replies Carruthers, who graduated from Sewanee with a classical education. "That was Juvenal and he didn't quite say that."

# JULY FOURTH

# ON THE WAY TO MEET MOIRA AT HOWARD JOHNSON'S

▰◣◤◣◤◣◤◣◤◣◤◣

**8:30 A.M. / JULY 4**

**O**NLY THREE HOURS' SLEEP AFTER MY NIGHT CALL TO THE love couple with the diarrheic infant in the swamp.

A cold shower and a breakfast of warm Tang-vodka-duck-eggs-Tabasco and I'm back to normal, which is to say tolerably depressed and terrified.

At the first flicker of morning terror I remember the modified lapsometer and fetching it from my bag, an odd-looking thing with its snout-like attachment, give myself a light brain massage.

Terror gone! Instantly exhilarated! The rip and race of violins. By no means drunk, clairvoyant rather, prescient, musical, at once abstracted, seeing things according to their essences, and at the same time poised for the day's adventure in the wide world, I achieve a noble evacuation and go forth, large bowel clear as a bell. Clay lies still but blood's a rover.

A hot still gold-green Fourth of July. Not a breath stirs. No squirrels scrabble in the dogwoods, no jaybirds fret in the sycamores.

Cutting now through the "new" 18, which is really the old since the construction of the Cypress Garden 36. Hm. Something is amiss. The Fourth of July and not a soul on the links. What with the Pro-Am using Cypress Garden, the "new" 18 ought to be jammed!

Weeds sprout in the fairways. Blackberries flourish in the rough. Rain shelters are green leafy caves.

Someone is following me. *Clink-clink.* I stop and listen. Not a sound. Start and there it is again: *clink-clink, clink-*

*clink*, the sound a caddy makes when he's humping it off the tee to get down to the dogleg in time for the drive, hand held over the clubs to keep them quiet but one or two blades slap together *clink-clink*.

But there's no one in sight.

Now comes the sound of—firecrackers? Coming from the direction of the school.

There is a roaring and crackling in the dogleg of number 5. Rounding the salient of woods and all of a sudden knowing what it is before I see it, I see it: the Bledsoe Spanish-mission house burning from the inside. The fire is a cheerful uproarious blaze going like sixty at every window, twenty windows and twenty roaring hearths, fat pine joists popping sociably and not a soul in sight. No fire department, no spectators, nothing but the bustling commerce of flames in the still sunlight.

I watch from the green cave of a shelter. Yonder in the streaked stucco house dwelled the childless Bledsoes for thirty years while golf balls caromed off the walls, broke the windows and rooftiles, ricocheted around the patio.

The house roars and crackles busily in the silence. Flames lick out the iron grills and up the blackened stucco.

Into these very woods came I as a boy while the house was a-building, picked up triangles of new copper flashing, scraps of aluminum, freshly sawn blocks of two-by-fours—man's excellent geometries wrought from God's somewhat lumpish handiwork. Here amid the interesting carpenter's litter, I caressed the glossy copper, smelled the heart pine, thought impure thoughts and defiled myself in the skeletal bathroom above the stuffed stumps of plumbing, a thirteen-year-old's lonesome leaping love on a still summer afternoon.

My chest is buzzing. Ach, a heart attack for sure! Clutching at my shirt, I shrink into the corner. For sure it is calcium dislodged and rattling like dice in my heart's pitiful artery. Poor Thomas! Dead at forty-five of a coronary! Not at all unusual either, especially in Knothead circles here in Paradise: many a good Christian and loving father, family man, and churchgoer has kicked off in his thirties. A vice clamps under my sternum and with it comes belated contrition. God, don't let me die. I haven't lived, and there's the summer ahead and music and science and girls—No. No girls! No more lewd thoughts! No more lusting after my neighbors' wives and daughters! No hankering after strange women! No more humbug! No more great vaulting lewd daytime longings, no whispering into pretty ears, no more assignations in closets, no more friendly bumping of nurses from behind, no more night adventures in bunkers and sand traps, no more inviting Texas girls out into the gloaming: "I am Thomas More. You are lovely and I love you. I have a heart full of love. Could we go out into the gloaming?" No more.

My chest buzzes away.

Clutching at my shirt in a great greasy cold sweat, I encounter it, the buzzing box. Whew. Well. It is not my heart after all but my Anser-Phone calling me, clipped to my shirt pocket and devised just for the purpose of reaching docs out on the golf links.

Whew. Lying back and closing my eyes, I let it buzz. It if wasn't a heart attack, it's enough to give you one.

It is Ellen Oglethorpe. Switch off the buzzer and move around to a shady quarter of the green cave to escape the heat of the fire.

Now resting in the corner and listening to Ellen and giving myself another brain message. I could use an Early Times too.

"What is it, Ellen?"

"Oh, Chief, where have you been? I've been out of my mind! You just don't know. Where've you been all night?" Comes the tiny insectile voice, an angry cricket in my pocket.

"What's the trouble?"

"You've got to get down here right away, Chief."

"Where are you?"

"At the office."

"It's the Fourth of July and I have an engagement."

"Engagement my foot. You mean a date. You're not fooling me."

"O.K., I'm not fooling you."

"I know who you have a date with and where, don't worry about that."

"All right, I won't."

"Chief—"

"Ellen, listen to me, I want you to call the fire department and send them out to Paradise. The Bledsoe house is on fire."

"Are you kidding?"

"Eh? I can hardly hear you." I incline an ear to my bosom.

"They're not taking calls out there, not the police or anybody. That's why I was so worried about you."

"What are you talking about?"

"There's some sort of disturbance out there. Riffraff from the swamp, I believe."

"Nonsense. There's not a soul here."

"Everybody out there has moved into town. It's an armed camp here, Chief. You wouldn't believe it."

"What happened?"

"It started with the atrocity last night—right where you are. At the Bledsoes'."

"Atrocity?"

"Mrs. Bledsoe was killed with that barbecue thing. Mr. Bledsoe has disappeared. No doubt he's dead too. The work of madmen."

Mrs. Bledsoe. Skewered with P.T.'s kebab skewer.

"Chief, you better get out of there!"

"There's no one here," I say absently.

"Oh, and we've got a roomful of patients."

"On the Fourth of July?"

"Your new assistant is treating them."

"Who? Speak up, Ellen, I can't hear you."

"I can't talk any louder, Chief. I'm hiding in the EEG room. I said Dr. Immelmann has a roomful of patients and some very strange patients, I must say."

"Dr. Immelmann! What the hell is he doing there?"

"Treating patients with your lapsometer. He said you would understand, that it was part of your partnership agreement. But, Chief, there's something wrong here."

"What?"

"They're fighting. In your waiting room and in the street."

"Who's fighting?"

"Mr. Ledbetter and Mr. Tennis got in a fight, and—"

"Let me speak to Art Immelmann."

"He just left. I can see him going down the street."

"All right. Ellen, here's what you do. Are the lapsometers still there?"

"Well, only half of them. And only because I hid them."

"Where did you hide them?"

"In a crate of Bayonne-rayon training members."

"Good girl. Now here's what you do. Take the crate to your car. Lock it in the trunk. Go home. I'll get back to you later."

"When?"

"Shortly. I have something to attend to first."

"Don't think I don't know what it is."

"All right, I won't."

Ellen begins to scold. I unclip the Anser-Phone and hang it in the rafters among the dirt-daubers. While Ellen buzzes away, I take a small knock of Early Times and administer a plus-four Sodium jolt to Brodmann 11, the zone of the musical-erotic.

Waltzing now to *Wine, Women and Song* while Ellen Oglethorpe chirrups away in the rafters, a tiny angry Presbyterian cricket.

"Chief," says the insectile voice. "You're not living up to the best that's in you."

"The best? Isn't happiness better than misery?"

"Because the best that's in you is so fine."

"Thank you." From the edge of the woods comes a winey smell where the fire's heat strikes the scuppernongs.

"People like that, Chief, are not worthy of you."

"People like what?" *People* pronounced by Ellen in that tone has a feminine gender. Female people.

"You know who I mean."

"I'm not sure. Who?"

People like that Miss Schaffner and Miss Rhoades."

"Are you jealous?"

"Don't flatter yourself, Doctor."

"Very well." I'm waltzing.

*Wien Wien, du du allein*

"Oh, Chief. Are you drinking?"

I must be singing out loud.

"Goodbye, Ellen. Go home and sit tight until you hear from me."

I turn off the cricket in the rafters and snap the Anser-Phone in a side pocket, away from my heart.

Again the popping of firecrackers. The sound comes from the south. Taking cover in the gloom of the pines, I look between the trunks down number 5 fairway, 475 yards, par five. Beyond the green are the flat buildings of the private school. The fire-crackers come from there. The grounds are deserted, but a spark of fire appears at a window, then a *crack*. Is somebody shooting? Two yellow school buses are parked in front. Now comes a regular fusillade, sparkings at every window, then a sputtering like a string of Chinese crackers. People run for the buses, majorettes and pom-pom girls for the first bus, their silver uniforms glittering in the sun. The moms bring up the rear, hustling along, one hand clamped to their hats, the other swinging big tote bags. A police car pulls ahead, the buses follow, a motorcycle brings up the rear. As soon as the little cavalcade disappears, the firing stops.

Was it fireworks or were people inside the building directing covering fire at an unseen enemy?

2

At Howard Johnson's.

Moira gives me a passionate kiss tasting of Coppertone. She is sunbathing beside the scummy pool. Her perfect little body, clad in an old-fashioned two-piece bikini, lies prone on a plastic recliner. Though her shoulder straps have been slipped down, she makes much of her modesty, clutching bra to breast as, I perceive, she imagines girls used to in the old days.

"A kiss for the champ," she says.

"For who?"

"You beat Buddy."

"Oh."

"Poor Buddy. Wow, what a bombshell you dropped. Total chaos. Did you plan it that way?"

"Chaos?"

"In The Pit, stupid."

"Yes, The Pit. Yes. No, I didn't plan it exactly that way." I notice that she has a dimple at each corner of her sacrum, each whorled by down.

"I heard the Director tell Dr. Stryker to sign you up and keep you here at any cost."

"What do you think that meant?"

"Before Harvard or M.I.T. grab you, silly."

"I'm not so sure. What was going on over there when you left this morning?"

"Quiet as a tomb. Everyone's gone to the beaches."

The golden down on her forearm is surprisingly thick. I turn her arm over and kiss the sweet salty fossa where the blood beats like a thrush's throat.

Spying two snakes beside the pool, I pick up a section of vacuum hose and run around the apron and chase them off, and sing *Louisiana Lou* to hear the echoes from the quadrangle.

"Are you going to take the job, Tom?" asks Moira, sitting up. The lounge leaves a pattern of diamonds on the front of her thighs.

"What job? Oh. Well, I'm afraid there's going to be some trouble around here. You're sure you didn't notice anything unusual this morning?"

"Unusual? No. I did meet that funny little man who was helping you yesterday."

"Helping me?"

"Helping you pass out your props. Wow, how did you do it?"

"He wasn't helping me. He was—never mind. What was he doing this morning?"

"Nothing. He passed me carrying a box."

"How big?"

"Yay big."

I frown. Ordinarily I don't like girls who say *yay big*.

The box. Oh me. Terror flickers. I take a drink.

"He was very polite, knew my name and all. In fact, he sent his regards to you. How did he know I was going to see you? Did you tell him?"

"Certainly not."

"Rub some of this on me, Tommy." She hands me the ancient Pompeian phial of Coppertone.

"O.K. But you realize you can't go in the pool."

"Ugh," she says, looking at the pool. "I can't. What'll I do?"

"I'll show you. But let me rub you first."

Foreseeing everything, I had earlier made an excuse and hopped up to the room, cranked up the generator and turned on the air-conditioner.

Now, when Moira's had enough of the sweat and the grease and the heat, I lead her by the hand to the balcony. From the blistering white heat of the concrete we come into a dim cool grotto. Fogs of cold air blow from the shuddering tin-lizzy of an air-conditioner. The yellow bed lamp shines down on fresh sheets. A recorder plays ancient Mantovani music—not exactly my favorite, but Moira considers Mantovani "classical."

Moira claps her hands and hugs me.

"Oh lovely lovely lovely! How perfect! Whose room?"

"Ours," I say, humming *There's a Small Hotel with a Wishing Well*.

"You mean you fixed it up like this?"

"Sure. Remember the way it was?"

"My heavens. Sheets even. Air-conditioner. Why did you do it?"

"For love. All for love. Let me show you this."

I show her the "shower": a pistol-grip nozzle screwed onto two hundred feet of garden hose hooked at the other end to the spigot in the Esso station grease-rack next door.

"And soap! And towels! Go away, I'm taking my shower now."

"O.K. But let me do this." I turn on the nozzle to get rid of two hundred feet of hot water.

While Moira showers, I lie on the bed and look at *The Laughing Cavalier* and the Maryland hunt scene in the wallpaper. Mantovani plays, the shower runs, Moira sings. I mix a toddy and let it stand on my chest and think of Doris, my dead wife who ran off to Cozumel with a heathen Englishman.

Doris and I used to travel the highways in the old Auto Age before Samantha was born, roar seven hundred miles a day along the great interstates to some glittering lost motel twinkling away in the twilight set down in the green hills of Tennessee or out in haunted New Mexico, swim in the pool, take steaming baths, mix many toddies, eat huge steaks, run back to the room, fall upon each other laughing and hollering, and afterwards lie dreaming in one another's arms watching late-show Japanese science-fiction movies way out yonder in the lost yucca flats of Nevada.

Sunday mornings I'd leave her and go to mass. Now here was the strangest exercise of all! Leaving the coordinate of the motel at the intersection of the interstates, leaving the motel with standard doors and carpets and plumbing, leaving the interstates extending infinitely in all directions, abscissa and ordinate, descending through a moonscape countryside to a —town! Where people had been living all these years, and to some forlorn little Catholic church up a side street just in time for the ten-thirty mass, stepping up on the porch as if I had been doing it every Sunday for the past twenty years, and here comes the stove-up bemused priest with his cup (what am I doing out here? says his dazed expression) upon whose head hands had been laid and upon this other head other hands and so on, for here off I-51 I touched the thread in the labyrinth, and the priest announced the turkey raffle and Wednesday bingo and preached the Gospel and fed me Christ—

—Back to the motel then, exhilarated by—what? by eating Christ or by the secret discovery of the singular thread in this the unlikeliest of places, this geometry of Holiday Inns and interstates? back to lie with Doris all rosy-fleshed and creased of cheek and slack and heavy-limbed with sleep, cracking one eye and opening her arms and smiling.

"My God, what is it you do in church?"

What she didn't understand, she being spiritual and seeing religion as spirit, was that it took religion to save me from the spirit world, from orbiting the earth like Lucifer and the angels, that it took nothing less than touching the thread off the misty interstates and eating Christ himself to make me mortal man again and let me inhabit my own flesh and love her in the morning.

Moira comes out wound up in a towel, rubbing her short blond hair with another towel.

"Feel me."

The flesh of her arm is cold-warm, the blood warmth just palpable through her cold smooth skin.

"Let me get up to take a shower." Moira is sitting in my lap. She won't get up so I get up with her and walk around holding her in my arms like a child.

"Don't," says Moira.

"Don't what?"

"Don't take a shower."

"Why not?"

"I like the way you smell. You smell like Uncle Bud."

"Who is Uncle Bud?"

"He has a chicken farm out from Parkersburg. I used to go see him Sunday mornings and sit in his lap while he read me the funnies. He always smelled like whiskey and sweat and seersucker."

"Do I look like Uncle Bud?"

"No, you look like Rod McKuen."

"He's rather old."

"But you both look poetic."

"I brought along his poems for you."

"Which ones?"

"The ones about sea gulls."

"You've thought of everything."

"You're a lovely girl," I say, holding and patting her just as

I used to pat Samantha when she had growing pains.

"Do you love me?"

"Oh yes."

"How much?"

"Enough to eat you," I say and begin to eat her kneecap.

"Enough to marry me?"

"What?"

"Do you love me enough to marry me?"

"Oh yes."

"Do you know what I've always wanted?"

"No."

"To keep some chickens."

"All right."

"Golden banties. You know what?"

"What?"

"That work at the clinic is a lot of bull. I'd love to stay home raising golden banties while you are doing your famous researches."

"All right." I suck the cold-warm flesh of her forearm covered by long whorled down. The fine hair rises to my mouth and makes a skein like the tiny ropes that bound Gulliver.

"Could we live in Paradise?"

"Certainly."

Eating her, I have visions of golden cockerels glittering like topazes in the morning sun in my "enclosed patio."

"When?"

"When what?"

"When will we do that?"

"Whenever you like," I say, marveling at her big littleness. My arms gauge a secret amplitude in her. She is small and heavy.

"No really. When?"

"When we leave here."

"When will that be?"

"A week, a month. Perhaps longer."

"My Lord," says Moira, straightening in my arms like a child wanting to be put down. "What do you mean?"

"I'm afraid something is going to happen today, in fact is happening now, which will make it impossible for us to leave here for a while. At least until I make sure it's safe for us either in Paradise or the Center."

"What do you *mean*? When I left there this morning, the place was dead as a doornail."

"For one thing a revolution may have occurred. There is a report that guerrillas from Honey Island are in Paradise. I fear too that there may be disorders today at the political rally near Fedville."

"You don't have to go to this much trouble to keep me here, you know."

"Let me show you something."

I carry her to the window, where she pulls back the curtain. Five columns of smoke come from the green ridge above the orange tiles of the ice-cream restaurant.

"There was only one fire when I was there earlier."

"What does that mean?"

"They're burning the houses on the old 18."

"O my Lord."

"But that's not the worst. I'm afraid my invention has fallen into the wrong hands."

"What does that mean?"

"Two things. Civil war and a chain reaction in the Heavy Sodium deposits."

"But I can't stay here." Moira straightens in my arms again.

"Why not?"

"I don't have anything to wear! All I have is the clothes on my back—the clothes in there, that is."

"Let me show you something else. Open the top drawer."

She opens it. "What in the world?" The top drawer has underclothes, blouses, slips. The other drawers have skirts, dresses, shorts, etcetera.

"Whose are they?" asks Moira, frowning.

"Yours."

"Were they your wife's?"

"No. She'd make two of you."

"Gollee." Moira gets down, opens the bottom drawer, sits drumming her fingers on the Gideon. "And what are we going to live on? Love?"

"Let me show you."

I take her to the closet. She gazes at the crates and cartons stacked to the ceiling, cartons of Campbell's chicken-and-rice, Underwood ham, Sunmaid raisins, cases of Early Times and Swiss Colony sherry (which Moira likes). And the Great Books stacked alongside.

"That's enough for a small army."

"Or for two people for a long time."

"Who's going to read all those books?"

"We'll read them aloud to each other."

Think of it: reading Aeschylus, in the early fall, in old Howard Johnson's, off old I-11, with Moira.

"What about Rod McKuen?"

"He's over there. Under the Gideon."

"There's no pots and pans," says Moira suddenly.

"The kitchenette's next door."

"Good night, nurse."

"Let me show you something else." We sit on the bed. "Put this quarter in the slot there."

The Slepe-Eze starts up and sets the springs gently vibrating.

"Oh no!" Moira's eyes round. "I guess they had to have this."

"They?"

"The salesmen."

"Yes."

"Those poor lonely men. Think of it."

"Yes."

Making love and dying in a place like this, far from home."

"Dying?"

"The Death of a Salesman."

"Right. Come sit in Uncle Bud's lap."

"All right. Honey?"

"Yes."

"Let's have children."

"All right." How odd. The idea of Moira and me having a child is the oddest thing in the world. But why? "First, let's fix us a drink."

"All right."

She sits in my lap and we drink. She insists on whiskey rather than her sherry since that was what the flappers and salesmen drank.

"This beats Knott's Berry Farm," she whispers.

"Yes."

One difference between Moira and my wife, Doris, is that Doris liked motels that were in the middle of nowhere, at the intersection of I-89 and I-23 in the Montana badlands. While Moira likes a motel near a point of interest such as Seven Flags over Texas.

Now we lie in one another's arms on the humming bed. She is as trim and quick as one of her banty hens. She's a West Virginia tomboy brown as a berry and strong-armed and -legged from climbing trees.

Cold fogs of air blow over us, Mantovani plays Jerome Kern. "I love classical music," whispers Moira. *The Laughing Cavalier* smiles down on us, hundreds of Maryland hunters leap the same fence around the walls.

Locked about one another we go spinning down old Louisiana misty green, slowly revolving and sailing down the summer wind. How prodigal is she with and how little store she sets by her perfectly formed Draw-Me arms and legs.

Now she lies in the crook of my arm, eyes open, tapping her hard little fingernail on her tooth. Her little mind ranges far and wide. She casts ahead, making plans no doubt, doing my living room over. I took her there once and it was an unhappy business, she keeping her head down and looking up through her eyebrows at Doris's great abstract enamels that went leaping around the walls like the seven souls of Shiva.

"Do you like my hair long?"

"Do you call it long now?"

"Yes."

"Yes."

When my daughter, Samantha, was a freshman in high school, she had her first date, a blind one for the Introductory Prom, the boys from Saint Aloysius drawing the Saint Mary's girls from a hat. Samantha and I sat waiting for the date, I with my instructions not to open the front door until she had a chance to leave the room so that she could then be a little late, she with her blue pinafore skirt tucked under her fat knees. We watched *Gunsmoke* as we waited. The boy didn't come. *Gunsmoke* gave way to the Miss America pageant. Bert Parks went nimbly back-stepping around snaking the mike cord out of his way. Samantha's acne began to itch.

"I wouldn't have missed this, Poppa," said Samantha as we watched Miss Nebraska recite "If" in the talent contest. But she was clawing at herself.

"Me neither."

I began to itch too and needed only a potsherd and dung-heap. Curse God, curse the nuns for arranging the dance, goddamn the little Celt-Catholic bastards, little Mediterranean lowbrow Frenchy-dago jerks. Anglo-Saxon Presbyterians would have better manners even if they didn't believe in God.

"Why are you crying?" Moira asks me, rubbing my back briskly. She wants to get up.

"I'm not crying."

"Your eyes are wet."

"Tears of joy."

But Moira, paying no attention, raises herself on one elbow to see herself in the mirror.

"Nothing is wrong with two people in love loving each other," says Moira, turning her head to see her hair. "Buddy says that joy not guilt—"

"Buddy says!" Angrily I pull back from her. "What the hell does Buddy have to do with it?"

"All I meant was—"

"And just when did the son of a bitch say it? On just such an occasion as this?"

"At a lecture," says Moira quickly. "Anyhow"—she levels her eyes with mine—"what makes you so different?"

"Different? What do you mean? Do you mean that you— that he—? Don't tell me."

"I won't. Because it's not true."

But I can't hear her for my own groaning. Why am I so jealous? It's not that, though. It's just that I can't understand how Moira can hold herself so cheaply. Why doesn't she attach the same infinite values to her favors that I do? With her I feel like a man watching a child run around with a forty-carat diamond. Her casualness with herself makes me sweat.

"It's just that—" I begin when the knock comes at the door.

For a long moment Moira and I search each other's eyes as if the knock came from there.

"The Bantus," whispers Moira.

"No," I say, but get up in some panic and disarray. Getting killed is not so bad. What is to be feared is getting killed in a bathtub like Marat.

Moira breaks for the bathroom. I finish off my toddy and brush my hair.

Comes the knock again, light knuckles on the hollow door. Somehow I know who it is the second my hand touches the doorknob.

It is Ellen, of course, in uniform, with the wind up, color high in her cheeks, head reared a little so that the curve of her cheek narrows her eyes, which are icy-Lake-Geneva blue. It is hotter than ever, but a purple thunderhead towers behind her. Her uniform is crisp. The only sign of the heat is the sparkle of perspiration in the dark down of her lip.

"Come in come in come in."

She's all business and a-bustle, starch whistling as if she were paying a house call. When she sets down her bag, I notice her hands are trembling.

"What's the matter?"

"Somebody shot at me," she says, leafing nervously through the Gideon, unseeing.

"Where?"

"Coming past the church."

"Maybe it was firecrackers."

She slams the Bible shut. "Why didn't you answer the Anser-Phone?"

"I guess I turned it off."

Ellen, still blinded by the sunlight, gazes uncertainly at the dim fogbanks rolling around the room. I guide her to the foot of the bed. I sit on the opposite bed.

"Chief, I think you better come back to the office."

"Why?"

"Dr. Immelmann found the box of lapsometers."

"I know."

"You know? How?"

"Moira told me she saw him."

"Oh. Chief, he's been handing them out to people."

"What sort of people?"

"Some very strange people."

"Yes, hm." I am eyeing the dressing room nervously. Moira is stirring about but Ellen pays no attention.

"I heard him send one man to NASA, another to Boeing."

"It sounds serious."

"When the fight started, I left."

"What fight?"

"Between Mr. Tennis and Mr. Ledbetter."

"Is that Ted Tennis, Chico?" cries Moira, bursting out of the dressing room. "Oh hello there!" She smiles brilliantly at Ellen and strides about the room, hands thrust deep in the pockets of the blue linen long-shorts I bought for her. They fit. "These really fit, Chico," she says, wheeling about.

Chico? Where did she get that? Then I remember. When we stayed in the small hotel with the wishing well in Merida, she called me Chico a couple of times.

"Yes. Ah, do you girls know each other?"

"Oh yes!"

"Yes indeed!"

Ellen then goes on talking to me as if Moira had not come in.

"And that's not the worst, Chief."

"It isn't?"

Ellen and I are still sitting at the foot of separate beds. Moira stretches out behind *me*. Both girls are making me nervous.

"I heard him tell the same two men that five o'clock was the deadline."

"Deadline?"

"I didn't know what he meant either. When I asked him, he said that was the time when we'd know which way your great experiment would go. What did he mean by that?"

"I'm not sure."

"He said you'd know. He said if worst came to worst, you had the means of protecting us and that you would know what he meant."

"I see."

"What do you suppose that means, Chico?" asks Moira, giving me a nudge in the back with her toe. I wish she wouldn't do that. "Is that why we have to stay here?"

"Ahem, it may have something to do with that."

"Give me a quarter."

"O.K.," I say absently.

Moira puts the quarter into the slot. The Slepe-Eze begins to vibrate under me. I jump up.

Ellen manages to ignore the vibrating bed.

"Chief, he said you would know what to look for at five o'clock."

"Right," I say eagerly. The prospect of a catastrophe is welcome. "Three things are possible: a guerrilla attack, a chain reaction, and a political disturbance at the speech-making."

"Pshaw," says Moira, gazing at the ceiling. "I don't think anything is going to happen. Idle rumors."

My eyes roll up. Never in her life has Moira said *pshaw*

before—pronounced with a *p*. She read it somewhere.

"That was no rumor that took a shot at me," says Ellen, looking at me blinkered as if I had said it. She hasn't yet looked at Moira.

"I imagine not," I say, frowning. I wish the mattress would stop vibrating. I find myself headed for the door. "I better take a look around. I'll bring y'all a Dr. Pepper."

"Wait, Chico." Moira takes my hand. "I'll go with you. Don't forget you promised me a tour of the ruins, the ice-cream parlor, the convention room where all the salesmen used to glad-hand each other." She swings around. "It's been nice seeing you again, Miss Ah—"

"I'll be running in," says Ellen, reaching the door ahead of us.

"No, Ellen." I take her arm. "I'm afraid you can't leave."

"Why not?"

"I want to make sure the coast is clear."

"Very well, Chief."

To my surprise, Ellen shrugs and perches herself—on the still-humming bed!

"You want to come with us?"

"No no. You kids run along. I'll hold the fort. I see you have food. I'll fix some sandwiches while you're gone."

"Let me show you where everything is, honey," says Moira. The two huddle over the picnic basket.

Oh, they're grand girls though. Whew. What a relief to see them get along! There's no sight more reassuring than two women working over food. Women needn't be catty! Perhaps we three could be happy here.

"We'll be back, Ellen!" cries Moira, yanking me after her. "If things get slow, there's always the Gideon."

Now why did she have to say that?

"You mean you didn't bring your manual from Love?" laughs Ellen, waving us on our way.

"Ha ha, very good, girls," I say, laughing immoderately. They are great girls, though. Whew. A relief nevertheless to close the door between the two of them and be on our way.

3

Moira was never more loving or lovable. By turns playful, affectionate, mournful, prattling, hushed, she darts ahead like a honeybee tasting the modest delights of this modest ruin.

"Do you think there's any danger, Chico?" she calls back.

"I doubt if there's anyone around."

"What about Ellen's sniper?"

"Well—"

"She spooks easy, huh?"

"No. On the contrary."

"Do you like her?"

"She's a fine nurse."

"But do you like her?"

"Like?"

"Or as you say, fancy."

"No. I fancy you."

We're behind the registration desk reading the names of long-departed guests, not salesmen, I notice, but families, mom and pop and the kids bound from the Gulf Coast or the Smokies or Seven Flags.

Now we're under the moldering Rotary banner in the dark banquet room arm in arm and as silent as we were last summer at Ghost Town, U.S.A. Moira reads the banner.

> *Is it the Truth?*
> *Is it fair to all concerned?*

I squeeze her pliant belted rough-linened waist. The linen reminds me of Doris. Was that why I got it?

"Let's stay here a while." I draw her behind the banner. What an odd thing to be forty-five and in love and with exactly the same pang of longing in the heart as at age sixteen.

Moira laughs. "Let's go get a Dr. Pepper."

In the arcade, dim and cool as a catacomb, she skips along the bank of vending machines pulling Baby Ruth levers. Pausing in her ballet, she stoops and mock-drinks at a rusted-out water-cooler.

I stoop over her, covering her, wondering why God gave man such an ache in his heart.

"You're a lovely girl," I say.

*CoooooorangEEEEEEEE*. The cinderblock at my ear explodes and goes singing off down the arcade. It seems I am blinking and looking at the gouge in the block and feeling my cheek, which has been stung by twenty mosquitoes.

*CooooooRUNK*. The block doesn't sing. But I notice that a hole has appeared in the lip of the basin where the metal is bent double in a flange. I fall down on Moira, jamming her into the space between cooler and ice machine.

"You crazy fool! Get off me! You're killing me!"

"Shut up. Somebody is trying to kill us."

Moira becomes quiet and small and hot, like a small boy at the bottom of pile-on. Craning up, I can see the hole in the lip of the cooler basin but not through to the top hole. The second shot did not ricochet. It is possible to calculate that the shot came into the arcade at an angle and from a higher place. No doubt from a balcony room across the pool. Perhaps directly opposite the room where Ellen is.

My feet feel exposed, as if they were sticking off the end of a bed. My arms tremble from the effort of keeping my weight off Moira.

The third shot does not come.

"Here's what we're going to do," I tell her, still covering her. "I think we can squeeze around behind the ice-maker and come out beyond the line of fire. You go first."

Moira nods, dumb, and begins to tremble. She has just realized what has happened.

"Now!"

I follow her. We wait between Coke machine and ice-maker.

"Now!"

We break for the far end of the arcade and the rear of the motel.

Out to the weedy easement where my water hose runs from the Esso station. The elderberry is shoulder high. We keep low and follow the hose. It turns up the wall to the bathroom window.

It is an easy climb up the panel of simulated wrought-iron and fairly safe behind the huge Esso oval.

"I'll go up first," I tell Moira, "take a look around and signal you."

I climb in the window and run for my revolver in the closet without even looking at Ellen, who is shouting something from the bed.

"Bolt the door, Ellen."

Back to the bathroom to cover Moira, who is looking straight up from the elderberries, mouth open. I beckon her up.

Turn off the air-conditioner.

We three sit on the floor of the dressing room. No sound

outside. Moira begins to whisper to Ellen, telling her what happened. I am thinking. Already it is hotter.

"He's going to kill us all," says Ellen presently. She sits cross-legged like a campfire girl, tugs her skirt over her knees. "It must be a madman."

"A very very sick person," says Moira, frowning.

They're wrong. It's worse, I'm thinking. It's probably a Bantu from the swamp, out to kill me and take the girls. It comes over me: why, the son of a bitch is out to kill me and take the girls!

Presently the girls relax. I stand at the front window and watch the opposite balcony.

Does the curtain move?

But there is nothing to be seen, no rifle barrel.

Ellen is leafing through a directory of nationwide Howard Johnson motels. Moira is clicking her steely thumbnail against a fingernail.

Whup! Something about the revolver looks wrong. I spin the cylinder. Something is wrong. It's not loaded. Heart sinks. What to do? Fetch my carbine. But that means leaving the girls. Then I'll have to take the sniper with me.

I think of something.

"Where is your car parked, Ellen?"

"Beyond the restaurant."

"Next to the fence?"

"Yes."

"All right. Listen, girls. We can't stay here like this—with him out there. Not for days or weeks."

"Weeks!" cried Ellen. "What do you mean?"

"Here's what we're going to do. Who can shoot a pistol?"

"Not me," says Moira.

Ellen takes the empty revolver. It'll make them feel better.

"It's cocked and off safety. Shoot anybody who tries to get in. If it's me, I'll whistle like a towhee. Like this. Now lock the bathroom window behind me. I'll have to undo the hose."

"What do you have in mind, Chief?" asks Ellen, all business. She's my girl Friday again. She's also one up on Moira.

"I'm going to get my carbine. I also have to check on my mother. Truthfully I don't think anybody's going to bother you here. I'm going to make a lot of noise just in case somebody's still hanging around, and I think he'll follow me. He's been following me for days. Ellen, let's check the Anser-Phones. We'll stay in touch. See what you can find out about what's going on. Sorry about the air-conditioner, but I think it's going to rain."

The girls look solemn. I take a drink of Early Times and fill my flask.

4

A simple matter to follow the weedy easement past the ice-cream restaurant to Ellen's neat little Toyota electric parked between a rusted hulk of a Cadillac and a broken-back vineclad Pontiac. No bullet holes in the windows.

Head out straight across the plaza making as big a show as possible, stomping the carriage bell and zigzagging the tiller —you sit sideways and work a tiller and scud along like a catboat. Ellen's car is both Japanese and Presbyterian, thrifty, tidy, efficient, chaste. As a matter of fact, Ellen was born in Japan of Georgia Presbyterian missionaries.

No one follows. Then double back, circle old Saint Michael's, bang the Bermuda bell—and head out for the pines.

Someone should follow me.

Now wait at the fork behind the bicycle shed where the kids parked their bikes and caught the school bus. One road winds up the ridge, the other along the links to the clubhouse. It is beginning to rain a little. Big dusty drops splash on the windshield.

Here he comes.

Here comes something anyhow. Rubber treads hum on the wet asphalt. He pauses at the fork. A pang: did I leave tracks? No. He goes past slowly, taking the country-club road, a big Cushman golf cart clumsily armored with scraps of sheet-iron wired to the body and tied under the surrey fringe. The driver can't be seen. It noses along the links like a beetle and disappears in the pines.

There is no one in sight except a picaninny scraping up soy-bean meal on number 8 green.

Why not take the ridge road and drive straight to my house?

I do it, meeting nobody, enter at the service gate and dive out of sight under a great clump of azaleas. Then up through the plantation of sumac that used to be the lawn, to the lower "woods" door. It is the rear lower-level door to the new wing

Doris added after ten years of married life had canceled the old.

It occurs to me that I have not entered the house through this door since Doris left. I squeeze past the door jammed by wistaria. It is like entering a strange house.

The green gloom inside smells of old hammocks and ping-pong nets. Here is the "hunt" room, Doris's idea, fitted out with gun cabinet, copper sink, bar, freezer, billiard table, life-size stereo-V, easy chairs, Audubon prints. Doris envisioned me coming here after epic hunts with hale hunting compan-ions, eviscerating the bloodly little carcasses of birds in the sink, pouring sixteen-year-old bourbon in the heavy Aber-crombie field-and-stream glasses and settling down with my pipe and friends and my pointer bitch for a long winter eve-ning of man talk and football-watching. Of course I never came here, never owned a pointer bitch, had no use for friends, and instead of hunting took to hanging around Para-dise Bowling Lanes and drinking Dixie beer with my partner, Leroy Ledbetter.

The carbine is still in the cabinet. But before leaving I'd better go topside and check the terrain. At the top of a spiral stair is Doris's room, a kind of gazebo attached to the house at one of its eight sides. An airy confection of spidery white iron, a fretwork of ice cream, it floats like a tree house in the whispering crowns of the longleaf pines. A sun-ray breaks through a rift of cloud and sheds a queer gold light that catches the raindrops on the screen.

Here sat Doris with Alistair and his friend Martyn whom, I confess, I liked to hear Alistair address not as we did, with the swallowed *n, Mart'n*, but with the decent British aspirate *Mar-tyn*. Even liked hearing him address me with his tidy rounded *o*, not as we would say, Tăm, but Tōm: "I say, Tōm, what about mixing me one of your absolutely smashing gin fizzes? There's a good chap?" Where's a good chap? I would ask but liked his English nevertheless, mine having got loosed, broadened, slurred over, somewhere along the banks of the Ohio or back in the bourbon hills of Kentucky, and so would fix gin fizzes for him and Martyn.

Alistair: half-lying in the rattan settee, tawny-skinned, tawny-eyes, mandala-and-chain half-hidden in his Cozumel homespuns, his silver and turquoise bracelet (the real article with links as heavy and greasy as engine gears) slid down his wrist onto his gold hand, which he knows how to flex as gracefully as Michelangelo's Adam touching God's hand.

Mar-tyn: a wizened Liverpool youth, not quite clean, whose low furrowed brow went up in a great shock of dry wiry hair; Mar-tyn, who gave himself leave not to speak because it was understood he was "with" Alistair; who mystified Doris with his unattractiveness and who when I gave him his gin fizz in a heavy Abercrombie field-and-stream glass, always shot me the same ironic look: "Thanks, mite."

Doris happy though, despite Mar-tyn. Here in her airy gazebo in the treetops it seemed to her that things had fallen out right at last. This surely was the way life was lived: Alistair sharing with her the English hankering for the Orient and speaking in the authentic mother tongue of reverence for life and of the need of making homely things with one's own hands; of a true community life stripped of its technological dross, of simple meetings and greetings, spiritual communions, the touch of a hand, etcetera etcetera.

"We're afraid of touching each other in our modern culture," said Alistair, extending his golden Adam's hand and touching me.

"You're damn right we are," I said, shrinking away.

He would discuss his coming lecture with Doris, asking her advice about the best means of penetrating the "suburban armor of indifference."

Doris listened and advised breathlessly. To her the very air of the summerhouse seemed freighted with meanings. Possibilities floated like motes in the golden light. Breathlessly she sat and mostly listened, long-limbed and lovely in her green linen, while Alistair quoted the sutras. English poets she had memorized at Winchester High School sounded as fresh as the new green growth of the pines.

> The world is too much with us; late and soon,
> Getting and spending, we lay waste our powers,

said Alistair, swishing his gin fizz.

"How true!" breathed Doris.

"Holiness is wholeness," said Alistair, holding in his cupped hand a hooded warbler who had knocked himself out against the screen.

"That is so true!" said Doris.

Not that I wasn't included, even after Alistair found out
that it was Doris, not I, who had the money. Alistair was
good-natured and wanted to be friends. Under any other circumstances we might have been: he was a rogue but a likable
one. Mar-tyn was a Liverpool guttersnipe, but Alistair was a
likable rogue. We got along well enough. Sunday mornings
he'd give his lecture at the Unity church on reverence for life
or mind-force, and Samantha and I'd go to mass and we'd
meet afterwards in the summerhouse.

They were a pair of rascals. What a surprise. No one ever
expects the English to be rascals (compare Greeks, Turks,
Lebanese, Chinese). No, the English, who have no use for
God, are the most decent people on earth. Why? Because they
got rid of God. They got rid of God two hundred years ago
and became extraordinarily decent to prove they didn't need
him. Compare Merrie England of the fifteenth and sixteenth
centuries. A nation of rowdies.

"I greatly admire the Catholic mass," Alistair would say.

"Good."

"I accept the validity of all religions."

"I don't."

"Pity."

"Yes."

"I say, Tōm."

"Yes?"

"We could be of incalculable service to each other, you
know."

"How's that?"

"You could help our work on mind-force with your scientific expertise in psychiatry. We're on the same side in the
struggle against materialism. Together we could help break the
laws of materialism that straitjacket modern science."

"I believe in such laws."

"We could oppose the cult of objectivity that science
breeds."

"I favor such objectivity."

"I have unending admiration for your Church."

"I wish I could say the same for yours."

"You know, Origen, one of the greatest doctors of your
Church, was one of us. He believed in reincarnation, you
know."

"As I recall, we kicked his ass out."

"Yes. And the poor man was so burdened with guilt, he cut off his own member."

"I might do the same for you."

"You're a rum one, Tŏm."

Mar-tyn laughed his one and only laugh: "Arr arr arr. Cut off 'is ruddy whacker, did he?"

Doris would have none of this, either Catholic vulgarity or Liverpool vulgarity, and she and Alistair would get back on reverence for life while I grilled rib-eye steaks on the hibachi, my specialty and Alistair's favorite despite his reverence for steers.

What happened was not even his fault. What happened was that Samantha died and I started drinking and stayed drunk for a year—and not even for sorrow's sake. Samantha's death was as good an excuse as any to drink. I could have been just as sorry without drinking. What happened was that Doris and I chose not to forgive each other. It was as casual a decision as my drinking. Alistair happened to come along at the right time.

Poor fellow, he didn't even get the money he wanted. He got Doris, whom he didn't want. Doris died. God knows what Doris wanted. A delicate sort of Deep-South Oriental life lived with Anglican style. Instead, she died.

Alistair was right, as it turned out, to disapprove my religious intolerance. I, as defender of the faith, was as big a phony as he and less attractive. Perhaps I'd have done worse than follow Origen's example, poor chap.

Feeling somewhat faint from hunger, I return to my apartment in the old wing and fix myself a duck-egg flip with Worcestershire and vodka. Check the phone. Dead. Call into Ellen on the Anser-Phone. The line is already plugged in. The Anser-Phone operator got frightened about something, Ellen said, and left. But all quiet at the motel. She and Moira are playing gin rummy.

Two lovely girls they are, as different as can be, one Christian, one heathen, one virtuous, one not, but each lovely in her own way. And some Bantu devil is trying to take them from me. He must be dealt with.

Back in the hunt room, I take the 30.06 from the cabinet. It is still greased and loaded. I pocket an extra clip. Get 38's for the revolver!

5

Take the Toyota onto the links, use cart paths next to the woods, cross the fairway to my mother's back yard, run under her mountainous Formosa azaleas and out of sight.

The back door is unlocked. All seems normal hereabouts. Eukie, Mother's little servant, is sitting in the kitchen polishing silver and watching Art Linkletter III interview some school children from Glendale.

"Eukie, where is Mrs. More?"

"She up in the bathroom."

"What's been going on around here?"

Eukie is a no-account sassy little black who is good for nothing but getting dressed up in his white coat and serving cocktails to Mother's bridge ladies.

Check the phone. Dead.

For a fact Mother is in the bathroom, all dressed up, blue-white Hadassah hair curled, down on her hands and knees in her nylons, scrubbing the tile floor. Whenever things went wrong, I remember, a sale fallen through, my father down on his luck sunk in his chair watching daytime reruns of *I Love Lucy*, my mother would hike up her skirt and scrub the bathroom floor.

"What's wrong, Mama?"

"Look at that workmanship!" She points the scrub brush to a crack between tile and tub. "No wonder I've got roaches. Hand me that caulk!"

"Mother, I want to talk to you." I pull her up. I sit on the rim of the tub. She closes the lid and sits on the john. "Now. What's going on around here?"

"Humbug, that's what's going on."

"Has anybody bothered you?"

"Who's going to bother me?"

"Then why are you scrubbing the bathroom floor in your best clothes?"

"My car won't start and I can't call a taxi. My phone's dead."

"Is that all?"

"What else?" She is sitting straight up, smoothing her waist down into her hip, wagging her splendid calf against her knee.

"I mean, have you noticed anything unusual?"

"People running around like chickens with their heads cut off. You'd think a hurricane was on the way."

"What people?"

"The Bococks down the street. He and the children threw their clothes in the boat and drove away."

"Boat? Oh, you mean on the trailer. Is that all?"

"What else? Then this trash backs up a truck to the Bocock house."

"Trash? What trash?"

"White trash. Black trash. Black men in yellow robes and guns."

"You mean they moved in?"

"Don't ask me!"

"Or did they take things and leave?"

"I didn't notice."

I sit on the tub thinking. Mother dips brush into Clorox.

"Mother, you're leaving."

"Leave! Why should I leave?"

"I'm afraid you're in some danger here."

"There's not a soul in the neighborhood. Anyhow Euclid is here."

"Eukie ain't worth a damn."

"I can't leave. My car won't start." I see she's frightened and wants to leave.

"Take my car. Or rather Ellen's. Take Eukie with you and go to Aunt Minnie's in town and stay there till you hear from me. Go the back way by my house."

"All right," says Mother distractedly, looking at her wrinkled Cloroxed fingertips. "But first I have to pass by the Paradise office and pass an act of sale."

"Act of sale! What are you talking about?"

"Then I'm coming back and stay with Lola. Lola's not leaving."

Dusty Rhoades, Mother tells me, had come by earlier, argued with the two women, had an emergency call, and left.

"You mean Lola's over there now?"

"She won't leave! She's a lovely girl, Tommy."

"I know."

"And she comes from lovely people."

"She does?"

"She's the girl for you. She's a Taurus."

"I know."

"Ellen is not for you."

"Ellen! Who said anything about Ellen? Last time you were worried about Moira."

"She doesn't come from the aristocratic Oglethorpes. I inquired. Her father was a mailman."

"My God, Mother, what are you talking about? There were no aristocratic Oglethorpes. Please go get your things."

My mother, who sets no store at all by our connection with Sir Thomas More, speaks often of her ancestor Sieur de Marigny, who was a rascal but also, she says, an aristocrat.

I give Eukie my father's twelve-gauge pump gun loaded with a single twenty-five-year-old shell.

"Eukie, you ride shotgun."

"Yes, suh!" Eukie is delighted with the game.

"If anybody tries to stop Miss Marva, shoot them."

Eukie looks at me. "Shoot them? Who I'm going to shoot?"

"I don't know." Euclid is sitting opposite Mother, holding the shotgun over his shoulder like a soldier. "Never mind."

Off they go in the Toyota, facing each other across the tiller.

6

Lola, in jeans and gingham shirt, is hoeing her garden at Tara. A straight chair at the end of a row holds a .45 automatic and a cedar bucket of ice water with a dipper. Her shirt-tails are tied around in front leaving her waist bare. The deep channel of her spine glistens.

I lean my carbine against the chair.

"What are you planting?"

"Mustard." Lola jumps up and gives me a big hug. "You're so smart!"

"Smart?"

"Yesterday. I didn't know you were a genius."

"Genius?"

"In The Pit. Lola's so proud of you." She gives me another hug.

"Do you think you ought to be here by yourself? Where's Dusty?"

"Nobody's going to mess with Lola."

"I see." I fall silent.

"Did you come to see me?"

"Yes."

"Well? State your business."

"Yes. Well, I don't think you ought to stay here." It's where she should stay that gives me pause. Lola sees this.

"And just where do you propose that I go?"

"Into town."

She commences hoeing again. "Nobody's running Lola off her own place. Besides, I doubt there is any danger. All I've seen are a few witch doctors and a couple of drugheads."

"There was another atrocity last night."

"Nellie Bledsoe? I think P.T. got drunk and let her have it with the shish kebab."

"I've been shot at twice in the last hour."

"Tommy!" cries Lola, dropping the hoe. She takes my hand in her warm, cello-callused fingers. "Are you hurt?" she asks, feeling me all over for holes.

"No. He missed me."

"Who in the world—?"

"I don't know. I think it's a Bantu."

Lola slaps her thigh angrily. Eyes blazing, she places her fists on her hips, arms akimbo. She nods grimly. "That does it."

"Does what?"

"You stay here with Lola."

"I can't do that."

"Why not?"

"I have, ah, other responsibilities." Such as two girls in a motel room, but I can't tell her that.

"Such as?"

"My mother."

"Very well." She waits, searching my eyes. She's waiting for me to ask her to stay with me. When I don't, she shrugs and picks up the hoe. "Don't worry about Lola. Lola can take care of herself."

"Why won't you leave?"

"I can't leave my babies." She nods toward the stables.

"You mean the horses? Turn them loose. They'll be all right."

"Besides that, I've just laid in one thousand New Hampshire chicks."

"Chickens, mustard greens. What are you planning for?"

"I think we're in for a long winter and I'm planning to stick it out here."

"Why do you say that?"

She shrugs and mentions the possiblity of civil disturbances between Knothead and Leftpapas, between black and white, etcetera. "So I think the safest place in the world is right here at Tara minding my own business."

I nod and tell her about my fears for the immediate future, about the mishap that befell my lapsometers and the consequent dangers of a real disaster.

Lola listens intently. It is beginning to drizzle. Suddenly taking my hands in hers, warms as a horn, and picking up her gun, she leads me impulsively to the great gallery of the house, where we sit in a wooden swing hung by chains from the ceiling.

"Tommy," she says excitedly, "isn't it great here? Look at the rain."

"Yes."

"Dusty's leaving. Let's me and you stay here and see it through, whatever it is."

"I'd certainly like to."

"You know what I truly believe?"

"What?"

"When all is said and done, the only thing we can be sure of is the land. The land never lets you down."

"That's true," I say, though I never did know what that meant. We look out at six acres of Saint Augustine grass through the silver rain.

The great plastered columns, artificially flaked to show patches of brickwork, reminds me of Vince Marsaglia, boss of the rackets. He built Tara from what he called the "original plans," meaning the drawings of David O. Selznick's set designer, whose son Vince had known in Las Vegas. Once, shortly after I began to practice medicine, I was called to Tara to treat Vince for carbuncles. Feeling much better after the lancings, he and his boys sat right here on the gallery shying playing cards into a hat from at least thirty feet, which they did with extraordinary skill. I watched with unconcealed admiration, having tried unsuccessfully to perfect the same technique during four years of fraternity life. I also admired the thoroughbreds grazing in the meadow.

"You like that horse, Doc? Take him," said Vince with uncomplicated generosity.

Now the swing moves to and fro in an almost flat arc on its long chains. We sit holding hands and watch the curtains of silvery rain. Lola smells of the fresh earth under her finger-nails and of the faint ether-like vapors of woman's sweat.

Her cello calluses whisper in my hand. At the end of each arc I can feel her strong back thrust against the slats of the swing.

"Now here's what we're going to do, Tom Tom," says Lola, ducking her head to make the swing go. "Lola's going to fix you a big drink. Then you're going to sit right there and Lola will play for you."

"For how long?"

"Until the trouble is over."

"That might take weeks—if it's over then."

"O.K. Lola will do for you. We'll work in the garden, and in the evenings we'll sit here and drink and play music and watch the mad world go by. How does that sound?"

"Fine," I say, pleased despite myself at the prospect of spending the evenings so, sipping toddies here in the swing while Lola plays Dvořák, clasping the cello between her noble knees.

"Tom Tom singing to Lola?" she asks and I become aware I am humming. "Là ci darem" from *Don Giovanni*. My musical-erotic area, Brodmann 11, is still singing like a bird.

I pick up the 30.06. "There's something I have to take care of first."

Lola shoves her .45 into her jeans. "Lola will go with you."

"No, Lola won't."

"I can shoot."

Before I know what has happened, she takes out the .45 and, aiming like a man, arm extended laterally, shoots a green lizard off the column. I nearly jump out of the swing. In the bare gallery the shot is like a crack of lightning in a small valley. Thunder roars back and forth. Brick dust settles.

My ears are ringing when I stand up to leave.

"Darling Tom Tom," whispers Lola, putting away the gun and giving me a hug, eye to eye, shoulder to shoulder, hip to hip. "Come back to Tara. Lola will be waiting. Come back and put down roots with Lola."

"All right. Now listen. If anything happens—if there is an invasion by the Bantus or if you see a peculiar yellow cloud—I want you to do exactly what I tell you."

"Tell Lola!"

"Come to the old plaza. To Howard Johnson's. I'll be there. You understand?"

"O.K.," says Lola, hugging me and giving me some hard pats on the hip. "But don't be surprised if you see Lola sooner than you think." She winks.

I frown. "Don't you follow me, Lola. I forbid it, goddamn it."

"Tom Tom act masterful with Lola? Lola like that. Howard Johnson's. Wow." She hands me my carbine. "Come back to Tara!"

7

Colonel Ringo's distinguished head is outlined in the window of the guardhouse at the gates of Paradise. A reassuring sight. Hm, things cannot be too bad. The colonel's armored Datsun is parked behind the guardhouse.

"Halt! Who goes there!" yells the Colonel from a crouch in the doorway, his revolver pointed at me.

"It's me, Colonel!" I hold the carbine over my head.

"What's the password? Oh, it's you, Dr. More." The Colonel holsters his revolver and yanks me inside. "You're in the line of fire."

"What is the password?"

"Lurline, but get on in here, boy."

"What's up, Colonel?"

Now that I take a second look, I perceive that all is not well with him. His silvery eyebrows are awry and one eye, which has been subject for years to a lateral squint, has turned out ninety degrees. His scarlet and cream uniform is streaked with sweat.

"Rounds have been coming in for the past thirty minutes." He nods toward the shattered glass of the far window.

"Rounds? From where, Colonel?"

"From the pro shop as best as I can determine," he says, scanning the distant clubhouse through a pair of binoculars.

"Did you notice a golf cart pass here a while ago?"

"No, but I've only been here half an hour. That's why I'm here, though."

"Why?"

"To mount a rearguard action until they could get the golf carts and swim trophies out. I'm also worried about the molasses cakes and soybean meal in the barn yonder." He looks at his watch. "The patrol is supposed to pick me up in fifteen minutes. You better get out too."

"Colonel, what's going on?"

"Son, the Bantu boogers have occupied Paradise Country Club."

"But, Colonel, I haven't seen any Bantus."

"Then who in hell is shooting at me, the tennis committee?" The Colonel slumps against the wall. "What's more, they got Rudy and Al."

Noticing that the Colonel's hands are shaking, I offer him a drink from my flask.

"I thank you, son," says the Colonel gratefully. "Reach me a Seven-Up behind you. They cut the wires but the box is still cold."

The Colonel knocks back a fair portion of my pint, chases it with Seven-Up, sighs. Presently he takes my arm, cheek gone dusky with emotion. One eye drifts out.

"Doc, what is the one thing you treasure above all else?"

"Well—" I begin, taking time off to fix my own drink.

"I'll tell you what I cherish, Doc."

"All right," I say, taking a drink and feeling the good hot bosky bite of the bourbon.

"The Southern womanhood right here in Paradise! Right?"

"Yes," I reply, even though 90 percent of the women in Paradise are from the Midwest.

"And I'll tell you something else!"

"All right."

"We may be talking about two gentlemen who may have laid down their lives for just that."

"Who's that?"

"Rudy and Al!"

"What happened to them?"

"Damnedest thing you ever saw," says the Colonel, settling down in his canvas chair and putting his good eye to a crack that commands a view of the clubhouse.

I look at my watch impatiently and then study the shattered window. Could a bullet have done it? Perhaps, but the Colonel is a bit nutty today. Taking no chances, I sit in the doorway and keep the heavy jamb between me and the clubhouse, even though the latter is a good four hundred yards distant.

The Colonel takes another drink. "I've never seen anything

like it, son, since I was with the Alabama National Guard in
Ecuador." The Colonel is from Montgomery.

As best I can piece out the Colonel's rambling, almost
incoherent account, the following events took place earlier
this morning. There is no reason to doubt their accuracy. For
one thing, I witnessed the beginning of the incident on the
golf links this morning.

The Colonel was in charge of the security and the transportation of the corps of Christian Kaydettes to Oxford, Mississippi, for the national baton-twirling contest. The Kaydettes
had put on an early show for the Pro-Am Bible breakfast,
immediately thereafter embarking for Mississippi in two
school buses, the first transporting the girls, the second their
moms, a formidable crew of ladies who had already fallen out
with each other over the merits of their daughters and had
boarded the bus carrying their heavy purses in silence. (It was
this boarding that I had witnessed earlier in the day.) Firecrackers (not rifles, as I had thought) had been discharged.
Banners on the buses read BEAT DAYTON, Dayton, Ohio,
being the incumbent champs. Colonel Ringo rode point in his
armored Datsun followed by the bus carrying the Kaydettes,
followed by Rudy on his Farhad Grotto motorcycle, followed
by the busload of moms, each a graduate of the Paradise karate school. The rear was brought up by Al Pulaski, formerly
of the Washington, D.C., police and now president of PASHA
(Paradise Anglo-Saxon Heritage Association), in his police
special, an armored van fitted out with a complete communi-
cations system.

Mindful of rumors, however preposterous, of a conspiracy
to kidnap the entire Kaydette corps and spirit them off to the
fastness of Honey Island Swamp, Colonel Ringo was careful
in plotting his route to the Mississippi state line, where the
little convoy was to be turned over to the Mississippi Highway
Police. Ruling out the interstate as the obvious site of ambush,
he selected old state highway 22. All went well until they
reached the wooden bridge crossing a finger of Honey Island
Swamp formed by Bootlegger Bayou. The Colonel, riding
point, felt a premonition ("I learned to smell an ambush in
Ecuador," he told me). Approaching the bridge, however, he
saw nothing amiss. It was not until he was halfway across and
coming abreast of the draw that he saw what was wrong, saw
two things simultaneously and it was hard to say which was
worse: one, the cubicle of the drawbridge was occupied by a

bridge-tender in an orange robe—Bantu!—two, the draw was beginning to lift. In the space of two seconds he did three things, hit the accelerator, hit the siren to warn the buses, and began to fire his turret gun ("You got to shoot by reflex, son, and I can fire that turret gun like shooting from the hip").

He made the draw, felt the slight jolt as he dropped an inch or so, shot up the cubicle with the turret gun and, he felt sure, got the Bantu. The girls made it too, though they were badly shaken up by the two-foot drop.

"I got ever last one of those girls to Mississippi, son," says the Colonel, taking another drink. I watch my flask worriedly. "You talk about some scared girls—did you ever see a school bus make eighty miles an hour on a winding road? But we made it."

"But, Colonel, what happened to the others?"

The Colonel clucks and tilts his head. "That's the only bad part."

Once across the bridge, he didn't have time to look back. But he saw enough. The Bantu bridge-tender was out of commission, dead or winged, but the draw went on lifting. Rudy, on his Farhad Grotto Harley-Davidson, saw he couldn't make the draw and tried to stop short, braking and turning. The Colonel's last sight of him ("a sight engraved on my memory till my dying day") was of the orange and green bike flying through the air, Rudy still astride, and plummeting into the alligator-infested waters of Bootlegger Bayou.

The moms? The second bus stopped short of the draw, Al Pulaski in his van behind them.

"You mean the Bantus have captured the mothers?" I ask.

The Colonel looks grave. "All we can do is hope." On the plus side, the Colonel went on to say, were two factors. Al was there with his van. And the mothers themselves, besides carrying in their heavy purses the usual pistols, Mace guns, and alarms, were mostly graduates of karate and holders of the Green Belt.

"Many a Bantu will bite the dust before they take those gals," says the Colonel darkly.

"Well, I mean, were there any Bantus attacking? Did you see any? Maybe the bus had time to turn around and get back."

"I didn't see any, but we must assume the worst."

We sit drinking in companionable silence, reflecting upon the extraordinary events of the day.

Presently the Colonel leans close and gives me a poke in the ribs. "I'll tell you the damn truth, son."

"What's that, Colonel?"

"I wouldn't take on those ladies in a month of Sundays. Whoo-ee," says the Colonel and knocks back another inch of my Early Times. He laughs.

"Ha ha, neither would I, Colonel," I say, laughing. "I feel sure they will be all right."

Suddenly the Colonel catches sight of something through the crack. He leaps up, staggering to the doorway.

"Stop thief!" he cries hoarsely.

"What's wrong, Colonel?"

"They're back, the little boogers!" he cries scarlet-faced, lunging about and picking up helmet and revolver and riding crop. "I'll fix the burrheads!"

"Wait, Colonel! The sniper!"

But he's already past me. Looking out the window, I catch sight of a dozen or so picaninnies and a few bigger boys running from the stables with armfuls of molasses cakes. One big boy totes a sack of feed. It's too late to stop the Colonel. He's after them, lumbering up a bunker. With his steel helmet and revolver, he looks like a big-assed General Patton. The culprits, catching sight of the furious red-faced Colonel thundering down on them, drop their ill-gotten goods and flee for the woods—all but one, the boy with the feed sack. The Colonel collars him, gives him a few licks with the crop and, dragging him to the shack, hurls him past me into the corner. "You watch this one. I'm going after the others."

"Wait, Colonel—!" I grab him. "You've forgotten the sniper."

"No, by God! I have my orders and I'm carrying them out."

"Orders? What orders?"

"To guard the molasses cakes and soybean meal."

"Yes, but, Colonel—"

He wrenches loose. "Here I come, you commonist Bantu burrheads!" cries the Colonel, charging the bunker and firing his revolver. "Alabama has your ass." Up he goes and—"Oof!"—as quickly comes reeling back. He stumbles and sits down hard on the doorsill. At the same moment there comes a slamming concussion, a rifle shot, very loud, from the direction of the clubhouse. The youths shrinks into his corner.

Gazing down at the Colonel, I try to figure out what hit him. He looks all in one piece.

"What happened, Colonel?" I ask, pulling him out of the line of fire.

"They got me in the privates," groans the Colonel. "What am I going to do?"

"Let me see."

"What am I going to tell Pearline?" he asks, swaying to and fro.

"Who is Pearline?" I ask in a standard medical tone to distract him while I examine him, and from curiosity because his wife is named Georgene.

"Oh, Lordy."

At last I succeed in stretching him out on the floor. There is a bloodstain on his cream-colored trousers. I borrow the youth's pocketknife and cut out a codpiece.

The Colonel is a lucky man. The bullet pierced a fold of scrotum, passed between his legs and went its way. I take out a clean handkerchief.

"You're O.K., Colonel. A scratch. Son, hand me a cold Seven-Up."

"Yes suh, Doc."

"Colonel, hold this bottle here and close your legs on it tight as you can. You'll be right as rain."

There is time now to examine the black youth, who has been very helpful, uttering sympathetic noises and an exclamation of amazement at the nature of the Colonel's wound: "Unon*unh!*"

"Aren't you Elzee Acree?"

"Yes suh!"

I recognize him now, a slender brindle-brown youth with a cast in his eye, the son of Ellilou Acree, a midwife and a worthy woman.

We make the Colonel as comfortable as possible, propping his head on his helmet. He lies stretched out the length of the tiny hut, the king-size Seven-Up in place between his legs.

"Elzee, what in hell are you doing here?"

"Nothing, Doc!"

"Nothing! What do you mean, nothing?"

"I heard they needed help unloading the barn."

"So you were unloading a few sacks to help them out?"

"That's right, Doc. I was stacking them under the tree so the truck could pick them up."

"Never mind. Listen Elzee. I want you to do something." I give him five dollars. "You stay here and tend to the Colonel until the patrol picks him up."

"I'll be right here! Don't you worry, Doc. But what I'm gon' tell the patrol?"

"The patrol won't bother you. The Colonel here will tell them you helped him, won't you, colonel?"

"Sho. I been knowing Elzee, he's a good boy. Bring me a Seven-Up, Elzee."

"Yes suh!"

"Now pour out the neck and fill it up from Doc's bottle there."

Collecting the carbine—the flask is empty—I stand in the doorway a minute, gathering my wits when: *thunk* ka-POW! Splinters fly from the jamb three inches from my nose. I sit down beside the Colonel.

"Why, that son of a bitch is trying to kill us all!" I say.

"Like I told you!" cries the Colonel.

"Unh unh tch," says Elzee, not unhappily. "Those some turrible folks over there."

"That fellow's been after me for three days," I mutter.

"It sho looks like it, Doc," murmurs Elzee sympathetically and hands the Colonel the spiked Seven-Up.

"What do you know about them, Elzee?" I ask, looking at him sharply. "Who all's down there?"

"I don't know, Doc, but they some mean niggers, don't you worry about that," says Elzee proudly.

"You mean there's more than one?"

"Bound to be."

"Or is there just one?"

"I just seen one pass by and I didn't know him."

I look at him in disgust. "Elzee, you don't know what in the hell you're talking about."

"That Elzee's a good boy, though," says the Colonel, who feels a lot better after taking a drink. "Aren't you, boy?"

"Yes suh! I been knowing the Colonel here!"

"Oh shut up," I say disgustedly to both. Between the two of them they've struck up an ancient spurious friendship and I've had enough of both. Let me out of here. I look at the clubhouse through the crack. The sun is out. The fairways sparkle with raindrops. Pennants fly from the pavilions set up for the Pro-Am tournament, but not a soul is in sight. The legend of the banner, Jesus Christ Greatest Pro of Them All, can't quite be read from this distance.

There must be a way of getting behind the sniper.

A drainage ditch runs from the higher ground behind the stable toward the clubhouse road and angles off across two fairways before it enters the strip of woods along the bayou.

"Elzee, how deep is that dredge ditch over by the tree there?"

"That grudge ditch at least ten feet deep, Doc!" cries Elzee.

Shouldering my carbine, I bid farewell to the drunk Colonel and the obliging Elzee.

8

The ditch crosses the road under a cattle guard directly in front of the guardhouse. The danger here is thirty feet of open ground between the door and the ditch. There's a better way. The north window of the guardhouse lets into a grove of live oaks whose thick foliage droops at the margins, the heavy limbs propped like elbows on the ground. The ditch skirts the far perimeter of the grove. Though the distance is a good hundred feet, at least ninety feet of it is covered by the grove.

Drop from the window, three long steps and dive for the grove. No shot. Once inside the oak, the going is good. The ground is still dry. It is like walking across a circus tent, the dusty twilight space sparkling with chinks of sunlight in the shifting canopy.

Elzee lied as usual. The ditch is no more than five feet deep, but it is dry and unchoked and walkable at a stoop. The worst part is near the cattle guard, where it rises to within two feet of the bars. Through the briars on hands and knees, cradling the carbine in my elbows Ecuador-style.

It takes ten minutes to reach the woods.

Once again in deep shade and walking is possible, through little bare swale and hollows studded with cypress knees, all the while angling gradually toward the water and diverging from the raised shell road. My objective is the marina some two hundred feet upstream from the clubhouse. My face, elbows, and knees are scratched, but I don't feel bad.

Aiming for a point on the bayou where, as I recall, the bank curves out and anchors the downstream end of the docks.

A piece of luck: a gleam of white directly ahead. It is fresh white sand deposited under willows that run out in a towhead. Here is both cover and footing where I expected muck.

My knees make musical rubs in the sharp cool shearing sand, which is wet only on top. Not bad: I missed the end of the marina by no more than a few yards, hitting the lower docks at the fourth slip. This end of the dock is unroofed and low-lying, designed for skiffs and canoes. A reef of alligator grass runs in front of the slips. Mullet jump. Gold dust drifts on the black water. The bayou is brimming from a south wind. Upstream, yachts and power boats drift in their moorings. Sunlight shatters like quicksilver against their square sterns.

I lie at the edge of the willows and watch. Three hundred yards upstream, at a point, two men are pole-fishing in the outside curve. A peaceful sight—but here's an oddity. Their caps are the long-billed mesh-crowned kind Midwesterners wear, pulled low, shadowing their faces; but they fish Negro-style from the bank out, poles flat. Something wrong here: Michiganders don't fish like that and Negroes don't wear caps like that.

From their spot on the outer curve I calculate that they command two reaches of the bayou.

The next-but-last slip has a child's pirogue of warped ply-wood. It is unlocked and dry. Next to it floats a locked canoe with a paddle.

Reach the pirogue, keeping lower than the alligator grass, and slip downstream lying on my back and paddling with both hands. Now past the reef of grass but under cover of the cyr-illa and birch, which, caving and undermined, slant toward the water. A smell of roots and fresh-sloughed earth.

Once round the bend and out of sight of the fishermen, it is safe enough to sit up and paddle straight to the water entrance at the rear of the clubhouse—but no! Downstream now, at the next point, sit another brace of fishermen, faces shaded, poles flat out!

Did they see me? Hardly, because I'm already behind the Humble yacht tied the length of the club dock and standing off just enough, two feet, to let me slip between. I can't see the fantail above me where white-coated waiters would ordinarily be serving up frozen drinks to Humble big shots. But today there is no sound but the slap of water. The yacht, I reason, must be empty because the ports are closed and the air-condi-tioning is silent. The cabins must be like ovens. Turning now into the dark boathouse that runs under the ground-level floor of the clubhouse.

Wedging the pirogue between the dock and the high water, I climb up, keeping an eye peeled for the fishermen. But the yacht blocks the entire boathouse. Anyhow, it is too dark to be seen under here.

Up the concrete service stairs, little used at best, but which ascend, I know, into a kind of pantry between the kitchen and the men's bar. (I was on the Building Committee.) If the sniper is still in the pro shop and the rest of the building is empty, it should be possible to slide open the panel at the rear of the bar where golfers in the pro shop are served, so saving the floors from their spikes (my sole contribution to the Building Committee).

Silence, the keeping of it, is the problem. The door at the top of the stairs is open a crack. I stand on the landing listening. The kitchen sounds empty. It roars with silence and ticks away like any kitchen in the morning. No motors run. A bird hops on the roof.

Will the door creak? Yes. But it can be opened silently, I discover, by warping it open, pushing high with one hand and pulling low with the other. The pantry is dark, darker than the Bayou Bar because the window in the swinging door makes a faint gray diamond. I look through, first from one side then to the other, using the obliquest possible angle without touching the door. The bar is empty, but the far door into the main hall is open. The Portuguese fishnet droops from the ceiling, its glass floats gleaming like soap bubbles in the dim light.

Test the swinging door for creaking. No creaks up to ten inches. Ten inches is enough.

Slip along pecky cypress wall to hinged section of bar. Don't lift, go under—damn! I trip and almost fall. Forgot the raised slatting on the floor to save the barman's feet. Will the slatting creak? Yes. Try the nailed joints. No creak. The quality of the silence is different here. A more thronging, peopled silence—as thick as last Christmas Eve's party. Perhaps it is the acoustic effect of the bottles.

The panel opening into the pro shop is closed. Take a full minute to unsling carbine and prop it against the cushioned edge of the bar. Wait and blink and get used to the light.

Listen.

The leather dice cup is in place, worn and darkened by sweat and palm oil. The bottles are visible now, the front row fitted with measuring spouts. Whitish tendrils of vine have sprouted through the simulated wormholes and twined around the necks of the bottles. I blink. Something is wrong. What? Then I see. What is wrong is that nothing is wrong. The bottles are intact and undrunk.

Someone clears his throat, so close that my breath catches. I open my throat and let my breath out carefully.

The sound comes from behind me, behind the panel.

Again the hawking: I breathe easier. It is a careless habituated sound, deep-throated and resonant with blown-out cheeks, the sound of a man who has been alone for some time.

A chair creaks. Something—its front legs?—hits the floor.

I listen—for a second man and to place the first. If you know a man, you can recognize his voice in his throat-clearings.

French windows, I remember open from the pro shop onto a putting green. Beyond, the shell drive winds through the links and joins the main road. A hundred yards farther is the gate and the guardhouse.

How does the panel fit in its frame? Does it run on channel bearings? Test its hang by putting a finger into the finger recess. The panel sits, simply, in a wooden slot. Test lateral motion: a faint grate. Lubricate it. With what? Spit? No, Benedictine. The liqueur pours like 40-weight oil. Test again. The panel moves an eighth-inch with a slight mucous squeak.

More hawking and throat-clearing. I do not recognize the voice. Wait for a long hawk and slide the panel a quarter-inch. But the panel clears the frame by no more than a crack: a bright line of light but not wide enough to see anything.

Another hawk, another quarter-inch.

I can see him but it's the wrong man: Gene Sarazen in plus fours and slanted forty-five degrees to the floor. To my nostrils comes the smell of the spike-splintered pine floor and of sweated leather. The sunlight is bright. I can hear the open window.

The hawking again but now I can also hear the liquid sound of throat muscles swallowing—and even a light click of the uvula popping clear of the tongue.

*Ahem.*

I reflect: better get the carbine in position now rather than later. The problem now is balance and position, clearing shelf space for my elbows. I calculate he is sitting ten or fifteen feet to the left of my line of sight and that the panel must be opened two or three inches to take the carbine at this angle.

Open it then: with right hand, forefinger in recess, holding carbine stock in left elbow. Open it till I can see him. It takes five minutes.

There he is. Up he comes swimming into view like a diver from the ocean depths.

I don't know him.

He sits at the window, back turned, but I see him at an angle. One cheek is visible, and the notch of one eye. His feet are propped on the low sill—it is not a French window, as I had remembered—the front legs of the director's chair clear of the floor. The feet flex slightly, moving the chair. The rifle lies on the floor under his right hand. It is an M-32, the army's long-barrel sniper rifle with scope. How did he miss me with that? He must be a poor shot.

He is dressed as an *inyanga*, a herbalist, in a *monkhu6*, a striped orange and gray tunic of coarse cotton. From his belt hangs an *izinkhonkwani*, a leather bag originally worn to carry herbs and green sticks but now no doubt filled with .380 mm shells. The foot propped on the sill wears a dirty low-quarter Ked, the kind pro ballplayers wear for scrimmage. His head, shaved, ducks slightly in time with the rocking. His right wrist, dangling above the rifle, wears a large gold watch with a metal expansion band.

I judge he was or is a pro. The lateral columns of neck muscles flare out in a pyramid from jaw to the deep girdle of his shoulders. The bare leg below the tunic is rawboned and sharp-shinned, as strong and stringy as an ostrich's. The skin is, on his neck, carbon-black. It blots light. Light hitting it drains out, it is a hole. The skin at the heel of the loosely flexed hand shades from black to terra cotta to salmon in the palm.

The front sight of my carbine is on his occipital protuberance. The sweetish smell of the Benedictine fills my nostrils. I must shoot him. He will experience light, a blaze of color, and nothing else.

Then shoot him.

He tried to shoot you three times and he would shoot you now. Worse, he wants to take your woman, women.

Saint Thomas Aquinas on killing in self-defense: Q.21, Obj. 4, Part I, *Sum. Theol.* But did he say anything about shooting in the back?

My grandfather on sportsmanship (my grandfather: short

on Saint Thomas, long on Zane Grey): Don't ever shoot a quail on the ground or a duck on the water.

Then what do I do now for Christ's sake, stomp my foot to flush him and shoot him on the fly?

Or in Stereo-V-Western style: Reach, stranger?

No. Just shoot him. The son of a bitch didn't call you out.

Shoot him then.

Wound him?

No, kill him.

The trouble is my elbow is not comfortable.

Get it comfortable then.

Now.

Consider this though: would Richard Coeur de Lion have let Saladin have it in the back, heathen though he was?

The trouble is that my grandfather set more store by Sir Walter Scott than he did by Thomas More.

What would Thomas More have done? Undoubtedly he would have—

"Hold it, Doc."

The voice, which is both conversational and tremulous, comes from close behind me.

"All right."

"Just set the gun down real easy."

"I will."

"You wasn't going to do it anyway, was you, Doc?"

"I don't know."

"You wasn't. I been watching you. Now turn around."

"All right."

It is Victor Charles. He sighs and shakes his head. "Doc, you shouldn't ought to of done this."

"Well, I didn't."

Victor stands against one flap of the saloon doors, single-barrel shotgun held in one hand like a pistol. The weak light from the hall gleams on his white ducks and white interne shoes.

The gun was aimed at my middle but now strays off. Victor, I know, will shoot me if he has to. But I perceive that an old etiquette requires that he not point his gun at me.

"Doc Doc Doc. You sho done gone and done it this time?"

"Yes."

"Doc, how come you didn't do like I told you and move in with your mama and tend to your business?"

"You didn't tell me why."

"How come you had to come over here?"

"That fellow in there has been trying to kill me."

"O.K., Doc. Now let's just move on out of here and up in the front."

It is odd: the main emotion between us is embarrassment. Each is embarrassed for the other. We cannot quite look at each other.

As he waits for me to get in front, Victor picks up the carbine and shoves it under the slatting!

We walk around to the pro shop. At the door I hesitate, wondering if the *inyanga* will shoot me. Victor fathoms this and calls out: "It's all right, Uru. It's just me and Doc."

Uru has swung his chair around to face us. His rifle is still on the floor, his hand clasped behind his head. I notice with surprise that he is very youthful. His pleasant broad face has a sullen expression. A keloid, or welted scar, runs off one eyebrow, pulling the eyebrow down and giving him a Chinese look.

"Well well well. The hunted walks in on the hunter."

"Then I was the hunted." I look at him curiously, shifting my head a bit to get a fix on him. What sort of fellow is he?

"Where did you find him, Victor?"

"He was in there." Victor nods toward the panel. "Fixing hisself a drink. Can't you smell it?"

I take some hope in Victor not mentioning my carbine and in Uru not picking his up. Perhaps they are not going to shoot me.

"What were you doing in there, Doctor?" asks Uru, straining his clasped hands against his head.

"Doc was picking up a couple of bottles," says Victor, shaking his head. "Doc he like his little toddy."

"I didn't ask you. I asked him."

Uru diphthongs his *I*'s broadly and curls his tongue in his *R*'s. I judge he is from Michigan. He sprawls in his chair exactly like a black athlete at Michigan State sprawling in his classroom and shooting insolent glances at his English instructor.

"So Chuck here was going to have himself a party," says Uru lazily. He turns to me. "Chuck, your party days are over."

"Is that right?"

"All right, Victor. You found him. You take care of him."

"D-D-Doc's all right!" cries Victor. Victor's stammering worries me more than Uru's malevolence. "When Doc give you his word, he keeps it. Doc, tell Uru you leaving and not coming back."

"Leaving your house?" Uru asks.

"As a matter of fact, I have left. Moved out."

"So we're taking Doc's word now," says Uru broadly, imitating Victor. He frowns. The chair legs hit the floor. "Victor, who are you taking orders from?"

"You, but I'm going to tell you about Doc here," says Victor, rushing his speech, a frightening thing. He is afraid for me. "Doc here the onliest one come to your house when you're sick. He set up all one night with my auntee."

Uru is smiling broadly—a very pleasant face, really. "So Chuck here set up all night with your auntee." He rolls his eyes up, past Gene Sarazen, to the ceiling. "I don't know. I just don't know."

"Do you mind if I ask you something?" I ask Uru.

"Make it quick, Chuck."

"Just what is it you all have in mind to do around here?"

"Doc," says Victor, sorrowful again. "You know we can't tell you that."

"Why can't we tell him? Chuck's not going to tell anybody, are you, Chuck?"

"Are you all taking over Paradise Estates?"

"No, we all not," says Uru, like any other Yankee.

"Not in the beginning, Doc," says Victor patiently. "All we wanted was the ridge houses since they were empty anyhow, all but yours and you wouldn't leave. We had to have your house."

"Why?"

"The TV tower, Doc."

"What?" I screw up an eye.

"We had to have the transmitter, Chuck," says Uru almost patiently.

"And there you setting under it, Doc." The pity of it comes over Victor. "How come you didn't move in with Miss Marva?"

"Then the shootings were to frighten me away?"

Uru looks at Victor.

"What about the kidnappings?" I ask.

Victor shrugs. "That was just insurance. We just going to keep the little ladies out in Honey Island till y'all sign the papers with us. Ain't nobody going to harm those little ladies, Doc! In fact, my other auntee out there looking after them right now. She raised half of them, like Miss Ruthie and Miss Ella Stone."

"I don't know," says Uru to Gene Sarazen. "I just don't know. They told me about coming down here." He shakes himself and looks at me with an effort. "Victor is right, Chuck. That's all we wanted in the beginning. But now it looks like all the chucks and dudes have moved out. So: we can use the houses."

"It won't work. How long do you think you can hold the place?"

"Just as long as you value your womenfolk."

I am wondering: does he mean the moms and does he know that the Kaydettes were not taken?

The chair legs hit the floor again. Uru looks straight at me.

"I'm going to tell you exactly how it is, Doctor. You chucks had your turn and you didn't do right. You did bad, Doc, and now you're through. It's our turn now and we are going to show you. As Victor say, we sho going to move your ass out."

"I didn't say no such a thing," says Victor. "I don't talk nasty."

"It won't work," I say.

"Doc, you don't know who all we got out there," says Victor. "And we holding enough folks so nobody's going to give us any trouble."

"That's not what he means," says Uru grimly. "Is it, Doctor?"

I am silent.

"What he means, Victor, is that even if we win, it won't work. Isn't that right, Doctor?" Uru has a light in his eye.

I keep silent.

"He means we don't have what it takes, Victor. Oh, he likes you and your auntee. You're good and faithful and he'll he'p you. Right, Doctor? You don't really think we got what it takes, do you?" Uru taps his temple.

"I don't know."

"Come on, Doctor, tell us the truth."

"Doc always tell the truth!"

"Shut up, Victor. Doctor?"

"I'm not sure what you mean."

"Do you always tell the truth?"

"Yes."

"Then tell it now."

"All right."

"You don't really think we're any good, do you?"

"How do you mean, good?"

"I'm talking about greatness, Doctor. Or what you call greatness. I'm talking about the Fifth Symphony, the *Principia Mathematica*, the Uranus guidance system. You know very well what I'm talking about."

"Yes."

"Well?"

"Well, you—"

"And don't tell me about music and rhythm and all."

"All right." I fall silent.

"Let me put it this way, Doctor. You know what we're going to do. We're going to build a new society right here. Right? Only you don't think we can do it, do you?"

I shrug.

"What does that mean?"

"Well—you haven't."

"Haven't what, Doctor?"

"You haven't done very well so far."

"Go on. Let's hear what you mean."

"I think you know what I mean."

"You're not talking to Victor now. You're talking to a Ph.D. in political science. Only I didn't choose to be a black-ass pipe-smoking professor."

"Didn't you used to play split-end for Detroit?"

"Don't change the subject."

"Aren't you Elijah Washington?"

"We have no Jew-Christian names, least of all Washington. I'm Uru. You didn't answer my question."

"What question?"

"About us not doing very well."

"You've had Liberia a long time."

"So?"

"Look at Liberia. You've had Haiti even longer."

"So?"

"Look at Haiti."

"You know something, Chuck. You got a smart mouth. We're liable to do to you what you did to the Indians."

"Do you mind if I have a drink?"

"We don't use it."

"I'll fix you a drink, Doc," says Victor.

"No you won't," says Uru, showing anger for the first time. "You're not his goddamn houseboy."

"You know, my name's Washington too," Victor tells Uru. "After George Washington Carver."

"Jesus Christ," says Uru to Gene Sarazen.

"Blessed be Jesus," says Victor.

"Look what you done to him," Uru says to me.

"What he done to me!" cries Victor.

"You did a good job, Doctor. It took you four hundred years but you really did a good job. Let me ask you something."

"All right."

"What would you do about it if you were me? I mean what with the four hundred years and Victor here."

"What's wrong with Victor?"

"You know what I mean. What would you do about the four hundred years?"

"I'd stop worrying about it and get on with it. To tell you the truth, I'm tired of hearing about the four hundred years."

"You are."

"Yes."

"And if it were up to you?"

"If it were up to me, I'd get on with it. I could do better than Haiti."

"That's what we're going to do, Doctor," says Uru in a changed voice. He picks up his rifle and rises.

Victor grabs my arm. "I'll take care of him, Uru. Like you aksed." He gives me a yank, pulls me close. "Goddamn, Doc, ain't you got any sense?"

Uru seems to keep on getting up. He is at least six feet nine. "All right, Chuck. Let's go."

"Very well, but please let me tell you one thing."

Quickly I tell them about my invention, about its falling into the wrong hands and the likelihood of a catastrophe. I describe the danger signs. "So even though your pigment may protect you to a degree, I'd advise you to take cover if you should sight such a cloud."

Uru laughs for the first time. "Doctor, Victor's right. You something all right. What you telling us is the atom bomb is going to fall and we better get our black asses back to the swamp?"

"Doc is not humbugging," says Victor.

Uru takes a step forward. "Take him, Victor. If you don't, I will."

"Let's go, Doc."

"Where're we going?"

"To headquarters."

"Man, don't answer his questions," says Uru furiously. "When did he answer your questions? He knows what he going to get."

Again Victor pulls me close. "Don't worry, Doc. We holding you for ransom. Ain't that right, Elij—, I mean Uru?"

The two look at each other a long moment. "Doc's worth a lot to us, Uru."

Uru nods ironically. "Very well. But I'm coming with you. I wouldn't put it past you to turn him loose—after fixing him a toddy."

"I ain't fixing Doc nothing, but I might pick me up a bottle," says Victor, disappearing into the hall. I look after him in surprise. Victor doesn't drink.

Uru waves me ahead of him with his rifle.

Victor is waiting for us at the armored Cushman cart. He's got a bottle under his arm. In the golf bag behind him, among the irons, are two guns barrels, his—and mine! Victor doesn't look at me. Uru pays no attention.

9

They take me to "headquarters," which is located in, of all places, the abandoned rectory of old Saint Michael's in the plaza. A good choice: its construction is sturdy and there are no windows to defend.

We drive through Paradise in the armored golf cart, I squatting behind Uru and Victor in the bag well. Victor drives. Uru keeps an eye on me.

Uru is feeling good. "Chuck, you have to admit that Victor here is a remarkable man. He still thinks he can get along with you chucks, sit down and talk things over."

"That's right!" says Victor sententiously. "You can talk to folks! Most folks want to do what's right!"

"Uh huh," says Uru. "They really did right by you, Victor. Here you are fifty years old and still shoveling dog shit. And Willard. Ten years with the U.S. Army in Ecuador and they're nice enough to put him on as busboy at the club. I'll tell you where right comes from—they know it, Chuck knows it, only you don't." Uru swings the muzzle of the M-32 into Victor's neck.

"Ain't nobody going to hold no gun on me," says Victor, frowning and knocking down the barrel.

"That's where they're smarter than you, Victor. They don't need a gun. They made you do what they want without a gun and even made you like it. Like Doc here, being so nice, sitting with your auntee. That's where they beat you, Victor, with sweet Jesus."

"What you talking about?"

"These chucks been fooling you for years with Jehovah God and sweet Jesus."

"Nobody's fooling me."

"And what's so damn funny is that you out-Jesused them."

"What you mean?"

Uru winks at me. "Doc here knows what I mean, don't you, Doc?"

"No."

"He knows the joke all right and the joke's on you, Victor. All these years you either been in trouble or else got nothing to your name, they been telling you about sweet Jesus. Now damned if you don't holler sweet Jesus louder than they do. What's so funny is they don't even believe it any more. Ask Doc. You out-Jesused them, Victor, that's what's so funny. And Doc knows it."

"Now Doc here is a Catholic," says Victor. "But that don't matter to me. I never had anything against Catholics like some folks."

"I'm sure glad to hear that you and Doc have composed your religious differences," says Uru, grinning.

"I don't see how a man can say he doesn't believe in God," says Victor. "The fool says in his heart there is no God. Myself, I been a deacon at Starlight Baptist for twenty years."

"Christ, what a revolution," mutters Uru, eyeing a burning house.

While he and Victor argue religion, I notice something: a horse and rider, glimpsed now and then through the side yards of houses. The horse must be on the bridle path that runs along the margin of the links behind the houses. His easy trot just keeps pace with the cart. It is—!

—Lola! on her sorrel mare Yellow Rose. She could be out for her morning ride, erect in her saddle, hand on her thigh, face hidden in her auburn hair. Foolish impetuous gallant girl! Beyond a doubt she's trailing me, out to rescue me and apt to get herself caught or killed or worse. Something else to worry about, yet worry or not and despite my sorry predicament I can't but experience a pang of love for this splendid Texas girl.

As we leave the pines and head straight out across the deserted plaza, I sigh with relief. Lola is nowhere in sight. At least she has sense enough not to show herself. But what is she up to?

The Anser-Phone buzzes on my chest. Feigning a fit of coughing, I switch it off. Uru doesn't seem to notice. Ellen is calling! Somehow I must reach her. At least she is well. And Moira, my love! Pray to God the Bantus don't search me and take my Anser-Phone. My heart melts with love and my brain sings in the musical-erotic sulcus when I think of Lola and Moira. How lovely are the daughters of men! If I live and love Moira, who's to love Lola and how can I tolerate it? Same with Lola-Moira. And will Ellen stand for it in either case? Only one solution: I must live with all three.

Victor parks at the cloistered walk between church and rectory. Up the steps past the Bantu guard in a dirty white belted *kwunghali* stationed behind the concrete openwork (has he been here for weeks?) who salutes Uru with respect. He carries a Sten gun propped in his waist.

Time for one quick glance toward Howard Johnson's: all quiet. The balcony is deserted.

Down the front hall of the rectory and through the parlor with its ancient horsehair nose-itching furniture. From his *izinkhonkwani* Uru takes out a key chain, unlocks the door to Monsignor Schleifkopf's office and without further ado bumps me inside—with a basketball player's hip-bump.

"Sweat it, Chuck," says Uru, closing the door.

"Sorry, Doc," says Victor as the latch clicks.

Try the switch. No lights, of course. No windows either, but a row of glass bricks under the ceiling mutes the July sun to a weak watery light like a cellar window.

The trouble is the room is as hot and breathless as an attic.

While my eyes are getting used to the gloom, I call in to Ellen. She and Moira are still in the motel, safe and sound but nervous.

"Chief," says Ellen in a controlled voice. "The news is

bad. We watched on TV. There is fighting on the highway."

"You mean the guerrillas have gotten that far?"

"No, Chief. It's the town people, fighting the federal people. Not two miles from here. And Chief," says Ellen, lowering her voice. "You better do something about your so-called friend."

"Friend? Who's that?"

"Miss S. She's getting a little hysterical."

"Where is she?" I ask in alarm.

"In the bathroom. I never saw anybody go to the bathroom so much."

"Hm. Have you seen anybody around there?"

"Not a soul. But, Chief, I think you better get over here. Things are coming unstuck."

"I'm tied up just now. Perhaps later. I was wondering—"

"Yes?"

"Perhaps the best thing for you to do would be to get back to town."

"Chief, you've got my car!"

"So I have." What did I do with it? Oh yes, gave it to Mother.

"Anyhow, there's fighting between here and town."

"Well, sit tight."

"All right. But it's so *hot* here."

"Here too. But don't make any noise."

"Very well, Chief."

"Over."

"Over and out."

My eyes have accommodated to the gloom. Rocking back in Monsignor Schleifkopf's executive chair, I survey the room. Evidently it has been used by the Bantus. A couple of ceremonial garlic necklaces hang from the hatrack. A Coleman gas stove sits on the coin counter. Baby Ruth wrappers and used TV dinners litter the wall-to-wall carpet; shreds of collard greens bestrew the desk.

Behind me the door of the walk-in vault swings open. In one corner stands a stack of boxes full of Sunday envelopes exactly as they stood years ago when I used to attend Holy Name meetings here. Good rough fellows they were, the Holy Name men. We'd meet once a month and mumble gruff embarrassed prayers for the intentions of the Holy Father and so that we might leave off swearing and using the name of our dear Lord in vain and uttering foulness in general.

The four walls are hung with huge Kodacolor murals of Monsignor Schleifkopf's native Alps. Tiny villages are strung out along narrow green valleys. Great snowy peaks indent a perfect cobalt sky. In the foreground rises a rude roadside crucifix.

I am sweating profusely and breathing through my mouth. I am losing water and there is no water here. They had better turn me loose soon. Or I had better get out.

The room swims in a watery heat. A thin tatter of cloud flies from one alp. Ice crystals. Hot as it is, though, and bad as I feel, my eye wanders around the room appraising its construction. The rectory was built, I remember, early in the Ecuadorian wars, when there were bomb scares and a lot of talk about shelters. The rectory was to serve as a bomb shelter in case of attack. It is windowless and double-walled and equipped with back-up electrical systems. Yes, I recall some restiveness in the congregation about the cost of the generator, which was the latest type and heaviest duty—the sort that could run indefinitely without a human soul to service it. Samantha liked to imagine it humming away for thirty years after everyone was dead. Yes, I remember the sight of Monsignor Schleifkopf presiding over the control panel with that special proprietorship priests develop for things they don't own. Here was an oddity: that in the latter days when laymen owned everything they didn't care much for anything, yet some priests who owned little or nothing developed ferocious attachments for ordinary objects—I once knew a monk who owned nothing, had given it all away for Christ, yet coveted the monastery typewriter with a jealous love, flew into rages when another monk touched it.

The Alps swim in the heat. My tongue swells and cleaves to my palate. Stale hot bourbon breath whistles in my nose.

Monsignor Schleifkopf used to hover over the panel, one hand caressing the metal, the other snapping switches like a bomber pilot . . .

The control panel. Wait. I close my eyes and try to think. Sweat begins to drip through my eyebrows. I remember. It is in the walk-in vault behind me. Here Monsignor Schleifkopf kept the valuables, gold chalices, patens, the Sunday collection, bingo money, and yes, even the daily gleanings of the poor box after the drugheads from the swamp began to break into it.

I feel my way inside. The vault door is open but it opens

toward the glass bricks and it is dark inside. The panel was in the tiny foyer, wasn't it? I stumble over a bingo squirrel-cage. Feel the walls. Yes, here it is: rows of switches in a console of satiny metal, switches for lights, air-conditioning, electronic carillon. Some are up, some are down. Is up on? I close my eyes and try to remember (I was on the Building Committee). What time of day was the rectory evacuated? The Christmas Eve riots started in the afternoon and the Monsignor barely got away with his skin—that night.

Panting and sweating in the dark. Somewhere in my head two ideas grope for each other but it is too hot to . . . I return to the chair and look at the alp and the banner of ice crystals. The panorama of the high alpine valley is spoiled by a large metal grill set in the wall beside the roadside crucifix. It is the main intake vent of the air-conditioner.

I look at it, sweat, pant, and sock my forehead, trying to think what it is I already know.

Well but of course.

At least it is a chance. And the chance must be taken. I've got to get out of here.

Think.

The compressor is in the garage. The return duct therefore must run along the wall past the vault, past the kitchen whose inside wall is, must be, continuous with the back wall of the garage. Yes. I was on the Building Committee.

Sitting on the floor. A bit cooler here. I feel the metal frame of the grill. Phillips screws. Hm, a dime is no good. Look around. Yonder is Saint Michael on a pedestal, a somewhat prissy bronze archangel dressed to the nines, berobed like Queen Victoria but holding a proper bronze sword. Which I know is loose in his hand because I used to fiddle with it during the Holy Name meetings.

Slide it out of the bronze hand, a foot-long papercutter and, as I had recalled, dull. Dull enough to turn a Phillips screw.

The grill out and set down carefully on the rug, I stick my head in the duct. Plenty of room to crawl. Close my eyes and try to remember whether the compressor stands against the back wall of the garage or a ways out. It better be the latter. Also: does the jut of the garage from the side of the rectory clear the corner so that it is visible from the front of the church, where, behind the concrete screen, a guard is almost certain to be stationed? I can't remember.

Back to the console in the vestibule of the vault. The problem is to create a diversion, sufficient noise to cover my exit in the garage, where I'll have to kick out a panel and make a racket. The trouble is I don't know how many Bantu guards are here or where they're stationed. Is there only the one in front?

Feel the switches again. Some are up, some down, but which position is on? Here's the emergency starter button. Monsignor Schleifkopf—God bless him for his love of manufactured things, their gear and tackle and trim, good Buicks, Arnold Palmer irons—bought the best nickel-cadmium battery money could buy, a $500 job with a self-charging feature guaranteed for ten years.

The four speaker electronic carillon sits atop the silo tower a good two hundred yards from here and even farther from the garage. If I could start the carillon, it would create a commotion and the guards would, surely, look for the trouble where the sound was and not here. But which is the carillon switch? No telling. The only thing to do is take a chance and throw all switches up—surely up is on—and turn all knobs to the right.

Flip all switches up.

Hit the starter button for a second just for the feel of it. *Urr*, it goes, the very sound of an old Dodge starting up of a winter morning.

Get ready then. Resisting an impulse to cross myself, I press the button.

*Urr-urr-urr* and then BRRRRROOM.

On goes the twelve-cylinder motor, God bless General Motors.

On goes the light.

On goes the air-conditioner compressor and blower.

On goes the carillon—

—a shriek of sound. The carillon resumes in the middle of the phrase of *O Little Town of Bethlehem* it left off five years ago on Christmas Eve:

> . . . *how still I see thee lie.*

I find myself running around the office with Saint Michael's sword, heart thumping wildly. The sound and the lights are panicking. The sound is an alarm, up go the lights and here's the burglar, me, caught in the act. The thing to do is get out of here, I tell myself, loping around the Alps. The hot air is moving out.

Thinking now: do this, pocket the screws, hop into the intake vent and pull the grill into place after me. If they see no screws, they won't notice.

It's tight in here, but a few feet along and I'm in a cloaca of ducts converging from the church. The air, thundering toward the 100-ton Frigiking (I was on the Building Committee), is already cooler.

Suddenly it comes over me that I am, for the moment, completely safe. Why not lie down in this dark cool place, an alpine pass howling with mountain gales, and take a little nap? *Indulgeas locum refrigerii*: refrigeration must be one of the attributes of heaven.

Now forty or fifty feet along and able to stand up. A cave of winds, black as the womb, but I'm against the unit, a great purring beast encased in metal filter mesh.

Press the panel to my right. Here I calculate is the garage. Metal bends and a chink of light opens. Daylight, moreover. At least the garage door is open. Try to see something. Cannot. Try to hear something. Nothing but the roar of the blower and compressor and soaring above, the piercing obligato of *White Christmas*:

> *May your days be merry and bright . . .*

Feel along the edge of the panel. It is fastened by sheet-metal screws, one every three or four inches and screwed in from the outside. Discard Saint Michael's sword. Try pushing one corner loose. No good.

Nothing for it then but to lie down, shoulders braced against the opposite panel (this panel against concrete), wait for the final major chord of *White Christmas*, and kick with both feet.

Out she goes with a heart-stopping clatter, metal against concrete, metal against car metal—now I know they'll find me—and out I come feet-first, born again, ejected into the hot bright perilous world—tumbling somehow forward until I am wedged between the inner wall and the bumper of Monsignor Schleifkopf's burnt-out Buick, a hulk of rusted metal and moldering upholstery. Mushrooms flourish in the channel between bumper and grill. A fern sprouts upside down from the crankcase.

The music, I tell myself, comes from the silo at the other end of the church and nobody will come here.

Wait and watch a minute. I have a cockroach's view under the Buick.

The broad three-car garage opens onto the plaza. Still not a soul in sight! How can this be with such a racket? A very loud noise needs tending to. Someone should do something about it and no doubt will. An unattended din in a fearsome thing.

The July sun blazes, the tar in the plaza bubbles, the green growth atop the storefronts shimmers and there is sky under it like the Hanging Gardens of Babylon.

*The Drummer Boy,*

*rumpa-pum-pum,*

thunders its artillery and echoes from the giant screen of the Joy Drive-In.

The questions are: Is there a guard posted at the rear of the rectory? If so, did he and the guard at the front of the rectory head for the silo when the sound commenced? My hope is that the Bantus do not know where the control panel is and will assume that the source of the mischief is in the church.

Creeping now past the Buick, to the wall and along it to the slight jut that frames the door now levered up along the ceiling. Slowly work around jut—still no one in the entire plaza —and around the outside corner of the garage: yes, here is the concrete screen ending flush with the garage door and—

—Jerk back almost before I see him, shutting my eyes against him in a magic gesture to make *me* invisible to him, jerking back around the corner and clear around the jut into the garage, and there in the dark corner I consult my retina's image of him: the same Bantu guard in the same dirty *kwunghali*—then he must have heard the clatter of my exit— six feet away and back turned, face in profile and Sten gun pointed at the four speakers: they're the villains!

It is strange but, belatedly, indeed only now as I consult the image of him, I recognize him. It is Ely, who was bagboy at the A & P for forty years. What a transformation! He's turned into a tough hombre. Forty years a favorite at the A & P, toting bags to cars for housewives, saluting the tips, now he looks as if he'd just as soon stitch me with Sten gun as not.

I need his gun, I need him out of the way, so I need a weapon of my own. The Buick's trunk is open, lock prized, tire swiped. I crane over the tail fin looking for a lug wrench. No lug wrench, nothing but Monsignor Schleifkopf's moldering golf bag grown up in fennel and bladderwort, pockets ripped, clubs all gone, no, all but one, an ancient putter passed over perhaps five years ago for its age and decrepitude even then.

It is possible to reach the club without exposing myself past the jut.

*Round yon virgin mother and child . . .*

The putter has a lead blade and a hickory handle. Test it for heft.

Inch around ell.

He's closer, within range. He's still looking back toward the silo. It is a simple matter, surely, to take one step and hit him, with the heel of the putter taking care not to kill him. Then step.

Sorry, Ely—and aim for the occiput, the hardest skull plate, a glancing blow at that. But I take too much care and he's moved suddenly, closer, and it's a bad blow and the shaft shudders like shanking a ball. Staggering less from hurt than from surprise and outrage, he's already swinging around toward me and I see the Sten muzzle swinging as slowly as a ship's boom and I'm shrinking into the inner corner of the jut and touching the steel of the door mechanism as if we were playing a game and it were base: safe! You can't shoot me now! But he is going to shoot me, I can see. It's a matter of getting the gun around.

We are looking at each other. I notice that he is going bald the way some Negroes go bald, his high studious umber forehead shading off into hair of the same color, and that he has a mustache like Duke Ellington of old with a carefully tended gap in the middle. We are looking at each other, I knowing him and he me and he even signifying as much but his only care is getting the Sten around, his face all screwed up with the effort, and I see all of a sudden that all he's thinking about is whether he's going to do it right, that he's exactly like a middle-aged British home guard who patrols Brighton beach against a possible Nazi and sure enough here comes a Nazi. My God, he's thinking, ɪᴛ has happened! Here's the real thing! Here's a Nazi in the flesh! Will I do right? Why is everything in slow motion?

He is shooting, too soon!—and I am flinching and touching base, no fair! The steel is ringing like a hammer on boilerplate. He's got me. But as I open my eyes, he's swinging away. How did he miss me or did he or, better still, how did bullets hit the *outside* of the steel I-beam at my elbow?

Who is shooting? He's not.

"Wait!" I'm yelling, having caught no more than one glimpse of the sorrel rump prancing sideways. "Don't shoot him! It's Ely!"—swinging the putter sideways and back-handed and not having time to aim and so of course catching Ely properly on the parietal skull, the Sten swinging away now and down and Ely going down and around with it.

I drag him into the garage and test his pulse and pupils. He's all right. I still haven't had time to look at Lola, who comes in leading the sorrel and holstering her automatic in her jeans.

"You almost killed Ely," I tell her.

"Why, you damn fool, he was trying to kill you!"

"I know. Thank you. How did you know I was here?"

"Yellow Rose and I were watching from over there." She nods toward the Joy Drive-In. "We saw you come crashing through the wall. Crazy Tom Tom! What would you do without Lola?"

"I don't know. Let's get out of here." We have to yell to be heard above the racket of the carillon with its guaranteed five-mile radius at top volume.

*We three kings of Orient are . . .*

"What is all that?" asks Lola, making a face.

"Christmas carols."

"Oh," says Lola, accepting it, July or not. "Where're we going?"

"Back over there. Where's the horse?"

Yellow Rose has wandered off. Lola gives an ear-splitting whistle through her fingers and here comes the mare, stirrups flying. I hop up.

Lola jumps up behind me and gives me a big hug. "Oh Tommy, I was so worried about you!"

"Keep worrying."

The nearest cover is the Drive-In with its tower of a screen and its speaker-posts gone to jungle, but a good two hundred yards of open plaza intervene, most of it clearly visible from the front of the church. How many Bantus are left?

We light out, my legs swinging free, for the stirrups are too short, past the concrete screen enclosing the cloister. Swallows nesting in the fenestrae take alarm and flutter up by the hundreds.

Many swallows but no shots, no outcries and no Bantus. Are they all in church trying to figure out what started the carillon?

> *The first Noel*
> *The angels did sing . . .*

Breathlessly we fetch up behind lianas of possum grape, which festoon the giant Pan-a-Vision screen.

"You like to fell off," says Lola, reverting to Tyler Texas talk.

Half off, I slide down. The noble girl faces me, arms as they say akimbo, breast heaving, color high in her cheek.

"What now?"

I explain that we'd best make our way to the motel, that indeed there is nowhere else to go.

"Wow!" says Lola, but as quickly frowns. "What about Rose?"

I shrug. "We can't take Rose any farther."

"Don't worry!" She loosens the girth and gives the mare a slap across the rump. "Back to Tara! She'll go home. We'll follow shortly, won't we, Tom?"

"Possibly."

Sure enough, the mare takes out for the pines, straight across the plaza, head tossing around as if she meant to keep an eye on us.

The firing begins when the mare reaches the drive-up window of the branch bank. Little geysers of tar erupt around her flying hoofs. Lola moans and claps her cheeks. "She's made it," I reassure her. Parting the grape leaves, I catch sight of the two Bantus, one kneeling and both firing, on the porch of the church. "Keep down."

But she's whipped out her automatic again. "What—" I begin turning to see what she sees behind me.

It's Victor!—standing in the doorway of the Pan-a-Vision screen structure. The screen is a slab thick enough to house offices.

"Don't shoot!" I jump in front of Lola.

"Why not?"

"It's Victor."

"Why not shoot Victor? He's got a gun." But she lowers her automatic.

"Here, Doc," says Victor and tosses me my carbine. "This is so you can protect your mama. I know you are not going to shoot people."

I catch the carbine like old Duke Wayne up yonder on the giant screen.

"Thanks, Victor."

"Now you all get on out of here. Some people headed this way. Go to town. You take care this little lady too."

"O.K."

Lola can't tell the difference between the real Victor and the fake Willard. She claps her hands with delight. "Isn't Victor wonderful! Tom, let's got to Tara!"

"No." I grab her hand.

We run at a crouch through the geometrical forest of flowering speaker posts, past burnt-out Thunderbirds, spavined Cougars, broken-back Jaguars parked these five long years, ever since that fateful Christmas Eve, in front of the blank and silent screen. The lovers must have found the exit road blocked by guerrillas and had to abandon their cars and leave the drive-in by foot. In some cases speakers are still hooked to windowsills and we must take care not to run into the wires.

No more shots are fired, and when we reach the shelter of the weeds at the rear of the Howard Johnson restaurant, I feel fairly certain we've made our escape unobserved. But why take chances? Accordingly, we follow the easement between the motel and the fence. Directly below the bathroom window I take Lola's arm and explain to her the circumstances that prompted me to fit out the motel room and stock it with provisions for months—all the circumstances, that is, except Moira. "There is some danger," I tell her, "of a real disaster."

"Darling Tom!" cries Lola, throwing her arms around my neck. "Don't worry! I don't think we'll be here that long but we can have a lovely time! Lola will do for you. We'll make music and let the world crash about our ears. Twilight of the gods! Could I go get my cello?"

"I've told you we can't go back to Tara."

"No, I mean over at the Center. I could be back in fifteen minutes."

"Where?"

"At the Center. Don't you remember? I played a recital yesterday before the students rioted. There was so much commotion I thought the best thing to do was leave it in a safe place over there."

"Yesterday?" I close my eyes and try to remember. "Where is it now?"

"Ken told me he'd lock it up in his clinic."

"Ken?"

"Ken Stryker, idiot. Think of it, Tommy. We'll hole up for the duration and Lola will cook you West Texas chili marguerita and play Brahms every night."

"Very good. I'll get the cello for you but not just now. Now I think we'd better go up and join the ah, others."

"Others?"

"Yes. Other people have sought refuge here. I couldn't turn them away." Thank goodness there are two girls up yonder and not one.

"Of course you couldn't. Who are they?"

"My nurse, Miss Oglethorpe, and a colleague, a Miss Schaffner."

"Ken's research assistant?"

"She was."

"Should be cozy."

"There are plenty of rooms."

"I should imagine."

"Are you ready to go up?"

"Can't wait."

I give the sign, a low towhee whistle. Above us the window opens.

# 10

The girls are badly out of sorts, from fright but even more, I expect, from the heat. After the rainstorm they did not dare turn on the air-conditioner, the sniper might be hanging around. The room is an oven.

Moira is hot, damp, petulant, a nagging child.

"Where have you *been*, Chico?" She tugs at my shirt. There are beads of dirt in the creases of her neck.

Ellen sits straight up in the straight chair, drumming her fingers on the desk. Her eyes are as cool as Lake Geneva. The only sign of heat is the perspiration in the dark down of her lip.

"I thought you were going to get your mother," she says drily, not looking at Lola.

"Yes. Mother. Right. But Mother, you know, has her own ideas ha ha. No, Mother is in town and safe. Lola was at Tara and alone. I made her come." I jump up and turn on the air-conditioner. "With all the racket at the church, I doubt if anyone could hear this." Sinking down on the foot of the bed. "I could use a drink. I've been shot at, locked up, pushed around."

Ellen comes around instantly, sits behind me, begins probing my scalp with her rough mothering fingers. "Are you hurt, Chief?"

"I'm all right," I say, noticing that Lola is eyeing me ironically, thumbs hooked in her jean pockets.

"Quite a place you have here, Tommy," she says.

"Yes. Well. Now here's where we stand, girls," I say, rising and pacing the floor wearily. I am in fact weary but there are also uses of weariness. "I'm afraid we're in trouble," I tell them seriously because it is true but also because there are uses of seriousness. The three girls make me nervous. "As I believe all of you know, there is a good chance of a catastrophe this afternoon, of national, perhaps even world proportions. You asked about my mother, Ellen. Here's what has happened."

Everyone is feeling serious and better. The air-conditioner blows cold fogs into the room. Hands deep in pockets, I pace the floor, eyes on the carpet, and give them the bad news, reciting the events of the day in sentences as grave, articulate, apocalyptic, comforting as a CBS commentator. Now swinging a chair around, I sit on it backward and give the girls a long level-eyed look. "And that is by no means the worst of it. No," I repeat as somberly as Arnold Toynbee taking the long view. "As I also believe each of you also know, the Bantu revolt may be the least of our troubles."

"You're speaking, Chief," says Ellen, "of the danger of your lapsometer falling into the wrong hands."

"Yes."

"I'm afraid it's already happened, Chief," she says as gravely as I.

"I'm afraid it has."

"And what you fear is both a physical reaction and a psychical reaction, physical from the Heavy Salt domes in the area and psychical from its effect on political extremists."

"That is correct, Ellen."

The room is silent save for the rattling of the air-conditioner. Outside, like distant artillery, I can hear *The Drummer Boy* again.

*Rumpa-pum-pum . . .*

Lola is sitting on the end of the other bed, cleaning her automatic. Moira lies behind her, flat, knees propped up, gazing at the ceiling.

"I'll fix you a drink, Tom. Where's the fixings?" says Lola.

"In there." I nod toward the dressing room.

"I'm afraid I've got bad news too, Chief."

"What's that?"

"It's the last message I got from Dr. Immelmann. Just before you came. On the Anser-Phone. Chief, how could he use the Anser-Phone? He didn't have a transmitter and he had no way of knowing our frequency."

"Never mind," I say hurriedly. "What did he want?"

"He said to tell you—now let me get this straight." Ellen consults her notebook. "To tell you that the program was third-generational and functional on both fronts; that he's already gotten gratifying overt interactions between the two extremes of the political spectrum, and that you would soon have sufficient data for a convincing pilot. Does that make sense?"

"I'm afraid so," I said gloomily. "Is that all?"

"I saved the good news, Chief," says Ellen, frowning at Lola, who is at the bar fixing drinks. "He also said to tell you—and this I wrote down word for word—that he's been in touch with the Nobel Prize committee in Stockholm, each member of which he knows personally, apprising them of the nature of your work, and that they're extremely excited about it. Chief, isn't the Peace Prize the big one? Anyhow, he's cabling them a summary of the present pilot and he closed with the cryptic remark that you should prepare yourself for some interesting news when the prize is announced in October. Does any of this make sense, Chief?"

"Yes," I say, frowning. "But October? What makes him think there'll be anything left in October? The damn fool is going to destroy everything." Then why is it, I wonder, that a pleasant tingling sensation spreads down the backs of my thighs?

"Here's your favorite, Tom Tom." Lola hands me a drink.

"Did she say 'Tom Tom'?" Moira asks Ellen.

I've tossed off the whole drink somewhat nervously before it comes over me that it is a gin fizz. Oh well, I've got anti-allergy pills with me. The drink is deliciously cool and silky with albumen.

"What are we going to do?" wails Moira, opening and closing her thighs on her hands, like a little girl holding wee-wee.

"Why don't you go to the bathroom?" suggests Ellen.

"I will," says Moira, jumping up. "No, I've just been. I have to go to the Center to get my things."

"Right," Lola agrees instantly. "And I have to get my cello."

"No no," I say hastily. "You can't. Moira, you have everything here you need. I mean everyone has. I'll get your cello for you, Lola."

"But my Cupid's Qui—" says Moira, coming close.

"Yes!" I exclaim, laughing, talking, hawking phlegm all at once.

"Her Cupid's what?" asks Lola.

"Moira, like the rest of us," I tell Lola, "didn't know we'd be stuck here."

"And besides, I can't wear the things you brought!" Moira is in tears and is apt to say anything.

"What things?" asks Lola.

"I, ah, laid in some supplies as soon as I had reason to suspect the worst."

"In a motel?" Lola's fist disappears into her flank.

"It's a logical shelter for an emergency," says Ellen, "because it's convenient to town, Center, and Paradise." Ellen is defending me!

"Right," I say, hawking and, for some reason, dancing like Ken Stryker. I hand my empty glass to Lola.

"If I may make a suggestion, Chief," says Ellen briskly, "I think we ought to find out exactly what is going on before we do anything."

"Absolutely right!" Ellen is a jewel.

Ellen turns on the old Philco. "It's a bad color and 2-D but it gets the local channel—the one over your house, Chief. In a minute they'll have the news."

Lola takes my glass to the bar.

No one ever had a better nurse than Ellen.

## 11

On comes the picture, flickering and herringboned, of green people in a green field under a green sky. There is a platform and bunting and a speaker. The speaker has a ghost. The crowd mills about restlessly. "Hm, a Fourth of July celebration," I tell the girls—until all at once I recognize the place. It is the high school football field on the outskirts of town, not three miles from here!

The camera pans among the crowd. I recognize faces here and there: a conservative proctologist, a chiropractor, a retired Air Force colonel, a disgruntled Boeing executive, a Texaco dealer, a knot of PTA mothers from the private school, an occasional Knothead Catholic, and a Baptist preacher sitting on the platform. The speaker is the governor, a well-known Knothead.

Nearly everyone waves a little flag. The crowd is restive.

A reporter is interviewing a deputy sheriff, a good old boy named Junior Trosclair.

"We cain't hold these folks much longer," Junior is telling the reporter.

"Hold them from doing what?"

"They talking about marching on the federal complex."

"Why are they doing that, Deputy?" asks the reporter, already thinking of his next question.

"I don't know," says Junior, shaking his head dolefully. "All I know is we cain't hold them much longer."

"Sir," says the reporter, stopping a passerby, a pleasant-looking green-faced man who is wearing two hats and carrying an old M-1 rifle. "Sir, can you tell me what the plans are here?"

"What's that?" calls out the man, cupping an ear to hear over the uproar. His face has the amiable but bemused expression of a convention delegate.

The reporter repeats the question.

"Oh yes. Well, we're going to take a stand is the thing," says the man somewhat absently and, catching sight of a friend, waves at him.

"How is that, sir?" asks the reporter, holding the microphone over and grimacing at the engineer.

"What? Oh, we're going over there and clean them out."

"Over where?"

"Over to Fedville." The man gesticulates to the unseen friend and drifts off, nodding and smiling.

The reporter grabs his arm.

"Clean out who, sir? Sir!"

"What? Yes. Well, all of them."

"All of who?"

"You know, commonists, atheistic scientists, Jews, perverts, dope fiends, coonasses—"

The reporter drops the man's arm as if it had turned into a snake. "Thank you for your comment," he says, coming toward the camera. "Now I'll return you to—"

"And I'll tell you something else," says the man, who has warmed to the subject for the first time. He catches up with the fast-stepping reporter. "The niggers may be holed up over yonder in Paradise but you know where they're getting their orders from?"

"No sir. Now we'll have a message from—"

"From the White House, otherwise known as the Tel-a-Viv Hilton on Pennsylvania Avenue."

"Yes sir! Take it, David!"

During the exchange I've been watching another reporter with transmitter and back-pack passing with his ghost among the crowd. But no. It is—Art Immelmann, a green Art plus a green ghost of Art. No doubt about it. There's the old-fashioned crew-cut and widow's peak. And he's carrying not a microphone but my lapsometer. And he's only pretending to do interviews: holding the device to people's mouths only when they are looking at him, otherwise passing it over their heads or pressing it into the nape of their necks.

"That's Dr. Immelmann!" cries Ellen, jumping up and pointing to the flickering screen, but at that moment the newscast ends and the afternoon movie resumes, a rerun of a very clean film, which I recognize as *The Ice Capades of 1981*.

"Did you see him, Chief?"

"It did look like him."

"And he had your invention."

"It did appear so."

Moira comes out of the bathroom, face scrubbed.

"I'm leaving," she announces and strides for the door.

"Wait!" I jump against the door, blocking her. "You can't go out there!"

"I'm going to get my Cupid's Quiver and my own clothes. That is, if I come back."

"Get her what?" asks Lola.

"You can't leave just now. It's too dangerous."

"I must get my own clothes."

"What does she mean, her own clothes?" asks Lola, frowning.

"We may be here quite a while, Lola," I explain earnestly.

"Yes," says Moira. "Chico and I had plans to stay only for the weekend."

"Weekend? Chico?" Lola has risen slowly and stands, one fist on her hip, pelvis tilted menacingly. "Who is this Chico?"

"Ha ha," I laugh nervously. "I'm sure everybody's plans for the Fourth were spoiled. I'll tell you what," I say quickly to Moira. "Give me your key and I'll go for you."

Now it's Lola who heads for the door. "Out of my way, Chico. I'm going too. I have to get my cello and look after my horses. A horse you can trust."

"I'll get your cello too, Lola. It's in Love, didn't you tell me?"

Both girls confront me.

"Well? Are you moving out of the way, Tom?" Lola asks.

I shrug and step aside.

Out they go— "I may not be back," says Moira over her shoulder—and back they come, reeling back as if blown in by a gale. They slam the door and stand, palms against the wood, eyes rolling up. Two girls they truly seem and very young.

Lola swallows. "He's there."

"Who?"

"A Bantu."

I peep through the curtains. It is Ely in his *kwunghali* standing with his Sten gun in the shadow of the opposite balcony. I recognize the classy Duke Ellington forehead. He is looking right and left but not up.

"I'll go, O.K.?" I say wearily, holding out a hand for Moira's key. "Lola, take out your automatic and sit here. Ellen, take my revolver and sit there."

Moira has collapsed on the bed, where she lies opening and closing her knees.

"Why don't you go to the bathroom, dear," says Ellen.

Moira obeys. She gives me her key without a word.

When she comes out, I open the bathroom window. Lola follows me.

"How are you going to get my cello through that window?"

"I'll put it in a safe place downstairs."

"What about the Bantu?"

"If he comes up on the balcony, shoot him."

"Very well, Chico," says Lola sarcastically. "Just you be careful with my cello—Chico."

I switch off the air-conditioner. "Sorry, girls."

"Be careful, Chief," whispers Ellen, helping me through the window. Absently wetting her fingertips with her tongue, she smooths out my eyebrows with strong mother-smoothings.

Before leaving, I give each girl a light Chloride massage over Brodmann 32 and pineal Layer I—to inoculate them against a Heavy Sodium fallout, an unlikely event in the next few hours, but who knows? After treatment, each girls looks so serene, both alert and dreamy-eyed, as sleepy and watchful as a waking child, that I do the same for myself.


# 12

A gaggle of unruly Left students mill about the main gate of the Behavioral Institute. Some drive nails into golf balls. Others fill Coke bottles with gasoline. They frown when they see me. I recognize several members of Buddy Brown's faction.

Professor Coffin Cabot, a famous scholar on loan from Harvard, is in their midst, a pair of wire-cutters in one hand and the flag of North Ecuador in the other, counseling, exhorting, and showing students how to clip the heads off nails after they are driven into a golf ball.

"What are *you* doing here, More?" he asks, his face darkening.

"What's wrong with my being here?"

"Haven't you done enough dirty work for the military-industrial-academic complex?"

"What do you mean?"

"You know very well what I mean. I suppose you didn't know that your cute little toy has been added to the Maryland arsenal along with its cache of plague bacilli and lethal gases."

"No, I didn't. By whom?"

"By your fascist friend, Immelmann."

"He's not a friend. But may I ask what you are doing?"

"We are organizing a nonviolent demonstration for peace and freedom in Ecuador."

"Nonviolent?" I ask, looking at the pile of spiked golf balls.

"We practice creative nonviolent violence, that is, violence in the service of nonviolence. It is a matter of intention."

Professor Cabot is a semanticist.

"When is this coming off?"

"This afternoon. We're marching against the so-called Fourth of July movement in town."

"So-called?"

"Yes. We recognize only the Fifth of July movement named in honor of the day Jorge Rojas parachuted into the mountains of South Ecuador."

"Jorge Rojas?"

"Of course. He's the George Washington of Ecuador, the only man beloved north and south and the only man capable of uniting the country."

"But didn't he kill several hundred thousand Ecuadorians who didn't love him?"

"Yes, but they were either fascists or running dogs or lackeys of the American imperialists. Anyhow, the question has become academic."

"How is that?"

"Because those who are left do love him."

I scratch my head. "Why are you carrying that flag?"

"Because North Ecuador stands for peace and freedom."

"But aren't you an American?"

"Yes, but America is a cancer in the community of democratic nations. Incidentally, More, my lecture on this subject last month in Stockholm received an even greater ovation than it got at Harvard."

"If that is the case, why don't you live in Sweden or North Ecuador?"

Professor Cabot looks at me incredulously as he adjusts a wick in a Coke bottle.

"You've got to be kidding, More."

"No."

He stands up, looks right and left, and says in a low voice, "Do you know what I'm pulling at Cambridge?"

"No."

"A hundred thousand a year plus two hundred thousand for

my own institute. And Berkeley offered me more. What do you think of that?"

"Very good," I reply sympathetically, setting as I do as high a value on money as the next man.

"Say, why don't you join us, More?" asks Coffin Cabot impulsively.

"No thanks. I've got to pick up a ah cello." For some reason I blush.

Cabot grins. "That figures. Fiddling while Rome burns, eh?"

"No. The fact is there are three girls over there in the motel—"

"What?"

"Never mind." I was on the point of telling him about the dangers of the misuse of my invention when I catch sight of—! It can't be but it is. There over Coffin Cabot's shoulder, moving about among the students with my lapsometer, is Art Immelmann!

"Excuse me," I murmur, but Cabot is already preoccupied with the next batch of golf balls and does not notice Art.

I watch him.

Art Immelmann, it soon becomes clear, is demonstrating my device to the students as the famous fake prop of The Pit, laughing and shaking his head at the preposterousness of it, like a doctor unmasking the latest quackery. The students laugh. Yet, as he does so, he makes passes over the students' heads.

In the instant he catches sight of me I lay hands on my invention and snatch it away from him.

"Oh, Doc!" he cries with every sign of delight. "Just the man I'm looking for!"

I gaze at him in astonishment. "How did you get here?"

"What do you mean, Doc?"

"I saw you on TV not ten minutes ago and you were in town."

Art shrugs. "Perhaps it was a tape."

"It was no tape." I am examining the lapsometer. "Do you realize you've got this thing set for plus ten dosage at the level of the prefrontal abstractive centers?"

"It's only for purposes of demonstration."

"Do you realize what this would do to a man, especially a student?"

"I know," says Art, smiling good-naturedly. "But I like to hear you say it."

"It would render him totally abstracted from himself, totally alienated from the concrete world, and in such a state of angelism that he will fall prey to the first abstract notion proposed to him and will kill anybody who gets in his way, torture, execute, wipe out entire populations, all with the best possible motives and the best possible intentions, in fact in the name of peace and freedom, etcetera."

"Yeah, Doc!" cries Art delighted. "Your MOQUOL surpasses my most sanguine expectations. I've already elicited positive interactions from both ends of the spectrum—"

"Goddamn, man, do you realize what you're saying?"

Art winces and turns pale. I swing him round to face me.

"I authorized you to use my invention to diminish, not increase tensions. It says so in the contract."

"Yeah, but Doc, this is the pilot. In the pilot you have to get the problem out on the table. Then when the pilot's completed—"

"Screw the pilot," I am yelling, beside myself with anger.

"How do you mean, Doc?" asks Art, mystified. "How is that possible?"

"Never mind. It's no use trying to tell you. I'm taking this lapsometer and I want the rest that you stole. Where are they?"

Art looks mournful. "I'm very sorry, Doc, but they're all in the hands of the interdisciplinary task force—"

"Listen, you son of a bitch, our agreement is canceled as of this moment."

"Excuse me, Doc." Art shakes his head regretfully. "In the first place, I don't understand your imputation about my mother when the fact of the matter is I don't—but that's neither here nor there. In the second place, I'm afraid the contract cannot be voided unilaterally."

"Get out of my way," I say, suddenly remembering the three girls in room 203.

"Don't worry about a thing, Doc!" Art waves cheerily. "Don't worry about the Nobel Prize either. You're in."

Though I fling away in a rage, a pleasant tingle spreads across my sacrum. Is it the prospect of the Nobel or the effect of the gin fizz?

## 13

I am surprised and dismayed to find Love Clinic humming with activity. Stryker explains that it was the volunteers themselves who, excited by a "new concept in therapy," had forgone the holiday in order to complete the research.

But how to retrieve the cello without awkward explanations?

Father Kev Kevin sits at the vaginal console reading *Commonweal*.

But I am blinking at the scene in the behavior room. What a transformation! Nothing is the same. The stark white clinical cube has been decorated in Early American and furnished with a bull's-eye mirror, cobbler's bench, rag rugs, and two bundling beds.

"What's going on?" I ask Stryker, who comes gliding up, one foot swinging wide in a tango step.

"You of all people should know!"

"Why me?"

"It's thanks to you we made the breakthrough."

"What breakthrough?"

"The use of substitute partners."

"The use of what?"

"Ha ha, don't be modest, Doctor! Your associate told me otherwise."

"My associate?" I ask with sinking heart.

"Dr. Immelmann."

"What did he say?"

"He showed us your paper in which you demonstrate that marital love often founders on boredom and the struggle to attain a theoretical orgasmic perfection."

"But I didn't suggest—"

"You didn't have to. We simply implemented your insight."

"With?"

"Substitute partners! A fresh start!" Like an impresario Stryker waves a graceful hand toward the viewing mirror.

Instead of the usual solitary subject, or at the most two subjects, there are four, two in each bed, J.T. Thigpen, Gloria, and Ted 'n Tanya. But Gloria is in one bed with Ted and J.T. in the other with Tanya. The couples are, for the most part, dressed: the women in Mistress Goody gowns, the men in Cotton Mather knee-britches.

"As you see, Tom, we also make use of your warnings about an abstract and depersonalized environment. We place our lovers in a particular concrete historical setting."

"But I didn't suggest—"

Dr. Helga Heine suddenly turns up the music, which is not Early American, however, but Viennese waltzes.

"Okay, keeds!" She speaks into a microphone, keeping time with her free hand. Though she is hefty, she balances lightly on the balls of her feet.

*"Zwei Herzen!* Now—bundling partitions up!"

"Hold it!" cries the chaplain from the vaginal console. "They haven't inserted the sensors! Rats!" He grabs Helga's microphone. "Hold it, kids! Bundling partitions down! Insert sensors!"

But it is too late. The couples are too engrossed with each other to pay attention. Nor do Stryker and Helga object.

"The important thing is the breakthrough," Stryker tells me. "The quantifying can come later."

"Go go go, keeds!" cries Helga, recovering the microphone and waltzing about in one place.

"Don't fret, Kev." Stryker tries to soothe the distraught chaplain. "We'll have the film and there'll be more sessions to collect data."

"Tch!" The champlain stamps his foot and rends his *Commonweal.* "I wish somebody would tell me why we're paying these people!"

But Stryker is standing beside Helga, the two of them suddenly quiet as they watch the lovers.

"Wow," says Stryker, lips parted.

"And how," says Helga.

They look at each other.

"Are you thinking what I'm thinking?" asks Stryker, touching Helga's elbow.

"The chicken room?" asks Helga softly, her eyes radiant. She pronounces it *zhicken.*

Linking arms, they disappear through the doorway of the Observer Stimulation Overflow Area.

But wait! That's where the cello is!

It's too late. The door closes. Father Kev Kevin and I watch in dismay.

"I have to get a cello out of there," I tell the chaplain for lack of anything better to say.

"What are we going to do?" asks the chaplain frantically, wringing his hands, starting now for his console, now for the chicken room. He is sweating profusely.

"I don't know about you, but I've got to get that cello."

"Oh dear!" cries Father Kev Kevin. "If there was ever an existential decision—! Kenneth, how could you!" He groans aloud and, thrusting me aside, disappears into the cubicle.

After a moment of indecision, I rush after him.

Despite the urgency, I find myself knocking politely at the door. No response. Try the knob. It is unlocked. Hm, nothing for it but to slip in, find the cello, and slip out with as little fuss as possible.

I do so, trying as best I can to pretend nothing is out of the way, but the cello is propped in the far corner and I have to bend over the cot to reach it.

"Pardon," I murmur, eyes rolled up into eyebrows.

But there is no not seeing a large rosy buttock. Stryker is at Helga, Father Kev Kevin is at Stryker, but Helga is also patting the chaplain as if to reassure him lest he feel unwanted. The three embrace like lost children trying to keep warm.

The encased cello is as bulky as a sarcophagus. There is no purchase on it and there is the devil's own time getting it over and across the populous cot without knocking the occupants.

"Pardon."

Puffing and straining, I make it at last. Whew!

I rush through the observation room without bothering to look at the volunteer lovers. Wheels whir, pointers quiver, unattended.

Now to find Moira's room, her Cupid's Quiver and underwear, and I'm on my way!


14

It's raining again when I return to the motel. No sign of Ely, the Bantu home guard. I store the cello in the Rotary dining room and go up through the bathroom window.

In my absence Moira has taken a shower and looks lovely, but she and Lola have fallen out. In their quarrel they hardly take notice of my return. Lola hardly acknowledges the news that her cello is safe and sound.

Ellen brings me a Spam sandwich and a glass of bitter hose water. Noticing her, Lola fixes me a gin fizz. I decide to drink the gin fizz before eating.

"Don't think I don't know what goes on in that so-called Love Clinic," Lola is saying with an ironic smile.

"And what might that be?" asks Moira.

Both women are smiling and speaking to Ellen but really through Ellen to each other. They have reached that stage of a quarrel where both still smile but neither can stand the sight of the other.

"Everybody knows about the atheistic psychologists who encourage immorality under the guise of research," Lola tells Moira through Ellen.

Moira is sitting cross-legged on the bed, doing her nails. She looks like a sorority girl. "At least there is no hypocrisy, which is more than I can say about the goings on in the so-called country-club set."

"Such as?"

Now they're looking at me!

"Well well, girls," I tell them. "You'll be glad to hear I brought everything you sent me for."

"Such as what goes on at night on the golfing greens and the skinny-dipping in the pool," Moira tells me with a wink.

"Sounds like someone's been reading girlie magazines, Tom," says Lola, to me.

"Yes. Well, to tell the truth"—I sip the gin fizz and close my eyes with every appearance of exhaustion—"you must excuse me. I can't concentrate on such matters. I'm afraid the situation outside has deteriorated badly." I relate the events of my excursion to the Center, omitting only some of the occurrences in Love. Disaster has its uses. "We may be here longer than you think. I'm afraid we're in for a long evening."

"How's that, Chief?" asks Ellen seriously. She pulls up a chair and absently plucks beggar's lice from my pants' leg.

"If there is going to be a major outbreak of violence, it will occur, I calculate, sometime this evening. I suggest that we all take a nap and prepare for what might be a bad night."

The grave news only partly mollifies Lola and Moira. Lola cants her pelvis and smolders, color high in her cheeks. Moira lies back on the bed, tucks her lip secretly, and holds up one pretty leg with both hands.

Ellen clears her throat and beckons me into the dressing room. "Chief, eat your sandwich!" she scolds and, as soon as we're inside, whispers: "You better do something about that pair."

"Yes," I say, noticing that Ellen is enjoying herself for the first time.

"Do you know what they did while you were gone?" she asks, scraping more beggar's lice from my sleeve. "They almost started scratching each other. I actually had to stand between them. They refused to stay in the same room, so what I did was fix up two other rooms. I had to! One's in 204 and the other in 205. I found some sheets and some Gulf spray, so we sprayed the mattresses and made them up."

"Then why are they back here?"

"Getting pillow cases!" Ellen nudges me. Her tone is the same she uses when she describes the antics of patients.

After a careful reconnoiter of the balcony, I tell the girls: "The coast is clear. Here's what we'll do. It's cool now, so everyone can go to his or her room and take a nap. I'll stand guard. Ellen, you keep this room."

"And where might *his* room be?" Lola asks *The Laughing Cavalier.*

"Don't worry, there are plenty of vacancies!" I say heartily.

"Then would you mind getting my cello?" asks Lola without looking at me.

"And I'll take my sachet," says Moira, stretching and yawning.

"Of course!" I say, laughing. Why am I laughing?


15


I take Moira and Lola to their rooms. The coast is clear. Ellen is agitated when I return. She paces the carpet.

"I didn't tell you that I talked to Aunt Ellie—the last message before the Anser-Phone broke down and the operator left for Mississippi."

"A fine woman, Miss Ellie."

Miss Ellie Oglethorpe, who raised Ellen, is a fine woman. She looks like a buxom President Wilson with her horse face, pince-nez, and large bosom. A virtuous and hard-working woman, she supported herself as town librarian, raised and educated Ellen, and still sends money to the African mission where Ellen's parents were killed by Nigerian tribesmen.

"She doesn't want me to stay out here alone, Chief."

"You're not alone."

"If I don't come back tonight, she wants to come out here."

"Good Lord, she can't do that."

"She's worried about my safety."

"We're perfectly safe here. Besides, I wouldn't let anything happen to you."

"It's not exactly that. She doesn't think it proper for me to stay here without a chaperone."

"Good Lord, of all things to worry about now."

"You know Aunt Ellie."

"Yes."

I am wondering whether to mix another gin fizz, eat, nap, or take a shower. Absently I mix a gin fizz.

"Aunt Ellie is something, isn't she?"

"Yes, she is."

"Do you know what she's been telling me for as long as I can remember?"

"No."

"You wouldn't believe it."

"No?"

"Here I am, twenty-four, and she still takes me aside and says: Ellen, think of yourself as a treasure trove that you're guarding for your future husband. Can you imagine such a thing?"

"No. Yes."

"For years I thought she was talking about Mama's silver service locked in the linen closet."

"Is that right?" Feeling a slight quilting of the scalp, I take an anti-hives pill. "Well, she's right, Ellen. And I envy the lucky man."

"Thanks, Chief."

"This is your room, by the way."

"What will your two girl friends say?"

I shrug. "Don't worry about them. Now. You take your nap. If you don't mind, I'm going to take a shower, put on some clean clothes, and eat your sandwiches. Then I think I'll feel better."

"I can't stand those on you," says Ellen, buttoning my unbuttoned collar tabs.

She lies on the bed, throwing the tufted chenille spread over her crossed ankles. How ill the chenille suits her! I blush at my summer's effort of fitting out this room as a trysting place. How shabby Ellen makes it all seem!

Take a shower. The water is hot at first from the sun, two hundred feet of bitter hot hose water between the motel and the Esso station, then suddenly goes cold.

A harsh toweling. Switch to an Early Times today. Eat Ellen's sandwiches? No, drink two gin fizzes.

Go fetch lapsometer, tiptoeing past Ellen, who sleeps, lips parted.

Now at mirror, set lapsometer for a fairly stiff massage of Brodmann 11, the frontal location of the musical-erotic.

The machine sings like a tuning fork. My head sings with it, the neurones of Layer IV dancing in tune.

The albumen molecules hum.

> Everybody's talking at me,
> I can't hear a word they saying,
> Only the echoes of my mind.

What does a man live for but to have a girl, use his mind, practice his trade, drink a drink, read a book, and watch the martins wing it for the Amazon and the three-fingered sassafras turn red in October?

Art Immelmann is right. Man is not made for suffering, night sweats, and morning terrors.

Doctor, heal thyself, I say, and give Brodmann 11 one last little buzz.

I feel much better, full of musical-erotic tenderness and gin fizzes and bourbon but fresh and clean and ravenous as well. I eat more of Ellen's sandwiches.

Time to fetch Lola's cello from the Rotary dining room.

The motel seems deserted. No activity at the church except for the carols still booming across the empty plaza:

> A partridge in a pear tree . . .

July or not, it all comes back, the old pleasant month-long Santy-Claus-store-window Christmas. It wasn't so bad really, the commercial Christmas, a month of Christmas Eves, stores open every night, everyone feeling good and generous and spending money freely, handsome happy Americans making

the cash registers jingle, the nice commercial carols, Holy
Night, and soft-eyed pretty girls everywhere—

The carol stops in mid-phrase. Someone has finally found
the control panel.

## 16

The rain slams in sheets against the windows of Lola's
room. It is a small tropical storm. Lola plays a Dvořák Sla-
vonic dance and ducks her head to its little lilt and halt and
stutter and start again.

The only clean place in the room is the mattress, which has
been Gulf-sprayed and spread with a fitted sheet snapped over
the corners and stretched tight as a drumhead.

I lie on the drumhead sheet in my stocking feet, toddy
balanced on my sternum.

Goodbye morning terror and afternoon sadness. Hello love
and Anton Dvořák.

Above the racket of the storm and in the reek of warm
bourbon and Gulf spray, old Dvořák sings of the sunny fields
and twilit forests of Bohemia.

Lola closes her eyes as she plays. Her long bare knees
clasp the cello's waist, her fingertips creak against the resin,
her deltoid swells, the vibrato flutter of her fingering hand
beats like the wings of a hawk.

> *Three French hens, two turtle doves*
> *And a partridge in a pear tree,*

shrieks the carillon like a wind in the storm. Some damn fool
has started it up again. Lola laughs and puts the cello away.

We lie entwined on the tight sheet, kissing persimmon kisses,
Lola twisting down and around in her old Juilliard torque style
of kissing. When she loves, even lying down, there is a sense
of her stooping to it. The cello is still but music plays on.
When we're not kissing, her tongue cleaves to the back of her
teeth and she hisses cello themes in a boy's way of whistling,
a paper-boy hiss-whistling through his teeth on his route.

Her warm callused fingertips strew stars along my flank.

My scalp quilts a bit, popping a hair root or two. But I can see well enough. Where are my pills?

She is both heavy and frail.

Now the idiot is fooling with the carillon controls, spinning the tape backward into fall football music. The storm roars but above it I recognize the Tarheel alma mater,

> *Hark the sound of Tarheel voices*
> *Ringing clear and true,*

played five years ago when Tulane played the Carolina Tarheels.

We close our eyes and go spinning back to those old haunted falls, the happy-sad bittersweet drunk Octobers. What needs to be discharged is the intolerable tenderness of the past, the past gone and grieved over and never made sense of. Music ransoms us from the past, declares an amnesty, brackets and sets aside the old puzzles. Sing a new song. Start a new life, get a girl, look into her shadowy eyes, smile. Fix me a toddy, Lola, and we'll sit on the gallery of Tara and you play a tune and we'll watch evening fall and lightning bugs wink in the purple meadow.

Our heads lie in each other's arms. My hand explores the tender juncture of her frailty and strength, a piece of nature's drollery, the flare of ribs from the massive secret paraspinal muscle columns.

"We'll live at Tara," says Lola past my arm in the prosaic casting-ahead voice of a woman planning tomorrow's meals. "While I'm showing horses and playing concerts, you can do your researches. You can have the garçonnière for your laboratory."

Lying cheek against the warm slump of her biceps, I am perceiving myself as she sees me, an agreeable H. G. Wells nineteenth-century scientist type, "doing my researches" in the handsome outhouse of Tara, maybe working on a time machine and forgetting time the way great inventors do so she has to remind me to eat, bringing a tray of collard greens and corn bread to the lab. "Darling, you haven't eaten all day!" So I take time off to eat, time off from my second breakthrough and my second Nobel.

Afterwards we sit on the gallery and Lola brings me toddies and plays happy old Haydn, whose music does not brook one single shadow of sadness.

Then we'll go to bed, not in the bunker to watch the constellations spin in their courses but upstairs to the great four-
poster, the same used by Rhett Butler and Scarlett and
purchased by Vince Marsaglia at the M-G-M prop sale in
1970.

Perhaps I'll even work at night. Happy is the man who can
do science at midnight, of a Tuesday, in the fall, free of
ghosts, exorcised by love and music of all past Octobers.
Clasp Lola on Halloween and howl down the yellow moon
and go to the lab and induce great simple hypotheses.

The rain slackens but still drums steadily on the orange tile
roof of Howard Johnson's.

"You're so *smart*," says Lola, giving me a hug.

"And you're a fine girl." I speak into the sweet heavy
slump of her biceps. "What a lovely strong back you have. It's
good being here, isn't it?"

"Lovely."

"You're such a good girl and you play such good music."

"Do you really think I'm good?" She lifts her head.

"Yes," I say, frowning, realizing I've stirred up her Texas
competitiveness. She's told me before about winning regional
cello contests in West Texas.

"How good?"

"At music? The best," I say, hoping to make her forget
about it and locking my fingers in the small of her back, a
deep wondrous swale.

But her horned fingertips absently play a passacaglia on my
spine as her mind casts ahead.

"You know what I think I'll do?"

"What?"

"Enter Yellow Rose in the Dallas show."

"Good." At least she's off music contests.

"Then take up Billy Sol on his idea of a winter tour."

"You have a truly splendid back. What a back. It's extremely strong."

"That's nothing, feel this."

So saying, she locks her legs around my waist in a non-
erotic schoolboy's wrestling hold and bears down.

"Good Lord," I say, blinking to clear the fog from my
eyes.

"What do you think of that?"

"Amazing."

"Nobody ever beat Lola at anything."

"I believe you." Sometimes I think that men are the only single-minded lovers, loving for love, that women love with the idea of winning, winning either at love or cello-playing or what. "Billy Sol? Winter tour?"

"Yes, darl. You want Lola to keep up her music, don't you?"

"Sure."

"This is Lola's big chance." Up and down goes the fingering hand warm as a horn on my backbone.

"Chance to do what?"

Billy Sol, it turns out, is Billy Sol Simpson of the music department at Texas A & M, who has offered her the "junior swing" for starters. It's a tour of the junior colleges of Texas, of which there are forty or fifty—with himself, Billy Sol, as her accompanist. After that, who knows? Maybe the senior circuit: Baylor, T.C.U., S.M.U., and suchlike.

"Well, I don't know," I say, thinking of this guy Billy Sol squiring her around Beaumont Baptist College and West Texas Junior College at Pecos. Should I trust her to a Texas A & M piano player?

"Shoot, you ought to see Billy Sol. Just a big old prisspot, but a real good boy. He's been wonderful to me."

"I'm glad."

"Don't you be like that—you want me to squeeze you again?"

"No."

"Anyhow, you're coming with us. You'll need a break from your researches."

"Yes!" All of a sudden I feel happy again.

For a fact, it doesn't sound bad at all, swinging out through all those lost lonesome Texas towns, setting up in Alamo Plaza motels and bejeweled in the dusk under those great empty heart-stopping skies. A few toddies and I'll sit in the back row of the LBJ Memorial auditorium behind rows of fresh-eyed, clean-necked, short-haired God-believing Protestant boys and girls, many dumb but many also smart, smart the way Van Cliburn was smart, who came from Texas too, making straight A's at everything and taking the prize in Moscow, while big prissy Billy Sol tinkles away on the Steinway and Lola clasps her cello between her knees and sends old Brahms singing out into the great God-haunted Texas night.

. . . And afterwards eat a big steak and drink more toddies

and make love and watch Japanese 3-D science-fiction late movies. (Dear God, I hope Lola won't develop an obsession about winning, winning horse shows and music contests, the way Doris got hooked on antiques, Englishmen, and Hindoo religion.)

I must have been shaking my head, for she raises hers and looks at me. "What?"

But I don't tell her. Instead I remind her that if worst comes to worst this afternoon, there may not be any horse shows or junior swings through Texas.

"Oh. You're right," she says, feigning gravity. She doesn't really believe that anything could go wrong with the U.S.A. or at least with Texas.

Her fingering fingers drift off my back. She's asleep. Her breath comes strong and sweet in my neck, as hay-sweet as her sorrel mare's.

Carefully I ease myself free of her slack heavy-frail body.

What a strong fine girl. If worst came to worst, she and I could rebuild Tara with our bare hands.

# 17

"Chief, the news is worse." Ellen watches me as I fix two gin fizzes. "Don't you think you're firing the sunset gun a little too early and too often?"

"What has happened now?"

"There are riots in New Orleans, and riots over here. The students are fighting the National Guard, the Lefts are fighting the Knotheads, the blacks are fighting the whites. The Jews are being persecuted."

"What are the Christians doing?"

"Nothing."

"Turn on the TV."

"It's on. The station went off the air."

"Then they've taken the transmitter," I say half to myself.

"What's that, Chief?"

"Nothing."

"Did you enjoy the concert?"

"What concert? Oh yes."

"I heard from Dr. Immelmann again."

"How did you hear from him?"

"On the Anser-Phone."

"I thought you said it was dead."

"It was. I don't understand it."

"What did he say?"

"He said to tell you 'it' was going to happen this afternoon."

"It?"

"He said you would know what I meant."

The gin fizz is good. Already the little albumen molecules are singing in my brain. My neck is swelling. I take a pill to prevent hives.

"What else did he say?"

"That if anything happens, we're to stay here. That we're safe with you because you can protect us with your lapsometer. He said you should watch and wait."

"Watch for what?"

"He said you would know. Signs and portents, he said. He told me, don't go back and get your coat."

"Hm. Did he say how long we should wait here?"

"He said it might be months."

"Did you ask him about your aunt and my mother?"

"He said they would be fine. Chief, do you know what is going to happen?"

"No. At least I am not sure."

"What are you going to do?"

"Right now I have to see how Moira is."

"Well, excuse me!"

"What's the matter?"

"Frankly I don't see what you see in either one of them."

"They're both fine girls. I'm very fond of them. I may as well tell you that I'm thinking of marrying again."

"Congratulations. But don't you have one girl too many?"

"Things are going to be very unsettled for the next few weeks," I say vaguely.

"What does that mean?"

I shrug.

Ellen uncrosses her legs and leans forward. "Well, what do you mean? Do you mean you want to—marry both of them?"

"Right now, I'm responsible for all three of you."

My scalp is beginning to quilt.

Ellen blinks. "I'm not sure I understand you."

"It's a question of honor."

"Honor?"

"I don't believe a man should trifle with a girl."

"Well yes, but—!"

"However, if a man's intentions are honorable—"

"But—"

"I mean if a man intends to marry a girl—"

"But, Chief, there are two of them."

"It is still a matter of intentions," I say, feeling scalp-hawsers pop.

"You mean you're going to marry both of them?"

"These are peculiar times. Abraham had several wives."

"Abraham? Abraham who? My God, you couldn't handle one wife."

"Never mind," I say stiffly. "The fact is I am responsible for all three of you."

"Ho ho. Include me out!"

"Nevertheless—!"

"With those two"—she nods toward the wall—"you need me?"

"That's right."

"You need something. Chief, I don't understand what is happening to you. You have so much to offer the world. There is so much that is fine in you. You're a fine doctor. And God knows, if the world ever needed you, it needs you now. Yet all you want to do is live here in this motel with three women for months on end."

"Yes!" I laugh. "You and I will spend the summer reading Calvin and Thomas Aquinas and let those two women squabble."

"Not me, big boy! I'm leaving this afternoon."

"You can't. You heard what Art said."

"It's Art who's picking me up."

"What?"

"Dr. Immelmann offered me a job."

"Doing what?"

"As his traveling secretary."

"What in hell does that mean?"

"He's going to Sweden to coordinate your MOQUOL program."

"You and Art Immelmann in Sweden!"

"What's wrong with that?"

"That's the goddamnest thing I ever heard."

"Your cursing doesn't help the situation."

"You don't want to go with him."

"No, I don't, Chief," says Ellen quietly. She sits bolt

upright at the desk, starchy as a head nurse on the morning shift, eyes blue as Lake Geneva.

"Stay with me, Ellen. Things will settle down. We'll go back to work. Somebody will have to pick up the pieces."

Ellen is silent.

"Well?"

"There would have to be some fundamental changes before I would stay," she says at last.

"Changes? What changes?"

"You figure it out, Chief."

What does she mean, I wonder as I give myself a light lapsometer massage, firming up the musical-erotic as well as pineal selfhood.

A better question: why do I want all three women? For I do. I can't stand the thought of losing a single one! How dare anyone take one of my girls?

Stepping out into the silvery rain, I notice a Bantu squatting cross-legged atop the Joy screen, looking toward the Center with a pair of binoculars.

The carillon has jumped back to Christmas.

*Silent night,*
*Holy night.*


18

Moira sits on the bed reading *Cosmopolitan*. Damn, I wish she wouldn't! I brought Rod McKuen and some house and home magazines for our weekend at Howard Johnson's, but no, she has to bring *Cosmopolitan*. Why? Because of Helen Gurley Brown, her favorite author. She's reading an article of Helen's now, "Adultery for Adults." Damn! For years now Helen has been telling girls it's all right to screw anybody you like.

But what if she likes Buddy Brown?

I hand her *House and Garden*. "You shouldn't read that stuff."

"Why not?"

"It's immoral."

She shrugs but takes *House and Garden*. "You didn't mind my reading it before."

"That was before."

"What's wrong with my reading it now?"

"Everything."

"What's the difference?"

"It's a matter of intention," I begin, but she's not listening. Something in *House and Garden* has caught her eye.

"I can't decide which I like better, the now look or the Vermeer look."

"What is the Vermeer look?"

"You know—Dutch doors with the top open, everything light and airy, tile."

"Very good."

"Myself I've always been partial to the outdoor-indoor look, green leaves in the kitchen, a bedroom opening to the treetops."

"We had that." I sit on the foot of the bed.

"Don't you love this kitchen?"

"Yes."

Moira must have had a nap. At any rate she's rosy and composed, her old thrifty self. Cross-legged she sits, lower lip curled like a thick petal. Above her perfect oval face, a face unwounded, unscarred, unlined, unmarked by sadness or joy, the nap of her cropped wheat-colored hair invites the hand against its grain. My hand brushes it. My heart lifts. I am in love.

She's the girl of our dreams, Americans! the very one we held in our hearts as we toiled in the jungles of Ecuador. She is! Sitting scrunched over and humpbacked, she is beautiful despite herself, calf yoga-swelled over heel, one elbow propped, the other winged out like a buzzard for all she cares. Prodigal she is with her own perfection, lip tucked, pencil scratching her head. She holds herself too cheap, leaves her gold lying around like bobby pins.

My throat is engorged with tenderness.

Planning a house she is, marking the margins of *House Beautiful*. She's beautiful too. A bit short in the limbs, I'll admit—I can stretch a hand's span from her elbow to her acromium—but perfected as it were in the shortening. Her golden deltoid curves in in a single strong arc, a whorl of down marking its insertion. Now she turns a page and supinates her forearm to hold the spine of the magazine: down plunges the tendon into the fossa at her elbow. Sweet fossa. I kiss it.

"See how the prints of the casual pillows pick up the daisies in the wall tile,.."

"Yes. I have any number of casual pillows at home."

"I like casual living."

"Me too."

"Could we do the whole house over?"

"What house."

"Your house."

"Sure."

"I think I'll collect Shaker tableware. Look at these."

"Very good. But I thought you were going to raise banties."

"I am. But my great-grandfather was a backsliding Shaker who got married."

"Is that so?"

"Here is something else I love: simple handcrafts."

"I do too."

She puts down her magazine, rises to stretch, sits in my lap.

"You are good enough to eat," I say and begin to eat her kneecaps, which are like beaten biscuits. My fiery scalp begins to pop hawsers.

"Your're just like my Uncle Bud," says Moira, burying her face in my neck.

"I know."

"Only I like you better."

"You're a lovely girl."

"What do you think of my taking up tennis at the club?"

"You'd look lovely in a tennis outfit."

"I want to join a book club too."

"There is a poetry club in Paradise."

"I love poetry," she says and recites a poem.

> There was a girl in Portland
> Before the winter chill
> We used to go a' courting
> Along October hill.

"Very nice."

"It's always had a special meaning to me."

"Why?"

"Because we used to live in Portland, West Virginia."

"I'd like to take you down October hill."

"You look just like Rod McKuen, only stronger."

"Younger too."

"Wait a sec, Chico."

"Where're you going?"

"Next door. To get my sachet."

"Ah. Hm. Actually I don't . . . I didn't mean . . . I . . ."

"Don't worry. I'll fool the battle-ax."

"Battle-ax?" I say wonderingly.

She turns at the door, dimpling.

"Aunngh," I say faintly. Segments of a road map drift across my retina, crossroads, bits of highway, county seats.

Sitting slouched and poetic, as gracefully as Rod, I wait for Moira before the winter chill.

What I need is a nap, I tell myself, and fall asleep immediately. Do I hear Moira come and go while I am dozing?

# 19

"I quit, Dr. More," says Ellen. "Now. As of this moment. I no longer work for you."

"I wish you wouldn't." I fix a toddy, lie on the bed, slip a quarter in the Slepe-Eze, and close my eyes.

"Of all the shameless performances."

"Whose?"

"Not yours. I don't blame you nearly as much as them."

"You don't?" Taking heart, I open one eye.

"Chief," says Ellen, concerned, "what's the matter with your eye?"

"I don't know. What?"

"It's almost closed."

"Probably hives."

"My goodness! It's awful."

"My throat is closing too."

"Wait, Chief! I've got a shot of epinephrine in my bag."

"Good."

I watch with one eye while she gives me the shot.

"At least, Chief, I give you credit for honorable intentions."

"You do?"

"I think you're confused and exhausted."

"That's true."

"Anyhow, I don't blame men as much as women."

"I'm glad to hear it."

"Are you feeling better?"

"Yes."

"Your eyes is opening. Now, Chief."

"Yes."

"We have to be clear on one or two things."

"Right," I say, cheering up. I've always taken delight in her orderly mind.

"First. Do you intend to marry?"

"Yes."

"Who?"

"I don't know."

"You really don't know?"

"I really don't."

"Do you want me to stay with you?"

"Yes."

Why do I take such delight in answering her questions? I remind me of Samantha, who used to come home from school letter-perfect in her catechism and ask me to hear her nevertheless.

"Why did God make you?" And she'd answer, faking a hesitation, slewing her eyes around to me to gauge the suspense. She liked for me to ask and for her to answer. Saying is different from knowing.

"Are we going to go back to work?" asks Ellen.

"Yes."

I look at my watch.

Ellen takes a damp washrag and scrubs my mouth with hard mother-scrubs.

"Tch, of all the shameless hussies." She scrubs motherhard with no mercy for my lip. "My word!" She grabs my shirt.

"What now?"

"They even pulled your shirttail out." Hard tucks all around.

"Thank you." The sugar in the toddy is reviving me.

"Now. What are the plans?"

"Here are the plans. In five minutes, as soon as I finish my drink, I'm going over to the high ground of the interchange. I'm taking the carbine and I'll be within sight and range of this balcony and these windows. From that point I can also see the swamp, the Center, the town, and Paradise. I know what to look for. It should happen by seven o'clock. If you need me here, wave this handkerchief in the window. And shoot any-body else who tries to come in."

"Right, Chief."

"After I leave, you can collect the others and bring them in here."

"Don't worry. I'll blow their noses and tuck them in. We've handled worse, haven't we?"

"Yes." I look at her. "And, Ellen."

"Yes?"

"You won't leave without telling me?"

"No. But wait."

"What for?"

"I'm going to fix you a sandwich to take with you to keep your strength up."

"Where are they?"

"Who?"

"The girls."

"Next door—in Miss ah Rhoades's room. All of a sudden they're thick as thieves."

"Hm," I say uneasily. What are they cooking up between them?

# IN A PINE GROVE ON THE SOUTHWEST CUSP OF THE INTERSTATE CLOVERLEAF

▰▱▰▱▰▱▰▱

## 7:15 P.M. / JULY 4

AWAKE AND FEELING MYSELF AGAIN, WHICH IS TO SAY, alert, depressed-elated, and moderately terrified.

My leg has gone to sleep. One eye is closed either by sleep or by hives. Albumen molecules dance in my brain.

It is almost dark, but the sky is still light. The dark crowns of the cypresses flatten out against the sky like African veldt trees. A pall of smoke hangs over the horizon, marring the glimmering violet line that joins dark earth to light bowl of sky. The evening star glitters like a diamond next to the ruby light of the transmitter.

No sign of a sniper.

Three windows are lit at Howard Johnson's. The girls then are safe and sound and waiting for me.

Closer at hand a smaller column of smoke is rising. It is coming from a bunker off number 12 fairway which runs along the fence bordering the interstate right-of-way. The links lights are on, sodium-vapor arcs concealed in cypresses and Spanish moss, which cast a spectral light on the fairway and big creeping shadows in the rough.

Two police cars are parked on the shoulder. A small crowd stands around the bunker, gazing down.

Forgetting about my leg, I shoulder the carbine, stand up to start down the slope, and fall down. The exposed leg between shoved-up pants and fallen-down socks is ghostly and moon-pocked. I touch it. It feels like meat in the refrigerator.

I wait until the tingling comes and goes.

* * *

The smoke is coming from the sandtrap under the bunker. Charley Parker, the golf pro, stands watering the sand with a hose.

P.G.A. officials run back and forth between Charley and his official tower, which also holds camera crews and floodlights. Players watch from their carts. One player, swinging his sand wedge, stands beside the bunker.

There are people from the Center and town. I recognize Max Gottlieb, Stryker, a Baptist chiropractor named Dr. Billy Matthews; Mercer Jones, a state trooper; Dr. Mark Habeeb, a Center psychiatrist; Elroy McPhee, a Humble geologist and a moderate Episcopal Knothead; Moon Mullins, a Catholic slumlord and Pontiac dealer.

"What do you say, Doc," says Charley as if we were teeing off on an ordinary Sunday morning. But I notice that his hand is trembling and his jaw muscles pop.

"All right, Charley. What are you doing?"

"Do you hear what that goddamn P.G.A. official said to me?"

"No."

"He said there was no rule in the book to cover this so I have to put the fire out."

"No rule to cover what?"

"A ball in a burning sand trap."

"Is that what's holding up the game?"

"I got to put the son of a bitch out!"

"I don't believe I'd do that."

"Do what?"

"Put water on it. It will only make it worse."

"I got to put it out. The sand is on fire."

"How could the sand be on fire? It's a Heavy Sodium reaction, Charley."

"What would you do about it?"

"Clear the area. The smoke contains Heavy Sodium vapor and could be extremely dangerous, especially if a wind should spring up,"

Charley makes a sound. With the thumb and forefinger of his free hand he flings something—tears?—from his eyes.

"What's wrong, Charley?"

"What's wrong," repeats Charley. He gazes sorrowfully at the sand trap into which he directs the stream from the hose in an idle ruminative way, like a man pissing into a toilet. "The greatest event that ever happened to this town, to this state, the Pro-Am, gets to the finals, forty million people are watching on stereo-V, nine out of the top ten all-time money-winners and crowd-pleasers are on hand, half a million in prize money has been raised, the evangelistic team has arrived, the President himself plans to play a round tomorrow—and what happens? The goddamn bunkers catch on fire."

"You mean more than one?"

"All of them, man!"

"That figures," I say absently. "Charley, it's not the sand that's burning and the water will only—"

"Don't tell me the sand is not burning!" cries Charley, dashing tears from his eyes with thumb and forefinger. "Look!"

Fortunately a brisk breeze from the north is blowing the smoke straight out to the swamp.

"Mercer, do you have a bullhorn in your car?" I ask the state trooper.

"What do you want with a bullhorn, Doc?" asks Mercer in the easy yet wary tone of an experienced policeman who is both at his ease in an emergency and prepared for any foolishness from spectators.

"I've got to warn these people about the smoke. Will you help me clear the area?"

"Why do you want to do that?" asks Mercer, inclining his head toward me carefully.

"Because it contains noxious sodium particles, and if the wind should shift, we could have a disaster on our hands."

"We have oxygen in case of smoke inhalation, Doc." Mercer looks at me sideways. He is wondering if I am drunk.

Stifling an impulse to recite the symptoms of Heavy Sodium fallout, I adopt the acceptable attitude of friend-of-policeman encountering policeman on duty and accordingly line up alongside him.

"Things pretty quiet this evening, Mercer?"

"More or less."

"Any other ah emergencies?"

The trooper shrugs. "An incident at the Center. A little civil disorder at the club."

"Haven't the Bantus taken over Paradise?"

Mercer clears his throat and cocks his head in disapproval. There: I've done it again.

"I wouldn't say that."

"What would you say?"

"There have been reports of vandalism at the old club-house, some shots fired, and a house or two burned on the old 18 and out on the bluff." Mercer's cheek is set against me. Only our long acquaintanceship draws an answer from him. Do we really have to talk, Doc?

I sigh. "One more question, Mercer, and I'll let you alone. Is there any news about the President and Vice-President?"

"News?" asks Mercer, cheek stiff.

"I mean, have there been any attempts on their— Have any incidents occurred?"

Mercer's eyes slide around to me, past me, to the carbine, which I had forgotten. It is crossing his mind: what is nutty Doc doing with a gun and do you suppose he's a big enough fool to—no. But didn't Dr. Carl Weiss, another brilliant un-stable doctor, shoot Huey Long?

"Not that I've heard? Been hunting rabbits, Doc?"

"Yes."

"With a thirty ought six?"

"As a matter of fact, a sniper has been shooting at me the last couple of days."

"Is that right!" says Mercer in a sociable singsong and swings his arms. "I'm telling you the truth unh unh unh!"—as if snipers were but one more trial of these troubles times.

Max Gottlieb, Ken Stryker, Colley Wilkes, and Mark Habeeb, all but Habeeb still wearing their white coats, stand leaning over the fence, their hands in their pockets. They have the holiday air of hard-working scientists who have been dis-tracted from their researches and lean on windowsills to watch a street accident.

They gaze down at Charley Parker, who is still watering the bunker. Charley is conferring with a member of Cliff Barrow's evangelistic team on one side and an Amvet on the other. The former wears a Jesus-Christ-Greatest-Pro armband, the latter an American flag stuck in his overseas cap.

The scientists greet me affably and go on with their talk. Not far behind them Moon Mullins and Dr. Billy Matthews stand silently. The sight of them makes me uneasy.

"The cross and the flag," Ken Stryker is saying.

Colley nods. "A nice example of core values and symbol systems coming to the aid of economics."

"The most potent appraisive signs in our semiotic," says Dr. Mark Habeeb.

Colley asks him: "Do you know Ted's work in sign reversal in *Gorilla gorilla malignans*? You take a killer ape who responds aggressively to the purple rump patch of a baboon. He can be reconditioned by using lysergin-B to respond to the same sign without aggression, with affection, in fact."

"Peace!" says Habeeb, laughing. "Maybe we could use electrodes here, Max." He nods toward the trio in the bunker.

But Max only shrugs. His mind is elsewhere.

"Right, Tom?" Habeeb turns to me.

"I couldn't say."

"Come on, Tom." Habeeb persists, nodding to the crowd. "You're perceptive."

"Perceptive? I perceive you are suffering from angelism," I say absently.

"Cut it out, ha ha. I was talking about the behavior over there."

"I was talking about you."

"Me?"

"You're abstracting and withholding judgment."

"I'm a scientist. We don't judge behavior, we observe it."

"That's not enough." I stagger a bit. "Blow hold or cot."

"Eh? How's that?"

"I mean blow hot or cold but not—" The road map, I notice, is breaking up again. Stretches of highway come loose, float across the sky.

"Are you all right?" asks Mark, taking my arm.

"Tom?" Max comes close on the other side, puts his arm around me.

What good fellows.

"I'm all right, Max. But it's happened."

"What's happened?"

"You know damn well."

"I'm not quite sure—"

"This." I point to the smoking sand.

"Colley thinks it's a fire in the sulfur dome."

"It's a slow sodium reaction and you know it."

"Oh." Max drops his arm.

"And you know the danger, Max."

"What danger?"

"My God, after what happened in The Pit, how can you ask?"

At the mention of The Pit, the other three smile at me with the greatest good humor and affection.

Ken laughs out loud. "That was something—the best of the year! Did you see the Old Man carrying on, ha ha!" They all laugh at the recollection, all but Gottlieb. Colley pays me a rare, for him, compliment. "You something else, Tom."

"What are you talking about?"

"What you did in The Pit, to old Buddy, to everybody!"

"And just what do you think I did?" I ask the four of them. "Max?"

Max's face is in shadow.

"Well, Max?"

"You always did have a gift for hypnotherapy, Tom."

"For Christ's sake, do you think I hypnotized them?"

"You take four hundred overworked dexed-up strung-out students at the end of the year—" Max breaks off.

"And what about my invention?"

"I thought it was an extremely effective objective correlative," says Ken warmly.

"Objective correlative my ass." I turn to Max. "Max, I'm putting it to you. If you don't help me clear this area immediately, I am holding you responsible."

"Tell me first, Tom. Have you reached a decision about coming back to A-4?"

"As a patient?"

"Patient-therapist."

"We'll talk about it, Max. But don't you see what is happening right here?"

"I see what is happening to you." Max is looking at my carbine, at my clothes gummed with pine resin, smeared with lipstick.

"Charley, listen to me. There is something dreadfully wrong."

"You're damn right there's something wrong. The Pro-Am is screwed up and we'll probably lose the Camellia Open next year. And the goddamn sand is still on fire."

"Moon, maybe you and Dr. Billy Matthews could help me. Unless we act now, the consequences could be nationwide and it will be too late."

"The consequences are already nationwide and it is already too late," says Dr. Matthews, shouldering between us. He is a tall heavy bald youngish man with shoulders and arms grown powerful from manipulating spinal columns in his chiropractic. His thick glasses are fitted with flip-up sun lenses, which are flipped up.

"What do you mean?" I ask fearfully. Has my lapsometer caused mischief in other places?

"The country has been taken over by our enemies and there is no respect for God or country," says Dr. Matthews menacingly. "Last Sunday some niggers tried to come into our church. And now this."

"Now what?"

"Those fellows," says the chiropractor in a loud voice and directly at the four scientists. "They're teaching disrespect for both the cross and Old Glory."

"Actually they were speaking of an experiment with primates."

"That's what I'm talking about! Monkeys! And that fellow there is a known Communist," he says in a lower voice, nodding toward Dr. Habeeb.

"I seriously doubt that," I say, remembering that Dr. Habeeb recently testified in a trial in which Dr. Billy Matthews had been sued by a woman whose husband had been treated for cancer of the liver by manipulating his spine.

"Where do you stand in this, Doctor?" asks Dr. Matthews, eyeing me suspiciously.

Moon shifts around uncomfortably. "Don't worry about Doc here. He's a hundred percent with us. Aren't you, Doc?"

"With you on what?"

"On God and country."

I am silent.

"You do believe in God and country, don't you, Doc?"

"Yes."

"I remember when Doc and I were in high school," Moon tells the chiropractor. "Doc wrote a prize-winning essay for the Knights of Columbus on how there was no real conflict between science and religion. You remember what you said about transubstantiation, Doc?"

"Yes."

"Transubstantiation is an invention of the Roman popes," says Dr. Billy Matthews, flipping his flip-ups down for some reason. "It's a piece of magic to fool the ignorant and has no basis in the Bible."

"Whoa, hold on, Billy!" cries Moon. "You don't know

what you're talking about. Christ said 'This is my body.' Didn't he, Doc?"

"Yes," I say and utter a groan.

"That's the Eyetalian translation," says Dr. Billy Matthews. With his flip-ups down he looks blind as a bat.

"No, it isn't, is it, Doc? Tell him."

"Later. Oh Lord. What am I going to do?" I ask them, rending my shirt. "What if the wind springs up?"

My eyes are swelling again. The world is seen through the slit on a gun turret.

"Max, something is dreadfully wrong."

"You're damn right there is. We've lost our N.I.M.H. funding for next year, thanks to our Ecuadorian venture."

"No, I mean something a great deal wronger than that."

"You look ill, Tom."

"I'm very tired and my eyes are swelling but I feel fine deep down. In fact, I've got a heartful of love, Max."

"Love?"

"Max, I'm a lucky man. I've got three wonderful girls waiting for me."

"Three girls. Look, sit down here on the grass and let me check you out. Just as I thought. You're going into anaphylaxis again. What have you been eating this time?"

"Gin fizzes."

"Oh no. Not again. *Why?*"

"I don't know. Lola fixed one for me. She's a lovely girl." Feeling very tired, I lie down on the velvety Tifton 451 Bermuda at the bunker's lip. "But that's not what bothers me."

"What bothers you?"

"You. And them. That is, you four and those two." I nod toward Moon and Dr. Billy Matthews, who are still arguing about transubstantiation.

"What about us and them?"

"You're both right and wrong."

"What does that mean?"

"I mean that it's almost hopeless now. One whiff of the vapor and you'll kill each other."

"What do you want me to do about it?" Max asks dryly.

I open my mouth to say something but can't utter a word. Max leans over and peers at me through the blue smoke and, suddenly seeing what is wrong, jumps up. "I'll be right back."

"Don't worry about—" I begin, lifting a feeble hand, and pass out.

There comes a familiar smell of sweat intricated by deodorant.

I open my eyes.

The smell comes from a push of air as Art Immelmann, who is sitting on the lip of the sand trap, leans over me and his bi-swing jacket flaps.

"I won't say I told you so, Doc."

"Told me what?"

"That nobody would believe you even if you showed them. Only two people in this world believe in you."

"Who?" Did Max give me a shot? My eyes open easily.

"I and your excellent nurse."

"Leave her out of it. She's no concern of yours."

"Then you'd better take care of her."

"What do you mean?"

"Get back to the motel, Doc."

"Why?"

"Because there is nothing you can do here and a great deal you can do there."

"But these people don't realize what is happening."

"And you can't tell them."

"They'll get hurt."

"Therefore you'd better save yourself for the long pull."

"I think you are somehow responsible, you and your god-damn foundations."

Art winces and shakes his head. "Doc, we operate on a cardinal principle, which we never violate. We never never 'do' anything to anybody. We only help people do what they want to do. We facilitate social interaction in order to isolate factors. If people show a tendency to interact in a certain way, we facilitate the interaction in order to accumulate reliable data."

"And if people cut each others' throats meanwhile, it's not your fault."

"Doc, we're dedicated to the freedom of the individual to choose his own destiny and develop his own potential."

"What crap," I mutter.

"Crap? Crap." Art searches his memory. "I'm not sure I understand—but never mind. Aren't you feeling well enough to go now?"

"Go where?"

"Back to the motel and look after the three ladies. Your lapsometer is still there. You can protect the three of them and yourself from any unfortunate little side effects from this." He glances at the column of smoke, which is thicker than ever. "Stay there three months."

"Three months?"

"It's your duty. By saving them and yourself, you can save millions later."

"What will we do for three months?"

"You have books, food, drink, music. But most of all you have your obligation."

"To whom?"

"To the three ladies."

"And what do you suggest that I do with three women for three months?"

Again the coat flaps as Art leans close. I'm enveloped by the smell of sebum and Ban.

"Love them, Doc! Believe me, it lies within your power to make all three of them happy and yourself too. Didn't God put us here to be happy! Isn't happiness better than unhappiness? Love them! Work on your invention. Stimulate your musical-erotic! Develop your genius. Aren't we all obliged to develop our potential? Work! Love! Music! That's what makes a man happy."

"True."

"Then you better get going."

"In a minute. One little nap," I say, closing my eyes with a smile as I think of the future.

Somewhat confused. I examine the contents of my pockets to get a line on the significance of the past and the hope of the future. Contents: 12 Phillips screws and one small dry turd folded in a clean handkerchief. I recall the latter but not the former. 12 Phillips screws . . .

A light hand touches my shoulder. It is Ellen. She squats on her heels, tucking her uniform under her knee.

"You all right, Chief?"

"Fine. Just taking a nap."

"You'll be all right. Dr. Gottlieb gave you a shot."

"What are you doing here?"

"There was no reason for me to stay over there."

"Where are Moira and Lola?"

"Your two little popsies have flown the coop."

Popsies. She's been talking to Max, all right.

"What happened?"

"Miss Rhoades went hiking off to Tara with the pistol stuck in her jeans and the cello slung over her shoulder. The last time I saw Miss Schaffner, she was getting in Dr. Brown's car in the plaza."

"Buddy Brown? How did that happen?"

"The Anser-Phone is working. She had me call him."

"I see."

"Now, come on. We're going home."

"Home?"

"Back to your house."

"What happened to the Bantus?"

"They've faded away."

"I think I'd better stay here a while."

"Come on. You're going to pick up your life where you left it. Dr. Gottlieb is wrong. You don't need to go to the hospital. All you need is good hard work and a—" She pauses.

"No. I can't go now."

"Why not?"

"The danger here is too great. I must do what I can. Did you bring my lapsometer?"

"Yes, Chief. But the important thing is to get you back in harness."

"Do you understand the danger?"

"Yes. I believe in you completely. That's why I want you to get out of here."

"And do what?"

"Go home and get some sleep. I'll meet you at the office tomorrow. We'll have our work cut out for us."

"I'm not going back to that."

"Back to what?"

"Back to my old life."

"It's your duty, Chief," says Ellen and means it.

"I still can't do it."

"Why can't you? You can. I'll help you. We'll do it."

I am thinking of my old life: waking up Monday Tuesday Wednesday as not myself, breakfast on Tang and terror in the "enclosed patio," Thursday Friday afternoons a mystery of longing. My old life was a useless longing on weekdays, World War I at night, and drunk every weekend.

"You wait here, Chief. I'll get my car. Your mother had

Eukie bring it to the plaza. She's safe. The Bantus are under control. There was no real trouble. All the trouble was caused by a few outsiders and some hopped-up swamp rats. Most people here, white and black, like things the way they are."

"I don't."

"You will. Wait here. I'm going to get the car."


Three pairs of legs dangle over the lip of the bunker, two on one side of me, one on the other. They belong to Chuck Parker with his golden curls, his Jeb Stuart fan of a beard and his clamshell necklace, and Ethel, his little dark Smithie Pocahontas, and Hester on my other side.

"Are you all right?" asks Hester in her lovely peculiar flatted New England vowels and laterals.

"I'm fine." With a bit of effort I hike up on my elbows and sit beside her. I look into her clear hazel eyes in which there is no secret or concealment such as causes one to look away. There is only clarity here and no shadow of the past. It's all gone, not only the old Priscilla-Puritan beginnings but what came later and opposed it: no Priscilla, no anti-Priscilla; no Puritanism, no transcendentalism, no -ism at all, not even an anti-ism, not even a going back like Ethel to Pocahontasism, no left or right. It's all gone, she's wiped the slate clean and now she sits in the wilderness and reads and rereads *The Case of the Velvet Claws*. She's waiting for something.

"What a sight, eh, Doc?" says Chuck, leaning out to see me. "I'm glad to be here, glad to have seen it."

"Seen what?"

"Seen the end. You're looking at it, Doc. The same is up." Chuck sweeps his arm past the smoking bunker, his father with the hose, the pros, the ams, the golf carts, the officials, the scientists, the stereo-V tower with its cameras, the sodium arcs. "A fitting end, wouldn't you say, Doc?"

"End to what?"

"Everything! Look at my poor father. His mind is blown, and you know why? Because of a game with a little ball and money. Money, Doc!"

"Actually it's not money at all."

"Look at him! It's too much for him. He thinks the sand is burning. But you and I know better, eh, Doc? We know why it's smoking and what is going to happen, wow! Doc, you are something else, you and your doomsday machine. What a way for them to go, in a golf game with the bunkers on fire, hee

hee hee. You set it, didn't you, Doc? You fixed 'em all, not only Pop but the others."

"What others?"

"All of them. Look at them, the scientists, the manipulators, the killers of subjectivity, the jig is up with them too and they don't even know it; and them too, the Christian flag-wavers and hypocrites, and it's all thanks to you—you may be forty-five but you're one of us."

"Yeah, well—"

"So we're leaving now and you're coming with us."

"With you?"

"With Hester."

"Hester?"

"Hester wants you to live with her in her chickee."

I look at Hester. She looks back. There is no secrecy in the clear depths, no modesty or boldness. She smiles and nods. She neither blushes nor not blushes. I look at her bare brown legs, unscarred, not fat, not thin, thighs simple and deep in youth. I look at my ghostly moonpocked shins. It is just possible that—

"Will you come, Doc?" asks Chuck.

"I have my profession."

"Practice it. We need you. We'll start a new life in a new world. We'll hole up in Confederate number 2 until the fallout settles—your doomsday machine will protect us, wow, whee, you're our shaman, Doc, then we'll live on Bayou Pontchata-lawa, which means peace, and love one another and watch the seasons come and smoke a little cannab in the evenings, hee hee hee, and live on catfish and Indian maize and wild grape and raise good sweet innocent children."

"Well—"

"Tell me the truth, Doc."

"All right."

"Have you ever lived your life?"

"Lived?"

"Lived completely and in the moment the way a prothonotary warbler lives flashing holy fire?"

"Not often."

Chuck laughs. "Hoowee! You know what I mean, don't you, Doc?"

"Yes."

"Hester, don't you want Doc to come live with you in your chickee?"

For her answer, Hester, who is hugging her legs and has laid her cheek on her knees, facing me, sways to and fro and lightly against me.

"All right. Here's the deal, Doc," says Chuck. "I have to see Uru and get some maize seeds and ammunition to shoot rabbits this winter. You go get your gear, medicine and all, and one book—we each have one book—and meet us in an hour at the landing near the slave quarters. What book will you bring?"

"Stedmann's *World War I*," I say absently.

"Oh yeah! Wow! We'll all read it, all about those bad old days, and lead our new life!"

A light breeze springs up, swirling the smoke column. A whiff of brimstone comes to my nostrils.

Now a tuning fork sings against my skull. Art whispers behind me. "Just a little vaccination, Doc. You understand."

"Did you vaccinate the others?"

"Positively."

"Ellen says you lie."

"I don't believe you. She's a lovely person. If you go to Honey Island, I should like to employ her."

"You keep away from her, you bastard."

"I am not illegitimate."

"If you vaccinated the others, how come they're acting like that?"

"They act like that normally."

Dr. Billy Matthews, perhaps because he can't stand it any longer, perhaps because the vapors have irritated his vagal nucleus, comes charging up the grassy hillock, where he confronts the scientists.

"I heard you rascals!" he cries.

"Heard us say what?" asks Stryker easily.

"You insulted the United States, Old Glory, and Jesus Christ!"

"When did we do that?" asks Colley, also smiling, but his voice is shaky. The scientists are astonished at the sight of the burly chiropractor, fists clenched, bald head gleaming malignantly in the sodium light, sunshades flipped in place like black eyepatches.

"Don't think I don't know what you people are," says the furious chiropractor, gazing into one face after another.

"What are we?" asks Max.

"I know!"

Dr. Habeeb adjusts his glasses and peers closely at Dr. Billy Matthews. "A perfect example of *Homo Americanensis politicus paranoicus*, would you say, Max?"

"Don't fight!" I cry from the bunker. "Billy is a good fellow. Once when he and I were in Ecuador—"

"Say that again," says the chiropractor to Mark Habeeb.

"Or would it be more accurate to classify him as coonass or redneck?" Mark asks Max.

It is difficult to say which is the greater insult to Billy Matthews, to be called a coonass, a derogatory term for a Cajun, or a redneck, equally unflattering for a North Louisianian.

"Kike!"

"As a matter of fact, I'm Syrian."

"Atheist!"

"Coonass!"

"Communist!"

"Holy Roller!"

"That's not true. I am a Southern Baptist."

"Christ, that's worse."

"Un-American!"

"Kluxer!"

"One Worlder!"

"Racist!"

"Nigger lover."

"Knothead!"

"Liberal!"

For some reason, these last two epithets, the mildest of the list, proved the last straw. In a rage, yet almost happily, the two fall upon one another, fists flying. They grapple for each other, fall to the earth with a thud and roll into the sand trap.

"No!" I cry, getting up and staggering around. "Don't fight!"

"Don't jump in there," says Max, grabbing my arm.

The brimstone smell is stronger. Smoke swirls between us. Stryker, I see, is most strongly affected by the noxious vapors. His eyes go vacant and lose focus. The Heavy Sodium ions hit his pineal body, seat of self, like a guillotine, sundering self from self forever, that ordinary self, the restless aching everyday self, from the secret self one happens on in dreams, in poetry, during ordeals, on happy trips—"Ah, this is my real self!" Forever after he'll live like a ghost inhabiting himself.

He'll orbit the earth forever, reading dials and recording data and spinning theories by day, and at night seek to reenter the world of creatures by taking the form of beasts and performing unnatural practices.

I even fancy that I see his soul depart, exiting his body through the top of his head in a little corkscrew curl of vapor, as the soul is depicted in ancient woodcuts. Or was it no more than a wisp of smoke blown from the bunker?

"Over here, Doc."

"What? Who's that?"

I open my eyes. A fog must have rolled in from the swamp. The sodium lights have turned into soft mazy balls. Voices come from the highway, but the bunker is deserted.

"Come over here, Doc."

It is Victor's voice. I follow it into the woods, staggering into a pocket of ground fog that has settled into a saucer-shaped glade.

"Is that you, Victor?" I say to a shadow tall as a cypress.

"No," says a different voice, muffled and flat. "Victor's gone. I sent him for you. Sit down."

It is Uru. He points to a stump. I sit down in a pool of fog, which is as thick and white as a $CO_2$ Transylvania fog.

"What do you want, Uru?"

"I want your machine."

"Why?"

"I don't know what's going on here but Victor and Willard say you know something and that your machine works. Let's have it."

"I don't have one."

"Well, I'll find one in your house."

"It wouldn't do you any good. You wouldn't know how to use it."

"We'll be the judge of that." Uru takes another stump. Hunched over in his *monkhu6*, he looks like a benched pro in a poncho. His face is in darkness.

"If we live through this, I'll bring the lapsometer wherever you like, test your people, and treat them if they need it."

"We can take care of our own."

"Very well. I'll be going."

"All we want from you is you off our backs."

"Very well. You got it."

Uru picks up his *izinkhonkwani*, which hangs between his

legs like a Scotsman's sporran, and slings it to one side.

"We're taking what we want and destroying what we don't and we don't need you."

"Is that what Victor says?"

"Victor's got nothing to say about it. Let me tell you something." Uru hunches forward on his stump. We sit knee to knee like commuters but I still can't make out his face. "We got two hundred Bantus just from this town and not one of them, not one, got any use for Victor or sweet Jesus."

"So?"

"So we don't need any help from you or Victor in what we're going to do."

"Then why did you send for me?"

"You want to know what's funny, Doc?"

"No."

"The way you chucks sold Victor on sweet Jesus and he out-Jesused you. You beat him with Jesus but you beat him so bad that in the end he out-Jesused you and made liars out of you and that was the one thing you couldn't stand. So Victor won after all."

"Victor wouldn't think that was funny."

"No, he wouldn't but Victor doesn't matter now, not you or Victor. What matters is what we're going to do."

"What's that?"

"Like I said. Take what we need, destroy what we don't, and live in peace and brotherhood."

"Peace and brotherhood." The map has come back, crooked capillary county roads and straight stretches of interstate arteries. "Well, you're right about one thing. I couldn't help you now even if you'd let me. We're not talking about the same thing. We're talking about different kinds of trouble. First you got to get to where you're going or where you think you're going—although I hope you do better than that, because after all nothing comes easier than that, being against one thing and tearing down another thing and talking about peace and brotherhood—I never saw peace and brotherhood come from such talk and I hope you do better than that because there are better things and harder things to do. But, either way, you got to get to where you're going before I can help you."

"Help us do what?"

"There is no use my even telling you because, Ph.D. or not, you wouldn't know what I was talking about. You got to

get to where we are or where you think we are and I'm not
even sure you can do that."

"Like I told you, Doc, we can do it and without your
help."

"Good luck, then." I rise.

"We don't need that either."

"Yes, you do."

"You better go back, Doc, while you can."


"Papa, have you lost your faith?"

"No."

Samantha asked me the questions as I stood by her bed.
The neuroblastoma had pushed one eye out and around the
nosebridge so she looked like a Picasso profile.

"Then why don't you got to mass anymore?"

"I don't know. Maybe because you don't go with me."

"Papa, you're in greater danger than Mama."

"How is that?"

"Because she is protected by Invincible Ignorance."

"That's true," I said, laughing.

"She doesn't know any better."

"She doesn't."

"You do."

"Yes."

"Just promise me one thing, Papa."

"What's that?"

"Don't commit the one sin for which there is no forgive-
ness."

"Which one is that?"

"The sin against grace. If God gives you the grace to believe in him and love him and you refuse, the sin will not be
forgiven you."

"I know." I took her hand, which even then still looked
soiled and chalk-dusted like a schoolgirl's.


I wonder: did it break my heart when Samantha died? Yes.
There was even the knowledge and foreknowledge of it while
she still lived, knowledge that while she lived, life still had its
same peculiar tentativeness, people living as usual by fits and
starts, aiming and missing, while present time went humming,
and foreknowledge that the second she died, remorse would
come and give past time its bitter specious wholeness. If only
—If only we hadn't been defeated by humdrum humming

present time and missed it, missed ourselves, missed everything. I had the foreknowledge while she lived. Still, present time went humming. Then she died and here came the sweet remorse like a blade between the ribs.

But is there not also a compensation, a secret satisfaction to be taken in her death, a delectation of tragedy, a license for drink, a taste of both for taste's sake?

It may be true. At least Doris said it was. Doris was a dumbbell but she could read my faults! She said that when I refused to take Samantha to Lourdes. Doris wanted to! Because of the writings of Alexis Carrel and certain experiments by the London Psychical Society, etcetera etcetera. The truth was that Samantha didn't want to go to Lourdes and I didn't want to take her. Why not? I don't know Samantha's reasons, but I was afraid she might be cured. What then? Suppose you ask God for a miracle and God says yes, very well. How do you live the rest of your life?

Samantha, forgive me. I am sorry you suffered and died, my heart broke, but there have been times when I was not above enjoying it.

Is it possible to live without feasting on death?

Art and Ellen help me to my feet.

"Ready, Chief?"

"Where are we going?"

"My car is over there."

"Dr. More is going to Honey Island," says Art.

"I haven't decided," I say, frowning.

"Then you and I can go to Denmark," says Art.

"Denmark!" I repeat with astonishment. "Why?"

"Our work here is finished." Art gazes down at the bunker, which is smoking more than ever. Charley Parker's hose is still running but Charley is gone.

"Why Denmark?"

"Number one, it is my home base. Number two, it is close to the Nobel Prize committee. Number three, it is the vanguard of civilization. Number four, I can get you a job there."

"What kind of a job?"

"Of course after the Nobel you can write your own ticket. Meanwhile you've been offered the position of chief encephalographer at the Royal University."

Art advances with his lapsometer. I can't seem to move.

"He's not going off with you!" cries Ellen.

"I think he wants to," says Art quietly. For a second the

tuning fork hums on my skull. I knock it away.

"Keep away from him!" warns Ellen.

"One little massage of his musical-erotic and he'll be right as rain," says Art.

He stoops over me. I watch him dreamily.

"Just a minute." Ellen touches his shirt. I frown but cannot rouse myself. "Step over here."

Ellen returns arm in arm with Art. She hands me her car keys. "You can go now, Chief."

I am peering at Art through the smoke. He nods reassuringly. "She's right. You can go home, Doc."

"Where do you think you're going?" I ask Ellen.

"With Dr. Immelmann."

"What do you mean?"

She shrugs. "I need a job and you evidently don't need me. It's nothing new. Dr. Immelmann offered me a position the first day he came to see you."

"Doing what?"

"As his traveling secretary."

"You're not traveling anywhere with this bastard." I grab her hand and yank her away from Art. "Why you evil-minded son of a bitch," I tell Art.

"I can't understand why he calls me those extraordinary names," says Art to no one in particular.

"Get away from here," I say uneasily, for now Art is advancing upon us with his, with *my*, lapsometer.

Slinging the device from his shoulder, he holds out both hands. "The two of you will come with me."

"We have to go," whispers Ellen, shrinking against me.

"No we don't."

"If we both go, Chief, maybe it will be all right."

"No, it won't," I say, not taking my eyes from Art, whose arms are outstretched like the Christ at Sacre Coeur in New Orleans.

"We'll all be happy in Copenhagen," murmurs Art.

*Beautiful beautiful Copenhagen.*

'Let's sing, Doc!"

What is frightening is his smiling assurance. He doesn't even need the lapsometer!

"Let's go, kids," says Art. One hand touches Ellen.

"Don't touch her!" I cry, but I can't seem to move. I close

my eyes. *Sir Thomas More, kinsman, saint, best dearest merriest of Englishmen, pray for us and drive this son of a bitch hence.*

I open my eyes. Art is turning slowly away, wheeling in slow motion, a dazed hurt look through the eyes as if he had been struck across the face.

"I think you hurt his feelings," whispers Ellen, trembling.

"How?"

"By what you called him."

"What did I call him?"

"S.O.B."

"Really?" I was sure I had not prayed aloud.

"What else were you mumbling? Something about a saint?"

"Nothing."

"Do you think you're a saint?"

"No." Then Ellen never heard of the other Thomas More.

"Look, he's leaving."

"So he is."

"Shouldn't we—"

"No." I hold her tight.

Art disappears into the smoke swirling beyond the bunker.

"Now what?" asks Ellen.

"I think I'll have a drink."

"No, you won't. Let's go home," she says, spitting on me and smoothing my eyebrows.

# FIVE YEARS
# LATER

# In the Slave Quarters

HOEING COLLARDS IN MY KITCHEN GARDEN.

A fine December day. It is cold but the winter sun pours into the walled garden and fills it up.

After hoeing a row: sit in the sunny corner, stretch out my legs and look at my boots. A splendid pair of new boots of soft oiled leather, good for hunting and fishing and walking to town. For the first time I understand what the Confederate soldier was always saying: a good pair of boots is the best thing a man can have.

A poor man sets store by good boots. Ellen and I are poor. We live with our children in the old Quarters. Constructed of slave brick worn porous and rounded at the corners like sponges, the apartments are surprisingly warm in winter, cool in summer. They are built like an English charterhouse, a hundred apartments in a row along the bayou, each with a porch, living room or (in my case) library, two bedrooms, kitchen, garden, one behind the other.

Waiting and listening and looking at my boots.

Here's one difference between this age and the last. Now while you work, you also watch and listen and wait. In the last age we planned projects and cast ahead of ourselves. We set out to "reach goals." We listened to the minutes of the previous meeting. Between times we took vacations.

Through the open doorway I can see Ellen standing at the stove in a swatch of sunlight. She stirs grits. Light and air flow around her arm like the arm of Velasquez's weaver girl. Her half apron is lashed just above the slight swell of her abdomen.

She socks spoon down on pot and cocks her head to listen

for the children, slanting her dark straight eyebrows. A king-fisher goes ringing down the bayou.

Meg and Thomas More, Jr., are still asleep.

Chinaberries bounce off the tin roof.

The bricks are growing warm at my back. In the corner of the wall a garden spider pumps its web back and forth like a child on a swing.

My practice is small. But my health is better. Fewer shakes and depressions and unnatural exaltations. Rise at six every morning and run my trotline across the bayou. Water is the difference! Water is the mystical element! At dawn the black bayou breathes a white vapor. The oars knock, cypress against cypress, but the sound is muffled, wrapped in cotton. As the trotline is handed along, the bank quickly disappears and the skiff seems to lift and be suspended in a new element globy and white. Silence presses in and up from the vaporish depths come floating great green turtles, blue catfish, lordly gasper-gous.

Strange: I am older, yet there seems to be more time, time for watching and waiting and thinking and working. All any man needs is time and desire and the sense of his own sover-eignty. As Kingfish Huey Long used to say: every man a king. I am a poor man but a kingly one. If you want and wait and work, you can have.

Despite the setbacks of the past, particularly the fiasco five years ago, I still believe my lapsometer can save the world—if I can get it right. For the world is broken, sundered, busted down the middle, self ripped from self and man pasted back together as mythical monster, half angel, half beast, but no man. Even now I can diagnose and shall one day cure: cure the new plague, the modern Black Death, the current her-maphroditism of the spirit, namely: More's syndrome, or: chronic angelism-bestialism that rives soul from body and sets it orbiting the great world as the spirit of abstraction whence it takes the form of beasts, swans and bulls, werewolves, blood-suckers, Mr. Hydes, or just poor lonesome ghost locked in its own machinery.

If you want and work and wait, you can have. Every man a king. What I want is no longer the Nobel, screw prizes, but just to figure out what I've hit on. Some day a man will walk into my office as ghost or beast or ghost-beast and walk out as a man, which is to say sovereign wanderer, lordly exile, worker and waiter and watcher.

Knowing, not women, said Sir Thomas, is man's happiness.

Learning and wisdom are receding nowadays. The young, who already know everything, hate science, bomb laboratories, kill professors, burn libraries.

Already the monks are beginning to collect books again. . . .

Poor as I am, I feel like God's spoiled child. I am Robinson Crusoe set down on the best possible island with a library, a laboratory, a lusty Presbyterian wife, a cozy tree house, an idea, and all the time in the world.

Ellen calls from the doorway. Breakfast is ready. She sets a plate of steaming grits and bacon for me on a plain pine table. Like most good cooks, she hasn't a taste for her own cooking. Instead she pours honey on an old biscuit.

We sit on kitchen chairs in the sunlight. With one hand she absently sweeps crumbs into the other. Her hand's rough heel whispers over the ribs of pine. She keeps her apron on. When she sits down, she exactly fills the heart-shaped scoop of the chair. Her uptied hair leaves her neck bare save for a few strands.

In my second wife I am luckier than my kinsman Thomas More. For once I have the better of him. His second wife was dour and old and ugly. Mine is dour and young and beautiful. Both made good wives. Sir Thomas's wife was a bad Catholic like me, who believed in God but saw no reason why one should disturb one's life, certainly not lose one's head. Ellen is a Presbyterian who doesn't have much use for God but believes in doing right and does it.

Sunlight creeps along the tabletop, casting into relief the shiny scoured ridges of pine. Steam rising from the grits sets motes stirring in the golden bar of light. I shiver slightly. Morning is still not the best of times. As far as morning is concerned, I can't say things have changed much. What has changed is my way of dealing with it. No longer do I crawl around on hands and knees drinking Tang and vodka and duck eggs.

My stomach leaps with hunger. I eat grits and bacon and corn sticks.

After breakfast my heart leaps with love.

"Come sit in my lap, Ellen."

"Well—"

"Now then. Here."

"Oh for pity's sake."

"Yes. There now."

"Not now."

"Give me a kiss."

"My stars."

Her mouth tastes like honey.

"Tch. not now," she whispers.

"Why not?"

"The children are coming."

"The children can—"

"Here's Meg."

"So I see. Kiss me."

"Kiss Meg."

2

Walk up the cliff to catch the bus in Paradise.

Up and down the fairways go carts canopied in orange-and-white Bantu stripes. Golfers dismount for their shots, their black faces inscrutable under the bills of their caps.

Recently Bantu golfers rediscovered knickerbockers and the English golf cap, which they wear pulled down to their eyebrows and exactly level. They shout "Fore!" but they haven't got it quite right, shouting it not as a warning but as a kind of ritual cry, a karate shout, before teeing off.

English golf pros are in fashion now, the way Austrian ski instructors used to be. Charley Parker moved to Australia.

"Fore!" shouts a driver, though no one is in sight, and whales into it.

"Good shot!"

"Bully, old man!"

"Give me my cleek."

Paradise has gone 99 percent Bantu. How did the Bantus win? Not by revolution. No, their revolution was a flop; they got beat in the Troubles five years ago and pulled back to the swamp. So how did they win? By exercising their property rights!

Why not? Squatting out in the swamp for twenty years, they came by squatter's rights to own it. Whereupon oil was struck through the old salt domes. Texaco and Esso and Good Gulf thrust money into black hands. Good old Bantu uncles burned $100 bills like Oklahoma Indians of old.

So they moved out of the swamp and bought the houses in Paradise. Why not? I sold mine for $70,000 and sank the money in my invention like many another nutty doctor.

Willard Amadie bought Tara and was elected mayor.

Uru, baffled by Southern ways, left in disgust, returned to Ann Arbor, and rejoined the Black Studies department of the U. of M., where life is simpler.

Others left. Many Knotheads, beside themselves with rage, driven mad by the rain of noxious particles, departed for safe Knothead havens in San Diego, Cicero, Hattiesburg, and New Rochelle. Many Lefts, quaking with terror and abstracted out of their minds, took out for Berkeley, Cambridge, Madison, and Fairfax County, Virginia, where D.C. liberals live.

Some stayed, mostly eccentrics who didn't't fit in anywhere else. I stayed because it's home and I like its easygoing ways, its religious confusion, racial hodgepodge, misty green woods, and sleepy bayous. People still stop and help strangers lying in ditches having been set upon by thieves or just plain drunk. Good nature usually prevails, even between enemies. As the saying goes in Louisiana: you may be a son of a bitch but you're my son of a bitch.

Only one woman to my name now, a lusty tart Presbyterian, but one is enough. Moira married Buddy Brown and removed to Phoenix, where he is director of the Big Corral, the Southwest Senior Citizens Termination Center. Lola, lovely strong-backed splendid-kneed cellist, married Barry Bocock, the clean West-Coast engineer, and removed to Marietta, Georgia, where Barry works for Lockheed and Lola is President of Colonial Dames, shows three-gaited horses, and plays cello for the Atlanta Symphony Orchestra.

I say Paradise is 99 percent Bantu. My mother is the remaining 1 percent. She stayed and made a second fortune selling astrological real estate to the Bantus, who are as superstitious as whites. Most of the younger and smarter Bantus are, to tell the truth, only nominally Bantu, having lost their faith at the Ivy League universities they habitually attend.

3

Borrow a newspaper from a tube near the bus stop. ATRO-CITIES SOLVED says the headline.

Read the story in the sunny quarter of a golf shelter. Hm. It seems the murderers who have terrorized this district for the past ten years turned out to be neither black guerrillas nor white Knotheads but rather a love community in the swamp. The leader is quoted as saying his family believes in love, the environment, and freedom of the individual.


4


Before the bus comes, a new orange Toyota stops to give me a lift. It is Colley Wilkes, super-Bantu. He and his light-colored wife, Fran, are on their way to Honey Island for the Christmas bird count. A pair of binoculars and a camera with massive telephoto lens lie on the Sunday *Times* between them. A tape plays Rudolf Friml. The Wilkes are dressed in sports togs. Fran sits around catercornered, leg tucked under her, to see me.

"You catch us on the crest of the wave," she tells me. "We are ten feet high. Our minds are blown."

"How's that?"

"Tell him, Colley."

"We found him, Tom," says Colley portentously. "By George, we found him."

"Who?"

"He's alive! He's come back! After all these years!"

"Who?"

This morning, hauling up a great unclassified beast of a fish, I thought of Christ coming again at the end of the world and how it is that in every age there is the temptation to see signs of the end and that, even knowing this, there is nevertheless some reason, what with the spirit of the new age being the spirit of watching and waiting, to believe that—

Colley's right hand strays over the tape deck. The smooth shark skin at the back of his neck is pocked with pits that are perfectly circular as if they had been punched out with a tiny biscuit cutter.

"Last Sunday at 6:55 A.M.," says Colley calmly, "exactly four miles west of Honey Island I—saw—an—ivory-billed—woodpecker."

"Is that so?"

"No question about it."

"That is remarkable."

"Do you realize what this means?" Fran asks me.

"No. Yes."

"There has not been a verified sighting of an ivorybill since nineteen-three. Think of it."

"All right."

"Wouldn't that be something now," muses Fran, breathing on her binoculars, "to turn in a regular Christmas list, you know, six chickadees, twenty pine warblers, two thousand myrtle warblers, and at the end, with photo attached: one ivory-billed woodpecker? Can't you see the Audubon brass as they read it?"

"Yes."

"Of course we have to find him again. Wish us luck."

"Yes. I do."

Colley asks politely after my family, my practice. I tell him my family is well but my practice is poor, so poor I have to moonlight with a fat clinic. At noon today, in fact, I meet with my fat ladies at the Bantu Country Club.

Fran shakes her head with an outrage tempered by her binocular-polishing. Colley pushes a button. The tape plays a Treasury of the World's Great Music, which has the good parts of a hundred famous symphonies, ballets, and operas. Colley knows the music and, as he drives, keeps time, anticipating phrases with a duck of head, lilt of chin.

"I don't get it, Tom," says Fran, breathing now on the telephoto lens, which is the size of a butter plate. "Everyone knows you're a marvelous diagnostician."

"It's very simple," I reply, nodding along with the good part of Tchaikovsky's *Romeo and Juliet*. "The local Bantu medical society won't let me in, so I can't use the hospital."

An awkward silence follows, but fortunately the love theme soars.

"Well," says Colley presently. "Rome wasn't built in a day."

"That's true."

"These things take time, Tom," says Fran.

"I know."

"Rest assured, however, that some of us are working on it."

"All right."

The *Anvil Chorus* starts up. Colley beats time with soft blows of his fist on the steering wheel.

"You've got to remember one thing," says Colley, socking

away. "You can sometimes accomplish more by not rocking the boat."

"I wasn't rocking the boat. You asked me a question."

"You're among friends, Tom," says Fran. "Who do you think led the fight to integrate the Bantu Audubon Society?"

"Colley."

"Right!"

Colley lifts his chin toward me. "And who do you think fixed a hundred Christmas baskets for peckerwood children?"

"Fran."

"Longhu6 baskets, dear," Fran corrects him. Longhu6 is the Bantu god of the winter solstice.

"Tell me something, Tom," says Colley quizzically-Amherstly, swaying in time to the good part of "Waltz of the Flowers" from *Nutcracker*. "Still working on your, ah—"

"Lapsometer? Yes indeed. Now that there is no danger of diabolical abuse, the future is bright."

"Diab—!" He frowns, missing the beat of *Nutcracker*. He's sorry he asked.

But he's full of Christmas cheer—or triumph over the ivorybill—and presently comes back to it, as if to prove his goodwill. "Someday you're going to put it all together," he says, directing *Barcarole* with one gloved finger.

"Put all what together?"

"Your device. I'm convinced you're on the right track in your stereotactic exploration of the motor and sensory areas of the cortex. This is where it's at."

"That's not it at all," I say, hunching forward between them. "I'm not interested in motor and sensory areas. What concerns me is angelism, bestialism, and other perturbations of the soul."

"The soul. Hm, yes, well—"

"Just what do you think happened here five years ago?" I ask his smooth punchcarded neck.

"Five years ago?"

"In the Troubles. What do you think caused people to go out of their minds with terror and rage and attack each other?"

Fran looks at Colley.

"The usual reasons, I suppose," says Colley mournfully. "People resorting to violence instead of using democratic processes to resolve their differences."

"Bullshit, Colley—beg your pardon, Fran—what about the yellow cloud?"

"Right. Well, here we are!" Colley pulls over to the curb and reaches around the headrest to open my door, which takes some doing.

"Merry Christmas," I say absently and thank them for the ride.

"Merry Longhu6!" says Fran, smiling but firm-eyed.


5


The office is lonesome without Ellen. Usually she comes with me, but Saturday is my fat-clinic day and I only spend a couple of hours here. Ellen is taking the kids to see Santy. It is Christmas Eve and I need a bit of cash. Ten dollars wouldn't hurt.

The solitude is pleasant, however. I open the back door opening onto the ox-lot. English sparrows have taken the martin hotel.

When I prop my foot on the drawer of Bayonne-rayon members, it reminds me of taking a drink. I close the drawer. No drink for six months. One reason is willpower. The other is that Ellen would kill me.

Across the ox-lot Mrs. Prouty comes out on the loading ramp of Sears. She smiles at me and leans against the polished steel pipe-rail.

I smile back. Most Saturdays we exchange pleasantries.

She wrote up my order for the new boots and Ellen's Christmas present, a brass bed, king-size (60″) with nonallergenic Posture-mate mattress and serofoam polyurethane foundation, Sears Best. The whole works: $603.95.

A year's savings went into it, mainly from my fat clinic. No Christmas present ever took more thinking about or planning for. Even the delivery required scheming. How to get a bed past a housewife? Ask housewife to take children to plaza to see Santy (Santy is as big with the Bantus as with the Christians).

Did the bed make it? I lift my head in question to Mrs. Prouty. She nods and holds up thumb and forefinger. The bed is on the way.

We've slept till now, Ellen and I, on single beds from my old house. A conceit of Doris's and much prized then, they are "convent" beds, which is to say, not even proper singles, narrower and shorter rather. For thirteen years my feet have stuck out, five with Doris, three alone, five with Ellen. Nuns must have been short. White-iron, chaste, curious, half-canopied the beds were, redolent of a far-off time and therefore serviceable in Doris's war on the ordinary, because at the time it was impossible to sleep in ORDINARY BEDS.

Did Mrs. Prouty wink at me? Across the weeds we gaze at each other, smiling. Her olive arms hug herself. A nyloned hip polishes a pipe-fitting. Mrs. Prouty is a good-looking good-humored lady. Whenever she used to see me buying a bottle next door at the Little Napoleon, she'd say: "Somebody's going to have a party. Can I come?" Her lickerish look comes, I think, from her merry eye and her skin, which is as clear and smooth as an olive.

When I ordered the brass bed, she swung the catalogue round on its lectern, leaned on it, and tapped her pencil on the counter.

"I know where I'd spend Christmas, huh, Docky?"

"What? Oh," I say, laughing before I take her meaning. Did she say Docky or ducky?

After I ordered the boots, she leaned on the catalogue again.

"These can go under mine any day," she says, merry eye roving past me carelessly.

"Ma'am? Eh? Right! Har har!"

These = my boots?

Mine = her bed?

Nowadays when a good-looking woman flirts with me, however idly, I guffaw like some ruddy English lord, haw haw, har har, harrr harrr.


Three patients come. Two Bantu businessmen, one with ulcers, the other with hypertension. Their own docs did 'em no good, so they want me to make magic passes with my machine. I oblige them, do so, take readings, hoard up data. They leave, feeling better.

The third is old P.T. Bledsoe. Even though he lost everything, including his wife, when the Bantus took Paradise and Betterbag Paper Company, he didn't leave and go to the Outback after all. Instead, he moved out to his fishing camp and took to drinking Gallo muscatel and fishing for speckles. All he comes to me for is to get his pan-vitamin shot to keep his liver going. Out he goes rubbing his shiny butt and rattling off in his broken-down Plymouth.

Hm. Eleven dollars. Not a bad haul. My patients fork over cash, knowing I need it, five from each Bantu and one dollar from P.T., who also brings me a sack of mirlatons and a fifth of Early Times. Not good. But he didn't know I had stopped drinking.

Mrs. Prouty is still on the ramp.

Now she points to her wristwatch.

Does she mean it is almost noon and she'll be off and why not have a little Christmas drink?

For she's spotted the Early Times. Rising, I unshuck gift box from bottle.

Comes again the longing, the desire that has no name. Is it for Mrs. Prouty, for a drink, for both: for a party, for youth, for the good times, for dear good drinking and fighting comrades, for football-game girls in the fall with faces like flowers? Comes the longing and it has to do with being fifteen and fifty and with the winter sun striking down into a brick-yard and on clapboard walls rounded off with old hard blistered paint and across a doorsill onto linoleum. Desire has a smell: of cold linoleum and gas heat and the sour piebald bark of crepe myrtle. A good-humored thirty-five-year-old lady takes the air in a back lot in a small town.

Insert thumbnail into plastic seal between glass rim and stopper. The slight pop is like a violation.

Comes a knock. Patient number four.

Put away the Early Times in the drawer of Bayonne-rayons.

It is a new patient, a young coffee-colored graduate student with intense eyes and a high bossed forehead like the late Harry Belafonte. Seems he has a private complaint. Nothing for it but to close the back door. He leans forward in a pleasant anxious way. I know what is wrong with him before he opens his mouth, but he tells me anyway.

Chief complaint: a feeling of strangeness, of not feeling himself, of eeriness, dislocation, etcetera etcetera.

Past history: native of Nassau, graduate of U. of Conn. and Syracuse. He tells me it is his plan to "unite in his own life the objective truths of science with the universal spiritual insights of Eastern religion."

Ah me. Another Orientalized heathen Englishman.

"Well, let's see," I say, and take out my lapsometer.

* * *

When he's gone, I open the back door.

The Sears ramp is empty.

Ah well. To my fat ladies, to the A & P for a turkey, to the toy store and home.

6

"Fore!"

"Good mashie, old man!"

In a bunker I notice that, December or not, weeds are beginning to sprout.

A tractor pulling a gang mower stops beside me. The driver is greenskeeper Moon Mullins, a fellow Knight of Columbus, Holy Name man, ex-Pontiac salesman. Moon stayed because he owns half the shacks in Happy Hollow, now inhabited by peckerwoods, and can't sell them.

"How goes it, Moon?"

The greenskeeper shakes his head dolefully. Really, though, he's fit as can be. What he doesn't remember is his life as a Pontiac salesman in a Toyota town, standing around the showroom grinning and popping his knuckles while his colon tightened and whitened, went hard and straight as a lead pipe.

"You want to know where it all began to go wrong?" Moon asks me, nodding toward a foursome of sepia golfers.

"Where?"

"It started when we abandoned the Latin mass."

"You think?"

"Sure. You think about it."

"All right."

Off he roars, whistling a carol and showering me in a drizzle of grass cuttings.

"See you tonight!" he hollers back.

He comes down to the chapel now. Most A.C.C. (Cicero) Catholics have moved away. Monsignor Schleifkopf was transferred to Brooklyn. Moon and others who stayed have drifted back to Father Smith.

7

After holding fat clinic at the club, I am served lunch in the hall. The placing of my table in the hall between the men's bar crowded with golfers and the dining room overflowing with Mah-Jongg ladies is nicely calculated not to offend me.

I eat with the English pro.

From one side comes the click of Mah-Jongg tiles, from the other the rattle of poker dice in cup. My Bantu ladies, the weight watchers, are a hefty crew. They are all dressed in the fashion of the day, in velveteen, mostly green and wine-colored with hats to match, hats with tall stove-in crowns and large cloche-shaped brims.

The food is good—it comes straight from the rib room and is the same roast beef and Yorkshire pudding everyone is served. I eat heartily. Better still, I don't have to listen to "Christmas gif, Doc!" and I don't have to worry about tipping. Instead I get tipped. Beside my plate I find an envelope with check for $25 and poem attached. From my fat ladies.

> *Merry Longhu6 for our Doc*
> *Who tries to keep us slim.*
> *Don't get discouraged, Doc, we'll try harder*
> *More power to him.*

Reading poem and nodding and chewing roast beef.

## 8

The bell rings for midnight mass. Ellen decides to come with me.

"Thanks again for the bell, my son," says Father Smith on the tiny porch of the chapel. With his deep tan from fire-watching and his hairy Spanish futbol wrists he looks more than ever like Ricardo Montalban.

The bell is the plantation bell from Tara. It is the original bell provided by David O. Selznik for the original Tara. Lola hid it in the well before the Bantus came.

There is some confusion in the chapel. The Jews are leaving—it is their Sabbath. The Protestants are singing. Catholics are lined up for confession. We have no ecumenical movement. No minutes of the previous meeting are read. The services overlap. Jews wait for the Lord, Protestants sing hymns to him, Catholics say mass and eat him.

Bessie Charles is singing a spiritual:

*He's got the little bitty baby in his hands,*
*He's got the whole world in his hands.*

Catholics join in self-consciously and off-key.

Father Smith looks at his watch as usual and as usual says: "Time to get locked in the box. Coming?"

"Very well."

Blinking with surprise, he lets out a groan and looks at his watch again. Must he hear my confession in the few minutes he allots to polishing off the week's sins of his practicing Catholics? Well, he will if he must.

"Don't worry, Father. It won't take a minute."

He nods, relieved. Perhaps I've been slipping off to confess elsewhere.

My turn comes at last. I kneel in the sour darkness of the box, which smells of sweat and Pullman curtain.

The little door slides back. There is Father Smith, close as close, cheek propped on three fingers, trying to keep awake. He's cross-eyed from twelve hours of fire-watching. A hundred brushfires flicker across his retina. These days people, convinced of world-conspiracies against them, go out and set the woods afire to get even.

"Bless me, Father, for I have sinned," I say and fall silent, forgetting everything.

"When was your last confession?" asks the priest patiently.

"Eleven years ago."

Another groan escapes the priest. Again he peeps at his watch. Must he listen to an eleven-year catalogue of dreary fornications and such? Well, he'll do it.

"Father, I can make my confession in one sentence."

"Good," says the priest, cheering up.

"I do not recall the number of occasions, Father, but I accuse myself of drunkenness, lusts, envies, fornication, delight in the misfortunes of others, and loving myself better than God and other men."

"I see," says the priest, who surprises me by not looking surprised. Perhaps he's just sleepy. "Do you have contrition and a firm purpose amendment?"

"I don't know."

"You don't know? You don't feel sorry for your sins?"

"I don't feel much of anything."

"Let me understand you."

"All right."

"You have not lost your faith?"

"No."

"You believe in the Catholic faith as the Church proposes it?"

"Yes."

"And you believe that your sins will be forgiven here and now if you confess them, are sorry for them, and resolve to sin no more?"

"Yes."

"Yet you say you do not feel sorry."

"That is correct."

"You are aware of your sins, you confess them, but you are not sorry for them?"

"That is correct."

"Why?"

"I couldn't say."

"Pity."

"I'm sorry."

"You are?"

"Yes."

"For what?"

"For not being sorry."

The priest sighs. "Will you pray that God will give you a true knowledge of your sins and a true contrition?"

"Yes, I'll do that."

"You are a doctor and it is your business to help people, not harm them."

"That is true."

"You are also a husband and father and it is your duty to love and cherish your family."

"Yes, but that does not prevent me from desiring other women and even contriving plans to commit fornication and adultery."

"Yes," says the priest absently. "That's the nature of the beast."

Damn, why doesn't he wake up and pay attention?

"But you haven't recently," says the priest.

"Haven't what?"

"Actually committed adultery and fornication."

"No," I say irritably. "But—"

"Hm. You know, Tom, maybe it's not so much a question at our age of committing in the imagination these horrendous sins of the flesh as of worrying whether one still can. In the firetower on such occasions I find it useful to imagine the brushfires as the outer circle of hell, not too hot really, where these sad sins are punished, and my toes toasting in the flames. Along comes Our Lady who spies me and says: 'Oh, for heaven's sake, you here? This is ridiculous.'"

Damn, where does he come off patronizing me with his stock priestly tricks—I can tell they're his usual tricks because he reels 'em off without even listening. I can smell the seminary and whole libraries of books "for the layman" with little priest-jokes. How can he lump the two of us together, him a gray ghost of a cleric and me the spirit of the musical-erotic?

More tricks:

"For your drinking you might find it helpful, at least it is in my case, to cast your lot with other drunks. Then, knowing how much trouble you're going to put your friends to if you take a drink, you're less apt to—though it doesn't always work."

"Thank you," I say coldly.

"Now let's see." He's nodding again, drifting off into smoke and brushfires. "Very well. You're sorry for your sins."

"No."

"That's too bad. Ah me. Well—" He steals a glance at his watch. "In any case, continue to pray for knowledge of your sins. God is good. He will give you what you ask. Ask for sorrow. Pray for me."

"All right."

"Meanwhile, forgive me but there are other things we must think about: like doing our jobs, you being a better doctor, I being a better priest, showing a bit of ordinary kindness to people, particularly our own families—unkindness to those close to us is such a pitiful thing—doing what we can for our poor unhappy country—things which, please forgive me, sometimes seem more important than dwelling on a few middle-aged daydreams."

"You're right. I'm sorry," I say instantly, scalded.

"You're sorry for your sins?"

"Yes. Ashamed rather."

"That will do. Now say the act of contrition and for your penance I'm going to give you this."

Through the little window he hands me two articles, an envelope containing ashes and a sackcloth, which is a kind of sleeveless sweater made of black burlap. John XXIV recently revived public penance, a practice of the early Church.

While he absolves me, I say an act of contrition and pull the sackcloth over my sports coat.

"Go in peace. I'll offer my mass for you tonight."

"Thank you," I say, dumping the ashes in my hair.

After hearing confessions, the priest gets ready to say mass. The pious black seminarian, who looks like Saint Aloysius Gonzaga, who never entertained a dirty thought, assists him.

Some of the Protestants stay, including Leroy Ledbetter and Victor Charles and his wife.

There is a flick of eyes as people notice my sackcloth. Ellen's cheek radiates complex rays of approval-disapproval. Approval that I will now "do right," be a better husband, cultivate respectable patients, remain abstemious, etcetera. What she disapproves is not that I am doing public penance. No, what bothers her is an ancient Presbyterian mistrust of *things*, things getting mixed up in religion. The black sweater and the ashes scandalize her. Her eyelid lowers—she almost winks. What have these *things*, articles, to do with doing right? For she mistrusts the Old Church's traffic in things, sacraments, articles, bread, wine, salt, oil, water, ashes. Watch out! You know what happened before when you Catholics mucked it up with all your things, medals, scapulars, candles, bloody statues! when it came finally to crossing palms for indulgences. Watch out!

I will. We will.

Father Smith says mass. I eat Christ, drink his blood.

At the end the people say aloud a prayer confessing the sins of the Church and asking for the reunion of Christians and of the United States.

Outside the children of some love couples and my own little Thomas More, a rowdy but likable lot, shoot off firecrackers.

"Hurrah for Jesus Christ!" they cry. "Hurrah for the United States!"

9

After mass, Victor Charles wishes me Merry Christmas and tells me he's running for Congress.

"The U.S. Congress?"

"Why not?"

He wants me to be his campaign manager.

"Why me?"

"I got the Bantu vote. They've fallen out with each other and are willing to go with me. Chuck Parker's helping me with the swamp people. Max is working on the liberals. Leroy Ledbetter's got the peckerwoods. You could swing the Catholics."

"I doubt that. Anyhow, I'm not much of a politician." I have to laugh. He sounds exactly like a politician from the old Auto Age.

"You organized the SOUP chapter here, didn't you?"

SOUP is Southerners and Others United to Preserve the Union in Repayment of an old Debt to the Yankees Who Saved It Once Before and Are Destroying It Now.

For, in fact, much of the North is pulling out. The new Hanseatic League of Black City-States—Detroit, New York, Chicago, Boston, Los Angeles, Washington—refused last year to admit federal election commissioners. D.C. had to remove to Virginia, home of Jefferson.

"You're a good doctor, Doc. People respect you."

"What's that got to do with politics?"

"Everything, man!"

"You running as Knothead or Left?"

"Doc, I'm running under the old rooster." In Louisiana the rooster stood for the old Democratic Party.

I laugh. Victor laughs and claps his hands. It's the same old funny fouled-up coalition. Kennedy, Evers, Goldberg, Stevenson, L.Q.C. Lamar.

"All right."

"All right, what?"

"I will."

We laugh. Why are we laughing?

"Merry Christmas, Doc."

"Merry Christmas."

# 10

Barbecuing in my sackcloth.

The turkey is smoking well. The children have gone to bed, but they'll be up at dawn to open their presents.

The night is clear and cold. There is no moon. The light of the transmitter lies hard by Jupiter, ruby and diamond in the plush velvet sky. Ellen is busy in the kitchen fixing stuffing and sweet potatoes. Somewhere in the swamp a screech owl cries.

I'm dancing around to keep warm, hands in pockets. It is Christmas Day and the Lord is here, a holy night and surely that is all one needs.

On the other hand I want a drink. Fetching the Early Times from a clump of palmetto, I take six drinks in six minutes. Now I'm dancing and singing old Sinatra songs and the *Salve Regina*, cutting the fool like David before the ark or like Walter Huston doing a jig when he struck it rich in the Sierra Madre.

The turkey is ready. I take it into the kitchen and grab Ellen from behind. She smells of flour and stuffing and like a Georgia girl.

"Oh, for pity's sake," says Ellen, picking up a spoon.

"You're lovely here."

"You've been drinking."

"Yes."

"Put my dress down."

"All right."

"What are you doing?"

"Picking you up."

"Put me down."

I'm staggering with her, a noble, surprisingly heavy, Presbyterian armful.

"You're drunk."

"Yes."

"Where do you think you're going?"

"In here. Put the spoon down."

She puts the spoon down and I put her down on her new $600 bed.

To bed we go for a long winter's nap, twined about each other as the ivy twineth, not under a bush or in a car or on the floor or any such humbug as marked the past peculiar years of Christendom, but at home in bed where all good folk belong.

## ABOUT THE AUTHOR

Walker Percy went to medical school and interned at Bellevue, intending to be a psychiatrist. After a bout with tuberculosis, he married and converted to Catholicism. He became a writer and his first novel THE MOVIEGOER, won the National Book Award and has never been out of print since its publication in 1961. He lived with his wife in Covington, LA where they operated a bookstore until his death in 1990.